The Charmer

Autumn Dawn

DEDICATION

To my husband John. Yes, you are.

To the librarians, who fed my hunger for books.

For my English teachers, who began the journey.

To Judy Stone, beta reader extraordinaire. You made it easier.

To my
readers; you know why.

CHAPTER 1

"Wait a minute, Lemming! Let me catch my breath," Jasmine gasped as she clutched a slender poplar for balance. A shower of bright leaves and water peppered her head and shoulders as the tree swayed. For a moment, her vision blurred and her legs trembled, but she stiffened them to wait out the asthma attack. The painful tightness in her chest nagged at her.

Grumbling, she dug out her inhaler and took a couple puffs. She hated resorting to medicine. Every couple of days it seemed, the TV would announce that people were getting cancer from some drug or another. Her favorite ads were the ones for male impotence that announced in fine print that the side effects included impotence. Next they'd announce that inhalers caused black lung.

She shook her head at her imagination and shoved the inhaler deep in her pocket. There was no sense being morbid.

Lemming trotted over to her, tail wagging, and sat gracefully at her feet. The black and white Border collie was used to such stops, but unlike her companion, she still had energy to burn.

Jasmine inspected a large rock that had washed free of the sticky clay, looking for ants. Satisfied, she shifted the holstered pistol on her hip and sat down gingerly. Cold seeped into her jeans from the lichen covered stone, even with the extra layer of long johns underneath. She ignored it and took in the view.

Densely wooded Alaskan hills rolled away in the distance without a sign of civilization. Autumn had hung her gold coins from every birch and cottonwood as far as the eye could see, and the golden wash of late evening sunlight showed them to their best advantage. Even the dark spruce covering the gentle slopes were sprinkled with the bright leaves.

She glanced at her watch, her breath frosting in the chill air. It was 7:44 P.M, and it would start getting dark soon. This late in September, it could snow at any time. Too bad it wasn't June. If it were then she wouldn't have to worry about the darkness at all, since the sun never set during the height of summer.

She stood and hefted her pack, her lungs giving a tired protest. To cheer herself, she counted her blessings. She could have been born allergic to chocolate, or dogs. She glanced at Lemming affectionately.

Come to think of it, if she'd been allergic to dogs, she wouldn't have to be out here.

Suppressing a groan, she pushed herself to her feet and started out again. Wiley better have something hot on the fire, or there would be war. The least her friend could do after coaxing her into the boonies was to make camp.

Rapidly losing steam, she trudged up the trail, really little more than a brushy track, noting the moose nuggets and cloven hoof prints in the soft turf without enthusiasm. She didn't fancy running into an irate cow with a calf. She didn't want to spend the evening stuck in a Mexican standoff while the cow tried to decide if she was worth trampling or better off ignored.

While she was looking down she noticed the bounty of cranberry bushes. It really was a shame she didn't have the energy to stop and pick some. They were plentiful this year and she could use a good batch of cranberry bars.

Hey, while she was dreaming, how about a hot date, an end cut of the Turtle Club's prime rib and a dry pair of socks?

Maybe she should be dreaming about a hot date for Wiley, she thought with disgust. If her friend and roommate paid more attention to her love life, maybe she wouldn't feel the need to run off to the woods at a moment's notice. It was all great and well if Wiley had the itch to commune with nature, as long as she didn't drag her friends into it.

The only itch Jasmine felt were the ones left by the hordes of gnats and mosquitoes. It was almost pointless using repellent—the mosquitoes mistook it for ketchup and came back for seconds.

Lemming barked from somewhere up ahead, signaling that she'd found Wiley's camp. Jasmine's head came up and she eagerly picked up her pace. In a minute she'd be sipping hot cocoa and roasting herself in front of a fire. Wiley would sweet talk her with chili and she'd forget she'd just spent the last hour stomping through the woods.

She entered the mossy clearing where Lemming waited and stopped, confused. It was empty.

Later, as Jasmine nursed a cup of cocoa by a fire she'd had to make herself, she tried to figure out what could have happened. At first she'd circled the area, calling Wiley's name and trying to find evidence as to her recent occupation. It occurred to Jasmine that her friend had played a trick, maybe hid higher on the hill and grinned as she watched Jasmine wade through stickers and brush. It wasn't like her to make Jas worry, though.

As full dark descended, she had known Wiley wasn't playing a game. Something had happened to her friend, and it was too dark to make her way back to the Jeep to get help. If Wiley had tumbled down a hill, it would be no help to her if Jasmine got lost herself. Instead she tried to reason out what might have happened.

Wiley might take off at a moment's notice on her perverse games of hide and seek, but she always left a map, and she never strayed from it. If she said she was going to be forty-five minutes east of the Dalton Highway that's where they'd find her. Or rather, Lemming would find her, and Lemming always found her quarry.

She glanced at the search and rescue dog Wiley had trained from a pup. Lemming rested quietly at Jasmine's side with her chin on her paws, content with a job well done. Jasmine had tried to get her to keep tracking, but she'd only sat down, looked at her in confusion, and thumped her tail once. As far as she was concerned, her job was over.

Jasmine sighed and scratched an itch under her black Road Runner stocking cap. She was worried, but tried not to dwell on it. It wouldn't help the situation. Besides, there might be a good explanation for this.

She noticed a sticker bush twig in Lemming's fur. Gently, she removed it and flicked it into the coals. So now what? She didn't plan to stay in grizzly and wolf infested woods any longer then she had to. At first light she'd pack up and go for help. Maybe if she kept her eyes open she'd see signs of her friend.

She coughed as smoke suddenly blew into her face and moved around the fire.

Well, there was nothing more she could do right now, and she was tired of having the fire roast her front end while the cold air behind froze her rear. Time to crawl into her tent, shuck down to her long johns and hope she wouldn't have to shiver too long before the down sleeping bag warmed up. Though come to think of it, the night almost seemed to be getting warmer.

Scoffing at her wishful thinking, she stood and kicked dirt over the fire. That's when she saw them.

Eyes.

Freaky, glowing golden eyes. Lots of them.

Lemming growled and pressed so tightly against her that she nearly tripped as the eyes evolved into wolves with eerie, alien faces.

Slowly she reached for the 357 Smith and
Wesson revolver strapped to her hip. She'd brought
the thing as a bear deterrent, but there was no reason
it couldn't take down a wolf.

The fur on the creature directly in front of her
hackled and it snarled a warning that made her own
hair stand on end. Lemming responded with a vicious
bark that made her jump.

"Touch it and they'll rip your throat out," a
man's voice said mildly. It came from the dark,
behind the wolves.

Jasmine emitted a strangled yell. Her nerves
were on the crawl as she thought of someone
watching her. She searched the darkness, but couldn't
see beyond the animals. "Who's there?"

As if in a nightmare, a man stepped away from
the camouflage of dark trees. He stood less than ten
feet from her and seemed to study her with faint
distaste. Maybe she didn't measure up to his twisted
fantasies. Maybe he liked tall girls, like Wiley. What
were the odds he knew where she was?

Her jaw hardened. She itched to draw and cock
the gun, but the slight movement of her hand brought
the snarling beast before her a step closer.

"Call off your dogs," she demanded hoarsely.
All the moisture that should have been in her mouth
decided to run down her back instead. Who'd turned
up the heat?

"Give up your weapon," the stranger ordered,
and his words were brushed with an odd accent.
"They don't trust you."

"The feeling is mutual, pal, but I'm not doing it.
They'll eat me alive if I do." She'd watched TV. She

knew what happened to the idiots who dropped the gun.

He glanced at the creatures. "Your choice."

Long moments passed while she held his gaze. Sweat plastered the hair under her hat to her scalp. For all she knew this guy had kidnapped Wiley and was keeping her somewhere nearby…if she was still alive.

It was that thought more than anything that made her give in. Swearing one of Wiley's favorite words, she gave a curt nod. Careful not to make any sudden moves that might set the wolves off, she unfastened the safety strap of the holster and eased the gun out. Surprisingly, she wasn't snarled at until she hesitated at the last moment.

"You'll never kill them all," the stranger said with a trace of impatience.

Reluctantly, she tossed down the gun.

While she'd been stalling, the heat had turned killer. That was one heck of Chinook blowing, or he'd done something to cause it. There was a faint shimmer in the night behind him, an odd pressure in the air. She'd swear she smelled ozone.

Fearful she'd die of heatstroke at any moment, she yanked off her hat, then unzipped her heavy coat and shrugged it off. If she had to die, at least it wouldn't be from the sudden thaw.

She glanced at the wolves, but they were no longer snarling. In fact, the one she thought of as the leader had backed off. He kept his eyes on her while the others wove in and out of the huge trees.

Huge trees?

Jasmine paused in the act of stripping off her Norwegian sweater, all the fine hairs on her body standing on end. Huge trees? There were no trees like that in Alaska. But there they were, gleaming in the light of the triple moons....

For a bad moment Jasmine's world tilted, threatening the first faint of her life. Just in time, her innate good sense kicked in. Now was not the time for wilting.

As she stared, ferns sprang from the undergrowth and the trees moved closer, as the shimmer behind the stranger seemed to grow, marching forward as if swallowing her world whole. She hadn't moved, but that shimmer behind him, that otherworldly window, had grown to encompass them both. She was afraid to look behind her, afraid to see it consume all the earth.

First things first. The heat was humid and tropical, murderous to blood thickened by a cold climate, and she was overdressed. With a deep breath to calm her jangled nerves, she sent the man a defiant look and pulled off the bulky sweater, tugging the black T-shirt underneath to keep it from riding up. Then she just stood there in the redwood-scented air and tried to make sense of the moment. Sweat rolled down her back, and she wished she could ditch her wool socks and the long underwear. Her feet were sweltering in her heavy boots.

The man shifted restlessly. "Come," he said, melting into the trees before she had a chance to argue.

"Wait!" she called, but he ignored her. She hesitated, wondering if she could possibly retrieve the small flashlight inside her jacket. No way did she want to go blindly charging off through the night with a spooky stranger without at least being able to see what he was doing. She bent a little, and the lead wolf snarled. "Easy, fella, I just need to get a light." His lips pulled even farther back and saliva flecked his muzzle. The other wolves took their cue from the pack master and stalked closer, showing hundreds of teeth.

Stumbling through the darkness following a possibly vicious stranger suddenly held appeal. She picked up her feet and hurried after the man before she found out if the pack had a taste for sweaty hikers.

Besides, who knew what else might come creeping out of the brush?

There might have been three moons in the sky, but none of them were full, and she'd never had the best night vision. The second time she nearly went sprawling while jogging after the stranger, she decided to call a halt. If she didn't slow down one of the branches hitting her in the face was going to put out an eye, and where would she be? Besides, Lemming could always track him.

The wolf things had other ideas.

"Look," she tried to explain to one of the creatures that inched slowly closer, growling, while Lemming nearly backed up her leg, "I'm trying, but I can't see where I'm going. Just give me a minute, okay?"

A hand shot out of the dark and gripped her upper arm, making her shriek.

"This way."

She gasped for breath, trying to calm her frantic heart while the stranger hauled her through the woods. "Did you have to do that?" she demanded, but he didn't answer and didn't slow down. She tried again. "Where are we going?" Still no answer. "You're a real jerk, you know that?"

His grip on her arm tightened and he picked up speed. "I will return you to your place come morning."

She dug in her heels and threw every ounce of her weight into it, jolting them to a stop. *No way, pal.* She didn't know what he planned, but when a strange man without an ounce of courtesy told her he was going to keep her for the night, she panicked.

As he spun to face her, she shot her fist into his nose, snapping his head back, then grabbed his shirt and rammed her knee into his groin with all her strength.

Or tried to.

The next moment he was holding her on her toes with two frighteningly controlled hands around her biceps.

His voice, when it came, was rough with menace. "You think to deny me anything?" His body was very tense, as if he longed to either choke the life from her or hurl her from him. Even so, she tried to kick him. Swearing, he shook her, making Lemming snarl. The stranger snapped something in a language she didn't know and Lemming subsided with a whine.

His eyes bore into hers. "You're fortunate you are a woman, or I would snap your neck and have done with it." As suddenly as he'd grabbed her, he released her, causing her to stumble. "You go back come morning."

Jasmine trembled, not daring to move for a long, sick moment. Never before had she felt so threatened by a man, so completely aware of her inferior size and puny strength. He had her alone, completely at his mercy, and if he decided to hurt her there was nothing she could do to stop him.

Lemming whined and slid up to her, seeking reassurance, and in that seeking, gave Jasmine a measure of strength. She wasn't a coward, and she was smart. There had to be a way out of this. Wiley needed her.

CHAPTER 2

He was overreacting.

Keilor watched her tremble, chiding himself. The girl was young and scared, barely even a woman by the looks of her, and he was a stranger who deliberately frightened her. Of course she would lash out. As he watched the girl gather her courage, he remembered that his cousin considered her a friend. He didn't have to like it, but he could refrain from terrorizing her.

He wiped the blood from his battered nose and his anger flared again. Blight that! He would if she would.

Nevertheless, his touch was gentler and his pace slower as he guided her through the darkness. Remorse stabbed him when she shrank a little at his touch. He ruthlessly repressed it. They didn't want her to like it here, nor to feel welcome, no matter what Rihlia thought. She would come to see the wisdom of remaining separate from the human world soon enough. If he and Jayems had their way, the girl would be going back this instant. Only Rihlia's need to reassure this girl that she was fine stayed their hands.

The memory of her stripping off her heavy clothes strobed through his mind, provoking a flash of heat. She glanced at him in surprise and a little fear when his grip tightened on her arm. He forced it to relax.

It was only the unexpectedness of it that had caused his body to react, he reassured himself. He hadn't expected the girl to start stripping. It hadn't helped to discover that her outer wrappings had concealed an exotically pretty woman—*girl*, he corrected himself firmly—underneath. His cousin had claimed they were of an age, but this female was barely up to his chest, with a youthful face, besides.

Not that it mattered what she looked like; the girl was going back as soon as Rihlia said goodbye. It was time for his cousin to rediscover her real family.

He ducked to avoid a branch, thinking how fortunate they'd been to find the long lost Rihlia at one of the rare gates between worlds. He shook his head in amazement. After years of fruitless searching, only to discover the child she'd been had crossed worlds! But now she was home and it was time for her to take her rightful place among her people and her family.

He glanced at the dark haired girl in irritation, the night no barrier to his keen vision. What Rihlia didn't need was reminders of the past weighing her down while she tried to readjust to her home world. Even if they were sweetly curved and just the right height to—

"I cannot see what she could possibly want with you," he burst out in frustration.

The girl's head snapped up and she stopped. "She? Are you talking about Wiley?"

"Her name is Rihlia," he corrected stiffly, stopping as well. He was annoyed at his outburst. It wasn't like him to be this edgy around a woman; even a beautiful woman; *especially* a beautiful woman, and he didn't like it.

"She's my age, very dark hair, looks Asian?"

"I know who she is," he said coolly, "And her name is Rihlia."

Her eyes snapped fire as she jerked her arm away, fear apparently forgotten. Really, for such a tiny creature, she was full of passion. Had she been anyone else, he would have relished that knowledge; but she wasn't staying.

"Her name is Wiley, you misbegotten—" she broke off and took a deep breath. "I need to see her."

"Then come." He took her arm again and set off. The sooner this chore was accomplished, the better. He had more important matters to attend to.

Apparently she wasn't content to travel in silence, for she said, "What is this place?"

"The Dark Lands," he answered shortly, hoping she'd be quiet. He glanced off into the trees and toyed with the idea of having the volti show themselves again to frighten her speechless, but refrained.

"Why is it called that?"

"To frighten off unwanted humans?" he suggested with exasperation. Were all humans this bothersome, or was it just her? She tripped over a plainly visible rock in the path and swore, forcing him to steady her yet again. He added clumsy and unobservant to the list of things he didn't like about her.

"What do you mean, 'humans'?" she asked suspiciously.

"What you are, and what I am not. What Rihlia is not," he informed her with satisfaction. That ought help drive her off. Humans were notoriously fearful of anyone alien, even their own kind. She would be no different.

"*Wiley* is as human as I am," she gritted out. "I ought to know. We were raised in the same orphanage."

The remembrance of how his cousin had been kept in a sterile home for abandoned and orphaned children enraged him anew. "She was raised there, but she wasn't born there. Your kind put her there."

"Yeah? Well, she wouldn't have been there if *your kind* hadn't lost her," she snapped back.

He grabbed her arm and jerked her to him, angry on such a deep level that he could barely verbalize his emotion. "You have no idea what you are saying, creature. Beware lest you test my mercy," he warned her softly, almost relishing her trembling. Hatred of humans was old and instinctive. Though he could not have named all his reasons, he wanted this one to fear him. He wanted her to leave.

There was something wrong about her.

Before he could identify what his instincts told him, his nose caught her scent, bringing with it a desire that flooded his senses in an entirely alien way. For a moment his mind stalled, and the closest he could come to breaking away was to shift his hand down her arm. Spellbound, the only thing that he wanted in that moment was to let his body speak to her in a language entirely its own.

Lightning traveled up his arms from her frozen body and he let go with a gasp. "Charmer!" he hissed, and gripped the hilt of his blade. It was all he could do not to kill her on the spot. Of all the woman in the world Rihlia had to call friend, why one of *them*, one of the few guaranteed to be trouble to the males of his kind?

"What?" She looked confused. Could she be ignorant of her curse? It would not save her. He had sworn not to harm her, but it would not stop the others. They would kill her. A charmer was a temptress, a siren, poison.

He needed to get rid of her, fast.

He reached out to tow her along again, thought better of it, and pointed with an unsteady hand. "There is the trail. Follow it." He thought of prodding her along with his blade for good measure, but perhaps that was going too far. After all, it wasn't as if she'd leap on him and attempt a seduction right there.

Probably.

Her head turned to follow his pointing finger and she squinted in bewilderment. "Where?"

"Right there," he repeated, wondering what was wrong with her. Could she really be this helpless in the dark?

The sultry wind ruffled her limp hair as she gave a weary sigh. "Look, I can't see a thing out here, ok? I can barely see you, so if you plan on getting where we're going tonight, you'll have to lead the way."

It was not worth arguing. The sooner begun… He started walking—not so fast that she couldn't see him, but far enough ahead to ensure zero contact. One couldn't be too careful with a charmer.

For thousands of years, her kind had been used by humans to lure and trap the men of the Haunt. The best of their warriors had been enticed by the unique, bewitching scent of the charmer and killed by their masters until there were few of them left. That combined with the unrelenting fear and hatred of humans had driven his kind to seek their own world, free of the hunters.

And now one of them was here.

Jayems would be furious.

As they approached the forest entrance to the hollowed volcanic mountain that served as the Haunt fortress, he kept a wary eye on the female, remembering Rihlia's unfortunate reaction to her first sight of the warrior Haunt. This girl was no different. The moment she saw the shadowy guards she stumbled back with a gasp, which was at least an improvement over the ear-shattering shriek he'd been braced for. Reaching back, he grabbed a fistful of her shirt and dragged her through the door. Once inside, he propelled her down the hallway with a business-like hand at her back.

"Wh-what…"

Badly shaken, she could barely get the words out. At least she wasn't hysterical. It had taken much longer to calm Rihlia down enough to make her believe the Haunt were not a danger to her. But then, she belonged to this world.

He would make no such assurances to this human.

"Wait here," he told the girl sternly, pointing to the cushioned bench set in the alcove opposite his lord's rooms. She sank limply onto the bench, obeying him without a murmur, but it wasn't him she was looking at. He turned to the pair of Haunt guards flanking the massive double doors and eyed them wryly. She was unlikely to attempt any mischief while under their baleful stare, but just to be sure...

"Eat her if she moves," he ordered, and watched with satisfaction as her eyes widened. Hiding his grin at the guards' puzzled glances, he entered the room.

"She is here," he reported, stepping into the large room.

Jayems looked up quickly from where he sat at his desk of polished, dark wood. The heavy ledger he'd been reading closed with a muffled thud, but his boots remained crossed on the desktop as he waited for more details.

Rihlia wasn't nearly as calm. She leapt off the couch where she'd been sitting and demanded breathlessly, "Where?" Her long dark hair had been braided with pearls and topaz, and someone had gotten her into a white silk robe. He wondered who'd worked the miracle. The last time he'd seen her she'll still been stubbornly clinging to her old clothes.

Keilor smiled slightly, amused. For all she looked like a princess, she was as bright-eyed and eager as a much younger girl. It was easy to see in her the child she'd been.

Grimness replaced his amusement as he recalled her friend. "There's a problem," he informed his lord darkly. "She's a charmer."

Jayems' feet uncrossed, dropping with unnerving deliberation to the floor. He slammed his palms down on the desk and leaned forward. "A what?"

Keilor shook his head slowly. "She could be nothing else. I'm certain of it."

Jayems swore and got to his feet, pacing with barely controlled anger.

His reluctant betrothed looked between them in angry confusion. "What's the matter? You told me she could—"

Jayems whirled to face her, his dark tunic riffling in the breeze. "I gave permission for you to say goodbye, and I will still allow it, but the minute you are finished, she goes."

Her eyes flared in temper. "Well, of course, *darling,*" she agreed acidly. "After all, we wouldn't want any unsavory humans loitering about, now, would we?"

He stalked her, stopping inches from her to pierce her with his stare. "I'm gratified we understand each other, wife." Before she could snarl out a denial, he snapped, "Bring her, Keilor. Let's finish this."

* * *

Jasmine sat where she'd been ordered and stared at the intricate mosaic patterns in the wood floor. It was hard not to gawk at her guards, and her gaze kept darting up to peek with horrified fascination. Lemming pressed against her leg, whining softly.

They made no bones about staring back.

They had the heads and flattened faces of wolves, and their entire bodies were covered in dark hair. Each guard wore a leather holster with a gun of some sort strapped to his thigh and a long knife sheathed at the hip. Combat boots, pants and buckled leather vests completed the ensemble. They looked frighteningly competent.

Frightening being the key word.

It was a relief when her warden opened the door and ordered her to, "Come." With forced courage, she got to her feet and edged swiftly past the guards, relaxing only when the door was safely shut behind her. She was going to have nightmares about this place.

Lemming gave a glad bark and charged forward.

Wiley laughed as she knelt down to hug her dog.
"Good girl!" she praised the collie and fondled her ears
affectionately. "You found me, didn't you?" She looked
up and saw Jasmine, and her eyes glittered with tears.
"Aren't you a sight for sore eyes," she murmured, and
embraced her in a crushing hug. "I thought you'd never get
here."

Jasmine pulled back and gave her a wobbly grin.
"Blame it on your map. You forgot to mention that last
curve in the road." Her smile faded as she glanced at the
two men who watched them impassively. She looked back
at her friend. "What's going on, Wiley?"

"It's…" Wiley broke off and looked at the dark
haired man Jasmine didn't know. He was perched on a
desk, his feet crossed at the ankles. Her erstwhile escort
stood near him, which was also as far from Jasmine as the
room allowed.

"I don't suppose we could have some privacy?"
Wiley asked coldly. The handsome stranger inclined his
head, indicating that he had heard her, but he didn't move.
She muttered something under her breath and led Jasmine
to the far end of the room, sitting down with her on a
couch. Lemming came up and nudged Wiley's hand, and
she absently stroked her while she explained.

"We're on another world," she began slowly.

Jasmine glanced at the triple moons visible through
the window comprising an entire wall and then back at the
door. She nodded slowly in agreement. She'd figured that
one out on her own.

Wiley watched her carefully. "I was born here."

Jasmine's eyes unfocused for a moment as she
pondered that. "It explains a few things. Go on."

Wiley took a breath. "The guy who brought you here
is my cousin, Keilor."

Jasmine's eyes darted in surprise to the man, and for
the first time she really looked at him, scrutinizing his

features. Black, silken hair framed high cheekbones, reminiscent of a Cherokee warrior, and the faint flare of his nostrils reinforced the impression. She couldn't see the color of his eyes from across the room, but the expression in them of wary distaste was all too clear. She was already far too familiar with the strength of his hands, and the excellent lighting in the room only confirmed that he was in excellent shape.

He raised a dark brow in mocking acknowledgment of the introduction.

"You have my sympathy," she told her friend.

Wiley smiled slightly. She didn't even look at the other man, just jerked her head in his direction. "The other guy is called Jayems." They were both quite for a moment. Wiley's hands twisted her skirt. At last she said stiffly, "They won't let me go home, and they want you to go back right away and forget you ever saw me."

Jasmine sat back, carefully controlling her anger. Her expression was cold, but a dangerous smile turned up one side of her mouth. "Two words, my friend." She twitched an eyebrow and switched to Pig Latin. "Avyna, Ealsay, anda eytha anca ovesha ita upa eirtha assa." *Navy SEALS, and they can shove it up their—*

Wiley laughed a little, relieved. She understood that Jasmine wasn't going to just leave her there.

Jasmine smiled slyly, squeezed her hand and stood up. "It's been real, Wiley, and I'm glad to see that you're all right." She turned to the one called Keilor. "I'm ready to go home now."

Keilor looked back at her with a knowing expression. He turned to Jayems and made a few signs with his hands. Jayems glanced at her assessingly and signed back. Keilor moved towards her. "Why so hasty? You just got here. Perhaps it would be best if you waited to return until morning." He watched her closely.

Jasmine felt the panic flash like a neon sign across her face and quickly looked down, doing her best to contain it. She swallowed and said as evenly as possible, "I thought you were in a hurry to get rid of me." She bit the inside of her lip, cursing herself for saying something so revealing, and hastily amended, "Not that I mind staying to talk to a friend or anything, but this place gives me the creeps."

Jayems straightened from the desk and sauntered towards her until both he and Keilor towered over her. She didn't dare look at him. "Friends," he mused. "That's not what Rihlia called you. Sister of her heart, she said. Closer than blood." He paused and looked her up and down with too knowing eyes the color of polished bronze. "Odd that such a one would desert her so quickly." Suddenly he grasped her chin and forced her to look at him. "Would you be planning trouble, little sister?"

She met his eyes with difficulty, and kept them there through force of will. "Who would believe my story?" she evaded and then mentally winced. Why hadn't she just lied? She might as well just blurt out that she intended to bring the entire U.S. Army with her if she could find her way back.

He studied her for a moment and then softly snorted. Releasing her, he told Keilor, "Find her a room down the hall and see that she's comfortable, would you cousin? And post guards at her door." His smile was less than pleasant. "We wouldn't want anything to happen to Rihlia's loyal little sister."

She stiffened as Keilor's hand closed around her arm. Wiley got in his way at once.

He paused to acknowledge her effort. "Cousin."

Alarmed, Wiley looked around him to rail at Jayems. "What are you doing?"

His eyes narrowed. "Sending her away before I break her neck for lying to me." He glanced at the wide-eyed

Jasmine grudgingly. "Though I suppose she can be forgiven, as she does it out of loyalty to you."

His gaze glittered at Wiley. "There is a limit to what I will forgive those who try to deceive me."

"You said she could go home."

His face hardened. "Keilor."

Keilor gently moved the resisting Wiley aside and continued toward the door, leaving Jayems to continue his battle in private.

"You be nice to her!" Wiley shouted after Keilor as they entered the gray stone hall.

CHAPTER 3

Keilor looked Jasmine assessingly. "Do you want me to be nice to you, Dragonfly?"

She glowered at him. "I doubt you know how." They paused at a set of double doors a short way down the hall.

He flashed her a wicked smile. "I can be very nice when I choose." His hand closed over the door handle, but he didn't open it just yet. He moved a fraction closer to her. Warm breath slid across her skin as he traced the iridescent dragonfly pendant at her throat. She dropped her eyes, shivering just a little as chills rushed through her.

"Be good, my Dragonfly. Be very, very good," he whispered, lifting her chin until their faces were only inches apart. He stroked his fingers lightly down her neck, making her breath catch. A warning glinted in his eyes. "You won't like it if I have to correct you."

Jasmine pulled away and looked pointedly at the carved panels of the door, resenting how he made her feel. He was the enemy. "You get off on trying to scare women, don't you?"

Not really. Keilor paused, considering their uninvited guest. Initially he'd agreed with Jayems that the most efficient way to be rid of the human was to frighten her silly. That plan had failed miserably. But who could have known about her courage? Rihlia had been ready to run, and without provocation. Perhaps it was time to find a new way of dealing with the human.

After all, like it or not, she was going to be here a while.

Opening the door, he gestured her inside with a flourish. "Lights," he called, and the lights came on. "Softer," he ordered, and they dimmed. His eyes swept down her body, noting her tousled hair. She smelled like sweat and fear, and her eyes were shadowed with exhaustion.

"Bath," he called, and steaming water began to fill a tub at the side of the large room. It was large enough for four people and reached by a series of steps chiseled of blue veined marble. A carved screen, now folded, stood between it and a handsome armoire of red wood and mirrored doors. He gestured toward the armoire. "Towels. The door next to it is a closet, not that you'll find anything in it at the moment." He turned slightly on the parquet flooring. "Bed."

Jasmine glanced at the large bed against the left wall and did a double take. Vines curled around a pair of lovers entwined in a standing position on each post. She rolled her eyes, grateful that she rarely blushed. Heaven help her. It would be a miracle if she could get to sleep in such a bed. She dared a glance at the headboard and quickly looked away, brain burning.

"Don't you have somewhere else I can sleep?" Her eyes skittered restlessly around the otherwise elegant room, and then up at the ceiling. She groaned. An enormous mirror in a golden frame was mounted above the bed. "I mean...with a less..." She waved her hand at the bed.

"I could," he answered agreeably. He looked amused. "Though I couldn't guarantee your bed would be solitary."

She glared at him. "Fine." He raised an intrigued eyebrow. "*This* is fine," she clarified.

He shrugged. "As you wish. If you need anything—something to eat, for instance—just raise your voice slightly and call for service."

Jasmine waited a moment after he'd left and then quickly opened the door. Two wolf guards looked down at her inquiringly. She growled in frustration and shut the door, locking it for good measure. Then she slumped against it, done in. Lemming had stayed with Wiley, so nothing disturbed the silence in the room, or her thoughts, such as they were. Her brain felt numb—temporarily shocked into immobility by the events of the evening. Her body ached from her climb up and down the Alaskan hills, and her feet throbbed and sweated unmercifully in her double layer of socks.

A click caused her to roll her head towards the tub. The water had stopped pouring. After a moment of contemplation she gave a fatalistic shrug. Ah, well. What else did she have to do?

Jasmine sighed and stretched luxuriously against the silky sheets, then forced herself to roll over. It took a bit more effort to pry her eyes open long enough to actually see and process her surroundings. She sat up with a start.

"Jas...are you awake yet?" Wiley's voice sounded from a hidden intercom near the door.

Jasmine groaned and brushed the sleep from her eyes, not certain she was ready to face the day. Remnants of her dreams, something involving mirrors and a dark haired lover, still haunted her mind. Well, she'd known this tacky bed was going to give her nightmares.

"Jasmine!" Wiley sounded impatient.

"Come in."

"I can't—it's locked."

"Ah, nuts." Surrendering to the inevitable, she crawled out of bed and covered herself with a soft robe she'd found in the armoire before going to unlock the door.

"About time," Wiley grouched. Lemming was at her heels. "I was beginning to fear they'd done away with you, even though Jayems insisted you were still in here." She gestured for the servants behind her to enter while Jasmine stifled a yawn. "I brought breakfast." She crossed to the wardrobe and set a bundle of folded clothes inside. "You can see if these fit you after we eat, if you want."

"Great." Jasmine pushed her shoulder length hair out of her face. A servant in a white and gold tunic and loose trousers set a large covered tray on the dining table and took off the lid. He set the table for two.

"Shutters," Wiley called out, and the wall directly opposite the door slid open like elevator doors, revealing a wall of clear glass with a breathtaking view.

Jasmine drew in a breath, distracted from the delicious smells of breakfast, and moved closer to stare in awe at the sheer drop below her window.

It was misty outside, the kind of thick fog that was almost rain, but even so she could make out the cove five stories below her room. Towering redwoods rose on every side, to the edges of the shore, though they were half hidden in the haze. Farther out, gray sea met smoky sky in a seamless melding that might have stretched forever, off unto the edge of the world. Or perhaps it was merely the hazy glass curve of the magician's crystal that held this strange dream world.

"It's an inlet of the sea—I forget what it's called. On a clear day you can see the mountains on the other side," Wiley said. Today she wore a sky blue robe with a long sapphire tunic trimmed in silver embroidery. She stroked a sleeve absently, in a faintly troubled way.

Jasmine shook her head, breaking the spell of the sea. "Beautiful," she said to Wiley, suitably awed. Then she grinned. "Let's eat."

Wiley laughed and moved towards the table. The male servant stood discreetly against the wall while the other made up the bed and collected Jasmine's clothes, depositing them in a machine hidden behind a wall panel. Jasmine observed that her white uniform didn't appear to be the best color for a maid as the woman began to clean the tub, and then dismissed the matter. Maybe they had superior methods of stain removal here. At any rate, she had more important things to worry about.

She spread a napkin on her lap and had just opened her mouth to broach those matters when Wiley gasped and began to giggle. "What?"

"You had to sleep there?" Wiley pointed an unsteady finger at the bed.

She glanced at it, and the mirror on the ceiling, annoyed all over again. "Your sweet cousin seemed to think it was funny." She surveyed the silver chopsticks and wide spoon beside her plate with consternation. Perhaps she should have tried harder to master the wooden ones in the Chinese restaurants back home. Picking up her spoon, she scooped a small taste of what appeared to be a sausage pilaf and nibbled on it experimentally. Satisfied, she took the serving scoop and piled a small mountain onto her china plate. "I won't be sorry to see the end of him."

"Here, have some almond milk." Wiley smiled almost nervously and handed her an insulated silver ewer.

"Almond milk?" She made a face as she accepted it and poured a little in a tall crystal glass. "What is this, planet of the health food junkies?"

Wiley shrugged in apology. "No dairy animals."

Jasmine's brows shot up. "What? No whipped cream, no butter?" Frowning, she took a cautious sip from her cup. "Ok, it's not bad, but if someone whips out a brick of tofu, I'm leaving."

Wiley toyed with her spoon. Addressing it, she said, "You can't." At Jasmine's puzzled expression, she clarified, "They won't let you leave. They think you're planning to cause trouble if they let you go."

"Rescuing you, you mean." She tossed down her spoon. "What right do they have to hold you here, anyway? Seems to me like they gave up on you a long time ago. Why take you back now, when you don't want to be here?"

Wiley sighed heavily. "It's worse. Jayems…. He claims he's my husband."

"*What*?" The table rattled as Jasmine shot to her feet. "For crying out loud, why?"

Wiley's lip began to tremble. "He claims we were 'joined in a betrothal ceremony' when we were kids."

Jasmine shoved her chair away, her robe flapping against her legs as she stood up and paced, the better to rant. "That's barbaric!" An awful thought occurred to her and she paled. "He hasn't tried to…"

Wiley's eyes widened, reading her mind with the ease of long acquaintance. "No! No, nothing like that," she hastily reassured her friend. "I don't think he'd…I think he'd rather…" She cleared her throat and blushed. "Anyway, it's the whole idea."

"I should say so," Jasmine agreed indignantly, pacing again. She spotted the male servant watching her. No doubt he was sent to spy on them. Well, two could play that game. "What's your name?" she demanded.

"Knightin, my lady," he said with a respectful inclination of his head.

She puzzled for a second over the lady—he made it sound like a title—but let it pass, assuming it was a substitute for ma'am in this neck of the woods. She studied his face for a moment, noting that his long rusty hair was tied back. Long hair appeared to be in fashion on this world. "How do you get a divorce here?"

28

A gasp came from her right, and she whipped her head around in time to see the maid fumbling for her dropped feather duster. Score one for the home team.

Good, she thought with fierce satisfaction.

Knightin's expression turned wary. "It is not done, my lady."

"It's not done, or it can't be done?"

He shifted a fraction and took a slight breath. "If a woman can prove she has no desire for her husband, then she may be released from her bond, however—"

Jasmine smiled triumphantly at Wiley and watched her shoulders begin to relax. "There, you see? Nothing to—"

"*However,*" Knightin interrupted, "in the Lady Rihlia's case, it would be almost impossible to obtain." He seemed almost angry, and Jasmine wanted to find out why.

She pretended to be distracted by the view for a moment, letting him stew. She needed to keep her temper down. When she was calmer, she said, "Okay, please explain why Wiley would have trouble divorcing this Jayems."

He looked like she'd forced a bite of Chinese bitter melon on him. "*Lord* Jayems," he emphasized the title like a nanny prompting diction, "Is the successor to Lord Rohmeis, but only through his bond with Lady Rihlia."

Jasmine winced a little at all the foreign terms and then looked at Wiley significantly. "So without *Wiley*, the leadership, or whatever it is, goes poof, huh? But would Wiley really be forced to stay with him if she didn't want to?"

Knightin relaxed and answered with a touch of male arrogance, "Considering the type of bond they share, it's unlikely that 'wanting' could even be an issue." When they just stared at him, he clarified with satisfaction, "Their marriage was determined by casting lots."

Jasmine's temper began to get the better of her again. "Are you telling me…" she paused to control her tone, "that my best friend's future husband was determined by essentially drawing straws?"

Taken aback, he tried to explain, unconsciously speaking with his hands in his agitation, as well as his voice, "The lots are holy, reliable instruments of—"

"I don't care about your holy mumbo jumbo!" she shouted. "How could her family do that to her? Where were her parents? Don't answer that," she cut him off, raising a hand in warning. "I might get sick." She glanced at Wiley, who looked worried again, and made herself calm down. Wiley didn't need her losing her temper. She had it rough enough already.

But it wasn't fair—none of it. Wiley had already been through too much. Growing up an orphan was tough enough. Suddenly finding an entire family and being snatched by an alien world was more than enough to deal with without watching her friend throw temper tantrums on top of it. What they needed was a plan, and she had just the thing.

She touched Wiley's hand gently. "Don't worry about it, Wile E. Coyote," she teased. "We'll just treat him like a wart—a little liquid nitrogen, a little discomfort, and *poof*, he's gone." Wiley laughed, as she'd intended.

Knightin turned an unhealthy shade of bing cherry.

She eyed him speculatively. "So, what exactly are your orders? Besides reporting every word we say, that is?" She watched in satisfaction as his jaw clenched, but he didn't rise to the bait. "Do you have to follow her everywhere she goes, or only when she's with me?"

Annoyance simmered in his manner, but his answer was straight forward enough. "Only when she's with you."

She smirked at Wiley, and said just to see her smile, "I guess you'd better step out while I get dressed. There's only so much I'd care to have reported about me."

Wiley chuckled and waved her hand, more like her old self. "Go use the dressing room, brat. I promise not to let anyone follow you."

Jasmine entered the dressing room and closed the door behind her. She wasn't nearly as calm as she pretended, but she didn't want the panic she felt to show. They had to get home!

Well, she'd feel better once she was properly dressed. She took a breath and examined the bundle of clothing Wiley had brought. There was a pair of black leather boots with breathable canvas panels in just her size and several pairs of socks. Comfortable black pants in a material similar to extremely thick silk with a button fly closure and a belt had been included. She set them aside while she searched for underwear.

That was when she hit the first snag.

In disbelief, Jasmine dangled a pair of silky panties up in the air. The material parted at the crotch, forming a butterfly. She'd never owned such a scandalous undergarment in her life, and she couldn't believe Wiley would actually bring her such a thing. Yet here they were, several pairs of them. Yep, she could choose to be risqué in fire engine red, pink, black, white *or* midnight blue.

It got worse.

Jasmine had once seen a picture of some ancient Mediterranean pottery where the women wore a type of short-sleeved bustier/vest that had boosted their breasts. The garments had been cut out around the breast itself, leaving the naked breast lifted up and exposed as if held in two cupped hands, rather like an offering.

If she wasn't holding an exact replica, it was dang close.

"*Wiley!*" she roared, "Get your butt in here!"

Wiley entered on the run. Jasmine held the offending garment up accusingly, and her friend blushed all the way to the roots of her hair. "Don't blame me," she said defensively. "They're standard issue here."

Jasmine's eyes boggled, dropped to Wiley's chest and then hurriedly away. She was *not* going to ask. "Fine," she said, her voice strained. "I still can't believe you brought them, though. As if I'm going to wear a bright red…" She dangled the garment on one finger. "What *do* you call this thing?"

Wiley crossed her arms. "I never actually asked, and for your information, I wasn't the one who picked them out." She paused a moment, letting the horror build. "Keilor got them for you after I mentioned you needed a change of clothes."

There was a long moment of silence. Then, "You let your cousin pick out my *underwear*?" She ended on a shout.

"He picked out your boots, too, and I don't hear you complaining about them," Wiley pointed out.

Jasmine shut up. Some humiliations in life were best not dwelt upon. Trying not to think about it, she put on some panties, socks and pants. At least the pants were comfortable, she consoled herself. That left the naughty tops to choose from and several long scarves of matching colors.

Still wearing her robe, Jasmine picked up a scarf and scowled at it. "What am I supposed to do with this, wrap it around my head and pretend I'm a pirate?"

Since Wiley didn't know, they called in the maid for a consultation. It turned out that the scarf was made to be worn crossed over the breasts and tied at the back of the neck for a bandeau. Somehow the maid convinced Jasmine to put the bustier thing—which she called an *overnji*—over the bandeau and at least look at it.

"It's very respectable," the older woman reassured her. "My daughters wear it all the time."

"I look like a harem girl," Jasmine muttered, staring at the midnight blue overnji and white bandeau she'd been conned into.

Wiley smirked and grabbed the dark blue sash. She wound it low about Jasmine's hips and knotted it. "There," she said, putting her hands on her hips and standing back to look over her creation. "Now you look like a harem escapee turned pirate."

"Why, thank you, Wiley," Jasmine sneered, stalking out. "That is so much better." She yanked open the armoire doors and extracted a brush she'd discovered there the night before. As she eyed the top in the mirrored doors while she worked the tangles from her hair, she decided that it wasn't so bad. At least her stomach was flat. Heck, she'd worn crop tops in public that bared about the same amount of skin and never thought twice about it. Of course, none of those had ever been chosen for her by a man.

With effort she chased the image of Keilor holding her new panties in his hands, perhaps imagining her in them. It was swiftly replaced by the image of him looking over the *overnji*, trying to guess at the size of her...

She took a deep, deep breath and then expelled it slowly. Keilor wasn't thinking about her breasts, or anything else for that matter. Men who looked like he did didn't need to fantasize. Shoot, for all she knew, he was happily married and had three kids, not that she cared.

What she needed to be thinking about was getting Wiley and herself back home where men were manageable and the local police force didn't look like the cast of *Howling III*.

They needed a plan.

CHAPTER 4

Keilor shook his head as Knightin's recording finished late that afternoon. "I think we can conclude that she's cagey, disrespectful, and definitely up to no good."

Jayems gave him a thoughtful look from where he sat, arms crossed, on the edge of his desk. He slanted a look at Knightin. "How did the charmer affect you?"

His captain frowned at the memory. "Like a panting boy with an armful of naked woman. It's making me wish I'd fixed my interest elsewhere long before she ever showed up."

Keilor snorted with agreement. "Ah, the bliss of a man already spoken for! Too bad our doctors can't replicate that protective little brain chemical. It would save us all a lot of grief. Short of becoming a Haunt with no sex drive or falling in love, the rest of us are stuck."

Jayems shook his head. "This is not good, Keilor. I don't like my options." He ticked them off grimly on his fingers. "I can send her back and pray she won't cause trouble." Their eyes met, and he closed that finger back into his fist. They both knew it wasn't worth the risk. "I can lock her away from all but my wife, women, and mated males."

"And have Rihlia resent you forever," Keilor concluded.

Jayems withdrew that finger, clenching his fist. "Never," he swore. "We will work past this. In the meanwhile…"

"Find her a lover, my lord," Knightin suggested reasonably, and they looked at him in surprise. He'd made no secret that he disliked the presence of the charmer and her subversive essence, dreading the influence that it would have on his men. Knightin hated disorder, and a charmer was the definition of it.

"That might work," Keilor agreed and looked hopefully at Jayems. He didn't care for the woman's influence on him, either. The sooner she was mated, the sooner her wretched power would be confined to one poor soul, and the rest of them could get on with their lives as before. He frowned, momentarily displeased by the thought of all those intensely erotic charmer pheromones being spent on just anybody. Then he shrugged it off. It was only the lingering affects of her remembered scent making him possessive, and an excellent example of why Knightin's suggestion was a good one. "I'm for it," he asserted firmly.

Jayems looked hopeful for a moment and then scowled. "It can't be just a lover. By forcing her to stay and accepting her as a guest of my lady, I've declared her my guest as well. Honor dictates that I can't scheme her into such a disreputable position. Besides, a lover wouldn't be good enough. As long as she's not securely attached, the men will still vie for her."

Knightin nodded thoughtfully. "You're right, it will have to be a mate," he agreed, practical as always.

Keilor noticed Jayems eyeing him thoughtfully, and the hair rose on the back of his neck. He scowled. "Forget it, cousin. I'm not wedding to solve your problems."

His lord shrugged. "It will have to be someone like you, a man of rank. Preferably a warrior of strong will." He grinned wickedly. "She would trample anyone less."

Decision made, he went to his desk, sat down, and pulled out a pen and paper. "Very well. What lambs shall we toss to the slaughter?"

Jasmine hurried through the giant trees at a fast walk. She was still amazed she'd managed to slip away from the guards during the game of 'go find'. Even with Wiley's long counts, and the fact that she'd only traveled half this distance before, it would be a matter of minutes before the Haunt guards caught on, and they would find her in no time. Lemming wouldn't know enough to be slow in her tracking, either. At least they'd managed to work their way deep into the woods for this last game, and she was certain the gate between worlds was just up ahead. With any luck, her stuff would still be there; if not on this side, then the other.

It had better be, otherwise, she was in trouble. She couldn't survive the September temperatures of Alaska for long without protection.

She caught a flash of wild animal eyes, and, thinking of the wolves, ran faster. She didn't want to end up a Jasmine burger.

Nothing smelled right. The exotic scent of the redwood forest seduced her brain, invigorating and enervating all at once. Odd calls sounded through the deepening twilight, and she felt something squish against her knee. Giving a little shriek, she looked down to discover she'd plowed over a huge mushroom. It had a brown cap the size of a Stetson hat.

Something skittered through the ferns. She whipped her head around in time to see a black beetle the size of a terrier heading away from her.

She ran.

Without warning a shadow detached itself from the forest and stepped into her path. She cried out and staggered back a step. Then she recognized him. Keilor.

Oh, oh.

"Going somewhere?" he asked, and electric intensity vibrated in his words.

Though he'd half expected it, Keilor wasn't thrilled at the position she'd placed him in. As a Master of the Hunt, it was one of his responsibilities to see to his people's safety. By running away, most likely to bring others of her kind into his world, she was endangering the Haunt and all he held dear. That he could not allow, and he would do what he must to keep her from doing it again.

Even if he wished things could be otherwise.

She hunched over, sucking in air and hiding her eyes. "We were playing 'go find'," she offered, knowing he knew the truth but hoping he'd accept her excuse.

He didn't.

He stepped forward. "I win." Her eyes widened in alarm as he invaded her space. "You seem to have a problem with authority," he observed with deliberate menace, and she swallowed. "Perhaps it's time to acquaint yourself with the law of your new land."

Jasmine wasn't immune to intimidation. Unfortunately, whether he knew it or not, Keilor's advance was playing havoc on her body. Nerve endings his dream-self had ignited in the night chose that moment to flash in Technicolor glory through her mind.

A reckless thrill raced through her and flashed in her transparent face, and she prayed he wouldn't notice. She didn't want to feel this way.

The answering flare of heat in his eyes, quickly banked, said he knew.

"Justice is swift," he continued, forcing them both to focus on his point. Whatever it had been. "Punishment, often cruel." His dark gaze swept her, sizzling with what lay unspoken between them. "So reckless, little Dragonfly. So eager to tease danger." He stepped back, holding out his hand. "Give me your sash."

Jasmine's hands clamped protectively around the sash at her waist. She took a step back. "Why?"

Arctic chill slipped into his voice. "Do you give it to me, or do I take it?"

She wanted to believe he wouldn't really hurt her. Swallowing hard, she slowly unwound it and gave it to him, her arm at full extension.

He grasped her wrists and raised her arms above her head as he bound them to a convenient branch.

At that point Jasmine should have struggled. She knew it. Maybe he knew it, too. She told herself he was bigger, and stronger, and she'd never get away. All lies. None of that had stopped her before. None of it would have stopped her now if she hadn't wanted...

The air was warm, but she shivered. *Let him think its fear,* she begged silently, closing her eyes. *Just this once I don't want to think about it.* Besides, it was too late.

His eyes on hers, he flicked open the clasp of her overnji. She flinched.

As if he owned her, he leisurely trailed his fingers over the fluttering vein in her neck, pausing just a moment to trace the dragonfly on her necklace. Her breathing picked up, and he smiled at the unmistakable scent of charmer desire. For a moment he forgot it was terror and not passion he was supposed to inspire, and he reveled in her response. With his eyes half closed, he drank deeply of her intoxicating perfume.

Whether he knew it or not, Keilor wasn't a man in control. No man could be so close to a charmer and remain his own.

He shook his head as he remembered this was supposed to be a lesson, not a seduction. He moved to kiss her.

She snarled at him.

"Behave," he warned her with sensual promise, "or I'll bite back." She nipped him anyway, and he nipped her back sharply on the bottom lip, careful not to damage her tender skin. She gave a shocked whimper and jerked back.

"Behave," he repeated, and licked the small hurt to soothe it. The soothing turned without warning into a commanding kiss, full of hot persuasion.

Jasmine was having second thoughts. Whatever had possessed her to let him do this? The man was arrogant enough as it was without her giving in to him like a fool. Now was a fine time for fear to start speaking sense! Never mind that it was a fear born of inexperience.

She tried to bite him, but it took only moments for thoughts of revenge to be swept away by the siren call of their desire. His was a kiss specially designed to overcome a woman's objections. She moaned and kissed him in return, then jerked back with a mortified gasp.

He laughed softly against her ear, and she shivered. Her response to him was flattering, and he knew she wasn't happy about it. It was not what he'd intended. He'd have done nothing more than scare her into obedience if she hadn't betrayed herself with her unmistakable desire. Now heat like a river poured through him, consuming restraint, daring him to test her limits.

Pulling back, he flashed her a predatory smile, and untied the knot of her bandeau. He left the ends draped loosely over her neck, still protecting her from his eyes, but the slightest movement on her part would cause them to slide right off. She held very still, but her pupils smoked over, and her body spoke of anticipation, not fear.

Barely breathing, she watched him warily as he traced a finger across her lips, to her temple and down her jaw. Ever so slowly it moved down her throat, her breastbone, and all the way down the stripe of skin exposed by her unfastened clothes. It circled her pretty navel and dipped slightly below the first button of her pants.

She shuddered, and it wasn't with fright.

He grinned with wicked delight.

With one hand he grasped the white bandeau where it crossed her back and slowly pulled it away to bare her breasts. She gasped as her nipples were exposed, visibly struggling to control her breathing. It didn't work, and her lovely breasts thrust forward with every inhalation, begging for his attention. The nipples tightened under his gaze. He met her eyes with a look hotter than molten gold. "Very nice," he approved hoarsely, and she shut her eyes and writhed against her constraints. He unfastened the buttons on her pants and heard her breath catch in anticipation.

He was killing her.

With excruciatingly erotic, nerve wracking slowness she felt the soft slide of heavy silk as he lowered her pants just enough to be able to trace the top line of silk he revealed. Another hot tremor seized her, and she sucked in a breath. To cover it, she snapped, "Enjoying yourself?"

His eyes were full of sultry promise. "Oh, yes, but not nearly as much as you're about to." He smiled when her hips jerked in randy enthusiasm at his words.

She swore, furious at the sexual control he had over her body. So I want him, so what? she thought angrily. Its just hormones. He was too arrogant, and he delighted in trying to scare her. Why should she give him even that much without a fight?

Unfortunately, to fight him was to fight her body, and it was showing signs of surrender under his tender assault that even a blind man couldn't miss.

Keilor wasn't blind. He flashed her a wicked smile that made a sheen of sweat break out all over her body. He lightly ran his nails over her hips, up her sensitive sides to cup her tender breasts. She cried out and her body surged forward, begging for more.

"With pleasure," he whispered, and rolled her nipples between his thumbs and fingers. She tried to hide her face against her arm, but could do nothing about her pleasured cries. He kept his touch light; just enough to tease, not enough to satisfy, and her body jerked as she tried to restrain it from thrashing. His hands trailed downward over her flushed skin, pushing her pants down just enough to bare the scandalous panties.

With his hands spanning her hips, his thumbs lightly stroked along the very edges. In a low, dangerous voice, he asked her, "Will you be toying with me again?" He didn't need to be more specific; they both knew he referred to her attempted escape, and now she knew he took it personally. Very personally.

She grit her teeth, unwilling to give him the words, knowing he already understood she wouldn't lightly defy him again. Her hips twisted once under his caressing hands and she let out a strangled sound of frustration and rage. Boldly, he reached down and lightly touched her erotic nerve center—once. Even braced for it, a scream tore loose from her sensitized body.

He removed his hand, but still she thrashed, fighting against losing all dignity and begging him for more. He waited until she regained some shreds of control and opened desperate, glittering eyes. Holding her gaze, he slowly pulled up her pants, savoring each uncontrolled jerk that told him how much her body fought the deprivation of his touch.

Pain, her body cried. Pain from needing it. His eyes told her he understood, and at the slightest word from her he'd ease the hurting, but that he knew better than to expect such a request from such a proud woman.

He dressed her as leisurely as he'd undressed her and set her loose. Without a word she turned on her heel and headed back the way she'd come.

He didn't try to talk, and he seemed content to let her set the pace. It wasn't much, as gallantry went, but she'd take what she could get. She wasn't up to idle chatter just then.

She'd felt desire in her life, she thought, wading through the fern fronds. Even hot, raging lust, but she'd never before walked through fire. The idea that a virtual stranger could do that to her, could make her nearly frantic with need, did not please her.

Maybe there's something in the air, she thought suspiciously, taking a discrete sniff. Maybe it's not me at all, but something to do with that thing he calls me. What was it, a charmer?

Glancing at him out of the corner of her eye, she asked, "What is this charmer business about, anyway?"

He looked at her; obviously surprised she would choose to speak to him. He took a moment to answer. "A charmer makes men want her. It's the special pheromone she produces that makes the Haunt male wild."

"I thought a Haunt was a guard," she said with a sharp glance.

"It is a guard, but also the term for our race," he explained, looking at her curiously. Her interest would have to be powerful indeed to cause her to seek knowledge from him so soon after his...chastisement.

She kept her eyes straight ahead, ignoring what his accent was doing to her insides. "So what does this pheromone do to me?"

He stopped in surprise, caught himself, and continued on. But his tone carried definite inquisitiveness as he answered, "Nothing. You've possessed it all your life and it's done you no harm."

She clenched her fists. "Then it doesn't make me…" she left the rest unsaid, not wanting to make a fool of herself. Too late.

She saw him grin out of the corner of her eye. "No," he answered with an insufferable note of male pride. "You can blame me for that."

Humiliated all over again, she kept her head down and walked faster.

CHAPTER 5

"Are you all right?" Wiley demanded the moment she and Lemming entered Jasmine's room. The door closed behind her, sealing off the illumination from the hall and enclosing them in the deepening gloom.

Jasmine looked at her broodingly from the couch she was lying on. "Where's your keeper?"

Her friend waved an impatient hand. "Gone. But how are you?" She knelt in front of the couch, concern etching her brow. "Did he hurt you?"

"No." Not wanting to pursue that path any further, she quickly asked, "How did he know? There shouldn't have been enough time for them to figure anything out." She'd been going over Keilor's dreadful timing, but had yet to understand how they'd given themselves away. They'd thought they'd been so careful.

Wiley snorted and moved to an armchair, tucking one long leg under the other. "Lights," she ordered and then, "Shutters." Satisfied with their privacy and the improved illumination, she said, "They figured it out right away." Her lower lip protruded just the tiniest bit. "The Haunt brought me back here and Jayems told me that they knew." She shivered, remembering what else he'd said. Her eyes swept down. "I was afraid of what Keilor would do when he found you." She peeked through her lashes to see Jasmine busily avoiding her eyes. Her voice ached when she asked, "What did he do, Jas?"

Hearing that note, Jasmine looked at her and then up at the ceiling. If she didn't tell her, she'd imagine the worst and spend days brooding about it, convinced it was somehow all her fault. Besides, this was Wiley. "He tied me up to a tree and kissed me," she confessed quickly, hoping she'd drop it, knowing she wouldn't.

"*What*?" Wiley looked as if she didn't know whether to be outraged or titillated. Her expression became thoughtful, even speculative, and her eyes moved as if replaying something in her head. As if thinking out loud, she asked, "How was it?"

Jasmine bounded off the couch, putting an armchair between them as if to stop the flow of curiosity. "Wiley! How could you ask me that?" A casual friend would have raged over Keilor's behavior and called lightning down on his head. Someone else would have made dire threats against his manhood and commiserated with her.

There were definite disadvantages to having a friend who knew you so well.

Wiley regarded her with a touch of skepticism. "I know you're attracted to him. I saw you eyeing his backside earlier." When Jasmine flushed and mumbled, she went on knowingly, "And if he'd hurt you, or you'd hated it, you'd be upset in a different way. So come on," she coaxed. "Spill the beans."

Jasmine kneaded the back of the chair and then grumbled, "It was...okay."

Wiley's eyes brightened and she sat up attentively, drawing her other leg under her. "Just okay?"

"Bah." Jasmine hunched her shoulders and then admitted with extreme reluctance, "All right! Better than okay. More like..." she hesitated as she allowed herself to recall the feel of Keilor's lips on hers, his gentle hands. A shudder passed through her and she admitted softly, "All the stars fell and lit up my sky."

Wiley's eyes widened. "Wow," she breathed.

"But it's not going to happen again." She walked around the chair and sat down. Drawing her knees to her chest, she hugged them protectively. "I'm not going to let that snake get within ten feet of me next time."

They sat in silence for a while, each with their own thoughts. Finally Wiley stirred and sighed with regret. "I guess we won't be going home any time soon."

Jasmine grunted. She wasn't the sort of woman who gave up easily, and it galled her to admit she felt cowed, but the memory of Keilor's brand of sensual domination was enough to wipe out any immediate plans for escape.

She groaned and buried her face in her knees as the memories flashed across the backs of her eyelids. "A gun," she muttered, scrubbing her face. "That's what I need the next time. A gun to shoot the son of a bitch before he gets his hands on me."

Wiley turned troubled eyes on her. "I don't want anyone to get hurt, Jas," she said slowly. "Besides, he doesn't seem like the kind of man to take it well if you turned a gun on him. He might...take it personally."

Jasmine stiffened, considering the ramifications of a really enraged Keilor. If he did what he'd done to her that afternoon over a minor infraction, what would he do to her for threatening his life? It didn't bear thinking about.

Besides, she didn't think she could shoot him, not even a warning shot. Just the thought of it turned her insides cold. She sighed, admitting temporary defeat.

She'd have to sleep on it.

"Of course it would work," Jasmine insisted. Gravel crunched under her new boots as she followed the path to the stables. Her brown ponytail swished across the back of her neck and her black T-shirt while she checked out the area, taking mental notes.

They were speaking in Pig Latin again to ensure their privacy. Acting on a suspicion, Jasmine had subtly tested her Haunt guard's hearing and found it amazingly acute. She didn't dare risk whispering as they had yesterday.

A groom led a haltered riding beast past them, and she saw Wiley raise a bare arm to shade her vision as she eyed the stocky creature. The lucky girl had the good fortune to end up in the Haunt world with a tank top. The beast turned too intelligent eyes back at them and stared evilly, snorting in contempt for good measure. It had the body of a horse, but it sported more muscles than a body builder. More disturbing, its gray hide was covered with scales, and it had the clubbed tail of an ankylosaur. Rhinoceros-like horns sprouted from its nose.

She nudged Wiley. "The Arnold Swartznegger of horses." Wiley's snort of laughter made her smile as well, and she felt her shoulders relax a bit. They could do this.

Jayems hadn't seemed to mind their request for riding lessons; in fact, he'd volunteered himself and Keilor as instructors. Keilor had seemed about to object until he'd noticed Jasmine's obvious displeasure, at which point he'd graciously agreed.

The man did love to torment her.

Jasmine spied a row of tightly capped bottles full of a milky liquid sitting in the sun. She hefted one thoughtfully. With a naughty smile she spun it by its neck and launched into the routine from the bar scene of *Cocktail.*

Wiley put one hand on her denim covered hip and chuckled as she watched her friend's antics. "You're going to break that."

She grinned and passed the bottle behind her back and up over her shoulder. "Never."

Wiley snorted and flipped the end of her French braid back over her shoulder. "That's what you said the time you dropped the shampoo bottle and it broke open all over the kitchen floor. We were skidding across the tile every day for the next three months."

"Shoddy craftsmanship," she retorted, but caught the bottle deftly and studied the cloudy liquid. "What is this stuff, anyway?" She looked up and saw their instructors approaching. Both were dressed for action in the black uniform and buckled leather vests of the Haunt guard, but with the addition of red embroidered patches on their left breasts, possibly an indication of rank. The patches looked like Celtic knot work. Jayems also wore a torque around his neck.

Of course the tanned skin in place of the pelts of the Haunt made an enormous difference in how she saw the package. Jayems' muscles flexed naturally as he walked, and for a moment Jasmine envied her friend. She looked up and caught Jayems surreptitiously admiring Wiley's backside. He noticed her noticing and raised a regal brow. What of it?

She refused to look at Keilor.

It was Keilor who answered her question. He took the bottle from her hands and considered it thoughtfully. "Partly digested feeder beetle and browse." He smiled faintly when Jasmine leaned back in disgust. "For the orphaned young stags." He nodded his head towards the nearby pen holding three of the young creatures and replaced the bottle with the others.

"Stags are omnivores," Jayems explained. Jasmine noticed he stood just close enough to Wiley to make her friend fidget, but not close enough to excuse her from seeming rude if she moved away. The fact that Wiley was fidgeting and not freezing made her frown. She almost acted as if…

"They nurse at birth, but as they grow, they need more nourishment than milk provides. Gradually their mothers wean them onto regurgitated browse and prey…" Jasmine gagged, and even Wiley made a sound of disgust, "until they are old enough to find and digest their own food," he finished wryly.

Jasmine, always the one with the weak stomach, looked at the stags with something close to horror and spoke before she thought. "And we have to ride these things?" She grunted when Wiley jabbed her hard in the ribs with her elbow.

"You need the exercise." Wiley told her, giving her a significant look. "You wouldn't want to lose the little muscle you've got, would you?"

Jasmine bristled. "Just because I can't run triathlons doesn't mean I'm not in shape. I work out."

Wiley snorted. "*Sweating to the Oldies* doesn't count," she said contemptuously. She regularly won triathlons, and she could be a bit of a prig about physical fitness. Unfortunately, she'd also decided to make keeping Jasmine in shape her life's work, in spite of Jasmine's asthma and the fact that Jasmine could care less about clogged arteries or decaying bone density.

"I never—" Jasmine protested hotly, but Jayems cleared his throat, cutting her off.

"Ladies." He looped his arm through Wiley's with smooth finesse, much to her consternation, and made a sweeping gesture with the other. "Adventure awaits."

Keilor reflected wryly that he was hanging himself with his own rope. Proximity to the charmer was what he needed to avoid, yet where was she? Nestled between his thighs and teasing him with her luscious scent.

Not that she'd wanted to be there. It had taken some well chosen baiting on Rihlia's part and a flat refusal on Jayems' to ride with anyone other than Rihlia to get her into the double saddle at all.

He poked her. "Stop slouching and straighten your back. The stag won't respect a spineless rider." She obeyed him, but persisted in leaning forward to avoid body contact. He sighed in frustration and pulled her back flush to his chest with a small jerk, holding her shoulders to keep her there. "Unless you're racing, you must sit straight in the saddle. You'll never have a proper seat otherwise, and the ride will be uncomfortable."

He released her, and she silently did as he instructed. If her muscles got any stiffer, though, he'd be able to take her off the stag and use her for a poker. With that in mind, he began to massage her shoulders.

She hunched them, trying to discourage him, but he persisted, and slowly she relaxed. "Better," he told her. "A relaxed body will obey you better and help to keep your mount calm."

As they continued down the deserted sunny road in the opposite direction from the gate site, her continued silence began to annoy him. "Are you sulking because we're nowhere near the gate or because you can't shove me off this stag and trample me?"

Her answer, when it came, was not what he'd been expecting.

Jasmine turned her head to look at him. "Why do you make her stay here?" she asked quietly. "I don't understand." They both looked to where Jayems and Rihlia rode, several lengths ahead.

Keilor had seen Jasmine display many emotions, but this aching quiet stirred an answering sympathy in him. He felt the need to comfort, and he hadn't felt such tender emotion in a long time. "Do you know anything of your family?" he asked gently, aware that the subject was likely painful for her.

She shrugged, but her voice was harsh. "Sure. My mother was an exotic dancer and my father was some guy she'd met at a party. She found out later he had a wife and three kids. He owned a used car dealership. What about it?"

He paused, taken aback by her revelation. "You met them?" he asked tentatively, almost dreading her answer.

"My mother," she paused and then admitted with great reluctance, "When she was drunk, before she died, she used to rant on about how I'd ruined her life." She was silent a moment. "It was a lot more pleasant when she was stoned. Then she just ignored me." What could he say to such a revelation? Would she even accept comfort from him? He cleared his throat. "It wasn't like that for Rihlia. She was the baby of the family, and very spoiled. Jayems and I adored her from the moment we saw her. She was terribly charming, and very bossy."

Jasmine shook her head and said in faint amusement, "I'm sure."

"The day she disappeared, we were all frantic. Jayems would not sleep for two days. In spite of the best efforts of the Haunt elite, we could find no trace of her. I didn't see a smile cross Jayems' face for months afterward."

Jasmine's voice was heavy. "That little girl grew up, Keilor. She's not the same person."

He stopped the stag. Splaying his fingers against her jaw, he gently turned her head to look up at him, leaning to the side so she could see him clearly. He held her gaze, letting her see how he felt. "She deserves the chance to find out for herself exactly what she is, don't you think?" He could sense her weakening, so he pushed harder. "Her family loves her and wants her, Jasmine. Give her the opportunity to learn that. Jayems will never let her go while she still thinks we threw her away." He released her and set the stag in motion, giving her a chance to think; glad he'd been able to explain to her how they felt.

He'd deliberately misled her a bit—Jayems would never let Rihlia go, regardless, but he knew if he said as much he might have closed her mind to everything he'd told her. At least this way they had the chance of winning her as a powerful ally in the battle for Rihlia's heart. If she chose, Jasmine could single-handedly win half the war, and he wasn't going to be squeamish about using her to do so.

He looked again at Jayems and Rihlia. More than one heart hung in the balance.

Jasmine couldn't sleep for a long time that night. She kept analyzing every nuance of her conversation with Keilor that afternoon. Everything kept coming back to his eyes, and the way he'd looked when he'd said that Wiley's family wanted her. Earnest. Sincere. But what was best for Wiley? *Was* she running away because she thought they'd abandoned her?

With an annoyed grunt, she tossed off the covers and got dressed. She really shouldn't have taken that nap earlier in the afternoon, but there was no help for it now.

She opened her door and immediately the two Haunt turned to look at her. She gave them both a rather sick smile. She still wasn't used to having werewolves guarding her door. "Can't sleep," she explained apologetically. She must be crazy to want to wander around in the dark with these two. "Um, is there any reason I can't take a walk out here?" When they glanced at each other but made no move to stop her, she eased out of her room and shut the door.

To the left were Wiley and Jayems' rooms. To the right, the great unknown. She chose the right. In no particular hurry, she meandered at a thoughtful pace down the well-lit stone hall, aimlessly watching the patterns on the parquet flooring. Her guard trailed behind, allowing her privacy. There was something to be said for silence, she decided.

She'd only been walking along for a couple of minutes when she was startled into looking up. Another silent Haunt with the same insignia she'd noticed on Keilor and Jayems blocked her path, and he seemed to have business with her. Uneasy, she looked to her own guards, only to see them salute the newcomer with a fist over their hearts and a slight bow. They gave her a slight nod as well and then returned the way they'd come.

Bewildered, she considered the Haunt in front of her. A replacement?

Deciding to test her theory, she took a step forward as if she intended to go around him and he fell into step with her. Relieved, she continued with her walk, gradually relaxing as he did nothing but accompany her. Her steps slowed and she settled back into an aimless meander.

The hallway opened up unto the head of a broad staircase leading to an inner courtyard, and she stared in awe at the view of the triple moons and scattered stars. Slowly she sank down to absorb the view. The evening breeze caressed her cheek, pleasant with the scent of flowers. Her guard settled unobtrusively against the wall.

After a time, curiosity got to her. "You guys don't talk much, do you?" she said softly, loathe to break the serenity of the night. To her surprise, the Haunt answered her in the sign language she'd seen the guards use. When she continued to watch him, he repeated himself slowly, fingers to chest, an inclination of his head and then fingers to lips.

"You do talk?" she guessed, intrigued. Hm. This could be fun. Maybe these guys weren't too bad after all. She eyed him and decided to accord him a healthy respect, just in case.

She gestured to the stair just above her, but he didn't move. Frowning, she chewed the inside of her bottom lip. "You're on duty?" He inclined his head again and she relaxed, leaning back against the wall and hugging her knees. Touching the spot over her heart, she asked, "The patch, is it an indication of rank?" One nod. "Are you higher ranking than the last guy?" Yes.

Well now, this wasn't so bad. As long as she asked yes or no questions, they'd get along just fine. Scratching her jaw, she stifled a yawn. "Are there Haunt women? I guess there are, but all I've seen are guards. Not that I've seen a lot of this place. Are you married?"

He started slightly, but slowly shook his head.

"Me neither. It's got its advantages, though. There's something to be said for only answering to myself. Though sometimes…" she trailed off. Her bones started to grate against the hard step through the padding of her muscles and she shifted.

The Haunt was an indistinct outline even in the moon-flooded night, and she squinted, trying to see him better. "You see better than I do at night, don't you? And hear better?" He affirmed it, and she considered the matter further. "And your sense of smell…is it much better than mine?" Yes. "As good as a dog's?" This time, when he agreed with her, she shivered, reminded of their differences. What else might be alien between them? Her toes curled. "Are you stronger than humans, faster? Is that why all the Haunt are guards?" He stared at her, and in the moonlight his eyes reflected red.

She shut up, and it was a long time before she got up the nerve to move.

CHAPTER 6

Jasmine slapped a deck of cards and a decanter of honey liquor on the table. "Prepare to lose, Wiley. I'm feeling lucky tonight."

"Ha!" Wiley plunked down a drawstring bag full of little snail shells. Next to it she set a platter of raw vegetables arranged around a hollowed red pepper filled with creamy dip. "You, my friend, are going down."

Jasmine made a face at the platter and got up to rummage in the pantry of the suite Wiley shared with Jayems. Emerging triumphant with a jar of hot pickles and a bag of sour candies, she packed them to the dining table and went back to search the cold pantry for some cold cuts. Already she missed cheese.

"What are you doing?" Jayems asked as he entered the kitchen with Keilor and Knightin in tow. For some reason, Wiley colored.

"Poker," Jasmine answered. She returned to the table, a large plate of sausages filling her hands and bottle of fiery mustard clamped under one arm. She set those down and went back to reconnoiter the kitchen cupboards.

"What are you doing, Jas, preparing to feed an army?" Wiley asked. She leaned one hand on the table and rested the other on her hip. "Keep this up and there won't be room to play."

"Nag, nag, nag," Jasmine muttered, her voice muffled in the depths of the cupboard, blissfully unaware of the two sets of interested male eyes wandering over her derriere. Twin fires sparked in Knightin and Keilor's eyes as she bumped her head on something and wriggled.

Knightin came to his senses first and jerked his eyes away in annoyance. "On second thought, Jayems, I'll pass on that drink. I just remembered I have some things to deal with before morning. Good evening."

Keilor barely spared him a glance before returning to savor the view. His vision fogged as he inhaled her scent. It was all he could do not to act on the fantasy playing out in his head.

Fingers snapped in front of his face and he blinked at the unwelcome intrusion.

"Your eyes were glazed, my friend," Jayems told him dryly.

Jasmine emerged with a package of savory rye chips, which she poured into a pieced wooden bowl. Munching on a handful, she took the bowl with her and settled into a chair. "Your deal," she told Wiley, leaning back in her chair. Glancing at the watching men she said briskly, "This is not a spectator sport, gentlemen. Play or get lost."

Jayems frowned with annoyance, but before he could remind her that she was in his kitchen, not hers, Wiley said, "Quit trying to rob them, Jas. You know they'd end up without a penny to their names." She poured a splash of liquor into two glasses, adding an extra splash in one of them.

Leering, Jasmine reminded her, "They use gold and silver here, remember?" She eyed the men calculatingly. "I think we ought to let them play, if they provide their own ante."

"Ante?" Keilor asked. He drifted closer and snagged a chip.

"Money, honey," Jasmine supplied, taking the glass with the least amount of liquor. "You'll also have to supply your own booze. I don't think there's enough here to put us all under the table."

"There isn't enough there to put one of me 'under the table'," Keilor said with disdain, and went in search of something stronger.

"We wager with real money while you use snails?" Jayems asked with a scowl, pulling out a chair.

"What are we supposed to wager, our virtue?" Jasmine retorted, getting up to grab a glass of juice. All that salt was making her thirsty. Keilor had just returned to the room as she said that, and he froze in his tracks.

Jayems looked at Wiley out of the corner of his eye.

Wiley's eyes narrowed. "Forget it."

"I don't know, I think the idea has merit," he answered smoothly.

"You would."

Keilor brought two glasses with silver crests to the table and poured a generous shot into each. "If I'm going to be playing with real coin against shells, I'd have to agree with Jayems. We should at least get a kiss if we win the game."

"No."

Jasmine hesitated for a moment. Their newest plan depended on robbing these two blind. The question was, what was she willing to do to get home?

Anything.

Well, almost anything. Taking a bracing breath, she negotiated, "No tongues."

"Jasmine!" Wiley cried in disbelief.

Eyes narrowed, Keilor bargained, "If you sit on our laps while delivering it."

Wiley slapped a hand on the table, embarrassed. "Stop it, you two!" She was ignored.

Cupping her chin in thought, Jasmine ran a thumb over her lips, considering Keilor with mercenary eyes. If she had to sit on his lap then she darn sure was going to make it count. "Gold coin for every shell."

Keilor smiled wickedly. "I'll give you two for every shell if you sit astride."

That gave her pause. Some of the fun of bargaining drained out of Jasmine as she considered whether possible bribe money was worth what he was asking. Her eyes flickered as she looked down, counting the cost to her pride.

"Don't you dare," Wiley warned her, breaking the tense silence.

"Oda ouya aveha anothera away ota etga oneyma orfa ibingbra ehta aurdsga, Wi?" *Do you have another way to get money for bribing the guards?* Jasmine asked casually and then added in English, "Don't be a baby, Wiley. It's just a little kiss." Even as she said it she could feel her hot face betraying her. The very last thing she wanted to do was kiss Keilor, even if it might help them find a way to get home. The thought of sitting on his hard thighs, wrapping her legs around him, with only inches separating significant body parts…. Well, they'd just have to make certain they won most of the time.

"The winner gets the pot, the losers take a shot," Jasmine told them and then explained the rules while Wiley shuffled the cards in nervous silence.

Predictably, the women won the first few hands, pulling in money hand over fist. Jasmine and Keilor had just folded and taken their shots, and Jasmine was watching Wiley with a smug and slightly inebriated smile when Jayems laid down his first winning hand. She blinked, but the cards didn't change.

Slow color flooded Wiley's cheeks. Jayems pushed his chair back and laced his hands together over his stomach, a warm flame of pleasure and expectation in his eyes. Taking a quick breath, Wiley gulped her liqueur, squared her shoulders and then with more haste than grace, she straddled him.

No doubt she'd intended to make the kiss a quick peck, but it quickly became apparent that she was not in command, and tongues or no tongues, when Wiley finally slid off of Jayems' lap, she was clumsy with more than alcohol. She knocked her chair sideways trying to sit down, and Jasmine couldn't help a snort of laughter as she helped set it to rights.

Then she lost.

"Huh," she said in consternation, and slowly tucked an escaping strand of hair behind her ear. She reached for her drink, attempting to stall.

Before her fingers could close around it, Keilor snatched it up. With a wicked glint in his eye, he toasted her. "I'd hate for your senses to be dulled for this, Dragonfly." With a quick toss he finished her drink and then scooted back his chair, waiting.

She looked away from the electric promise in his eyes and told herself sternly to move. Just a little kiss, she reminded herself, rising. It wasn't helping. Reluctance slowed her every movement and made the slide onto Keilor's lap torturous for both of them. When she would have stopped halfway, he grasped her hips and pulled her flush, sending a shockwave of thrill through them both.

Jasmine grit her teeth and gripped his shoulders, stiff with willful desire. He grazed his cheek against hers once in acknowledgment and then slowly slid his mouth to her own. Invisible sparks flew as their lips touched softly. Her mouth parted a little of its own accord, and Keilor sipped, drawing delicately on the soft, damp interior, dragging his lower lip across hers. Her heart thumped like a piston as she slid her fingers into his dark hair, instinctively finding the clasp and freeing the silken strands.

So caught up was she that she failed to remember their audience until Jayems said with amusement, "Do you think we should leave him to her mercy or have pity and toss water on them?"

With a groan of heartfelt reluctance, Keilor ended the kiss and set her back. Aching, Jasmine scooted off his lap and felt her way back into her chair, her eyes still too dilated to focus properly. As her left hand connected with the back of her chair, she heard a clink. Dropping down heavily, she opened her hand to investigate and flushed. It was Keilor's hair clip.

"Keep it." He mimed a kiss. "A memento."

The tide had definitely turned in favor of the men, and Jayems and Keilor kept stealing the ladies' drinks in the name of sharp senses, though the liquor had little noticeable effect on them.

"You must be cheating," Jasmine muttered, eyeing the pile of shells in front of their opponents with suspicion. They were on their last hand, and her cards were good. Almost unbeatable. As time went on she became less willing to take the chance of losing again. As it was she started trembling just thinking about the consequences of defeat.

Still...It was a lot of money. Maybe enough to get them home again. Could she afford to lose this chance when the odds were so completely in their favor?

Keilor raised the bet and Jayems folded. Wiley was already out, and Jasmine couldn't cover the bet. Taking the last shot straight from the bottle for courage, she cleared her throat and asked huskily, "Would you be willing to take a promissory note on a game of strip poker for my ante?"

Wiley drew in a shocked breath of protest, but choked on her own saliva. While Jayems thumped her on the back, Keilor regarded her intently. "Strip poker?"

Jasmine looked down and tapped her finger on the table, her nerves jangling a warning. And whether she liked it or not, a dangerous thrill of anticipation. Would it be so bad to lose?

Mentally chastising herself for daring to think such a stupid thing, she said, "I'll tell you after the cards are on the table." If things went as planned, it wouldn't matter anyway, because she wouldn't be in a position to pay up.

He looked skeptical, but one look at Wiley frantically waving, "no, no!" and shaking her head at Jasmine and his expression turned speculative. With a graceful gesture, he tipped his cards onto the table.

"Heh, heh!" Jasmine gloated as she tossed her own hand down and raked in the pot. She threw back her head and hooted. "Whoo, hoo!" Jumping up, she did a little war dance, then grabbed Wiley in a headlock and rubbed her head with her knuckles, chortling. "I win, I win!"

"Is she always like this?" Jayems demanded in disbelief, watching Jasmine dance a jig around the room.

Wiley snorted. "Only when she wins."

Breathless, Jasmine came back to the table and began raking coins and shells into the drawstring pouch. Keilor dropped his hand over hers, pinning it to the table. When her startled eyes met his he asked, "What did I just lose?"

Pinned at an awkward angle over the table, Jasmine had nowhere to hide her hot face. "Ah…" Heat licked at her from his touch, making her tongue thick, and for a moment she felt a pang of regret. Losing might have been the smartest thing she'd ever done. She cleared her throat. "Strip poker is played in private. The ante is…the player's clothes."

Keilor sucked in a breath and his fingers tightened. He slowly let her go and leaned back, contemplating the ceiling with a resigned expression. Somewhat subdued, Jasmine finished collecting her loot and then helped to clear the table. With everyone working at once, everything was quickly put away. As soon as it was done, the ladies took their winnings and left.

Keilor poured them both another drink and then saluted Jayems. "A greedy man would regret letting them win that last hand." Their people had brought the game from Earth long ago, and cards were a popular pastime among their people. The ladies should have been more suspicious when they found the cards in Jaymes' room.

Jayems smiled faintly. "Caught you by surprise with her offer, did she?" Keilor swore softly and gulped his drink, making Jayems laugh. His expression sobered. "How else am I to give them an allowance? Rihlia won't accept anything from me."

"Hm, well, she seemed to be accepting your kisses well enough at the end."

A half-smile curved Jayems' mouth. "And Jasmine yours."

Keilor took a deep breath as desire flashed through him. "Bite me, I didn't think I'd survive much more of that. The charmer had to win, and swiftly."

Jayems chuckled and poured them both another drink. "To women," he proposed, raising his glass.

"To relief." Keilor countered wickedly, and clinked his glass to Jayems'. A thought occurred to him and he cocked his head, causing the loose strands of his black hair to brush across his shoulders. "How do you intend to let the charmer spend her allowance? It's not as if she can wander through the markets."

Jayems frowned and propped his chin on his fist. "I hadn't thought of that. I suppose I'll have to invite the merchants to bring their wares here." He brushed his thumb across his lower lip, squinting. "What sorts of things do you think two women raised on Earth might be tempted by?"

"How should I know?" Keilor waved a hand in dismissal. "Females seem to wallow in silks and satins. Send for a dressmaker. Arrange for fittings. Find a perfumer and jewelers—any merchant selling fripperies should do."

Jayems shook his head at him. "Such promising husband material," he mocked. "Yet so ugly."

"Tell that to Jasmine." He preened. "That woman couldn't keep her hands off me."

Smirking, Jayems pointed out, "She was drinking. You might have been a stag for all she knew."

Keilor's smile flashed. "I certainly felt as randy. Too much more of her and we would have both disappeared under the table."

"And Rihlia would have been after you with a knife…"

CHAPTER 7

"There is no justice," Jasmine grumbled the next morning when she entered Jayems' suite and saw her chipper poker companions. Her head felt ready to split and her mood was rotten. She felt as if she'd had ten shots instead of just three.

Wiley's lips twitched as she poured them both a cup of tea. "Pain killer hasn't kicked in yet, huh?"

Her answer was a grunt as Jasmine rested her elbows on the table and pressed the heels of her hands to her eyes.

"I should have warned you," Jayems told her, contrite. "Haunt are notoriously difficult to inebriate. Our liquors are made strong to compensate. I did not remember at first that you might become ill."

Jasmine glowered at Wiley. "Scruffy alien. Should have known all these years that you were cheating."

Wiley chuckled.

Slitting her eyes, Jasmine peered at Keilor, who was dressed casually in loose trousers and a dark green, long sleeved shirt. His hair was loose today, and he looked better than she could bear to look at so early into a hangover. "What's the occasion? Are all your uniforms in the wash?" she asked nastily and then winced when her head throbbed in rebuke.

He raised a brow. "Our family is arriving today, and I've taken the day off." He nodded at Wiley. "Her mother, Lady Rhapsody, will be here in time for dinner."

Wiley blanched.

Jasmine jerked upright and hissed at the crushing pain. She grabbed her head. White lights flashed behind her eyes and she grit her teeth, panting. Someone picked her up and carried her to the couch. Something sweet and cloying was waved under her nose, and then she was out.

"She's better off asleep until the medicine kicks in," Keilor explained in a business-like manner as he capped the vial of dream flower oil.

Rihlia was still pale, and Jayems touched her shoulder in concern. She knocked his hand away and turned her back on him. "I don't want to see her."

"Rihlia—" Jayems began, concerned. He hadn't seen her this upset since before Jasmine arrived.

"My name is *Wiley*," she snapped viciously, "And I won't see her!" Her eyes took on a dangerous golden glint.

Undaunted, Jayems tried again. "She's your mother," he said, his body tense. "She's waited almost twenty years for the chance—"

Wiley's answering response raised the hair on the back of his neck. No one should say such things about their mother. Shocked momentarily dumb, Jayems watched her storm off and winced when she slammed the door to her room. There was a moment of silence.

Keilor touched his shoulder. "She didn't mean it, surely," he said quietly.

"How can I keep Lady Rhapsody from her own daughter?" Jayems asked in agony. "She's done nothing to deserve this." He began to pace. "She's coming here tonight, thinking she's about to meet her beloved daughter, not confront a waking nightmare. This will kill her, Keilor."

Keilor said nothing. Jayems spoke the truth. Better that her daughter had never been found than to be returned to her full of misplaced hatred. Worse, who could understand such loathing?

His gaze fell on Jasmine, and his eyes flared. "Our little gem," he breathed, and grabbed Jayems. "What do you see?" he demanded, pointing to the unsuspecting girl.

Jayems frowned. "A menace, usually."

"A girl," Keilor paused significantly, "who knows Rihlia better than anyone alive. A confidant, a beloved friend. Someone with untold influence over your wife. And if need be, a bargaining chip."

Jayems studied the girl. A slow, determined smile lifted his mouth. "Perhaps the girl might be of some use after all."

Jasmine felt a great deal better when she woke up. Sure, her mouth felt like dryer lint and her head was fuzzy, but nothing hurt. She opened her eyes, feeling almost optimistic, and turned her head.

Jayems and Keilor were staring at her.

"What?" she asked defensively. She scooted up into an upright position. Keilor handed her a glass of cool water, and she gulped it down gratefully.

"Why does Rihlia hate her mother?" Jayems asked without warning, staring at her intently.

Caught off guard, she said the first thing that came to mind. "Wouldn't you be mad at someone who dumped you in the woods and never came back?"

"That is not what happened!" Jayems snapped, making her jump.

Keilor touched his arm, but he didn't look any happier. "We've told her that she was lost, not abandoned."

Jasmine shrugged. "As if that matters to a child."

"She's no longer a child," Jayems argued, looking like he wanted to jump up and pace.

She looked at him for a long moment. "Wiley never knew her mother growing up. Emotionally, when she thinks of her, it's with the feelings of a small child. She's stuck in a time warp, with no frame of reference to deal with the woman as an adult." Her thoughts turned inward. "You just don't erase all that in a day," she finished softly.

"How can I do that if she won't even talk to her?" Jayems demanded. "How can she learn to get over this if she keeps running away?"

Jasmine was silent. Mothers weren't a topic she cared to dwell on. Her own hurts were infected, painful wounds, and she didn't care to probe the hurts of others, especially Wiley's. Still, it was different, wasn't it? Wiley's mother wasn't going to drive her off.

Wiley's mother wanted her.

Feeling a little sick, she wandered over and gripped the back of a kitchen chair, very tight. Wiley's mother wanted her, and why wouldn't she? Wiley was a wonderful person. Anyone would be glad to have her for a daughter. And deep down, past the pain and the fear of rejection, Jasmine believed Wiley wanted to know her mother, too—needed to know her.

She walked over to the bedroom and knocked on the door. "Wiley." Her voice lacked enthusiasm.

There was a rustling noise inside. "I know you can hear me, long ears." No response. Jasmine slumped against the door, feeling ninety years old. She braced one palm against it and rested her head against the wood. She felt so tired. "You're going to see your mother, Wiley, because you're not a coward. If you need to hate her, at least have the decency to call her a bitch to her face."

A growl came from Jayems' direction, but she ignored it. Eyes closed, she said hollowly, "I'd do it for you, Wi, but dealing with one mother in a lifetime is all I have the energy for. Just get it over with." Utterly drained, she shuffled off to her room; not caring as much as she should've that others saw her weakness.

Two hours later, she cared.

Keilor found her wedged in a corner behind a wing chair in her darkened room. She was curled on a cushion, nursing her sense of worthlessness.

He'd feared something like this, but a sense of self-preservation and the need to keep Jayems from storming into his wife's room had stopped him from following her. Kisses were one thing, but he was not ready for emotional intimacy with her, now or ever.

The sight of her so broken pained him in frightening ways. To preserve his distance and to maintain control, he responded with callousness.

After all, it had worked so well on Rihlia.

"Lights." He folded his hands behind his back and regarded her with a cool stare. "It appears your tactics were successful, charmer. My cousin has agreed to dine with her mother this evening. She is selecting a dress as we speak, and she wishes you to come and choose your own."

She closed her eyes and shook her head. "It's not my mother."

"I see. You're content to prod her into facing her demons, but too cowardly to stand at her side?" He watched with satisfaction as her lip curled.

She stood up slowly, one hand braced against the wall as if to hold her back from kicking him. "I did this once, and by myself," she told him defiantly, before her eyes clouded. "Wiley's an adult, and she doesn't need—"

Not about to let her slip back into self-pity since he'd gotten her this far, he stepped into her space. Boxed in on all sides, she had no choice but to look at him.

He let his eyes light with golden fire and spoke with contempt. Fear would serve her better than pity, would stir up constructive anger. "I order you to serve my cousin tonight," he told her with soft menace. "If you doubt my authority to do so, I will gladly demonstrate why the Haunt are so feared."

Anger narrowed her eyes, and just a trace of doubt. He could see she was thinking, considering, and that was bad. If he let up now, she'd slide right back into her depression.

"You don't know me, woman," he whispered harshly in her ear, careful not to touch her, but close enough to vibrate the fine sensors on her skin. "And you don't know what I'm capable of." He gave her a couple of seconds to dwell on that and then lied through his teeth. "It's no secret the Haunt male is excited by the sight of his lover's blood. And charmers blood…" he let his voice drop an octave, savoring her heady scent. "…is said to be the sweetest of all." Her perfume curled around him, beaconing, lulling. He lost the battle with his control and leaned in that extra fraction to touch his lips to her silky neck.

She giggled.

He pulled back, indignant. "What is so amusing?"

She caught sight of his face and clamped a hand over her mouth to muffle her laughter, but it didn't help. Instead she raised her hands and attempted to keep a straight face. "All right, O Fearsome One. Far be it from me to disobey the big scary Haunt." She brushed past him and sauntered over to her armoire, presumably in search of a washcloth for her face.

Unwittingly, she drew his eyes after her. He was still deeply submerged in her sensual scent, and it was all he could do not to follow her. Hunger curled in his belly, wound him tight. He wanted to stop her laughter his mouth. Let her be the one ensnared, he thought angrily, taking a step toward her. She shouldn't have this power over him.

A flicker of common sense stopped him. She was doing as he had asked, no, *ordered* her to do. A wise man would let that be enough.

He was beginning to fear he wasn't wise.

Lust was clouding his thinking. He leaned against her bedpost and watched her. He knew what she was, yet he lingered in her presence, allowing her more and more sway over his will. Knightin lusted after her, too, yet he had no trouble in distancing himself from her at every opportunity. Why did he find it so difficult?

Keilor stiffened, appalled at what he was doing. He'd given up standing around like a lovesick cadet years ago, and he wasn't going to take it up again for a human, of all things. It was time he took another lover, someone to clear his mind and satisfy his body, to give him back control.

Determined this night would not be spent alone and unsatisfied, Keilor walked out.

Wiley's eyes were glazed as she stared at the door. The late afternoon sunlight from the hall windows gave it an almost holy glow. It was covered with mother-of-pearl and inlaid with golden scrollwork, but it was doubtful she even saw the art. "I can't do it. My mother's in there."

She turned and gripped Jasmine's arms. Her hands trembled.

Jasmine wore a Grecian inspired gown of dark red with slit silk sleeves. Three tiny gold clips held the seams together, and her grip caused one of them to dig into Jasmine's arm.

"You'll be fine." Jasmine pried her fingers loose one by one and smoothed the spot the clip had bruised. Her ribs felt oddly constricted, even though the wide black sash around her waist wasn't tight. She adjusted the tasseled golden cord that was wound on top of the sash and forced herself to stop fidgeting. She looked fine. Wiley looked fine. They could do this.

She studied Wiley critically. "You're right. You're not ready." She gripped Wiley's shoulders and straightened them. With the back of her hand she chucked Wiley's chin up gently and used her thumbs to draw the corners of her friend's lips into a smile. When she took her hands away, the smile stayed, and grew. "Now you're ready."

The Haunt guards began to open the door. They flinched as Wiley suddenly slammed it shut. With her hands on the door, she hurriedly told Jasmine, "I forgot to tell you, you need to pick a male dinner partner when we go in." She backed off and the door started to open again.

Jasmine slammed it shut.

The Haunt looked at her strangely.

"What do you mean, I have to pick a male partner? What for?" she demanded.

Wiley shrugged her ignorance. "Custom. Just pick somebody. Anybody."

Jasmine didn't budge. "This is some sort of social trap, right? I pick the wrong guy and I offend someone for life." She shook her head. "No way. You pick for me."

Wiley shifted, impatient, and gestured to the guards to open the door. They tried to obey.

Jasmine braced her back against it and glared at them.

"You won't offend anybody, just pick someone," Wiley insisted.

As Jasmine opened her mouth to argue, the door was forced open from the inside. Keilor stood there, frowning.

Wiley's laugh was high-pitched. "Jasmine's a little nervous. We're ready to go in now." Jasmine glowered, but kept her mouth shut as Keilor took her arm and led her into the banquet hall. She felt like the opening band at a rock concert as three brightly robed women and one man looked her over curiously, then turned their attention eagerly back to the door.

Well, the women looked back.

The stranger's eyes froze on her face, then drifted down her body, retracing their path no faster than they had to. His loose, navy blue trousers and gold trimmed tunic were cut in the Chinese style and edged in gold. His blond hair was pulled back neatly with a clip and fell to his shoulders. By his bearing, he was a commander of some sort.

Keilor's touch at the small of her back fell away as the man took her hand and slowly raised it to his lips. "Fallon, sweet lady." His intense green eyes sizzled. "Your servant, day or night."

A little shocked, mostly because such a risqué comment was directed at *her,* she stammered, "Uh, thanks." She looked back at the door and he reluctantly parted with her hand. It was difficult to pay attention, since he remained close enough for her to feel him breathe.

Wiley stared at an older woman with braided silver hair, and the woman looked back at her with sky blue eyes alive with emotion. Wiley had a look of consternation fixed on her face, but the other woman…

The queenly lady glided forward, entranced, until she stood blinking fiercely at Wiley. Her voice was hoarse when she whispered, "Daughter?" Suddenly she hugged the stiff young woman, shaking her head over and over. "Rihlia," she said, and her eyes were wet with tears.

CHAPTER 8

Jasmine hadn't meant to drink so much, but as she looked up and saw Wiley seated at the opposite end of the table with her family, she felt the need for fortification.

Something had to warm her insides.

Wiley's family consisted of her mother, Lady Rhapsody, Rhapsody's sister Lady Portae, and two cousins. Urseya, a young woman about their own age, was a sloe-eyed beauty of perfect dimensions and practiced poise, while her older brother, the handsome Fallon, looked to be in his late twenties. They were all that was left of the extended family who had existed before the devastating assassinations swept the Haunt. The murders had wiped out most of their bloodline and resulted in the loss of Rihlia, as Rhapsody explained during dinner.

Quite a loss, if the stunning male specimens present were any indication.

Fallon, who'd single mindedly secured her for his partner during the blessing, favored her with another one of his sexy smiles. The benediction had been spoken with a man standing protectively behind every woman, hands on shoulders, giving thanks and promising to use the strength given by the nourishment to protect and provide for their family and loved ones. Fallon's hands had settled on her shoulders with a definite sensation of promise.

The man was gorgeous and ruthlessly charming, and at another time he would have had her falling at his feet.

Tonight his interest left her cold. It was the last thing she needed.

He lifted the green glass wine decanter—a work of art with its woven rush covering—and offered silently to pour for her. She covered her glass with her hand and gave him a faint smile. "No, thank you. I think I've had too much of a very good thing."

In a voice as smooth as molten caramel, he countered, "Ah, but is there ever too much of a good thing?" He refilled his glass and set the decanter aside, and she tried very hard to not to feel anything at all.

Keeping her eyes on the pale amber liquid that remained in her glass, she answered, "In the case of wine, yes, of course."

He sipped his wine and watched her with the lazy gaze of a hunter. "And in the case of men?"

What could she say to make him stop? Men didn't play these kinds of games with her.

Keilor was useless as a distraction. He was deep in conversation with Urseya on his left and unconcerned with her torment. The bits and pieces she caught of the flirtatious exchange did not help her peace of mind. It seemed Keilor wasn't above playing with whatever new toys came his way. The knowledge that she held no more interest for him than a night's diversion sent dark eddies through her. As a result, vinegar seasoned her response. "A curiosity best left...unexplored."

Green eyes full of amusement studied her as he swirled his wine in its crystal cup. "Hm. How do you know the unexplored isn't hiding pleasures you might find to your liking? Perhaps you might sample a little excitement and find it's to your taste?"

She snorted, and the wine must have rotted her brain, because she told him candidly, "The last guy who promised me a little excitement turned out to have a

73

tongue like a slug. No thanks." Conversations stopped, and even Keilor turned to look at her.

Fallon looked startled. "A slug?"

Perhaps she'd taken the right tack after all. At least he'd stopped flirting. "A cold, wet slug, and once was quite enough, thank you. I'm swearing off men. You're all a pack of trouble."

Jasmine stood up and nodded at Wiley's mother. "It was a pleasure to meet you, ma'am, and congratulations on your reunion, but your wonderful wine has gone to my tongue, and you'd be better off without my company. So if you'll excuse me…"

Astonished she'd managed to pull off such a diplomatic speech, she left before the poor woman could reply.

It seemed like the smart thing to do.

She dreamed of her mother that night.

Jasmine lay curled on the tile next to the commode, waiting for the next upheaval from her stomach. She tried not to think, other than to chant the mantra, "I will never touch Haunt alcohol again. I will never…" Then the knocking began.

"Jasmine, are you ok?" Wiley sounded worried. Maybe she'd noticed how much she'd been drinking the night before.

"Hung over. Go away," she croaked, and she was left in peace for a little while.

She was in stage two with a horrendous headache and a cold, soggy cloth over her eyes when Wiley tried again. "You'll feel better if you eat something," she coaxed.

Jasmine groaned a denial and tossed a pillow at the door.

By stage three it was late afternoon. She'd taken a bath and her body was beginning to function better, but unfortunately so was her mind. She'd just sent Wiley away again and was lying on the couch in her jeans and t-shirt, staring at nothing, when she heard Keilor's deep voice over the intercom.

"Open the door, Jasmine."

Immediately she got up and padded across the hardwood floor with bare, silent feet. She didn't even think of telling him to go away, not when he was using that tone.

He entered her room and strode to the table with a covered tray. He set it on the table while she shut the door. "Sit down and eat."

Her feet dragged as she moved toward him, but the moment he uncovered the steaming sweet and sour fish and snowy rice underneath, her mouth began to water. She devoured everything on her plate.

Keilor opened the shutters and sat in the chair opposite her. He kept his eyes mostly on the view, though occasionally he glanced at her to gauge her progress. As she finished the last few bites, he stood up and walked around the table.

She rubbed the edge of the table with her thumb. What would he say first? That she'd made a fool of herself last night? That she ought to be nicer to Wiley? "What if I promised you I wouldn't cause any trouble if you agreed to take me home?"

His eyes glinted dangerously. Her scent was making him feel aggressive. He needed to touch her. "I'd tell you to stop sulking." In a lightning fast maneuver, he snaked his hand around her waist and pulled her roughly up to him. She pushed against him, but was no match for his large, battle-toned body.

Giving her nowhere to run, he voiced a suspicion that budded in his mind while watching her drink more than was good for her. "Admit it—you're jealous of Rihlia."

She struggled, but he wouldn't give an inch. "Wiley is my friend! I've never been jealous of her in my life." She grunted, twisted, but his arm was a rigid restraint.

With a strangled shriek of rage, she aimed a bite at his shoulder, but he seized her hair and imprisoned her head.

"Admit it!" His nostrils flared as his eyes shot sparks at her. A hot tremor shot through him, but they both ignored it. "You...are...*jealous*!" He'd spent another sleepless night *alone*, thinking of her, and he was not about to back down until they'd dealt with this. Maybe then he'd get some peace.

Furious at her restraint and battered by emotions she could no longer contain, she shouted back, "All right! I'm jealous, ok? I've never been more jealous in my life." At her admission, his arm relaxed. She took every inch of distance he offered.

As her words registered, shame filled her. Her hands curled into fists, clutching his shirt, and her head slowly bowed. "I love her like a sister and I've never wanted to outrun her so badly in my life. God help me." Blood pounded in her ears, and she felt lower than low. Hah! Some friend she was.

"She needs you, you know."

She nodded and tried to keep the moisture burning her eyes inside. The last thing she wanted was his pity.

Almost reluctantly, he separated their charged bodies and led her over to the living area. He chose a velvet armchair and sat down, tugging her down to sit in front of him. With gentle hands he massaged her shoulders.

She sighed, an aching kind of sigh, and let her eyelids drift shut. "Why are you being so nice?"

His voice, when it finally came, was husky, and it sent little firecrackers off up and down her nerves. "I'm not being nearly as nice as I'd like to be, but I'm trying to behave." His thumbs eased up to work the knots out of her neck. "Fallon would think I'm a fool."

She angled her neck to give him better access. "What's he got to do with it?"

"He's a determined man. Don't underestimate him. Just when you think you've driven him off, he'll come back and surprise you."

She tensed, and his fingers pressed more firmly into the bunched muscles. "I don't know why he bothers."

"I told you—you're a charmer." He was matter-of-fact, as if the topic were as unremarkable as the dawn rising in the eastern sky. "He couldn't do anything else."

She frowned. "It doesn't seem to be bothering you."

His hands tightened on her shoulders. He turned her around until she was kneeling in front of him. Taking her hand, he put it on his warm erection, holding it there when she would have jerked back in surprise.

He held her gaze. "I'm a man of action, of discipline. The Haunt follow my orders, and sometimes lives depend on my making hard decisions and keeping a level head." His hard length burned into her palm. Her fingers curled around it.

"I won't be led around by a woman, or by anything else." He pressed her hand more firmly to him and held her eyes for a moment while he got bigger, and harder.

Then he stood up and walked away.

Keilor set the empty tray down on the table while Rihlia watched him with anxious eyes. "She ate."

Rihlia sank down in a wing chair. A new concern filled her face and he shook his head, guessing its source. "Give her until morning. I think you'll find her in better spirits and more pleased with company."

The unhappiness didn't leave her face as she twisted the end of a long black lock. She touched the silver hair ornament holding her hair up and off her face as if she wanted to remove it and then dropped her hand. "She never drinks so much, Keilor. Last night was hard for her."

He tilted his head slightly. "It was hard for you as well, but I don't see you sulking."

She grimaced and slouched in her chair. "I need to, I think. I just haven't had the chance." She raised troubled eyes. "I don't remember her at all. My mother, I mean. She looks at me with such hunger, and all I want to do is push her away. I feel guilty, like I'm doing something wrong— what kind of person doesn't love her mother? Then I get angry because she makes me feel that way, and it starts all over again."

He nodded, just listening, and she went on. "And then there's Jayems." She smiled without humor. "Do you know he told me I was everything he ever wanted in a wife? How could he say something like that? He hardly knows me."

Keilor's smile held real humor. "Love does not take long among our kind—we know."

She leaned back and looked at him skeptically. "Love, Keilor? I think you're getting it confused with— no, don't shake your head. You know I'm right."

He sat down on the couch so she wouldn't have to look up at him. "Cousin, I've known Jayems all his life and seen him with more than his share of women." She scowled at him, but he went on, "Never once have I seen in his eyes what they hold for you."

She clasped her hands over her stomach and stared at her knees. "I don't know what I feel for him." She frowned. "I don't want to have to feel anything at all." There was silence for a moment. "Speaking of feelings, what are you doing to my friend?"

He blinked. "Nothing."

"I know better than that." She folded her arms and her foot started tapping. "There's something going on between you two. Every time you're in the same room the air starts crackling."

Best to cut this inquiry at the quick. He threw an arm over the back of the couch and adopted a nonchalant expression. "Your friend is a charmer, cousin. If I show sexual interest in her, it's no more than can be expected of any man in the room. You'll have noticed Fallon was no different."

"That's a bunch of bull!" Rihlia's eyes shot sparks as she sat forward, gesturing angrily. "She might be a little shy with men, but Jasmine has always been a pretty girl. I don't think it's fair of you to blame some mythical pheromone just so you can have an excuse for being attracted to a human!"

"What I feel, what Fallon feels, what Knightin feels," he answered with grim conviction. "What every unattached male above the age of puberty will feel whenever she is near." He leaned forward, determined to make her understand. "She is pretty, and it doesn't help, but it wouldn't matter if she were fat and bald and covered with boils, men would still want her." She tried to interrupt, but he cut her off ruthlessly. "Fallon likes his women, true, but I've never seen him pursue one with the tenacity he displayed last night. If she hadn't surprised him with that comment about tongues," he grimaced, "then we might have had to leash him to keep him from following her to her room." He paused to give his words weight. "Do you really think her beauty alone would bring three grown men to their knees?"

Rihlia's lips were tight with anger. "Prove it."

"Very well." He strode towards the door. "Give me fifteen minutes to arrange an escort, and I'll meet you in the courtyard. We'll take a tour of the cadet's dining hall." He slammed the door behind him, giving vent to his frustration, and strode quickly down the hall. Jayems might have his head later, but by fire, he'd hear no more complaints about imaginary pheromones!

Word spread about what he was about to do, and by the time he met Rihlia and Jasmine in the bricked courtyard the rest of his female relations were there as well. They'd gathered by a fountain, and the spray from the small waterfall misted the air. It sparkled around his aunt Portae as she talked, gesturing expansively.

Jasmine was coolly confident in the nondescript white uniform of a servant, and even Rihlia looked disdainful, but there was nothing chilly in the greeting Urseya granted him.

"Keilor! This is so exciting," she greeted him, smiling, and put her hand on his arm. When he merely nodded an acknowledgment her smile faded a little, and her hand fell away. "Well." She bounced a bit on the balls of her feet and looked over to their family. "I must warn you, Keilor, we've placed wagers on the outcome of your charmer's unveiling." She smiled up at him through her long lashes. "As a vote of confidence, I've placed my money on you, but I must say, I think Rihlia's friend is cheating dreadfully. Just look at what she's done to her face."

Jasmine's face was coated in something that made it pasty gray, and she'd greased her hair so that it hung in limp strands on her shoulders. Dark circles dimmed her green eyes and she smiled at him, revealing three blackened teeth. She looked like something two days in the grave.

"It won't matter," he said grimly. Jasmine's confidence visibly wavered a bit at those words, and he felt a sharp pang in his chest. He didn't think she was going to enjoy this.

He knew he wouldn't.

Gesturing sharply to the fifteen mated Haunt he'd brought with him, he turned and strode resolutely towards the cadet barracks built into the curving arm of the mountain.

Jasmine told herself she had nothing to worry about. This whole thing was foolish. Keilor had made a mistake, and she'd prove it to the idiot. She'd show him that what he felt, what *she* felt, had nothing to do with a stupid legend and everything to do with a man and a woman who were attracted to each other, and had been from the first. After that...

Her mind shied away from the 'after'. First she had to prove her point. There was no mysterious, seductive pheromone, and even if there ever had been, she didn't have it.

She was butt ugly today and confident that Wiley and the beautiful Urseya outshone her by a mile.

No one would look at her twice.

CHAPTER 9

From the moment the double doors opened for the noble party and her scent was carried into the hall, all eyes were on her. They remained on her throughout the introduction that excluded her, even though she tried to hide behind the others. The necks of cadets at attention craned to watch her as she walked by, in spite of sharp words from their superiors and the warning growls of her tense guard. One dazed young man even broke rank to watch her walk by and was forcibly escorted from the hall.

Jasmine shivered as the cold of dread seeped into her bones. Keilor wasn't imagining it, and it was far worse than she could have dreamed. She edged forward and gave his uniform a frightened tug. His he raised his arm. Instantly their tour was over, and the Haunt guards closed ranks and got them out of there as swiftly as protocol allowed.

"Jasmine…" Wiley's voice was concerned, stunned. Jasmine began to walk very fast. "Jasmine!" She began to jog. In a moment she was running back the way she'd come, the warm, damp sea air burning her lungs as she tried to out run this thing she'd become.

No one stopped her.

Jasmine burst into Jayems' room and skidded to a stop on the polished wood. Eyes wild, she demanded, "How do I make it stop?"

"What?" He looked up from a map he and Knightin had been studying and frowned.

She gestured violently. "This charmer thing!" Raising a trembling hand to her forehead and closing her eyes, she continued, "They were all looking at me like..."

Jayems glanced at Knightin, dismissing him. Tossing his pen aside, he leaned back in his chair and regarded her. "Like they desired you?"

She threw her hand down, but could only hold his eyes for a second. "It was worse than that! They—" She grabbed the back of a chair for support, feeling like she just might fly apart. "I want it to stop. Now."

Knowing eyes considered her. "Is it so bad to be desired?"

She clenched her fists and shouted at him. "Yes! *Yes*. I don't want men to look at me like that!" She moaned in frustration and swept her fist through the air. "I was afraid genetics would come back to haunt me."

He tilted his head in inquiry, and she swallowed hard. Addressing the carpet in front of his desk, she said, "My mother was a stripper. She...ah, when she danced, she...stripped."

"Ah." He examined his desktop as if it held the secrets of the universe.

"In front of people. Male audiences," she finished bitterly.

"I see."

"Good. Then send me back." His face took on that stubborn look and she didn't wait for his denial. "Listen here, you pigheaded son of a bitch! I...." To her horror, her throat closed on the words, and she could only stand there in humiliation, reduced to the helplessness of a child. A single tear tracked down her cheek.

She bowed her head and clenched her fists. Now was not the time to lose her composure. She might as well concede defeat if she did.

"It won't be forever, Jasmine." His voice was soothing.

She wanted to scream.

"It will stop as soon as you take a mate."

Bile churned in her stomach. "You think I would…" Her world blackened on the edges. "I don't even have a boyfriend!" *Breathe, Jas, just breathe.*

"Fallon—" He didn't flinch when the priceless black diamond statue of a volti splintered against the front of his desk, nor even when the heavy crystal decanter followed. His door crashed open, but he waved the Haunt guards back as she insulted first his mother, his ancestry and finally himself in graphic, lurid detail, then stormed out, rolling on her own thunder.

Jasmine started violently when Wiley touched her shoulder.

"It's just me," Wiley assured her softly. She bit her lip. "It's getting close to dinnertime." She paused, hope in her eyes. "The family is eating together again."

Jasmine shook her head. "I'm not hungry."

"Feign it," Keilor told her flatly, announcing his presence. "Jayems expects you to be there, and your lady desires it." He ordered the bath to start up. "I'll be back to escort you to the table in half an hour."

Jasmine jumped to her feet. "Get out of my room, you jerk!"

He didn't budge. "Are you going to be ready?"

"I don't think so," she said with biting sarcasm, and made the mistake of adding a sneer. In a heartbeat he'd crossed the room and tossed her over his shoulder. Striding over to the tub, he dumped her swearing self into it, clothes and all. She surfaced, spitting water, and furiously raked the hair off of her face. "You son of a—"

He hefted the soap in warning, and she clamped her mouth shut. It was tough to glare and blink away the water spiking her lashes at the same time.

He gave her a pleasant smile. "Now, you can either finish this yourself, charmer, or I can climb in there with you..." his voice roughened a fraction, and she swallowed hard, "...and I won't be wearing my clothes when I do." Fire shot into her cheeks, and he handed her the soap. "I'll be back in...." He glanced at the clock on a wall shelf. "...twenty-six minutes. Be ready."

The door shut behind him, and Jasmine looked at Wiley.

Wiley looked at her. She offered a weak smile. "Need help with your hair?"

He knocked on the door exactly twenty-six minutes from the time he'd left, clad in his own formal wear. Rihlia opened the door and entered the hall, followed by a sulky Jasmine.

Her jade gown deepened the green of her eyes and made the red of her glossy, pouting lips all the more inviting, not that he would tell her. She ignored his politely offered arm and tried to walk around him, so he took her hand and tucked it into his left arm, clamping his right hand over it.

Her jaw tightened. "Shouldn't you be escorting Wiley? Doesn't she outrank me?"

"Her name is Rihlia, and Jayems will escort her." He nodded to Jayems as he stepped out into the hall and offered Rihlia his arm.

"I've called her Wiley for years now and I have no intention of—oh!" She gasped as the backs of his fingers brushed against her breast.

"Rihlia," he repeated with as much patience as he'd use training a new villi. "It is her name, and I expect you to address her as such." Jayems and Rihlia rounded a corner and he deliberately lagged. Their footsteps began to fade.

There was far more to Jasmine's refusal to acknowledge Rihlia's name than sheer stubbornness. Too many shocks had hit her too quickly, and she was still trying to retreat. If he continued to allow her to call his cousin Wiley then he was tacitly allowing her the illusion of a return to life as she knew it. Such a thing would be a cruel tease, and the sooner she forgot the idea and moved on the better off she'd be.

The woman on his arm sent him a withering look. "I'll call her whatever I wish, and what I wish to call her is—" she broke off with a yelp as he spun her back to the wall and bared her left breast. A hot, wet mouth closed over her nipple. She cried out and grabbed his hair.

"What will you call her?" he demanded. He gifted her nipple with a long, fiery lick.

She tugged weakly at his head, gasping, "Stop! They'll see—Oh, Keilor…" If anyone else had touched her like that she'd have done her best to draw blood, but this was Keilor. Though she'd have taken a beating rather than admit it, she'd wanted this. Dreamed of it…

His teeth raked her peak and she squirmed against the wall. Her scent rose around him, entered into him, permeating the chinks in his defenses, calling to him to take her fast, now, against the wall.

Keilor forced himself to pull away and glance pointedly down the hall, reminding her they lacked privacy. "You want to call her Rihlia, don't you, Dragonfly?"

Reminded of his game, she shoved against him and tried to knee his groin, but he twisted and trapped her with his hips against the wall. A handful of silky hair stilled her head for him and a massaging hand at her naked breast gained him entrance to her mouth. With all the pent up passion she aroused, he kissed her, stealing her breath and making it his own.

With one last lick to her luscious tongue, he drew back, keeping their bodies locked together. Fighting for breath, he warned her, "I can go all night, sweetheart, but I can't guarantee we won't draw an audience."

She slowly closed her eyes. She'd done it again; let him use her body against her. When would she learn? "Rihlia," she said, and it tasted like ashes.

"Rihlia," he agreed, but didn't withdraw as they both expected. Instead he kissed her again, softly, washing away the ashes with the sweet tenderness of his kiss. Desire washed through her like a warm rain, and when he withdrew this time, both were trembling.

Keilor stepped back while he still had the will. It took strength to straighten her bodice, tucking her away from his sight. His hand fell away, and for a tortured moment, neither could move.

"Your hair is loose," Jasmine observed from where she sagged against the wall.

He gave her a rakish smile and ran both his hands through it, smoothing it back. "So is yours."

"Yeah, but mine started out that way." A corner of her mouth tugged up, and she looked down shyly, uneasy with this thing between them. Somehow, with their second kiss, a wall had shivered and collapsed, and she was afraid to look beyond the swirling dust to see what the darkness might conceal.

Jayems and his lady walked around the corner. Jayems' eyebrow shot up as he surveyed the pair; Keilor with a gleam in his eye and reeking of possessive dominance, Jasmine leaning against the wall as if afraid her knees would fail her. It didn't take much imagination to figure out what had been going on. "Should we expect you at dinner?" He addressed the comment to this cousin with some amusement.

Rihlia jabbed him in the ribs and scowled at Keilor as she looped her arm protectively through Jasmine's. "She's coming to dinner, and I'm escorting her." She shot Keilor a look of disgust. "At least that way I'll know she'll get there."

Lady Rhapsody smiled when they entered the room. Her eyes rested first, as always, on her daughter, and then settled on Jasmine with kindness. Taking her hands, she asked with concern, "You must be in better spirits to be joining us this night, Jasmine. I am glad to see it." Her eyes rested with love on Rihlia. "My daughter's face casts a shadow whenever you aren't near."

Jasmine smiled wryly. "Thank you. I'll try to behave myself this evening."

Lady Portae huffed and waved a perfumed hand. Jasmine tried not to stare at the soft flesh that oozed around her many rings. "I certainly hope not, my dear. You livened things up the other night. I can see why our Rihlia adores you."

As they moved towards the table to begin the blessing, Jasmine was a little surprised when Fallon moved to stand behind her.

He gave her a charming smile, lifting her hand for a gallant kiss. "I was unaware of your unique...gift last evening, dear lady, but I'm quite certain I would have been equally devastated without it. May I have the pleasure of sharing this blessing with you?" He took her smile for assent and placed his strong hands on her shoulders while Jayems blessed the meal.

She did her best to ignore Keilor as he stood across the table, sheltering Urseya.

"You can do better, you know."

Mildly startled, Keilor dragged his eyes back to his dinner companion, who was frowning at the remaining curry on her plate, absently poking it with her chopsticks. He didn't pretend not to know what Urseya was talking about. This was the third time he'd lost the thread of her bright chatter and let his eyes rove across the table. "Could I?" No one was listening to them—all were caught up in a boyhood anecdote Fallon was sharing.

Urseya set down her chopsticks, laying them across her plate to signal that she was finished. A servant immediately collected her plate, and Urseya waited until she was done to continue. "The charmers I have heard tales of are not known for their fidelity. Why take only one lover when one can have the adoration of hundreds...as well as the gifts."

He answered carefully, being certain to keep his voice low. Jasmine would certainly never hear it. "And you fear she would betray me?"

She shrugged. "One cannot say. Frankly, I'm a little surprised at our cousin allowing the charmer around Jayems. I'm not certain I would trust her around my man."

Keilor felt a stab of impatience at her thinly veiled jealousy, and was about to reply when Rihlia suddenly said, "Hey, Jasmine—you never did tell me what happened on your date with Chris. How did it go?" When Jasmine just blinked at her in confusion, Rihlia prompted teasingly, "You know, the hot date you had Friday night. I wasn't there to hear a report, and in the confusion, I forgot to ask. How was it?"

Her friend shrugged. "It was dead on arrival. I should have known better."

"No way!" Rihlia paused to thank the servant who brought her dessert before turning her attention back to Jasmine. "He was such a sweet guy. Cute, too. What happened?" She took a bite of coconut mousse, watching Jasmine from the corner of her eye.

Jasmine squirmed under the family's scrutiny. She had never liked the hot seat. Deciding that a short answer might turn away curiosity, she said succinctly, "He was thirty-five and he still lived with his mother."

"So? She was ill," Rihlia replied, indignant. "I think it's great that he took care of her in her old age. Lots of people would have packed her off to a nursing home."

Jasmine drummed her fingers on the tablecloth in irritation. It wasn't like Wiley to play devil's advocate. "The man just couldn't cut the cord, Wi—" She glanced at Keilor's raised brow and scowled. "*Rihlia*. He wouldn't even buy a car without consulting her."

Portae frowned at her. "There is absolutely nothing wrong with consulting one's elders before making important decisions, young woman." She lifted a brow at her son Fallon, who rolled his eyes. "Frankly, I wish more young people would have the wisdom to do so."

Jasmine continued on as if there had been no interruptions, feeling rather like the subject of an inquisition. "Actually, he told me he was afraid of offending her because she might cut him out of her will and give everything to his sister." She paused for effect. "Apparently his mother is loaded."

Portae had no reply for that.

"This was after he told me that he couldn't consider marrying someone his mother disapproved of," she said indignantly. "I mean, the guy hadn't even made it to first base yet, and here he is talking about marriage! Not only that, but when dinner arrived, he didn't like the way they'd cooked his steak. But does he do anything about it? No. Instead he spends the rest of the meal whining about the poor service and the lousy food." She made a face. "By the time the jerk stiffed the waitress for the tip and walked me to my car, I was more than happy to see the end of him."

Fallon gave her a lazy smile and let his eyes drift down to her mouth. "I don't suppose this was the slug kisser, was it?"

Jasmine grimaced. "This guy didn't rate a kiss."

Grinning mischievously, Rihlia asked, "How is Michael, anyway?"

"I don't know and I don't care." Why was Wiley baiting her? Jasmine scowled at her untouched dessert, muttering, "At least now I won't have to worry about avoiding him, either."

Urseya raised a brow at Keilor. *You see? Now the truth comes out.* He frowned at her. "Was it a very bad ending?" she inquired with cheerful interest.

Rihlia laughed and shook her head. "Only if you count telling the poor guy—on the phone, mind you—never to call her again and then hanging up before he could say anything about it."

"There was no point in dragging it out," Jasmine said with stiff dignity. Wiley was painting a rather ugly picture of her romantic life, and she didn't care for it one bit. Besides, what was she doing, dragging all the skeletons out of her closet in public like this? She didn't notice that the others at the table were beginning to look at Rihlia, wondering the same thing.

Rihlia did notice, but ignored it with determination. Jasmine would thank her later for dampening the interest of the males present. She didn't need their kind of attention. Jasmine deserved better, and she was determined to see her get it. "I guess it's like that poem you dedicated to poor Josh, huh? "'If they're gutless when you meet them, they'll be gutless 'til they die; the man was a mama's boy, so I left him there to cry.'"

Dead silence greeted her recital. Finally Jasmine said slowly, "You know, B.B., if you'd like to rehash old flames, I'm sure I could come up with a tale or two to amuse your family. Like that time I found you getting it on hot and heavy with—"

"Uh, that's ok, Jas," Rihlia hastily interrupted. Jasmine's threat was clear. Not only was she threatening to spill all of her secrets—not that they were excessive, just potentially embarrassing—but she would start calling her Blue Balls as well, the name given to her by frustrated boyfriends, and seal the humiliation. "We don't want to bore them with that." She glanced at the glowering Jayems and gulped. "Why don't you try the custard? It's really very good."

Jasmine gave her a look, but slowly lifted her spoon and tasted the treat.

Rihlia asked Jayems to refill her wineglass.

Noting her friend's distress and eager to lift the tension that had settled over the table, Jasmine snatched the glass before it could make it to Rihlia's trembling lips. She gave her a roguish smile. "Royalty really ought to have a taste tester, don't you think?" Grinning, she took a large swallow of the golden wine.

Rihlia laughed in grateful relief and looked down, shaking her head. "Are you sure it's not the job of court jester you're after?" When there was no answer, she looked up and saw Jasmine frozen with an odd look on her face. "Jasmine?"

Jasmine blinked, but didn't move.

Rihlia touched her arm. It was rigid with strain. "Jasmine? Are you okay?"

Colors swam before Jasmine's frozen eyes. Her muscles went weak and then spasmed without warning, shattering the glass in her hand. Someone screamed. Male voices cursed as strong arms wrapped around her, giving her support. She felt the blood and wine flow over her hand, but could neither unclench her fist from the shards nor see, for the room began to blacken. Past the roaring in her ears she dimly heard Rihlia shouting...something...

And then the screaming began.

CHAPTER 10

Keilor swore and leapt over the table the moment the glass shattered, but in spite of his best efforts and Fallon holding Jasmine steady, he could not unclench her hand, short of breaking it. Her body shuddered and the cords of her neck stood out with the strain as her muscles contracted, driving the shards deeper into her hand. Fresh blood flowed.

Rihlia screamed and fought against Jayems' hold as she struggled to reach her friend. In the background Keilor heard him telling her, "They are helping her! We have to stay out of their way."

"She's hurting!" she shrieked, nearly wild, and he dragged her back even farther.

"Love, sweet love…" he soothed, and his words faded into a murmur as Keilor pressed the tendons in Jasmine's hand to force it open. He worked quickly to pick out the largest fragments.

Jasmine moaned, a low, tortured sound. She rolled into a tight ball.

The first shriek caught him off guard. He saw Fallon pale and press his lips tightly together. Vengeance took up a war drum in his blood. He saw the same need mirrored in Fallon's hard eyes. Someone would pay for harming this woman, and pay dearly.

"She'll live," The medic announced as he entered the clinic waiting room. He nodded respectfully to the party of

93

four who'd been waiting more than two hours for his verdict.

Keilor had just sat down from his last circuit of the room. He closed his eyes as some of the tension drained from him.

Rihlia lifted her head from her hands, exposing tear-swollen eyes. Her voice hoarse, she asked, "Will she be all right?"

The medic sighed and crossed his arms, rocking back on his heels. "There is unlikely to be brain damage, and I believe that most of her organs will make a full recovery, but it's bound to be slow. The chemical we found in her blood is most deadly to humans. Frankly, I'm surprised she survived it."

Keilor sucked in a breath. Fallon swore softly and Jayems put a supporting arm around his wife. She allowed him to hold her as he kissed her hair and murmured soothing words, slowly shaking her head.

"What was it?" Keilor demanded.

The medic's lips tightened as he stared at the polished stone floor. "Its scientific name is Libran, but you might know it better as Sweet Surrender." He smiled without humor. "It would seem someone tried to slip your charmer an aphrodisiac, and ended up with a nasty surprise instead."

Keilor turned lethal eyes on Fallon, who was watching him with an equally savage expression. Each assessed and dismissed the other as suspects. Fallon was far too proud to resort to such an underhanded scheme, and as for Keilor...he held no love for Libran.

"But...it happened after she drank from my glass," Rihlia ventured uncertainly.

"The dessert," Jayems said with grim conviction. "She took a bite of the dessert just before she drank from your cup, Rihlia. If you hadn't been distracting her..." He glanced at Keilor. "But who and why? No one was going to get past the guards at her door without my permission, so even if she was drugged, they would have had a hard time seducing her. And if it wasn't one of us…"

Keilor frowned at Fallon. "Your mother does want you to wed." There was a silence as they considered just how far the manipulative Portae would go to secure a daughter-in-law. Considering the lengths she'd gone to in the past to manage her only son's life, there was no telling what she was capable of, and Jasmine was the first woman he'd ever shown a serious interest in.

"Had the drug been in your dessert, Keilor, I would have suspected Urseya." Jayems smiled faintly. "Under the circumstances, I can't see her wishing to inflame Jasmine, lest she be forced to toast the pair of you at your wedding feast."

His cousin gave him a sardonic smile.

"You give up on me too soon, Jayems," Fallon interjected smoothly. "The lady might have preferred to spend the night in my bed."

Rihlia stood up, fists clenched. "You leave her alone!"

Surprised by the fury of her command, the three men regarded her with uncertainty.

Fallon tried to soothe her. "We jest, cousin," he assured her. "No one is going to treat Jasmine with less than honor and courtesy. Surely Jayems has explained to you—"

"Just this morning you told me, Keilor, that the only thing you men feel for Jasmine is lust." When he didn't respond to her challenge, she continued tightly, "Well, I'm taking you at your word, and I'm telling you, *commanding* you, to leave her alone. She deserves far better than a man whose only interest in her is as a one night stand."

"Keilor speaks for himself if he said such things, Rihlia." Fallon glowered Keilor, who said nothing to defend himself. "I admire your friend, respect her, and I…"

"Admiration is not enough," she answered him coldly. "She deserves a lot more."

Fallon was silent for a moment. His jaw ticked when he said, "If you are looking to know my heart, it's not yours to know." The expression on his face when she tried to interrupt him was so savage, she stopped before uttering a word. "If your friend wishes to know, I will speak truthfully with her. Until then…" He softened his voice a little. "Be satisfied that she is in good hands."

Rihlia stared at one of the many potted plants dotting the room. "What about the other? What will you do when she finds out about the Haunt?" Silence followed her comment.

All three men had been there the night Rihlia had been found. She had been wary from the beginning of the three strangers who had suddenly appeared in her camp, emerging from the shadows as if they owned the night, and she had not gone willingly to the Dark Lands. Worse than that, when she had attempted to use the only weapon she had left, the one thing that they now knew she feared above all else, Jayems had shown her the true nature of the Haunt.

Tonight had been the first night since that she had willingly suffered his touch.

Keilor waved a hand irritably, dismissing her fears. "Jasmine's made of stern stuff, Rihlia, and loyal. I think she'd settle down quickly after she became used to the idea." He gave her a level look. "Your friend is the type to face her problems, not to turn and run."

"Have you seen how she looks at the soldiers?" she countered. "She's never relaxed around them, never forgets their presence for a moment. If one of them makes an unexpected move, she tenses and watches him as if she expects him to try and eat her." Keilor winced, and she nodded, vindicated. "How do you think she'd react to the announcement that you were one?"

Rihlia was curled up in a fat chair beside Jasmine's bed, knitting, when Jasmine finally woke up. She immediately set aside her needles and came to sit on the big bed.

"How are you doing, Jas?" she asked softly. She felt Jasmine's forehead with the back of her fingers and smiled. "You look better, and your skin's not clammy anymore."

Jasmine frowned, sifting details through her sleepy brain. She lifted her bandaged hand, staring as memories trickled through her awakening brain. "The glass," she croaked. Her throat was still sore from screaming.

"Yes. It took the medics a long while to get all the pieces out." Rihlia helped her take a sip of water, adjusting the straw so she could drink without sitting up.

Jasmine closed her eyes and relaxed back into the pillows. Her whole body hurt. "Did they figure out who tried to poison you?"

There was a pause. "It wasn't poison."

One eye opened and looked at her.

"It was an aphrodisiac."

Jasmine's eyes opened wide and she started to sit up. She groaned when her sore muscles and tender stomach protested. Temporarily defeated, she flopped back down, allowing Rihlia to fluff the pillows behind her head. "Someone gave you an aphrodisiac?"

Rihlia sighed. "Someone gave *you* an aphrodisiac, Jas, only it backfired. It acted on your body like a poison."

Jasmine stared at her for a long moment. Her face darkened.

Before she could explode, Rihlia hastily said, "It wasn't one of the men. You should have seen their faces;

they were so upset. Nobody has any proof, but we think it might have been Fallon's mother."

A queer look passed over Jasmine's face, and Rihlia smirked. "Not for herself, silly! Apparently she wants Fallon to get married pretty badly. She might have used the stuff for that, never dreaming she might kill her future daughter-in-law."

There wasn't much Jasmine could say to that without a great deal of thought, and she felt too drained at the moment to engage in lengthy internal debates. Instead she grumbled, "So I'm going to be all right? There's no lasting effect to this stuff?"

Rihlia studied the quilt. "The medic said that you'll be all right, except for…" She cleared her throat uncomfortably and shifted on the bed. "You might have a few hormonal problems at first."

Jasmine narrowed her eyes. "Like what?" Sudden visions of sprouting facial hair taunted her. If Wiley's aunt had made her into a bearded lady, Jas was going to have to hurt her.

"Your sex drive." Rihlia waffled a hand in the air uncomfortably. "Uh, you may not be able to feel, er, arousal for a while."

Jasmine squinted one eye. This was getting worse and worse. Not that she wasn't grateful to be alive, and she'd never been a sexual dynamo, but not to feel any desire at all? Sheesh! "How long?"

"A few weeks, maybe. Or months." Rihlia cringed. "Or maybe never."

"Never!" Jasmine tried to shout, but it came out more of a croak. *Never?*

"Don't worry!" her friend hastened to assure her, laying her hand on her arm. "They can give you hormone therapy if it doesn't come back on its own, which your doctor is almost sure it will. You'll be fine."

"Great," Jasmine rasped, furious. "Viagra for women." She smacked her damaged hand on the bed and yowled with the pain. She'd forgotten it was injured.

While she was still mouthing curses and holding her wrist, the door tone sounded, and Rihlia went to answer it. "All right. Bring it on in." Jasmine glanced in irritation at the doors as Rihlia swung them wide and stood back. A man pushed a wheeled platform into the room. A giant granite pot rested on the platform, and inside it grew a six-foot fruit tree, loaded with ripe avocados.

She looked at Rihlia in bewilderment. "What—"

The deliveryman stepped forward and nodded his head respectfully. "Lady Jasmine, may I present a gift from the cadet Marcus Bustos? He sends his hopes that you might recover swiftly and prays that his gift will cheer you in your convalescence."

When she only blinked stupidly at him, Rihlia apologized, "Jasmine's voice is almost gone at the moment, but if she could speak I'm certain that she would say thank you, the tree is very lovely. Why don't you set it right at the foot of the bed, where she can have a good view of it?"

She grinned at Jasmine while the man slid the heavy pot off the platform. "They've been arriving all morning." She gestured to the window, where three other potted plants and a small waterfall surrounded by mushrooms formed a miniature grove. "So far you've collected a banana, an *ulu ristu* fruit and an apple tree, and I can't wait to see what shows up next." She rubbed her hands gleefully. "Apparently, instead of 'say it with flowers', here they say it with fruit."

"It's an old tradition," Jayems said, entering the room as the deliveryman left. He walked to Rihlia. Jasmine's eyes widened as he slid an arm around her friend's waist and then kissed her neck in greeting. Rihlia blushed and avoided her eyes.

"Your suitors are very organized, Jasmine. I've heard they have a list going at the barracks to avoid duplicating any gifts." He smiled in good humor and she reflected with surprise that she'd never seen him so relaxed.

It could only mean one thing.

Before she could speculate further, he continued, "Keilor searches every gift to be certain that it is safe and Fallon scowls every time another delivery is made." He flashed her a wicked grin. "I haven't had so much fun just watching them in years."

Jayems, wicked? Feeling a little disoriented, Jasmine just grunted a reply. How much had she missed while she'd been sleeping, anyway? "I guess I'll have to see them and tell them thank you." She blinked sleepily at her hand. "Thank you notes are out of the question."

Rihlia gave her a bright smile and adjusted the covers. "I'm sure they'll be thrilled to hear it, Jas, but you might want to wait a couple of days. How about I make up a schedule for you?" Rihlia grinned. "You're quite the celebrity. I don't think you'd want all your fans mobbing you at once."

Jasmine murmured something in the affirmative and closed her eyes. In moments she was asleep.

Keilor watched Jasmine sleep, deep in thought. Three citrus, an *illupe* vine, a pineapple plant and a hairy sugar fruit later, her room looked and smelled like a garden. As Jasmine's public liaison, Rihlia had finally suggested that Jasmine's admirers switch to another form of gift, and since then baskets of blooms and bushels of tempting treats—all carefully and discreetly tested for dangerous additives— had begun to arrive in place of the plants. Not that she would be able to taste any for a few days—her tender stomach wouldn't be able to process much than liquids for a while.

He smiled mischievously and popped a truffle into his mouth. No sense letting them go to waste.

Jasmine opened her eyes, smiling a little when she saw him, and he felt a warm wave slide through him. The girl had a way about her.

"Morning," she murmured, and elbowed herself into a sitting position. He adjusted the pillows for her. "Are my guests scheduled to arrive yet?"

He surveyed her tousled hair and slumberous eyes ruefully. "I don't think you'll want to greet them just as you are."

She yawned behind her bandaged hand. "You're right. I guess I probably ought to do something about my hair and at least wash my face. I probably look kind of scary."

A fire kindled in his eyes as they brushed over her body. Even hidden under a soft sleep shirt and a velvet quilt, her pull on him was strong. "That wasn't my concern." He handed her a glass of thick, almond milk eggnog. "Your breakfast."

She sighed. After two days of subsiding on near liquids, even that tasty concoction lacked appeal. She eyed the truffles in the crystal dish near her hopefully. "Those look good."

He flashed a devilish grin at her and selected a chocolate ball coated in nuts. He bit into it slowly. "Mmm. They are." He licked his fingers as she scowled at him. "Hazelnut filling, I believe."

She harrumphed and sipped her eggnog.

"I brought you something." He lifted a small package from the floor and placed it on her lap, pleased to see her eyes light up.

She traced the smooth surface of the silver paper. With a shy smile, she teased, "It's not a plant, is it?"

Keilor raised a brow. "You do not enjoy your new garden?"

"Actually, I love it, though I'm a little afraid of killing everything off," she admitted. "I've never had a garden before. Do you think I might be able to find someone to teach me how to take care of it?"

He propped his chin on his fist and leaned on the arm of his chair. "I'll teach you."

Surely he was teasing. Men like Keilor did *not* run around with pruning shears and weed flowers. "You, a gardener?"

He winked at her. "It impresses the ladies." He waved a graceful hand towards her present. "Open your gift." He watched as she awkwardly held the package steady with her right wrist and worked at the seams with her left, making no move to interfere. When the paper parted, spilling a cool wash of ivory silk across her lap, he gently removed the paper and helped drape the straps of the chemise over her bandaged hand.

He lowered his eyes, feeling an unaccustomed touch of self-consciousness. "For your comfort, when you sleep. Do you like it?"

"It's very pretty, thank you," she said, coloring faintly. "But if...Keilor," she whispered, and there was a touch of pain in her voice, "I can't feel...the doctor said…" She had nearly died, and at the moment she felt no reason to hide her feelings. Besides, what else could he mean with such a gift but that he cared?

His brow cleared as he understood what she was saying. For a moment, he'd feared something else entirely. "It doesn't matter," he assured her. "It is a gift, freely given." He brushed the backs of his fingers over her cheek. "Enjoy it. I hope for only your pleasure in return."

She lowered her gaze. "You Haunt men must take lessons in charm. Thank you. I will enjoy it."

He leaned back and gave her a lazy grin. "Of course, I have to admit the thought of you wearing it may cause me to loose sleep—" he laughed and caught the pillow she tossed at him, "—but the gift of your smile makes the sacrifice worth while."

She wagged a finger at him and he chuckled. "I will call for Rihlia. She will wish to help you prepare to meet your admirers." He kept the pleasant expression on his face until he was safely out of the room. The moment the doors closed behind him, he lost all traces of amusement.

He looked critically over the two Haunt captains he'd personally selected to guard Jasmine while she thanked her admirers. Each had achieved a reputation for vicious ferocity in battle during the years before Jayems officially came to power. Isfael had guarded his back during the ambush that had taken Keilor's father and the rest of his family. When the battle had been over, only the two of them had been left standing; bloody, but alive. Isfael had been by his side ever since.

He turned his eyes to Raziel. That Haunt had been feared as the most devastating warrior in the realm before an attack by jealous rivals had brought him down. They tortured him and left him for dead, going on to slay the rest of his family. Raziel had recovered and single-handedly destroyed his enemy's entire clan. He was fearless, soulless.

The Haunt knew him as the Immortal.

Those two were the only ones in the entire garrison who could hope to best him in battle, and Jasmine couldn't have been safer if he'd been standing by himself. But just to be sure…

"Her visits are to be short, safe, and pleasant. If she so much as looks distressed, remove the irritant at once. Take care of her." He began turn away, but paused. These might be his friends, but still… "One other thing, comrades. If you take a liking to her, I'll have to slit your throats."

Isfael growled and made an obscene sign. Raziel gave him toothy grin. Satisfied, Keilor walked away, smiling.

CHAPTER 11

"Stop fussing. You're not my nurse."

Rihlia grunted and shifted her grip around Jasmine's waist. Jas had one arm flung around her shoulders for balance. She'd already threatened to dump her friend on the floor or have one of their escorts carry her. "No, and I'm not a pack mule, either. I told you to let me get the books for you. I would have been there and back by now."

With an effort, Jasmine straightened and took most of her weight on her own feet, hiding what it cost her. It had seemed like a great idea to go check out the library. What better way to while away the long hours she was forced to stay abed than with a stack of books? Besides, she was sick of staring at her own four walls.

She'd unfortunately overestimated her stamina and was relieved when they staggered into the library and she was dumped onto a bench. Breathing heavily, Rihlia dropped down beside her. "Somebody else is carrying you back."

"Oh, knock it off," Jasmine grumbled, panting for real. "I'm not that heavy."

Rihlia grinned and dropped the act, hopping up with a sickening amount of energy. "What would you like me to get first?"

The immense old library had few patrons that day, and the silence peculiar to such hallowed halls of books made Jasmine feel right at home. The room was octagon in shape. Shelves of books rose to the carved panels of the arched ceiling. Trees grew right out of the floor. Benches had been built around them to provide seating. High, arched windows filled the western facing wall and provided plenty of reading light.

She sighed in delight. It was perfect. No doubt everything she ever wanted to know about these people was in here, and she couldn't wait to get her hands on it.

One of the little giraffes—villi—that were such popular pets in this world walked up and gravely sniffed at her. Lemming wagged her tail politely and returned the greeting. Amused, she watched as it sauntered off, curiosity satisfied.

Independent little creatures, she thought.

"Can I help you?" A voice inquired, and she turned to find an older man with the expression of someone trying to keep his thoughts to himself. He bent to pet the villi who'd greeted them, creaking with the movement.

"I was hoping to learn a little more about the history of the Haunt, and especially about charmers. I don't suppose you would know much about it, would you?"

If anything, the librarian grew more severe, but he moved off to find the books. Uneasy, Jasmine murmured, "I don't think he likes me, Ri."

Rihlia cleared her throat and sat down beside her on the bench. "Not everyone here likes humans. It's especially bad because you're...uh—"

"Charmer," Jasmine supplied, saying the word like a curse.

Rihlia bit her lip. "It would have been worse if Jayems had let you go back home and anyone had found out. There might have been war. As it was he had to deal with an uproar once word spread that a...uh, that you were here." Her face darkened. "Some people even wanted to kill you."

"What!" Jasmine stared at her in alarm. "What did I do?"

Upset, Rihlia rubbed her arms and wouldn't meet her eyes. "Nothing. It's just that too many of the older generation still remember what it was like before they came here. They're worried you might be some kind of danger to them."

"That's ridiculous," Jasmine scoffed. "What am I going to do, single-handedly annihilate the entire Haunt race? Give me a—" she stopped in mid-tirade, suddenly realizing what else Rihlia had said. "Ri," she said slowly, "They've been here for over two hundred years. You told me that yourself. How could they possibly remember anything?" Rihlia was silent. Jasmine swallowed hard. Addressing the floor, she asked, "Just how long do you guys live, anyway?"

"Three hundred years is considered a good, old age," the librarian supplied, returning with a stack of books and a register for Jasmine to sign. It took her a moment, but she scrawled her signature with a heavy hand at the bottom. He set the books on the bench beside her and went about his business.

She rubbed her face, wondering if she'd ever get used to living in an alien world. Three hundred years!

"You don't look so good," Rihlia said, worried. "I think we'd better get you back to bed."

Without being asked, Isfael picked her up like an infant and Raziel followed with her books. Jasmine squirmed and grumbled at the indignity of it, but she truly was too tired to argue. Even with the annoyance of Isfael's fur tickling her nose and making her want to sneeze, she was asleep by the time they reached her room.

The books were a revelation.

Jasmine traced the leather scrollwork on a book's blood red cover, admiring the craftsmanship. The gilt edges of the pages and the gold title winked in her reading light. The Haunt were a people who took pride in their literature and wrote even their histories with passion. No bloodless recitals of bare facts here.

She scooted down against her raised pillows, seeking a more comfortable position. It was after midnight, but her mind was too seduced by the glory of Haunt history to give in to slumber. The first book she'd read had barely mentioned charmers, but this one seemed more promising.

Hours later, she closed the book and set it on her nightstand. The trouble with reading a no-holds-barred version of history was that unflattering views of one's self or people were often printed. She had to admit, humans did not look good from a Haunt perspective.

In her opinion, it had been a good idea to separate the two races. Nothing but tragedy had resulted from their mixing. The charmers had been taken from their homes and families by other humans, mostly warlords, whether they were willing or not, and used to lure Haunts to often grisly deaths. If they possessed any kind of beauty, they were often disfigured to ensure that the males chasing them were actually Haunts. She shuddered, thinking of the descriptions of branded and noseless women. If they were lucky, their masters only forced them to wear masks for the rest of their lives.

The captured males had been tortured—mostly for the thrill of it, if she understood the text correctly. Any useful information had been obtained by "the suggestive power of the charmer herself" whatever that meant. Useful information usually consisted of where to find and annihilate any remaining Haunt, women and children included. Sometimes the captured one was "enspelled" and forced to lead the way to the others. As a result, the Haunt took to assassinating any known charmers, and they were notoriously successful. There were long lists of charmer kills and their assassins. Such stalkers were treated with great honor, and hailed as heroes.

If she had been born a Haunt, could she have blamed them? In the case of charmers, mutilated and forced to participate in torture and genocide, maybe some of them preferred to be dead.

She would have.

The blackest of the charmers, those who participated willingly in the slaughter of Haunt for the chance to wallow in ungodly wealth, were singled out for vilification in the history. The author seemed to relish listing their various crimes and the measures taken to bring them down. It wasn't pretty.

Eventually the Haunt became so successful at killing charmers that efforts had been made to breed them, but that had proved unsuccessful. Charmers were a wildcard mutation, and defied all efforts to recreate on demand. Thank God.

Now she understood why Keilor had been so repulsed by her in the beginning, and so angry. He and Jayems must have truly cared for Rihlia to go through all the effort to first humor her, and then to protect the dreaded charmer from their countrymen.

And speaking of their countrymen, just how opposed to her were they? Could she expect a lynch mob if she tried to wander out alone? She shivered, knowing she could never hope to outrun any Haunt who wanted her blood.

Taking a deep, calming breath, she reminded herself of the cadets. *They* certainly had no aversion to her. Maybe it was just the older generation she had to watch out for. It would pay to be wary, though. Now that Rihlia had accepted her role as Jayems' wife, there was no reason to go back to Earth. There was nothing there for them now.

Besides, she sort of liked it here. The weather was mild, the people interesting, and if she discounted the poisoned desserts, the food was the best she'd ever had. In fact, if she could just figure out how to live two hundred and fifty more years, life would be just about perfect.

"Tell me about your cousins."

Jayems looked up from the stained glass he was soldering, not the least bit startled, and Jasmine knew that he'd heard her outside the door of his hobby room. She pulled a stool up to his workbench and looked with interest at the vice. Grinding and polishing tools and sundry pieces of colored glass were neatly arranged on the work surface.

"Your wife is taking a nap." She shook her head. "I think the privileged life is going to her head. I swear she spends half her days napping."

Jayems grinned with satisfaction. "Her new duties as my lady are demanding."

Jasmine decided not to touch that one.

Noting her interest, he laid another line of soldering wire and heated it with his torch, shaping the frame of his project. With his eyes still on his work, he asked, "What was it you wished to know?"

She flicked away a speck of ground glass on the bench top. "Keilor and Fallon...they're about the same age?"

"Keilor is two years older."

"Oh." She propped her elbow on her knee and rested her chin on her fist. She'd adopted the comfortable loose trousers and tunic of the male formal attire, and she was much more comfortable in those clothes than she'd been in the beautiful gowns she'd been given to wear. It was difficult to relax in a dress that probably would have taken a month's pay—back when she still had a paying job—to buy. All she could think of when she wore one was how guilty she'd feel if she damaged it.

There were times when she felt like a maid mistaken for a movie star and put up in a fancy hotel on credit. She kept waiting for the day when the management figured out she was an impostor and came to collect on the bill. "What happened to Keilor's parents? I never hear anyone talk about them."

Jayems reached for another piece of glass with a trace of a frown. "They were murdered in an ambush when he was eighteen. He and one of his friends were the only ones left alive." He glanced at her stricken face. "He still visits his family's memorial on the anniversary of their death. He brings his mother jasmine flowers. They were her favorite."

She looked down, unable to say a word.

"She would have liked you." He chuckled. "Had she been still alive the night you became ill, I would have suspected her immediately of slipping you the Sweet Surrender."

She grinned wryly. It was good to find humor in that night.

The mood didn't last. There was something else she needed to ask, something that had been keeping her up nights. "Jayems...are your cousins always so...flirtatious with women? Or is it the charmer thing, do you think?" Her eyes darkened with painful wisdom. "I'm not naive enough to think it's my great beauty and charm that attracts them."

Jayems turned to face her. "If you wish to know their hearts, ask them, Jasmine. They will tell you the truth."

She sighed. "That's not how it works where I come from."

"Here it is a matter of honor for a man to speak honestly to a woman who asks his feelings for her. I know my cousins. They would not lie to you."

He frowned at her thoughtfully. "I don't think you realize what your position is. Rihlia claimed you as a sister, and I accepted her claim. You became my family. No one would dare treat you lightly." He slanted her a mischievous look. "Nor will they court you without my permission."

She eyed him. "You approved all the men who sent me gifts?"

He laughed. "No. Each was told before hand that no match would be permitted with the Lady Jasmine, but the Haunt are stubborn men, and much taken with you. Besides, Rihlia thought their gifts would cheer you." A sly look crossed his face. "What did Keilor bring you?"

Jasmine felt her face flush. "N-nothing much." That was true. There hadn't been much to that nightie.

Jayems looked down at his project, and she could tell he was trying to hide his smirk. She hastily made her excuses and left.

She made it to her room without mishap and called for the lights. She made a tour of her indoor garden as she considered her problems.

They were both good men. She skittered away from the knowledge that her midnight fantasies always revolved around the dark haired cousin. He wasn't the type to commit. She knew the danger of wishing for things that weren't meant to be.

Keilor was impossibly sexy, and Fallon too charming for his own good. The men were like champagne and dark rum; one was bright and sparkly and made her insides bubble, while the other burnt the throat going down, but— oh! It lit a fire inside.

She'd always been a champagne girl, but lately she craved a more potent brew. Frightened, bold, sexy—that's how Keilor made her feel. He had her teetering on the brink of a fatal loss of common sense. What if he pushed and she admitted her feelings?

She traced the centerline of a lemon leaf with her stiff right hand. Perhaps she was obsessing. What she needed was to get out of this room, collect Rihlia and hunt up an adventure. Jasmine grinned. After all, if she wasn't having fun, she had only herself to blame.

CHAPTER 12

"This isn't what I had in mind," Jasmine muttered. She watched Rihlia's aunt, mother and cousin shuck their robes and wade, buck naked, into a pool of warm mud.

Rihlia already sat in the repulsive stuff, her arms stretched out along the rough granite edge. The same stone formed the pools privacy wall. Large, roughly squared stones wove in a path through the spa's neatly clipped grass.

A waterfall splashed down over one wall and collected in a circular pool. The wall directly opposite it held tall arched niches with stone statues representing the four seasons. Thinking to delay—indefinitely, if she had her way—playing in the mud, Jasmine decided to take a closer look.

She hadn't taken two steps when Rihlia called out playfully, "Coward!"

Jasmine scowled. "I was just going to look around." If she'd happened to take all day about it, that was all right, too. Rihlia gave her a knowing look, and she sighed, admitting defeat. She shucked her robe and got hastily into the pool, not nearly as comfortable with her nudity as the others.

Modesty not withstanding, it still took an effort of will to sink into the warm, clinging mud, and she was grateful she'd pinned her hair up in a twist.

Rihlia took one look at her face and burst out laughing. Even Urseya and Rhapsody chuckled.

"Don't be such a sour pickle, dear," Portae chided, dipping down to coat her chins in the mud. "Volcanic mud is famous for its healing properties. You'll love it once you get used to it."

Urseya smiled, catlike, and leaned back, dipping her long, dark hair into the muck. "It's also extremely good for the skin." She raised her head and sighed, leaning back against the edge of the pool. She looked entirely too satisfied. "Some of us need all the help we can get."

Jasmine's eyes narrowed and she saw Rihlia frown. If she'd suspected Urseya had no use for her before, it was confirmed now. Unfortunately, the subtle insult seemed to be lost on the older women, or at least Urseya's mother.

"Don't be silly, dear, you know you're beautiful," she told her daughter fondly, "and if I've read the signs right, Keilor has noticed as well." She sent Rhapsody a sly look. "Perhaps we'll be celebrating two weddings this year."

Jasmine stiffened. "I thought Keilor was her cousin."

"Oh, he is, dear, but not a first cousin," Portae explained with a touch of condescension. "It would get very tiresome if we insisted on calling him 'third cousin Keilor' all the time, don't you think?"

"Definitely," a deep voice responded.

Jasmine looked up in shock to see Keilor standing at the edge of the pool. Embarrassed, she sank a bit lower in the concealing mud.

No one else seemed to take his presence amiss. Rhapsody inclined her head. "You have some message, Keilor?"

He nodded respectfully. "Your friend, Lady Liselle, is here. You said you wished to be notified the moment she arrived."

"And you rushed over here to bring the message yourself?" Portae gave her daughter a significant look. "How thoughtful."

"I was nearby," he explained, extending a hand to assist Rhapsody from the pool.

Jasmine's eyes got wide as the older woman thanked him as politely as if he'd just handed her a cup of tea. She walked over to the waterfall to rinse, as poised as if she were out for a stroll. When the procedure was repeated with his aunt, Jasmine hastily looked away. Even reminding herself that lots of cultures saw nothing wrong with nudity did little to help.

Urseya extended her hand, along with a sultry smile, and slithered out of the pool. She murmured something to Keilor that Jasmine didn't quite catch, proudly standing before him in all her mud-slicked glory.

"I'm sorry, cousin," Keilor answered politely, with just a touch of distance. "I'm afraid it would be only courteous of me to assist the other ladies as well." He extended a hand to Rihlia while Urseya walked off, trying to hide her disappointment.

Much to Jasmine's amazement, Rihlia took it.

"When in Rome," she murmured, and hopped out of the pool with all speed. She jogged off to the falls.

Jasmine boggled at her.

Keilor looked at Jasmine. He extended his mud-dampened hand.

Jasmine slouched a little deeper into the muck. "Um, I think I'll just hang out here for a while."

Keilor cocked his head. "Is there some problem?"

She closed her eyes and jigged her head a little, arguing with herself. She decided to just tell him. "I'm naked."

His voice deepened with amusement. "I had assumed as much."

She swallowed. Suddenly nerve endings she'd sworn were fried began hopping. Yippee, I'm healed, she groaned silently. Talk about bad timing. "Where I come from we're taught not to walk around naked in public." It sounded prissy, under the circumstances. It was obvious he was just being polite.

He raised a brow. "We're hardly in public."

"You're the public," she said, hoping he would take a hint before she managed to die of embarrassment. She risked a glance at the others. They were leaving. That did it. She was definitely staying put until someone came to rescue her. No way was she going anywhere near him covered in only a thin layer of mud.

He was silent a moment. "Has anyone spoken to you of the mud borer?" he asked gravely.

She looked at him as if he were insane. What was the man talking about?

"It's about this long—" he measured a space of about nine inches between his index fingers, "—and hollow, like an intestine. About that texture, and slimy as well."

Jasmine shuddered. What nasty little creatures they had on this world!

He looked at the mud and then around at the manicured lawns. "Not that we've had any here in nearly a month," he murmured, almost too softly to catch.

Jasmine gulped. He was pulling her leg, wasn't he? He made to leave.

"Wait!" He looked at her inquiringly and she bit her lip, reluctant to play the fool, but... "So what does this mud borer do? Suck blood?" she said, attempting to joke.

Keilor frowned. "I thought no one had mentioned it." He glanced at the smooth surface of the mud. "It *is* hatching season, but still…" He shrugged. "I wouldn't worry about it." He turned away.

He didn't get three steps before she called urgently, "Wait!" There *were* little swirls in the viscous pool now and then, and sometimes she almost though she felt a brushing...like...a soft little body….

"Yiieee!" she yelped, and leapt out of the mud, splashing brown gunk everywhere. Hastily she backed away from the pool, actually forgetting for about five seconds that she was stark naked.

He didn't.

For all of five precious seconds Keilor could neither think nor move as his entire attention riveted to her gloriously mud slicked body.

She crossed her arms over her breasts and spun around, giving him her back.

It was every bit as enticing as her front had been. This was a body he would have wanted even without her charmer spice. With it… "Beautiful," he murmured.

Her shoulders hunched. "Go away!"

Instead he moved beside her and offered his hand. She turned her back on him again, and he sighed. "This could get dull."

With an exasperated breath, she spun around and marched towards the pool. It felt like the longest walk of her life. The water was waist deep, and she immediately sank down to her neck. The foaming water made a nice screen. "You're a real jerk, you know that?"

He made himself comfortable on a small boulder beside the pool. "It seems you've said that to me before…near a tree, as I recall."

She gaped at him, shocked he would bring *that* up. "I've probably called you that on more than one occasion. Difficult to remember them all."

He gave her a slow, heated smile. "I remember everything about you." His voice dropped an octave. "I remember the fire in your eyes as you first fought me. I've never been so challenged by a woman. You excited me."

She looked down, unable to meet his eyes, but he could see the telltale rise and fall of her chest. "I can almost see the curves of your sweet body, and the way it twisted as you fought to deny my touch and your own passion." She shuddered, and a ghost of a smile touched his lips. "I'll never forget the fury in your eyes when I dressed you, denying us our release. I dream of it."

She didn't interrupt.

"I was cruel that night," he admitted. "To both of us." He waited until she chanced a look at him out of the corner of her eye. "I knew you'd claim yourself forced, that you'd fight us both until release and after. It was tempting to do it anyway."

He reached out and released her hair from her twist. She stiffened as the mass tumbled softly down her back. His eyes were glowing golden with proof of his desire. His hand traced the curve of her ear. "Even now I know you feel it. Your trembling speaks for itself."

She pulled away. "I'm not a dog, Keilor. I don't do tricks, and I won't lie down on command." Her jaw clenched. "Nor will I be petted by whoever takes it into their head to play with me."

He let his hand fall. "You think I play with you?"

"I've seen you with Urseya. Tell me you haven't played this game before." She gave him a hard look.

He was silent too long.

She'd expected as much. "What is it excites men like you, huh? The thrill of the chase? Some stupid male need to stalk and conquer?"

His eyes narrowed, but she didn't care. "Save it for someone who appreciates it." Her gaze swept past him and focused on Rihlia, who stood at the end of the path. "I'll be right there," she called. Without sparing him a glance, she exited the pool. She passed very close, and unwittingly teased him with the scent of charmer desire.

His hand shot out to grip her upper thigh, uncaring of who watched. She jerked to a halt with a gasp.

His gaze traveled slowly to hers. "Tell Rihlia to leave, Dragonfly. Give me one minute to prove to you this is one hunter you wish to be caught by." She trembled, and he knew she was tempted.

Then her eyes shifted to Rihlia, who stared at the ground with a fierce blush. She moved away, escaping. As she did, his fingers slid up and brushed the edge of her curls. Jasmine gasped and jumped sideways, staring at him in shock.

He winked at her.

"So you love Jayems, huh?"

Rihlia nearly dropped her cup. Jasmine had been so quiet since they got back from their spa adventure that the sudden question caught her off guard. Her eyes darted around the room to make certain her husband was out of earshot. "I...don't know what I feel for him."

Jasmine gave her a knowing look. "I've seen the way you look at him, Ri."

Rihlia set her cup down carefully. "It's not what you think."

Jasmine waved that away. "I know the difference. You're in love. Any day now I expect to see little Jaymeses running around in nappies."

Rihlia stiffened and Jasmine's eyes widened. "What? You're not—" she asked suspiciously.

Her friend quickly shook her head. "No, no...I don't think so, anyway."

"You don't *think* so?" Jasmine demanded. "Haven't you been...ah, there's ways of..." she stumbled to a stop, aware that she was entering deep waters. She didn't really want to know the details of Rihlia's sex life, not when the partner was her husband.

"I know that," Rihlia ground out. "But it's not always...sometimes there's just no time to..." She waved her hand in embarrassment. "He's a good-looking man. I'm no saint. Sometimes I just don't remember." Jasmine grinned, and Rihlia said a little testily, "You should talk. What about you and Keilor?"

The grin disappeared. "What about us? I mean, there is no us. No Keilor and me. I can hardly stand him."

"That's not what it looked like earlier. He might have been the instigator this time, but I'm not the only one who's noticed you checking out his assets." She dipped a slice of apple in caramel sauce and popped it in her mouth. "Urseya gets greener by the day."

Jasmine rolled her eyes. "Can I help it if the man has a fine rear end?" Her friend snickered, and Jasmine smiled. It faded fast. "But it doesn't mean I plan on pursuing him." She lifted her face to the afternoon sunlight, enjoying the warmth. "I'll leave that to his fan club."

"Jealous."

"Smart," she retorted. "A guy like that doesn't need another woman to inflate his ego." She lifted her glass and gestured with it. "What I need is a nice, steady guy who'll respect me. Someone who wants to get serious. Someone who doesn't have half the palace population drooling at his feet." She scowled.

"Be fair," Rihlia chided her. "The only ones you've actually seen chasing him are Urseya and maybe yourself."

"I do not chase him! And you have to admit, the man got that ego somewhere."

Rihlia considered her friend thoughtfully. "What's it like? Being a celebrity." She smiled when Jasmine made a face. "I'm serious! If half the female population is chasing Keilor then the male half is chasing you. What's it like?"

"A nuisance. It's fun at first to get all the gifts and flowers and things, but after a while it starts to feel like you're the only one at Christmas who forgot to buy gifts. It's not like I can bake cookies for that many guys, and I don't have a dollar to my name."

Rihlia smiled. "That's easy. What's the one thing all these men have in common?" When Jasmine just gave her a blank look, she prompted impatiently, "You. They all want you."

Jasmine shrugged. "So?"

"So I propose we give them what they want. Not that!" she insisted when Jasmine opened her mouth to object. "A contest, with the winner receiving a date with you."

Jasmine bit her lip. "I don't know…"

"It's perfect! We'll just go to Jayems and ask him to help us set it up."

Jasmine wavered.

"Ah, come on, Jas, it'll be fun! Just like being the prom queen." Rihlia jumped up to get a paper and a pen. "Let's see...we're going to need…"

CHAPTER 13

Lady Liselle had six daughters, and all of them appeared to be in heat.

Jasmine shook her head as Fallon sauntered past on his way to the buffet table, dripping women. Keilor was nearly as bad. True, he seemed to be subtly holding the women at bay, but his aloofness only made them more determined.

They were outside on a lawn, so it would have been difficult to escape with the excuse that she needed some air. She pondered what would get her out of this affair. She eyed the torches. Could she set herself on fire?

"A fruit jelly, Lady Jasmine?"

Jasmine sighed and turned her attention back to Lady Liselle's son, the ever-annoying Joffre. With a forced smile, she answered, "Why not?" When she tried to take it from the lanky young man, he smiled teasingly and placed the treat at her lips. Awkward. She bit it in half with one quick, efficient bite.

He popped the remaining half into his mouth, savoring the treat. "Mm. Delicious," he purred in imitation of a deep, sexy voice. "How do you like it?" he asked, as if he'd really been talking about candy.

The jelly was delicious, but she answered the real question. "It's very nice, but a little too sweet. I think a little would go a long way."

Joffre was either a trifle stupid or foolishly overconfident, for his smile deepened. "The more you taste, the better you'll like it."

Jasmine clamped her teeth and looked away before she succumbed to the urge to find another jelly and stuff it up his nose.

A delicate dessert glass was thrust into her hand and she looked up with surprise at Urseya's voice saying, "Be gone, Joffre. You're annoying the girl." He opened his mouth to protest, but a single raised brow from Urseya silenced him. With a resentful nod to her and a deeper one to Jasmine, he left.

"Pestilence," Urseya murmured with distaste. She sipped her wine as she watched him go. "He never did understand when he was unwanted." Her eyes shifted to Keilor, and she grimaced. "Disgusting, isn't it?"

Jasmine followed her gaze. One of the daughters placed a manicured hand on Keilor's shoulder. "Very."

Urseya eyed her with undisguised curiosity. "Did you know Keilor is very wealthy?" At Jasmine's surprise, she nodded. "His wealth rivals even Jayems', and Jayems is not a poor man."

"I hadn't realized," Jasmine looked down, uneasy. She didn't want to know about this part of him. "I never thought about it."

Urseya swirled the wine in her glass. "Mmm. He is also widely famed as the best warrior in the realm. His prowess and absolute fearlessness on the battlefield are legend. All of that, combined with his handsome face and prominence among the lords make him irresistible to women."

"Hence his large head," Jasmine returned tartly, and Urseya smirked. If Urseya was trying to make her feel bad, she was succeeding. What would a handsome, famous, wealthy warrior possibly want with someone like her, long term? Not that she was chasing him, of course. "Why are you telling me this? I thought…"

"That I was jealous? Of course I was. Until this afternoon." She smiled with self-deprecation. "Keilor made it abundantly clear I was not his choice and never would be. Even my mother, bless her ambitious soul, got the message." She looked at Jasmine appraisingly. "But I think you wish to know why I would bother with you now. Clan pride, of course." When Jasmine just stared at her, she said dryly, "You're making us look bad, my dear."

"And how is that?" she asked, skeptical. She couldn't remember doing anything embarrassing today, but maybe that was the trouble. It was possible her ignorance might have tripped her up.

Urseya sent a scathing look Joffre's way. "Men," she informed Jasmine. "Galling as it is, the mindless fools can't seem to stay away from you. It's plain you don't care for their attentions, yet here I see you, time and again, biting your tongue to keep from offending them."

"I was being polite!"

Urseya grinned. "Here is the first thing you must learn; speak your mind. You are part of the most powerful clan in the Dark Lands. Cultivate some arrogance and pride. You'll need it." Urseya moved away to speak with one of the daughters not currently attached to either Fallon or Keilor, leaving Jasmine to consider her wisdom.

She didn't know about pride and arrogance, but perhaps Urseya had a point. She had been biting her tongue, and it was beginning to gall. Considering her unique position, perhaps it would be smart of her to be a little harder on would-be suitors. After all, a walking aphrodisiac would have to use strong measures to kill the attraction, wouldn't she?

Noticing Joffre heading her way, she quickly put her new strategy into motion and moved off in Keilor's direction. He couldn't miss the fact that she was avoiding him.

If nothing else, watching the spectacle over there ought to provide some entertainment. She chose a spot on the fringes of Keilor and his harem, and eavesdropped with shameless interest.

Keilor hardly spared her a glance. He was still annoyed with her over her dismissal that afternoon. He'd been particularly enjoying watching Joffre torment her, though if Urseya hadn't intervened when she had, he might have had to step in and drive the whelp off. Whatever her motive, Urseya had allowed him to continue pretending to ignore Jasmine. Let the girl learn that she would rather be the one receiving his attentions, not watching as others took her place.

Unfortunately for his plan, Liselle's eldest daughter, Cara, noticed the charmer right away, and she was not known to tolerate rivals. "Don't stand in the corner, Lady Jasmine. Do come join us."

Jasmine took one look at Cara and decided they were unlikely to ever be friends. "Actually, I'm quite comfortable here," she answered. She took a bite of her dessert. "Besides, I wouldn't like to interrupt your...conversation." She glanced at Cara's hand on Keilor's arm, and something came over her. Power flooded her veins, power and possession. It happened so quickly, she didn't have time to analyze it.

She lifted a careless shoulder, the power giving her matchless confidence. "If Keilor wishes for fresh conversation, he can *come to me.*" Jasmine didn't know what made her use that particular tone of voice, or that precise look, but suddenly she felt like Lady Dracula, *because Keilor came to her, and she knew he hadn't planned to.*

She could see it in his eyes, the realization she had compelled him, and fury that she would dare. But the foremost, most frightening thing of all was the golden flame of desire in his eyes, the promise of absolute, unrestrained passion.

It terrified her.

Keilor planted one hand on the tree behind her, barely leaving her room to breath. "What would you have, my lady?" he breathed against her lips.

"B-back off!" she squeaked, but he didn't move an inch, and the fire in his burning gaze didn't cool one degree. "J-Jayems!"

Jayems was beside them in an instant. He took one look at Keilor and seemed to know. He placed a calm hand on his shoulder. "Keilor, my friend, I need some advice on a certain matter. Do you think you could spare a moment to confer with me?"

Keilor moved his head slightly.

"It really is quite urgent. Would you mind?"

Jasmine held her breath as Keilor slowly peeled away, allowing Jayems to lead him off. Only when the door closed behind them did she dare to breath.

"That bitch!" Keilor raged. "She actually enspelled me!"

Jayems took a deep breath. "She is as shaken as you are angry—"

Keilor bared his teeth. "I doubt that is possible." He shook with fury, and when he looked around his room, he did not see the dark, heavy furniture or notice the lack of light. He saw her face, heard her voice calling, *come to me,* and rage spurred him anew. "Send her away," he told his cousin harshly, slashing his hand through the air. "Send her back to her world."

"That might have been possible, if I hadn't promised Rihlia they could have their tournament."

Keilor's eyes narrowed. "What tournament?"

"It was Rihlia's idea. Jasmine wished to thank her suitors for their gifts, but since she had no money to send gifts in return—" He rolled his eyes.

Both men knew that as her lord it was his duty to pay for her expenses, and he would have rather bought a hundred foolish gifts than deal with the trouble his wife's fine idea would bring. "I immediately arranged for an allowance, but Rihlia would have none of it. She insisted that 'Jasmine didn't want to cost me any money'."

He shared a sardonic look with Keilor. Rihlia had no idea what it would cost to hold a tournament worthy of the Haunt. Jayems shook his head in disgust. "By the time we left the others, Rhapsody was already planning to hold the tournament as a prelude to our wedding feast."

Distracted from his ire, Keilor allowed himself to sink into his favorite chair. The leather had worn away on the armrests, but it was still serviceable. He couldn't be talked into throwing it out.

Why was it that all the trouble in their lives of late came in the form of a woman? A woman, he thought angrily, who'd called the undefeated Lord of the Hunt to heel with one phrase from her traitorous charmer lips? *Come to me...* He closed his eyes at the humiliation of it. How could he insure the safety of what family he had left if the Haunt knew that their Warleader could be brought to his knees by the voice of a woman?

"And what is to be the prize in this 'cost nothing' tournament?" Keilor asked bitterly. "A chance to drink wine from the charmer's cupped hands? A sash of scarlet embroidered with her name?"

Jayems laughed without humor. "Nothing so traditional, my friend." He paused, knowing he was about to hear an explosion. "The victor receives a night with Jasmine."

Keilor was on his feet in an instant. "*No.*"

"They will be chaperoned, Keilor. By two of the strongest Haunt I can find," Jayems assured him.

"I said no!" Keilor shouted. The thought of another man being allowed so intimate a time with her, even with others nearby, sickened him. "I will not allow it."

Jayems' eyes hardened. "Who speaks to me now, Keilor? The Master of the Hunt, or the man?"

Stricken, Keilor clenched his fists and turned his back on him, a thing he had never done.

Jayems continued relentlessly. "You speak to me this way, and yet you have made no binding claims on the girl. Why shouldn't I allow this? She needs a mate with all speed, and to find one, I must allow her time with any man of her choosing." He paused to lend his words weight. "Make your claim or stand aside. I've been patient long enough."

Keilor's voice was hoarse with years of pent up anguish. "I will not be bound by a woman." Just saying the words conjured dark memories

Jayems closed his eyes; hurting for the man he loved like a brother. "That was years ago, Keilor. Jasmine has nothing to do with it." He softened his voice. "She's nothing like Yesande."

"Nothing?" Keilor growled. "What was tonight?"

Haunt did not tolerate self-pity. Jayems' tone became implacable. "Then bind her to *you*. Make her ache for you. Seduce the charmer until she is the one waking in the night, crying out *your* name. But either way, let this now be finished."

Jasmine wandered the halls, long after she should have been asleep. She never noticed when Keilor took the place of her guard, wearing the unadorned black uniform of a lower ranking soldier. Silent, he followed her to the moonlit steps she'd visited before. He watched as she chose a stair and bent one knee, her back against the wall. She stared at the moons for a long time.

"There is only one moon on Earth," she said softly, at last. "It is very strange. It's never really dark here in these Dark Lands. I think I'm homesick." She took a ragged breath, and her head sank down to her knee. "I want to go home," she whispered, sounding very young. She sat there for a long time with her arms wrapped around her knee, her breathing shallow and uneven. "I just want to go home."

Jasmine sat cross-legged on the grass and waited for one of the villi to come to her. All she had to do was sit still until one of the tiny giraffe-like creatures decided she might make a good playmate—or so the morning maid had assured her. No one else had been about, and Jasmine assumed Rihlia and her mom were off on another shopping expedition.

She sighed, rubbed a thumb along her knee and glanced at the villi. Every once in a while one of the black and tan spotted creatures would eye her. They always went back to browsing on their long manger of brush.

It would have been nice to see a little more of the citadel, especially the merchants, but Jasmine never said as much. Sometimes merchants brought their wares to Rihlia's room, but it wasn't the same. Jasmine hadn't bought much.

Even if she could have gone to the bazaar, she didn't want to. Who could enjoy shopping with every male in the vicinity gawking at you? Thinking of males naturally brought Keilor to mind, and she slouched. She hadn't seen him in two days, and tomorrow was the day of the tournament. She wondered if he would avoid the event, and her, altogether, or go just so he could cheer on the victor.

One of the villi lifted its head and stared her, then went back to its browse.

Against her vigorous protest, Jayems had upped the stakes of the tournament, and the entrants now numbered in the hundreds. Not only were the cadets she'd originally wished to thank invited, but several men she'd never heard of had also been asked to join the contest on the second day. The first was reserved for those who simply wished to prove their skill, though Jasmine would be awarding the prize.

The little villi that had stared at her took a step her way. It dropped its head to nibble at the grass as soon as it saw her looking.

Jasmine looked back at her hands.

She hadn't liked it when she'd found out the tournament would be a trial by combat. She didn't want men getting bloody over her.

Jayems had lifted a brow and asked what other kind of tournament there was. When she'd explained she'd been thinking of games, sports, he'd snorted disdainfully and looked back at his guest list. That had been the end of it.

Jasmine felt something soft graze her cheek and looked up to see the little villi. "You are a darling, aren't you?" she murmured, and stroked his silky mane. "Would you like to come home with me?" To her surprise, the little villi reared and whipped his head back and forth.

Alarmed, she looked to her bodyguards, but they seemed unconcerned. The rearing turned to crow-hopping and she scrambled to her knees, prepared to run if the little guy got really rough. In her rush to get up, her feet slipped on the grass, twisting her leg. She crashed to the lawn and bit her lip on impact.

Dazed, she blinked up at the turquoise sky. Two Haunt faces and an inquisitive villi peered down at her. She gave them a weak smile. "Let's just keep this one to ourselves, shall we?"

CHAPTER 14

"What happened to you?" Rihlia demanded as Jasmine limped into dinner that evening. She was late. Everyone was present, even Keilor, and all conversation came to a halt as they waited for her answer.

Jasmine gave her a rueful smile as she lowered herself into a seat, wincing a little as her sore lip pulled. Feeling mischievous, she lowered her eyes and allowed a shy, satisfied grin to curl the corners of her mouth. "I found a new playmate—he likes it a bit rough." Stunned silence fell on the room.

"J-jas?" Rihlia finally ventured in disbelief, "Are you saying some guy hurt you? And you *let* him?"

She fought to keep a straight face as she toyed with her chopsticks. "I decided to take a walk on the wild side." She swallowed to force down her laughter. No doubt Rihlia would pick up on the odd note in her voice at any second and demand in on the joke. To her surprise, it wasn't her friend who questioned her.

"Who was it?" Keilor demanded.

Jasmine's eyes flew up, startled into looking at him. Other than noting his presence, she'd intended to ignore the ill-tempered brute. Without thinking, she answered, "I left him in my room."

Keilor was on his feet and to the door before she'd finished saying, "my." Jasmine gaped at the empty doorway. It took her a moment, but she grinned. It became a giggle. The giggle became a full borne laugh the minute

Rihlia demanded with suspicion, "What are you up to, Jasmine?"

Jasmine threw her a wicked grin. "My new playmate—" she snickered, "—is a villi."

Jasmine wasn't the only one snickering when Keilor returned several minutes later. He threw her a lethal glance as he took his seat between Rhapsody and Portae.

"How is the little villi, Keilor?" Fallon asked with amusement. "Jasmine's been telling us all about her new companion, Casanova."

Keilor's stare was not amused. "A foolish name for a villi." He took a vicious bite of meat.

"Do you think? I considered calling him Brad Pitt, but now he's happily married, it didn't seem quite right." She smiled slyly at Rihlia. "Besides, he hasn't been nearly as hot since he cut his hair." She glanced flirtatiously Keilor, just to annoy him. "Lost that bad boy look." Something hot leapt in his eyes, and she hastily averted her own. Her stomach clenched with excitement. He was jealous!

"What's got you in such a spirited mood this evening?" Fallon inquired, letting his appreciative gaze linger. "I don't think I've ever seen you quite so radiant."

Jasmine waited until Keilor took a sip of his wine and then quipped, "I'm in love with one of my bodyguards?" One cue, her victim choked and coughed fit to bring up a lung. "No?" she inquired, raising a brow at his glare.

She smiled sweetly at Fallon. "Actually, I'm just happy to have a pet of my own. *Wiley*—" she didn't even need to look to feel the heat of Keilor's glare, "—always had one, and that was fine when we lived in the same place, but now...I find I'm really enjoying it, and Casanova is so sweet." She batted her eyes at Fallon. "Sometimes a woman just needs someone to cuddle with on a lonely night."

Out of the corner of her eye, Jasmine saw Jayems lean back in his chair with an expression of fascination. Rihlia just peered at her as if she'd suddenly transformed into an alien. The rest of the woman remained breathlessly still, waiting for her drama to unfold.

Keilor she ignored.

Fallon's response was everything she could have hoped for. His smile was slow and infinitely sexy. "You might have said as much."

Jasmine very deliberately folded her napkin and stood up. Addressing the table at large, she said, "I really can't wait to introduce you all to Casanova. Would you mind escorting me to my room to get him, Fallon?"

His eyes slid over to gage Keilor's reaction. Fallon rose with a roguish smile. "Anything you desire, sweet Jasmine." He extended his arm, and Jasmine linked hers through it.

The door had barely closed behind the pair when Urseya grinned wickedly and asked, "Do you think they'll be back?"

"You should have a care," Fallon advised, slanting her a shrewd look. "Teasing Keilor can be a dangerous pastime unless you're able to deal with the consequences."

She shrugged. "What can he do? He can't beat me. I think Jayems would be annoyed at that."

He shook his head, chuckling dryly. "I doubt very much that *beating* you is what he's contemplating at the moment. Or is that what you had in mind?" She said nothing, and they walked in companionable silence until they reached her door. As she moved to open it, she suddenly found herself pinned between it and Fallon's strong arms. He placed a finger on her lips, stilling her protest. "He's watching," he said softly.

Jasmine's breath quickened with the thought of Keilor hiding in the shadows. It could only mean one thing.

Fallon laughed. "Mm," he whispered against her ear, making her shiver with the vibration. "You like that idea. But perhaps..." He placed a small kiss just in front of her ear, and then another, making her eyes go wide, "...perhaps I could make just a small suggestion."

Jasmine's hands came up to press against his chest. He was starting to worry her. Maybe she'd miscalculated. After all, how well did she know this man?

Fallon didn't move. "In the future, if you wish to torment my cousin..." His hand slid up along her arm and she sucked in a breath, "...don't use another man to do it. It's not safe; for you or him." He paused with his hand on her upper arm, a hair's breadth away from her breast, and she held her breath in dread.

He met her gaze with eyes of fire, letting her see the dangerous extent of his desire. "Understand?" She nodded like a robot, and rueful satisfaction filled his eyes. "Good." He gave her a fast, smacking kiss and withdrew. "Go get your villi, woman."

Keilor stepped around the corner the moment she'd scurried through the door. He surveyed his cousin with disgust. "I should rip your lungs out."

Fallon snorted. He leaned against the wall as if it were the only thing holding him up. A sheen of sweat slicked his skin. "Too much trouble. Besides, you should be grateful; had I done as I wished to do—"

Keilor grabbed him by the shirtfront and jerked the dazed warrior nose to nose. "Say it and I *will* maim you," he warned. His little charmer had put him through enough torment that night.

He set his jaw. Agony had shot through him when she'd declared, no, *implied,* she had not only taken a lover, but she'd chosen one who abused her. He'd had the sickest feeling of failure and loss, and a grief so fresh that furious searching for the lover had been the only thing to keep it at bay. All of that, only to discover her new 'playmate' was a villi! If he hadn't already spoken to Jayems for her hand, he would have right then just to have the right to beat her!

Enunciating very clearly, he said, "I am going back to the others. *You* will be right behind me. If you are not…"

Fallon sighed and freed himself from Keilor's grasp. He straightened his shirt and smiled wryly. "Rest easy, cousin. I have myself in hand. We'll be right behind you. After all, I am rather fond of breathing."

The first day of the tournament dawned bright and clear. Jasmine was nervous, but excited as well. Today promised to be an event to remember.

Their party, which consisted of Rihlia and Jayems, as well as Rihlia's family, walked out to the stands, which had been set up around the training grounds. They were to be seated in a raised pavilion where they would have an excellent view of the event.

Keilor stood behind the pavilion, holding the reins of a stag. He was dressed in the uniform of the Haunt, with the red symbol of rank above his heart. He was talking to Knightin.

With a twinge of unease, she noticed he seemed to be armed with an unusual number of weapons. An engraved tomahawk hung from his wide black belt, and he had several throwing knives in addition to the gun and long knife the Haunt regularly carried. "What's he doing?"

Jayems answered, "Keilor is Master of the Hunt. Naturally he's overseeing the event, and he'll be opposing the contestants, along with several of the men who will be competing tomorrow."

"Several?" she asked, surprised. "But won't they be outnumbered? You said there are over a hundred cadets in the tournament today."

Jayems snorted. "If they could be tired so easily by mere cadets they wouldn't be in the ring tomorrow. Today will merely be a warm up for Keilor and the rest of your suitors."

A frisson of alarm shook her at his words. "What do you mean, '*and* the rest of my suitors'?" she demanded, uncaring that they were close enough for Keilor to hear. Surely he didn't mean—

Giving her a sexy smile, Keilor answered for her. "Jayems gave me his permission to win you, of course." His smile turned down right scintillating. "Wear something silver tomorrow night, Dragonfly."

She blushed. A little bit scared, and more than a little bit excited, she ground out, "You can't play!" What if he actually won? It was one thing to tease him into noticing her, another for him to be elevated to suitor. That was serious business. She wasn't sure he was ready to belong to one woman. She hadn't had long enough to convince him.

Keilor raised a brow and studied her with lazy possession. "Why not? I did give you a gift, didn't I?"

Jasmine huffed even as her temperature shot up ten degrees. "You don't count!"

With a husky laugh, he flicked a butterfly caress across her lips with his thumb. "I'm the only one who does." He flashed perfect teeth at Jayems, full of good humor. "Your suitors can still have their reward. All they have to do is go through me."

Jasmine stamped her foot, which would have shocked her if she'd been paying any attention. She couldn't name the source of her acute agitation. "Why must you be so difficult?"

He just winked at her.

"This is hardly fair," Jayems told him with a smirk, putting his arm around the seething Jasmine as he steered her firmly towards their family pavilion. "I ought to just hand the girl over to you, gift wrapped."

Keilor grinned as Jasmine twisted futilely in an attempt to turn around and blast him. Telling that she would direct her ire at him instead of Jayems. "Where's the fun in that?"

The cadets had not been warned what to expect during the beginning of the tournament, except to be ready for anything, the Master of Ceremonies announced.

The stands were filled with a restless crowd of thousands. People had traveled for up to a week to see this tournament, and to see the skill of those under Jayems' command. The measure of their warriors was the measure of their strength, and this exhibition was much more than just entertainment.

The only prohibition placed on the men had been no shifting, which had surprised most of them, since the Haunt *always* fought shifted.

Speculation had run wild over the first command until a rumor had sprung up that Jasmine wouldn't recognize the warriors in Haunt, and she wished to remember the exploits of her favorites. After that all murmuring ceased, and the cadets walked around giving each other sly looks, each more sure than the last that the charmer would wish to remember *him*.

Jasmine didn't need to know any of that. For her, this was only a day of excitement and thrill, and Keilor intended to make certain it was a day she would long remember.

Nervous and bright eyed, she stood in the pavilion and looked down over the banner-draped guardrail to the regimented soldiers. "I wanted to thank you for the gifts you sent when I was ill." One corner of her lips tilted up,

"It was almost worth being so sick if it meant I could look at such beautiful plants and flowers. And those candies!" She shook her head, plainly awed. "I think I'm ruined."

The cadets were forbidden to even smile, but the audience chuckled. "Boys will be boys, I know, or men will be men, but for the sake of your mothers, guys, please be careful out there today." She grinned wryly. "I'd hate to make enemies of half the Haunt population." More laughter. She raised her fist over her head. "May the best man win!" The crowd roared in approval, and she laughed, looked down, and sat.

The games began.

With a roar like thunder, riders burst out of the gates to the left of Jayems' pavilion, charging straight toward the black blocks of cadets. Jasmine barely had time to note Keilor and the commanders move to the far side of the field, leaving the sub-commanders to handle their units. A single shouted command from five different throats caused the ranks to whip out their knives and turn en masse to present a solid wall of resistance to the oncoming hoard. Jasmine barely had time to wonder at the folly of facing horsemen—or stagmen—with nothing but knives when with a zap!, a hundred blades suddenly elongated into three foot lengths of blue light.

"Light sabers!" Jasmine gasped, her eyes enormous.

Jayems' eyes flicked to her briefly. "Energy blades. Blue Death." He returned his attention to the fray.

Faced with a solid wall of lightning, the riders sheered off, shouting blood curdling war cries as they tossed glowing white balls into the mass of soldiers. Unless struck from the air with a sword, dazzling white light exploded where they hit, coating the soldiers with glowing powder. Only one grenade struck, and those soldiers immediately removed from the field.

"Acceptable, for cadets, though Keilor will have them doing drills for a month." Jayems murmured.

The riders made two more passes with the bombs, and one struck, narrowing the field by five more men. The riders, all men with red insignia and red sashes, condensed into a menacing wedge with a fierce, dark haired warrior riding point. The wedge shot into the squadron. Jasmine gasped as the living missile impaled the square of soldiers and forced the box to burst open.

"Mathin the Mad," Urseya breathed reverently from Jasmine's left. "Every mother's daughter would give away their wedding night for a chance at him."

Jasmine's eyes opened wider and she watched the fierce soldier with even more interest.

There was much to see. With a snarl of animal bloodlust, Mathin cut his way through men who outnumbered him ten to one, and those men were definitely resisting. Plainly, merely outnumbering men like Mathin and the warriors who rode behind him was not enough to ensure victory, or to even offer the hope of it. In minutes the field was reduced by half, and some of the men were being helped off the battlegrounds.

"These are only cadets," Jayems offered, almost in apology.

Jasmine just stared at him. If these were only cadets, she shivered to think of his army in action. To her eyes, there had been nothing remotely restrained in their defense.

The riders dismounted, pointed towards the gates and told their mounts to go. Expressions grim, the fearsome ten advanced, swords drawn, on the remaining fifty cadets. Shouted commands from the sub commanders, most of whom were still on the field, locked that remaining fifty into a strong, determined opponent. Not a flicker of fear or hint of wavering showed in the entire division.

Yet the ten caused it to fold like a house gutted by fire.

Jasmine winced and flinched each time an energy blade descended and decimated a cadet. She could tell they were trying valiantly, yet heart and soul alone just wasn't enough to stop the ten. They were invincible.

When the dust cleared this time, ten of the original hundred soldiers who'd begun the tournament remained on their feet, and of those ten, two were sub commanders.

"Tailor and Seris," Jayems explained in an aside to her. "Our leaders earn the right to lead with cunning and skill. Nothing is given here." He rose. "Well done," he told the remaining ten, and they saluted him. The crowd cheered. To Mad Mathin and his men, he nodded, and received a nod in return. The soldiers left the field, and fire dancers and drummers took their places for intermission.

"The ten who have lasted until the end will now have the honor of exhibiting their skills for you," Jayems explained politely. "It won't be anything like what you'll see tomorrow, of course, but these men are not unskilled. I think you'll find it entertaining."

"I thought they did very well, considering the men they were facing," Jasmine protested, feeling the need to defend the men she'd originally set out to thank. She winced a little, thinking of the humiliating defeat they'd just suffered on her behalf. Would they still feel as charitable towards her now?

The last half of the tournament passed quickly in a stunning display of riding ability, marksmanship, and sheer daring. Jasmine was particularly fascinated by one cadet's uncanny ability to cling to his bareback, racing mount while assuming an astonishing number of positions. By the time she was presented with the sweating, disheveled victor of the day, she was truly in awe.

Jasmine looked closely at the young sub commander who stood before her, the one called Seris. He must have been close to her age, whereas all the men who would compete tomorrow were unanimously older, though still in their prime. She felt a tug of sympathy for the cadet, who'd fought so hard against such impossible odds, and after a moment, she recognized him. "Aren't you the one who gave me truffles?" she asked, frowning a little in thought.

Seris nodded his head in respect. "Yes, my lady. I made them myself."

Her eyes lit up. "You didn't tell me that when I thanked you for your gift!" she exclaimed. "Had I known, I would have asked you to show me how right away. Is it too late to ask now?"

"Never, my lady," Seris breathed, his eyes widening in disbelief at his stroke of good fortune. He'd never dared hope for so much when he'd made the admission.

Jasmine gave him a dazzling smile and awarded him with a red sash embroidered with her name. She hadn't made it herself, but she felt it was best not to share that with him. Why ruin his moment of glory?

Formally, she gave him the traditional words Rhapsody had taught her. "I give you a token of my pleasure. May you wear it in honor of your victory today, in all your triumphs, until you take a wife who demands the same honor." And then she added a touch of her own, kissing him lightly on the cheek as she presented the sash.

Poor Seris looked like he might swoon. "A tradition from my own country," She explained in the stunned silence, fearing for a moment she'd committed a grievous social faux pas.

The crowd erupted into wild cheers and began chanting, "SERIS! SERIS!"

To a man, Mad Mathin and his men sent the dazed cadet looks of death as he stumbled his way from the pavilion.

She did not see Keilor's face.

CHAPTER 15

Keilor slammed his sheathed blade down on his scarred and slightly dusty table, scattering stray papers with the slight breeze. "Bath!" he snarled, unbuckling his belt. The sound of splashing water immediately filled the room. He stalked towards the enormous tub, leaving a trail of clothes in his wake, and sank deeply into the steaming water.

Tie her to a stake and fire that girl! Custom of her country or not, there had been no call to show such favoritism to a mere cadet! Now the fool was in love with her, and all the true suitors for her hand seethed with jealousy. Tomorrow might well degenerate into a blood-fest, with all the warriors expecting to receive the prize of her lips.

Certainly, the crowd had loved it. The Haunt were a highly sensual people, often given to strong emotion. With one touch of her mouth, Jasmine had elevated a lowly soldier–clearly not the match of any of the ten!—to the status of a hero. It would be a wonder if Seris didn't develop an insufferable ego.

Keilor's eyes narrowed. Perhaps he ought to make time to give Seris a little personal training.

He'd just dunked his hair, savoring the thought of taking Seris through some particularly punishing drills, when a knock sounded at his door. "Who is it?" Unless it was Jayems himself—

"Jasmine," came the answer, causing his brows to shoot up in surprise. Could the little innocent be foolish enough to brave his den?

"Can I come in?"

He debated. There was still one day of the tournament left, and much as he wanted the woman, word would travel quickly of their mating, and the rest of the suitors would surely be enraged. Blood would be a certainty then, and if tempers flared hot enough, entire clans might get involved.

He snarled in frustration. For the sake of peace, he dare not risk it. "No," he called with reluctance.

There was a suspicious pause. "Is someone in there with you?"

A crack of laughter escaped him. As if! It soothed his temper enormously, though, to hear the note of jealousy in her voice. "No." There was a pause. He knew she hadn't left. He could practically hear her thinking.

"I have to talk to you," she told him, annoyance plain in her tone. "I don't think you want to discuss this through a door."

Very well, he thought fatalistically. If she was foolish enough, he was game. Settling back with his arms on the rim of the tub, he called, "It's unlocked."

Jasmine gasped. Keilor was immersed in steaming water, his long, dark hair slicked back. His eyes glowed in the dim light.

"I didn't know you were... I'll leave," she croaked out, reaching for the door she now realized she'd closed much too fast. Trust the arrogant jerk not to warn her! *Arrogant, discourteous and gorgeous,* a traitorous inner voice insisted gleefully.

He was out of the water and at her side so quickly, she barely had time to be shocked with the unprecedented view. She quickly averted her eyes, but six feet of prime naked warrior standing directly in front of her, dripping water, was not a sight any healthy young woman was able to block with ease. The point became moot, though, when said naked man reached out and whisked off her dress with business-like efficiency.

"What are you doing?" she gasped in alarm. She tried to snatch it back, but he'd already tossed it over her shoulder and reached for the hem of her chemise.

"I need someone to wash my back," he explained, as if it were of no consequence that he'd stripped her to her underwear. Her chemise sailed past her head to join the dress and she squealed as her lacy panties slid down her legs with frightening efficiency.

"Not me! Stop!" she squeaked, shocked at the speed of her disrobing.

"I'm not hurting you," he said calmly. He picked her up without effort and carried her to the bath. He released her the moment they were immersed and settled on one of the low seats built into the tub. She scrambled to the far end and sunk to her neck as she watched him. It was clear she was not the one in charge.

His lips twitched with amusement. "I'm not going to rape you, woman. If that was what I wanted, better to have taken you on the floor."

"You are vile!" she hissed. "I'm going to tell Jayems what you did." It sounded pitiful and childish, but what other defense did she have? He was too strong to fight, and she certainly couldn't drown him, much as she'd like to.

Keilor chuckled. He captured her wrist and plunked a bar of soap in it. "Scrub."

She glared at him, but she didn't have much choice. For all of his humor, there was a chilling hint of steel in his command, and she didn't have the guts to disobey. He propped one leg expectantly up on her knees, ignoring her embarrassment. She made quick work of it, stopping at mid-thigh. When she'd done both, he flashed her a smile and dunked his hair. He knelt in the bottom of the tub so she could lather it.

Desperate to take her mind off of the long, silky mass, she brought up the reason for her visit. "What did you mean when you said you got permission from Jayems to 'win' me?"

Keilor hummed and relaxed into her hands, enjoying the rare sensation of being pampered. "I bed you, I get to keep you," he explained, not mincing words. No sense in her not having a perfect understanding the first time.

Jasmine's fist tightened around a hank of his hair and she yanked, hard. Keilor's head disappeared under the water before he tore himself lose and surfaced. He whisked the water from his face and slicked back his hair, giving her a warning look through water-spiked lashes. It said clearly that once would be dismissed as funning, but twice would bring consequences.

"I am not a slave," she told him, displeased, and not the least bit cowed. "I'm not going to be passed around like some—"

"I had a wife in mind, not a slave," he assured her. Far too easily, he grasped her waist and lifted her, setting her down to straddle his thighs. The position raised the tops of her breasts out of the water. She struggled, but he held her waist firmly. "Be still. You haven't washed my chest. This will make it easier for you," he explained. Slowly he took his hands away from her and put them on the rim of the tub, holding her with his incredible black eyes.

Upset in more ways than one, she roughly scrubbed his neck, or tried to. It was difficult to do much damage with a slippery bar of soap. "You don't want a wife," she told him with bitter certainty. She twisted a little to wash his left arm, trying to block out its solid strength, and the hard muscles under his smooth, warm skin. She couldn't hide her fine trembling. He was so beautiful!

Unfortunately, his beauty was not for her. "What you want would burn out in a couple of days, maybe a couple of weeks. Then what? Divorce?"

She had reached his chest. Against her will, her hands were getting slower. It was all she could do not to squirm in agony from the fierce, demanding ache he caused. The man was killing her!

"My marriage will be forever," Keilor told her with quiet assurance, holding her eyes.

Distracted, Jasmine's hand slid lower, brushing against something hard under the water. She jerked her hand away even as her body shuddered. She knew exactly what that was.

When he said nothing, just watched her, she reached to put the bar of soap on the rim with the intention of leaving his lap, but he straightened up. "Wash my back."

She could not have told him no for all the yen in China. Since he didn't move, only remained leaning forward, she had no choice but to embrace him. She hissed and as her nipples brushed his chest, and it was all she could do not to moan. She refused to look at him. Bad enough that her breath quickened as her hands, slippery with soap, slid over his back. His rasping breaths in her ear were the only sign of his own arousal, as long as she didn't look into his face.

She didn't. She couldn't, not then.

By the time she reached his lower back her breasts were flattened against him and she didn't care. Head swimming, she reluctantly sat up and put the soap in its place. Steam rose around them. Slowly, eyes glazed, she looked at him. Twin, smoking furnaces gazed back at her. "I'm done," she whispered.

"Only if you want to be." Deceptively relaxed, he waited. When she said nothing, he gripped the tub a little more tightly. "Move forward."

Taking a breath for courage, she placed her hands on his ribs and did. She gasped at the feel of him caught tight between them.

He hissed.

Greatly daring, she slid her hands around his neck and rested her chin in the crook. His skin was so hot, so silky and damp, and she could not resist placing a light kiss on the hollow of his throat. He hummed deep in his chest, exciting her, making her ache.

"Do you want me, Jasmine?" he whispered in her ear.

"Yes," she moaned, rocking instinctively against him, abandoning all pretense of restraint. "Oh, yes!"

He nuzzled her ear. "Do you want my kisses?"

"Mm," she agreed, but he moved away as she tried to claim his lips. Frustrated, she rubbed her head against his shoulder. He lightly stroked her spine in response, causing her to gasp and arch into him. They both groaned.

Breathless, he asked, "Do you want me inside?" he moved against her and she cried out with need, nodding frantically against his neck.

"Good. Remember that." Before she could blink, he was out of the water. He didn't bother with a towel, just scooped up his clothes.

And then, without a backward glance, he left.

Keilor wanted to kill someone.

He'd probably start with himself.

He wrapped his trembling hands around a stone column in the gardens and pressed his hot forehead to it. He locked his jaw. She smelled so good! With an oath he pushed from the pillar and forced himself to walk before he lost the battle with his knees and sank to the ground.

As he strode through the gardens, he stumbled on a rock and kicked it angrily out of his way. There was nothing he could do for himself, and there were not enough women or liquor to purge the need from his blood.

He needed *her.* Yet he couldn't have her, not until he won tomorrow.

He needed a battle. Something fast and painful and bloody to tire him enough for sleep. As his feet took him to the guest barracks where the alternative suitors were, he found it.

Or rather, him.

Mathin's nostrils flared as the wind carried Keilor's scent to him, mixed with the provocative smell of soap and charmer. He'd never scented anything like it. The stuff of silken sheets and moonlight, naked skin and a lover's cries. The scent of legend.

One look at Keilor's savage face was enough to see that whatever he'd been doing with the charmer, he hadn't bedded her. That was good, as Mathin intended to do that himself, and once he had her, he didn't intend to share.

Just because he was Mathin, he called out in his gravelly voice, "Have you prepared yourself for your humiliation tomorrow, Keilor?"

Keilor checked in mid-stalk and pivoted to face his antagonist. Teeth bared in a savage smile, he answered, "Mathin. Defeating cadets has gone to your head. You'll have to have a real warrior rid you of your delusions." Once, years ago, he and the indomitable Mathin had been something of friends, even though they had often been rivals.

He did not know if they were friends tonight.

Mathin laughed recklessly. "Know any?" he asked, disparaging them both. He made no move to secure his waist length black hair into a queue, signaling that whatever his intentions, they didn't include a battle.

They would save that for tomorrow.

However, it was plain that Mathin wouldn't mind a bit of mischief while the opportunity presented itself. Keilor smiled grimly. Perhaps he would provide a distraction after all.

Amber mead flowed into Keilor's paper-thin stone cup, filling it to the brim. Mathin also replenished his own glass. Keilor's mouth lifted sardonically. No doubt Mathin would get him drunk as an elf if he let him. Granted, there wasn't much else to do in Mathin's Spartan room.

A narrow bed with a plain chest at the end of it, a small table and two chairs made up the sum of the soldier's guest room. A single window let in light. Mathin could have had better, but like most warriors, was satisfied with the bare essentials.

Mathin shot back half his cup and sprawled in his chair with a satisfied sigh, using one scuffed boot to tilt himself back. He laced his hands over his flat stomach, cradled the cup, and studied Keilor with curiosity. "So tell me about the charmer."

"She's a pocket full of trouble," Keilor answered immediately, his scowl reborn. Trouble and then some.

The corner of Mathin's lip curled up. "But worth it?"

Keilor drummed his fingers on the table. "I spoke with Jayems for her."

The warrior's brows shot up. "Here is news. The untamable Master of the Hunt, captured at last by a woman?" Mathin studied him. "You have no desire for children?"

Keilor rubbed his thumb over the rim of his cup. "I accept that I will not have them." He could have explained he planned on adopting a child, but the sudden tightness in his throat prevented it. A forceful swallow of mead cleared it enough for him to ask, "What of you? I had always assumed you liked children. Why would you court a human?"

A humorless smile traced Mathin's lips. "Perhaps, in my case, it would be better to remain childless." There was a moment of silence. Mathin's line was not called the Mad for nothing.

"Besides, legend has it that to lie with a charmer is to experience pleasure worth dying for. Is it not said that more than one Haunt went to his death, smiling, after a night with a charmer?" He leaned forward, disregarding Keilor's black look. "I'm no mewling virgin, Keilor. I've known satisfaction many times, but never have I—" he broke off, looking frustrated, as if the words eluded him. Or perhaps it was only that he realized the personal nature of what he'd been about to reveal. He finished gruffly with, "I'd like to test the legend."

"To legends," Keilor toasted him, not bothering with childish denials. Jasmine would be his tomorrow, and he was man enough to let his jealousy go, even though he wanted nothing better than to bare his teeth and launch himself across the table. To distract himself, he asked, "And what do you think drives her other suitors? Other than lust?"

Mathin snorted and refilled their cups. "Bloodless politics, my friend. A man can adopt children, but how many get the chance to ally themselves with the strongest family in the realm?" Keilor grunted, and he grinned. "Though no doubt the lady has some attraction."

Keilor ignored him.

"Speaking of women, where is your cousin, Fallon?" A wolfish gleam glimmered in his eyes. "Off on one of his mysterious journeys?"

Keilor gave him a bland look. Mathin knew full well where Fallon had gone, and he'd give his right nut to be able to follow. Even Mathin would have to have a powerful reason to use the gate uninvited, however. Volti were known for their savagery.

Obviously using great restraint, Mathin said nothing more. He was a proud man, and he wasn't going to sulk. "I marvel at his timing." He refilled their empty glasses. "Is he still determined to keep his freedom, or has your loyal cousin ceded the game to you?"

Before Keilor could open his mouth to retort, a knock sounded on the door.

"Come," Mathin called. A messenger entered and handed him a slip of paper. A slow, wicked smile curved Mathin's lips as he scanned the note. "Tell her yes," he told the messenger, who nodded with respect and disappeared.

Mathin tossed Keilor the note and tilted his chair back to watch his face.

He wasn't disappointed.

Two glowing slits were all that remained of Keilor's eyes when he finished and tossed the note to the table. His nostrils flared wide as he stared at it, wishing he could incinerate it and the nine others like it. No doubt the little witch did it just to torment him.

"It would seem the Lady Jasmine is curious about the Ten," Mathin needled him, the devil in his eyes. "Or perhaps just *one* of the Ten?"

Keilor snarled at him.

CHAPTER 16

"Were you invited?" Jasmine murmured coldly to him the next morning as he joined her and the Ten for breakfast. They were on the opposite side of the formal dining room from the rest of the gathering, which also included the female members of his family, most likely to help insure good behavior.

Keeping his voice equally low, he leaned forward and breathed in her ear, "After the private invitation you extended to me last night, I had no reason to think you'd exclude me this morning. Or are you afraid to face me?"

There were so many things Jasmine wanted to say to that, the numerous messages temporarily paralyzed her tongue. Keilor just smiled at her and joined the rest of the men. For a moment she didn't dare turn around, afraid the rage coursing through her would make her behave like a fool. She considered, strongly, calling the guards and having him thrown out.

The man had left her—*left her*!—shaking and huddled in his bath, suffering the twin agonies of humiliation and blistering desire. He had made her want him, and then been cold enough to leave her there to suffer. The man was cruel, and after she'd stumbled back to her room with two Haunt guards watching her with suspicion, she'd let out her anger and hurt in a flood of bitter tears.

Never again.

Rihlia snared Keilor into standing with her to say the blessing. She knew all about last night, and her lightly veiled anger shimmered in her eyes. He couldn't have missed it, but other than one wary look, he made no comment.

Inviting the Ten to breakfast this morning had been her idea. *"He wants to play games with you, fine,"* she'd said, furious on Jasmine's behalf. *"We'll skewer the rat and roast him over a fire made of the sexiest men we can find. We'll teach the arrogant jerk not to play games he can't win."*

Somehow, the idea had seemed much better last night.

The smile she offered Mathin, the handsomest of her guests, and the most likely to defeat Keilor today, was a pale imitation of the flirtatious smile she'd meant to deliver. She felt too bruised to offer more.

Something odd flashed in Mathin's eyes when she looked at him, almost as if he saw the truth behind her smile. His eyes flickered to Keilor, an indecipherable expression in them. When he looked at Jasmine again, though, his expression was clear. "May I share the blessing with you, Lady Jasmine?" he asked, and his rough voice sent a pleasant shiver down her spine.

"Please," she answered, mentally swearing at herself as his large, warm hands closed over her shoulders, making her nerves jump with awareness. She closed her eyes, shutting herself in solitary darkness as the blessing was said.

It's just a side affect of last night, she assured herself. The more she thought, the angrier became. *So I feel a little thrill when a handsome man touches me. I'm young, and healthy, and it's not as if—* She broke into a cold sweat. Even in her mind, her heart wouldn't let her complete the sentence. Panicked, she thought with desperation, *I don't* belong to him! He doesn't have any claim on me! Her eyes opened. She saw Keilor looking straight at her, and her heart condemned her for a liar.

The meal began, and it was all she could do at first simply to hide her trembling hands. Eleven hungry men made quick work of the quiche and sweet pastries, thinly sliced roast and steaming asparagus. No one seemed to notice that she barely nibbled at her own breakfast.

In an effort to make conversation, she asked Mathin, "Are you nervous about the tournament today?"

Chuckles broke out around the table, and one of Mathin's dark brows quirked. With great amusement, he answered, "Should I be?"

A touch annoyed at his arrogance, she answered with mock innocence, "Haven't you heard?" she paused a moment, dragging out the suspense. Even the women looked at her with curiosity. "Urseya has vowed to take to the field and show you all up as bumbling boys."

Urseya's eyes widened in shock, and it was all Jasmine could do to keep a straight face as the men stared at the young woman in astonishment. "I understand she's a wicked hand with a energy blade."

Urseya surprised her by leaning back in her chair with regal calm. "You hear correctly, cousin." She tilted her head, and without the slightest trace of humor, told Mathin, "I'm quite certain you'd find me unconquerable."

An appreciative gleam appeared in his eyes. "Then I'll have to ask you to beg off, warrior queen. I'd hate to risk public humiliation at your hands." He gave her a mischievous smile, and at his words the snorts and muffled snickers broke into full-blown guffaws. Even Urseya allowed a slight smile to touch her mouth.

Jasmine and Rihlia looked at each other, and Jasmine raised her brows. *This was interesting.* "Well, maybe I can talk her into a private duel with the winner," Jasmine said.

"So long as it's not directly after the tournament," Keilor interjected. "I'll be otherwise occupied this evening." Silence descended on the table.

Jasmine stared at him. Had the man been born with that ego, or had it taken years to inflate to such mammoth proportions? When the eyes of all of the warriors bugged out, she realized she'd said as much aloud. Even Mathin stared at her, incredulous.

Nuclear winter stormed behind Keilor's eyes, but his voice was calm when he answered, "Name a warrior who has defeated me since I became a man, Lady, and I will give you everything I own."

Jasmine held his gaze, refusing to give ground. She might not be able to take him with a blade, but she wouldn't be the first one to give way now.

"Which is a great deal, by the way," Rhapsody broke in, almost babbling.

Startled, Jasmine's eyes leapt to her, breaking her standoff with Keilor. It took nearly a minute for Jasmine to understand that Rhapsody was doing her best to break the tension, and another for her to turn to Mathin and attempt to converse politely. Choosing the first topic that came to mind, she asked, "So...do you like kids?"

Looking puzzled, he answered, "I fail to see why it would matter." When she just frowned at him, he said warily, "You don't know, do you?" When her frown got deeper, he told her, "Humans and Haunt never produce children."

Eventually she blinked. She had no choice—her lids simply closed over her burning eyes and opened of their own accord. Her lungs pumped and drew air into her starving lungs, and even her heartbeat began again, even if it did lurch and bump erratically.

But she did not feel. Her head nodded once, and then she calmly returned to eating her breakfast, a perfectly calm expression on her face.

She did not taste a crumb.

The meal ended shortly after that, and she thanked everyone cordially for coming and watched as they filed out of the room, shooting her wary glances.

As the last one closed the door behind him, Keilor said from beside her, "Jasmine."

Without a thought, she turned and slapped his face as hard as she could.

She'd almost thought she'd heard emotion in his voice.

Mathin was waiting for him in the hall. "What happened between you two last night?" he asked with deceptive quietness.

Keilor looked back at the door, but he was clearly picturing the woman within. "Apparently, not enough."

Jasmine did not give a speech that day.

She watched with dispassion as the Master of Ceremonies announced the events and the names of the participants. Yesterday all of the Ten had worn Jayems' colors; today each wore the uniform of their own clan. Only two wore the familiar black uniforms of Jayems' guards. One of them was Mathin.

The other was Keilor.

Rihlia and the others were with her in the pavilion, but she refused to look at anyone. She could easily believe her friend had no knowledge of...the child thing, but apparently it was common knowledge among the others. Rhapsody had explained that she hadn't thought of it exactly because it *was* such common knowledge. That did not excuse Jayems. It did not excuse Keilor.

She hadn't been under any illusions. She'd known exactly what her so called 'suitors' wanted from her. It was upsetting, though, to be so casually slapped in the face with the fact that none of them had cared enough about her to be upset that she couldn't have children. Wouldn't a man who felt something for a woman have the courtesy to at least *tell* her he could never give her a child?

A blazing wall of fire flared up directly in front of the gates, and eleven riders charged out, up the ramp, and through the flames. Jasmine glowered at them. She was determined not to be impressed no matter what antics they pulled.

That idea lasted all of three minutes.

When the first stag beast sailed over Keilor, he raked its belly with the tip of his sword, just cutting through its rider's girth. Jasmine thought she would have heart failure. When the rider managed to shed his saddle in mid-air, and regain his seat on his stag, she knew this was going to be nothing like yesterday.

The stags were as vicious as their masters, and astonishingly limber. It was amazing the men could even keep their seats, let alone still have the ability to strike at one another with such strength and speed. Blue sparks showered from each strike, but perhaps they didn't burn, for the unprotected arms of the warriors never flinched.

Jasmine did their flinching for them.

The battle raged hot and furious, and it didn't stop until one rider ended up in the dust. Drums sounded and a shofar blew, and that battle was over.

The men barely had time to wipe the sweat and grime from their faces with the backs of their hands when fireworks exploded practically under their stag's feet. Jasmine gripped her chair, afraid she was going to see guts. An opaque blue haze rose up, obscuring the scattered riders from view. When the sound of battle rose from the blue smoke, Jayems explained without prompting,

"They're fighting blind, using scent, hearing, and kinetic sense to find their opponents. The stag is particularly useful for such combat, as its kinetic sense and bravery match that of a Haunt. A horse would be worse than useless in such a fight."

Jasmine wanted to ask what kinetic sense was, but she was busy. She gripped the arms of her chair and strained in vain to catch a glimpse of what was going on in the cloud.

"Man down!" someone shouted, and immediately the haze began to clear. Nine riders appeared out of the smoke, and one man limped off the field, holding on to his stag.

Dread snaked through her, and Jasmine bit her lip. Before she could think, she said to Jayems, "Make them stop. I'm not worth this." Jayems looked at her, but didn't say a word.

It was too late anyway.

With an ominous creak, the gates opened again and spawned a new horror. Thirty Haunt soldiers marched out and surrounded the riders, who backed their mounts into a loose ring. These were not cadets. Jasmine began to rise to her feet, but Jayems clamped a hand on her arm and dragged her back down. He kept it manacled around her wrist, too, just as a precaution.

Jasmine could not sit still. The Haunt advanced with eerie silence, and the only sounds were the grunts of the fighters and the clash of blades. She tried to remind herself that no one was going to be killed, that this wasn't a real battle, but there was nothing feigned about the cat-like maneuvers and powerful strikes of the Haunt.

A man was finally dragged, swearing, off his mount. Several women screamed as the Haunt swarmed over him, and only Jayems' hand on her forearm kept her in her seat. Incredibly, the black sea seemed to struggle for several long seconds, and at least one Haunt drew back with a roar of rage before the warrior was bound and drug off. The procedure was repeated until only six riders and precious few Haunt remained.

"They're fighting under a handicap," Jayems explained, perhaps trying to distract her. "If not for that, we would have needed to use more than twice as many Haunt."

Jasmine's lips parted. *More than twice?*

For the first time, she noticed that the three captured men had been dragged over to the wall next to the gates, and now hung there, chained with their hands over their heads. Their feet barely touched the ground. More Haunt poured onto the field, surrounding them. The six remaining riders briefly conferred, and then they attacked.

Flash grenades exploded. Mathin swept in close on his stag and swung a whip at the legs of the Haunt front line, dragging several down. One of the other riders had a cord with weighted ends, and he took out a soldier by throwing it around his neck as he rode by, letting the weight at the ends twist around his neck. Unfortunately, the Haunt had the same cords, and one of the stags went down with it wrapped around his legs. His rider continued to fight on foot while the stag was freed and rushed out of battle.

A commotion started at the back of the line, and Jasmine gasped. Somehow, one of the chained warriors had gotten loose, commandeered a blade, and freed one of his brothers. They were wreaking havoc from the back of the line.

Deafening cheers broke out from the crowd, and this time Jayems let her go as she rose to her feet, urging the fighters on at the top of her lungs. They were winning!

Keilor thundered by and with a powerful move that could have severed the man's wrist if he'd missed, he flung his tomahawk at the chains binding the third man. The mob went wild with exuberance when the head buried itself deeply in the wall, severing the chains and freeing the prisoner.

The cheering turned to boos and hisses of outrage as more Haunt poured out of the gates in an endless black wave. It took them a considerable amount of effort, but finally, only Keilor and Mathin were left mounted.

Drums pounded and Jasmine settled back into her seat as the Haunt receded, taking its prisoners along with it. Mathin and Keilor dismounted and sent their stags off the field.

"Now they fight to determine the winner," Jayems explained to her.

She tried to calm down, a little shocked at how difficult it was. This morning she'd been determined to hate the men who were fighting so heroically, convinced she was worth nothing to any of them. How could she still believe that after seeing them today? How could any woman be unmoved by the sheer magnetism of such powerful, masterful men?

And they fought for her! These primal, beautiful men fought over *her*! She'd never even been given flowers before she came here, and now men fought for her as if she were a prize worth dying for. The enormity of it made her thoughts spin like a top.

Keilor and Mathin did not waste time dithering. At the signal, both men unsheathed their swords with lightning fast moves and had at it.

The individual moves were a confusing blur. Both men fought as if they'd just came fresh from their beds, not spent the morning fighting off hoards of opponents. The men were nearly equal in size, strength and endurance. What would tip the scales of the fight?

Mathin on a normal day was difficult to defeat. Mathin with charmer scented victory in his nostrils was a demon.

Keilor fought him with every ounce of energy and concentration at his command, sparing no thought to Mathin's increase in prowess since last he'd sparred with him, years ago. The boy had held the promise of greatness. The man surpassed it.

But Mathin was making no progress against him, either. Time and again their blades struck, and neither man faltered or so much as blinked.

Until their swords locked.

For a moment, they strained against one another, steel hilts biting into the flesh of their hands, neither willing to give an inch. Then Mathin said, "Rumor has it you've been at the charmer." He paused a moment to make certain his comment fully penetrated Keilor's battle haze. When he was certain he had his full attention, he asked suggestively, "Tell me, *how does she taste?*"

He never had a prayer after that.

CHAPTER 17

"I can't believe you fainted," Rihlia said again. She shook her head.

"Be quiet," Jasmine grumbled from her position on the couch. She did *not* want to talk about it.

Urseya smiled smugly. "I thought it was romantic. The beautiful, love-sick damsel, swooning at the feet of her lover…" She sighed, putting a wrist to her forehead and ignoring Jasmine's glare. "Everyone will be talking about it."

Jasmine sat up on her elbows and snapped, "He is not my lover!"

"Your warrior, then."

"He's not my anything!" she protested, but was interrupted by a snigger in the corner. She glared at Fallon, who had arrived earlier in the day and had watched from the crowd. She pointed a finger at him. "You be quiet, too."

He held up his hand, palm out, in a gesture of innocence. With a straight face, he said, "Don't worry, your secret is safe with me." He grinned. "However, I think there are several hundred other witnesses who might possibly slip and tell him."

Snorts and open laughter greeted those words. Why was it that the one and only time she ever fainted had to happen in front of hundreds of witnesses?

She cringed just thinking about how Keilor had been presented under her pavilion as the champion. She'd stood to acknowledge him, and suddenly the blood had drained her head with sickening speed. The next thing she'd known, Rihlia was patting her cheeks and demanding to know if she was all right. And the look on Keilor's face once he'd realized she had swooned! *Swooned*!

She'd tried to tell everyone it had been just a little head rush, caused by standing up too fast, but perhaps she'd protested too much, because no one believed her. Portae had scoffed and insisted it had definitely been a swoon, caused by too much excitement, and stated with authority the only cure was lie down and have some nice, sedative tea.

So here she was, lying on her couch with her feet up, gagging on a truly awful tea, and being tormented by a roomful of insensitive clods.

After a bit Rihlia took pity on her, or perhaps she got tired of her friend's mulish expression, because she began shooing people out of the room. Urseya, however, wasn't leaving without a parting shot.

"Don't worry!" she called out as she left. "If you swoon at his feet again, I'm sure Keilor will find some way of reviving you." Fallon grabbed his sister's arm and started dragging her.

"I can still sic Mathin on you!" Jasmine yelled back as the door shut behind them. "Great," she muttered as the tea cup she'd been precariously balancing on her stomach spilled on her dress. Oh well, at least she didn't have to finish it.

With more muttering, she clinked the cup and its saucer down on her coffee table and got up to rummage in her wardrobe. She emerged dressed in her jeans, black T-shirt and bare feet. She snagged a glass of juice and flopped down on the couch again. Casanova butted her hand, and she absently scratched around his nubby horns.

Rihlia sprawled in an over-stuffed chair opposite her and propped her chin on her hand. Eyeing Jasmine's clothes, she asked, "Are you planning to wear that for Keilor?"

Jasmine grinned and wriggled deeper into the couch. "Why not?" She stifled a yawn. "He won't be here for a while yet. No doubt his fan club has him busy signing autographs." No one had asked him to sign anything, but he *had* been surrounded by a rather large group of women the last time she'd seen him.

"Jealous, huh?" When Jasmine just sighed and twisted her glass on her leg, watching the orange juice lap at the edges, she prodded, "If you don't like it, what are you going to do about it?"

Jasmine leaned her head back and let out a slow breath of air. "Stake a claim, I guess." She thought for a minute. "This morning I thought he was pond scum; this afternoon, he's looking pretty good. Tomorrow, I might want to kill him again, but maybe this way I can get him out of my system." She rolled her head toward Rihlia. "Avoidance just seems to aggravate the condition."

Her friend smiled. "I wondered how long it would be before you gave it up." Her smile died, and a very serious expression came over her face. "There are some things you ought to know about the Haunt, Jas." She paused. "I don't think it's fair that you should go into any relationship with Keilor without knowing the truth about the guards outside the door—" she gestured, "—and the other soldiers you've seen."

Jasmine watched her without blinking, and she cleared her throat. "They've got a lot more in common than you think."

"They're the same. I know." Jasmine's expression never wavered as she sat up and put her juice on the coffee table. "I've known for a while now." When Rihlia looked uneasy, she sighed and laced her hands together. "You were afraid I'd be scared, weren't you?"

"You are scared!" Rihlia dropped her feet to the floor and leaned forward. "I've seen you watching the guards. It scares you spitless, and don't pretend it doesn't!" she finished, almost defiant.

Jasmine bent her neck towards both shoulders, popping the joints and stalling. "Sure, it scares me. It's weird, and I'd be a liar if I said otherwise. But," she interjected before she could be interrupted, "I'm not afraid of you, or your family. It's just going to take a while to get used to." She searched for a comparison. "Kind of like having someone you care for get in a really bad wreck and mess up their face, or become a burn victim, or—"

"Burn victim!"

"Hey, don't take it personally," Jasmine admonished her. "You know what I'm trying to say." She looked deep into Rihlia's eyes. "I've known you how many years, now? Should I start believing that suddenly you're going to go nuts and kill me, or let anyone else hurt me?"

"No! You know I'd never let that happen. They'd have to get through me first," she vowed. "I know you'd do the same for me, too."

Jasmine smiled and looked down. "All right." She took a deep breath. "I will try not to be so jumpy around the Haunt, but I can't promise overnight results, ok?" She slanted a teasing look at her friend. "You could have warned me sooner, though." She cupped her hands around her mouth and said, sotto voce, "Hey, Jasmine, watch out for these guys, because when the moons are full they turn into Wookies!"

"They are not Wookies!" Rihlia protested, laughing. "They're more like—" she stumbled.

"Werewolves?" Jasmine supplied, lifting a brow.

She winced. "They are not werewolves. They won't eat you."

Grinning, she said slyly, "Poor girl. First you get kidnapped, tricked into marriage, told you couldn't go back *or* have any visitors, and then to top it all off, you find out that you married a Wookie."

Rihlia choked. "They are *not*—" She giggled, unable to finish.

Jasmine continued blithely on. "I wish I'd been there to see his face when you told him you were not going to allow a walking carpet to sleep on the bed." Rihlia hooted and she chuckled. Waving a hand, she said with drama, "They say that men are animals, but really, this is going too far."

Rihlia wiped her eyes and smiled at her friend. Then her smile faded. She said soberly, "The first time I saw him change, I freaked out."

Jasmine nodded with understanding.

"He looked at me as if I'd lost my mind. When I cringed away from him, he changed back and tried to calm me down. Later he explained he'd only shifted to ease my mind, to let me know that he was like me."

She winced. "The things I said to him."

She laced her hands together and was silent a moment. "Things didn't go well for a while. After everything that had happened, I couldn't trust him. Everything was so strange and scary, and it took a long time for me to figure out that he wouldn't hurt me."

She looked through the window and smiled faintly. "He's not a very patient man, my Jayems." She said 'my Jayems' as if unused to admitting the sentiments revealed by that simple designation. She continued softly, "It was seeing him fight so hard to be patient, to wait for me, that made me feel about him the way I do."

She looked so poignant, one leg drawn up pensively, hands clasped around it.

She looked like a queen.

Jasmine frowned and dismissed the disturbing image. This was her friend, always her friend, and no disconcerting, newly discovered rank was going to come between them. Her voice gruff, she said, "Well, I guess after the way you reacted, Keilor should consider himself lucky I haven't been chasing him around with a wooden stake and a mallet."

Rihlia shook her head at her. "It's a silver bullet for werewolves, at least in the movies." Jasmine waved that away negligently, and Rihlia stood up. "I guess I'd better take off. Keilor's going to be here soon. I expect a full report in the morning." She waggled her brows.

Jasmine threw a pillow at her.

Keilor gazed down at Jasmine's small form curled on the couch. It seemed the events of the day had worn her out. Another man might have been offended, and he was a touch disconcerted that he hadn't found her flushed and nervously awaiting his arrival. After this afternoon...

"Jasmine," he called softly, not wishing to startle her.

She moaned something incoherent and snuggled deeper into the cushions, seeking warmth.

He grinned. It seemed his woman did not like leaving her dreams. Feeling mischievous, he said loudly, "After you swooned so prettily for me earlier today, I had hoped for a more enthusiastic reception."

That did the trick. She blinked and gave him a grumpy glare. "I didn't swoon. It was a head rush. How many times do I have to say it?" She stretched with unconscious seduction, and whatever he'd been about to say evaporated from his mind. She was so beautiful.

"Sorry," she apologized. "I didn't mean to fall asleep on you. If you can hang on five minutes, I can change and—"

He cut her off with a light, tender kiss, a touch of his lips only against her parted lips. When he withdrew, she blinked at him in surprise. There were advantages to catching her befuddled from sleep, he decided. "Come as you are. I wished to take a walk through the gardens, if you're willing."

He left her side for a moment, searching, then returned with a pair of black, woven leather sandals. When he knelt to slip them on her feet, she stared at him in bewilderment.

"What are you doing?" She sounded almost...frightened.

He slipped the other shoe on and fastened a light silver chain around her ankle. Jasmine tilted her foot to get a better look at it. The light glinted off the alternating silver links and flashing opal stones. She looked at him for an explanation, something vulnerable in her eyes, and he had the feeling that gifts had been few and far between in her life.

That would change. "I suspected if I wished for you to wear something silver, I'd have to dress you in it myself." He allowed his eyes to smoke, just a little. "Unless there's something else you'd rather wear for me?"

Jasmine coughed and stood up fast, dusting her hands busily on her pants. "It's very pretty, thank you. Uh, let me just comb my hair." Avoiding his eyes, she hurried to the armoire and took out a brush, sweeping it through her hair before putting it up in a fast twist. She paused in the act of fastening the clip, her eyes flashing to his reflection. "I'm not really good with hair styles, but—"

He smiled. "You can wear it down for me at dinner."

Jasmine lowered her eyes and rubbed the sole of one sandal into the floor.

Ah, now this was the reaction he'd been hoping for, he thought with satisfaction. Lust seemed to be commonplace for her, but proper courtship turned her into an inexperienced girl, out of her depth.

He rather liked the thought of teaching her to swim.

He could have raised her hand to his lips, but didn't.
Instead he took it in his own and walked with her to the
door. Her small hand trembled lightly in his.

Obviously, he'd chosen well.

This wasn't at all what she'd expected.

The hedge enclosed gardens smelled heavenly.
Beautiful, exotic white birds with red, blue and green
crests chattered in the trees, filling the air with their music.
Every once and a while they would pass an exceptionally
nice smelling flower or herb along the stone paths, and
Keilor would stop and tell her its name and perhaps a little
about it. Once he'd even picked a small spray of blossoms
and tucked them in her hair.

Jasmine couldn't figure out what he was up to. She'd
never seen him so gentle, so considerate of her needs and
wishes. This morning she'd expected to be the one who'd
entertain the winner, and when he'd woken her from her
sleep she'd felt guilty for not being ready for him. Now he
was the one going out of his way to make their time
pleasurable. It confused her, and left her feeling vulnerable
and so feminine and...soft.

For a woman who'd had to be strong from infancy
just to survive emotionally, the sensation left her off
balance, and she found herself looking hesitantly to Keilor
for guidance.

He seemed to like it.

"We brought what we could of the familiar with us,"
he explained, unaware of her distraction. "Books and
seeds, especially. Good fortune was with us, and we found
mild winters here. What could not be grown outdoors
thrived under glass." He nodded towards the enormous
green houses they approached. "All of our children are
taught something of horticulture in school. The knowledge
of agriculture is a powerful thing, and our people are well
fed as a result of it." He held the door open for her.

This was no utilitarian space. Everything was orderly, but the tropical plants didn't stretch in long, boring rows. Instead they were arranged much like plots, with attention paid to both attractiveness and maximum productivity. Jasmine was enchanted. Many of these plants she'd never seen before.

"What is this?" she asked, gingerly touching a coconut sized, hairy brown fruit. It hung from a tangle of stems connected to a trunk. She tapped it experimentally and found the rind to be as hard as a nut.

Keilor laughed. "It's a cannonball tree, though it has been bred to remove the stench and improve the flavor. The plant it's descended from smells much like sewer sludge.

"When I was a boy I decided to cultivate one for an academic project. Somehow, the plant I grew reverted back to its original form. Imagine my surprise when the lovely scented blossoms produced fruit edible only for a stag," Jasmine chuckled, and he added impishly, "They made very useful stink bombs, though. It took weeks to get the smell out of our rival cadet's barracks."

She smirked. "Making friends and influencing people even then, huh?"

He gave her a sidelong glance but didn't take the bait. Instead, he gestured to another plant, an interesting specimen with long pods growing directly from the trunk. "The cacao tree. The chocolate you love so much grows in these pods."

"Really?" She looked at the tree with interest. Forget the kale and turnips—someone had been thinking when they brought seeds for this thing along. Excited, she turned a little too quickly to ask him a question and lost her balance. When she grabbed onto his arm to steady herself, he hissed. Fearing she'd hurt him, she quickly let go, then frowned. She'd felt a bandage under the long sleeve of his shirt. She touched the midnight silk carefully. There was definitely a bandage under there. "You hurt yourself."

He shook his head. "It's nothing."

"But—"

"A medic looked at it. You don't have to worry, it will be fine." When the worried expression didn't leave her face, he teased, "Would you like to see for yourself?"

For a moment she looked as if she would say yes. Instead she looked down and thrust her hands into her pockets, nudging the crushed shell of the pathway with the toe of one sandal. "I guess the tournament was a bad idea."

He raised her chin and looked into her troubled eyes. "The tournament was a very good idea. I enjoyed it. So did everyone else." When that didn't help, he added playfully, "Besides, if you hadn't seen me today, I wouldn't have had the chance to see you fall at my feet. Think how my ego might have suffered."

She snorted and turned away, but he could tell she was trying to hide a smile.

Dinner was fun. When he brought her back to her room a short while later, they found the table had been prepared with the ingredients for a Chinese hot pot. A steaming wok on a stand with a small flaming lamp underneath graced the center of the table. A platter of raw meats and seafood sat at one side, a matching one of sliced vegetables on the other.

Crystal condiment servers and a covered glass stand containing sweet confections had been placed on one end of the lace tablecloth. Candles had been lit, casting a romantic glow. Jasmine asked Keilor to light them while she changed into a simple, yet elegant, white tunic with loose harem pants. The sleeveless silk top reached almost to her knees, but the split bottom seams made it very comfortable to move in. Even with a chemise underneath it and a wide silver sash hugging her waist it was so weightless she almost felt naked.

172

Keilor's heart almost stopped when he saw her. The thin silk, though opaque, molded to her body in a way that made him very glad that it was he and not another man who was with her tonight. She wore her hair down, and it was all he could do not to drop what he was doing and forget about dinner.

There was something very intimate about saying the blessing with just the two of them. At first he placed his hands, as was customary, on her shoulders, but he couldn't resist allowing them to slide down her soft skin. He was so close; he felt her lungs expand to take in a silent, deep breath. When he laced his fingers with hers and wrapped his arms around her, she shivered. It was very difficult to let her go after the blessing was done.

"Can I look at your sword?" Jasmine asked after they'd finished their dessert.

He unsheathed it and handed it to her. "Be careful," he cautioned as she moved towards the couch to study it in comfort. He followed and sat beside her.

"How does it work?" she asked, turning the long knife this way and that, looking for a way to activate it. He took it away from her and slid his thumb against the guard. Instantly a blade of blue energy appeared, eclipsing the razor edged steel. She didn't try to take it back, just looked it over carefully, catching his eye and nodding when she was done. The blue hummed back into the blade, and he gave it back to her.

"The energy source is inside the haft. I release the beam when I slide the catch."

She looked it over a little longer and gave it back to him to be sheathed.

She settled back against the pillows plumped against the arms of the couch and bent her knees, bringing her bare feet up on the cushions. For a moment, she watched him. "I know why Rihlia didn't tell me about the Haunt. Why haven't you?"

CHAPTER 18

When he frowned, uncertain what she was asking, she elaborated, "You shape shift."

"Ah." This was definitely a subject to be approached with caution. He didn't want to foster any more distrust than she must already be feeling. "If you had known in the beginning, what would you have done?"

She snorted. "Run screaming for the woods?"

He rolled his eyes. "And at what point after that would I have known it was safe to tell you? Your people used to burn mine at the stake, Jasmine," he told her, very serious. "I was not eager to see you hate us."

There was nothing she could say to that.

He searched her face. "And now that you know what I am, do you fear me?" Every muscle in his body tensed, waiting for her answer.

She kept her eyes on her knees. "Are you willing to be patient with me? It's the same with Rihlia. I know better than to fear the woman, but I don't know the Haunt."

He slid over her, careful not to let his weight crush her. "You know this Haunt." He let his lips slide across her parted mouth, once, twice. "He burns for you," he whispered, and slowly withdrew. Exercising great restraint, he took a deep breath and placed her feet in his lap. They needed to talk, and he needed some kind of contact. "You know I can't give you children."

Jasmine swallowed hard. "If I had met you when I was forty-five, we might not have had kids, either."

"You are not forty."

"I might not be able to have kids anyway, for all we know," she reasoned, biting the inside of her lip.

"That's not likely," he answered with grim logic. Delusions would not serve them. "I would like children, but I'm not adverse to adopting them. I need to know how you feel." So much depended on this, and he was not willing to let it wait for another day.

She closed her eyes, was silent for a long moment. "It depends. I can do it, but…." she took a ragged breath. "It's painful." They were silent for a moment. "I know this sort of thing needs to be discussed, but isn't it just a little premature?" She tried to smile. "This is only a first date, after all."

Keilor slid back down next to her. "That depends on whether you're ready for this." His kiss was light but full of passion and power. It did not take long before her hands slid into his hair, asking for more.

It cost him much not to give it to her.

He broke the kiss and moved back just out of reach. When she tried to pull him back, he resisted. "Are you ready to make promises to me, Dragonfly?" he asked before words could leave her opened mouth. "Are you ready to be mine and no other's?" She lowered her eyes, and he persisted, "Not just for a time, but for all time?"

A rush of breath left her mouth. "I haven't had time…you're asking for some serious things, Keilor."

"I'm a serious man."

She pushed him back and sat up, scrubbing her face with her hands. "I didn't know you were going to ask me this." She clasped her hands and rested her weight on her forearms, which were propped on her knees. Staring at the floor, she said, "I'm not sure I know you well enough."

Keilor forced his muscles to relax. He'd hoped to see this through tonight, but he had more mettle than she did. He could out wait her.

Freeing one of her hands, he kissed it and stood up. "As you wish. I can give you time."

"Wait!" she called, as he turned away. She stood up. "Let me walk you to the door." They paused in front of it, and he looked at her expectantly. She was blocking the exit.

She shifted a little and then dropped her eyes. "Goodnight," she murmured.

"Goodnight," he answered, wondering what else she had to say. It must be something, or she would move.

She cleared her throat and muttered something. Looking anywhere but at him, she said, "It's customary where I come from to end a date with a kiss."

She didn't see the wolfish grin, but she couldn't miss it when his arms slid around her. He pressed her up against the door. Before she could draw another breath he was inside her, kissing her mouth with a ruthless determination that left no doubt in her mind just how much he wanted her. She moaned when his thigh slid between her legs, and he didn't care that her guards could hear them. His hand slid down and cupped her bottom, pulling her more firmly to him.

"Keilor!" she gasped and then bit his neck, sucking with mindless need as he rubbed against her.

"Promise me forever," he ordered her savagely. This was almost more than he could take. "Give me the right to stay."

She pressed her forehead against his chest and sobbed for breath.

In the end, she waited too long to answer.

"What are you doing?"

Jasmine and Rihlia stopped practicing the self-defense move they'd been working on and looked at Keilor. He was back in uniform today and his bandaged biceps, and a few fading nicks and bruises, showed clearly. Jayems was right beside him in the empty courtyard. He looked grave.

"Practicing getting out of grabs," Jasmine answered and wiped her forehead. It was difficult to look him in the eye after last night.

"Don't go," she'd begged, even as she'd slowly allowed him to step back.

He'd closed his eyes and drawn his hands away. "When you're ready," he'd promised, and she'd moved away, disappointed, as he'd opened the door and left.

He was making a bad habit of that, she thought. Bringing her attention back to the question at hand, she said, "Before that we were doing kicks. Why?"

The late morning sunlight didn't quite reach the floor of their open air chamber, and cool shadows played across his face. "Do you really believe it will help you?"

"It saved me from being raped once and robbed twice," Jasmine returned tartly. "Yeah, I think it will help."

"Twice?" Rihlia demanded sharply. "When was the second time?"

Jasmine waved her off.

Something painful flashed across Keilor's face. Jayems looked at him in sympathy and motioned for his wife to follow him. Some things were better dealt with in privacy.

"I'm glad for that, then," Keilor said, coming closer. "But you aren't dealing with humans, now. A Haunt would literally tear you apart with his bare hands, Jasmine." He looked at her gravely. "I could rip your body open with nothing but my hands."

It was his quiet manner that disturbed her the most. Keilor might be arrogant, but he never boasted. He didn't need to. She looked down at his hands. They looked ordinary enough, but she'd seen him in action. She believed him.

Agitated, she freed her ponytail, swept the loose strands back into place and twisted the band back around it. "So what do you suggest? If I've learned anything over the years, its bad guys don't strike when the good guys are in shouting distance. What am I supposed to do, let them hurt me without a fight?"

A muscle ticked in his jaw.

She saw it, and wrapped her arms around herself, sheltering her heart. "It's not that I don't think you'd help me if you were there, but you can't be there all the time," she persisted. She could tell he didn't like it, but he was listening. "I know I can't match any of you physically. I'm not stupid. Still, even you got caught by surprise when I punched you in the nose that one time."

He snorted, but she thought she saw a hint of a smile. "Blind luck."

"Maybe, but what if I'd done something more deadly than just bloody your nose?" she argued. "What if I'd had a knife? The point is, the fact that I seem so completely helpless might just work in my favor."

Keilor eyed her, attempting to distance himself from the situation and think of her as a scrawny, stunted cadet with a sharp mind and a healthy respect for her life. It was true, she would never come close to matching a Haunt in battle. The idea was completely ludicrous. However, when it came to sheer nerve and craftiness...perhaps there might be something. First things first, however.

Before she even knew she was in danger, he had her by the throat. He did not hurt her, but he was not polite about it, either. "You are dead," he informed her grimly. "Your neck is broken and you are dead. As long as you expect nothing less, I can try to teach you something that might give you a few more minutes against a Haunt, as long as you are very quick and very sly. A minute might be long enough to let me reach you. Someone else might save your life. The odds of you escaping more than one man, unaided, are laughable. Do you understand?" She nodded, and he released her.

Enveloping her in a crushing hug, he told her, "I don't want this." He kissed her temple and rubbed his head soothingly against her. "I will never leave you unguarded for a second. I know you are brave, but my heart stops when I think of you resisting an assassin, because I see the ending." His voice roughened. "But I won't deny you your chance for revenge, and I won't force to you to remain ignorant if you truly wish to learn." He pulled back to gauge her reaction. "This isn't necessary. Are you sure you wish to learn?" A touch of humor lit his eyes. "I'm known as a critical teacher."

"Hmpf." She drew back and straightened her scarlet tunic. "If you get too annoying I can always get Mathin or Fallon to teach me. Or even Jayems."

A crack of laughter escaped him. She had no idea. "If you think any of them would be an easier master, you're in for a rude disappointment." He drew her closer. "Besides, if you think I'm going to allow another man so much access to you, you're sadly mistaken." His voice lowered to a seductive purr. "I'm a very possessive man."

"Are you?" she breathed against his lips, opening hers in invitation and sipping from his mouth.

"Are you ready to marry me?" he asked.

She drew back in frustration. "I like you better when you don't open your mouth." Why did he keep doing this? She knew what blue balls were, but what did they call it for a woman?

His eyes glimmered. "You like my open mouth."

"Not when words are coming out," she griped, pulling away. Fine, if he was going to be difficult then they might as well get down to business. "Show me how to use that," she ordered, pointing to his holstered gun.

Jasmine creaked into her room that night and shut the door stiffly behind her. She eyed the bed and bath, debating whether or not she could stay awake long enough to soak away some soreness, or if it would be better to flop down on the bed, sweat and all, and pray for oblivion. Reluctantly, she decided on the bath.

He was trying to kill her, she thought as she hobbled over. She sat down on the marble bath steps and plunked her head down into her hands. All right, he probably wasn't, but she strongly suspected he was trying to drive her so hard that she'd give up on learning self-defense all together. Only sheer mulishness had kept her at it for the last half hour, and when her legs had finally given out and dumped her on her butt, Keilor had just raised an eyebrow and inquired if she were finished for the day.

Sometimes she hated that man.

The only thing that consoled her, she thought as she gingerly stripped off her shirt, was the knowledge that she'd proven herself today. He now knew she meant business, and he'd ease up and get on with it at a more reasonable pace. After all, she wasn't one of his grunts. And if he didn't, she thought with dour resolution, he'd be sorry.

"You'll have to do better than that."

Jasmine lowered the laser gun in her aching arm and gave him a *look*. She knew how to use a gun, and she was a good marksman. He hadn't said a word the last five times she'd nailed the impossibly small dot on the stone wall he'd designated as her opponent's heart. Her jaw worked and she said tightly, "I hit the target." One more patronizing, arrogant comment out of his mouth, and she'd—

Completely uninterested, he shrugged. The movement caused muscles to ripple in his bare arms, but she barely noticed, or told herself she didn't. "If you're satisfied with merely nicking the center, instead of striking it dead on, then I bow to your womanly judgment." Boredom colored his every word and it was all she could do not to slap his indifferent face.

The morning had been difficult, at best. Keilor had run her through her paces with all the enthusiasm of one indulging a pampered child. With each patronizing bit of praise, or sigh of tolerance, her fury had uncoiled, and now it was barely under control. Unfortunately, Keilor made the supremely stupid mistake of treating even that with blasé disregard, which only added gunpowder to the fire.

Cradling her pistol in one hand, she gently tapped the black muzzle against her palm. Giving him an insincere smile, she said sweetly, "Since I'm such a lousy shot, I guess it's a good thing you only gave me a practice gun, huh?" She eyed him with malevolence. "Wouldn't want me to miss and actually damage anyone, would we?"

He smirked. "You aren't...quite that bad." He squinted up at the sun. "After a time I may even allow you to practice with a real weapon." A short laugh escaped him. "Then we will see if it will do you any good."

She shot him.

Standing sideways, with her arm angled across her stomach, she rotated the gun and shot the arrogant fool in his solar plexus. Then she stood over him and gloated.

Haunt guards surrounded her immediately, and she looked up with immense satisfaction and proffered the butt of her pistol, inquiring, "Would any of you like to be holding the bag when he wakes up?"

They checked.

"No?" She quirked a brow and holstered her weapon. Arms crossed, she stared down at him as she waited for the stun to wear off.

As the minutes ticked by, her temper cooled, and she began to feel a touch uneasy. Pacing helped, but she couldn't keep from glancing at Keilor's prone body and wondering what he'd do when he woke up. Men weren't very forgiving when it came to public humiliation.

That fact that he'd trampled her pride in front of witnesses wasn't irrelevant, but it began to seem less and less important as time dragged by.

"What is this?" A rough male voice demanded. Mathin strode onto the practice field with long legged efficiency. "Why have you left him there?" he demanded of the small gathering of Haunt and one sullen human.

"He's fine," Jasmine said as he squatted down to check for a pulse. "He's just taking a little nap."

Mathin's look froze her blood.

"He was being a jerk," she defended herself, her eyes widening with indignation. Sheesh, it wasn't *that* big a deal. Everyone was acting like she'd just robbed a bank.

"So you shot him in the back," he said with contempt.

She raised a brow and affected hauteur. "Actually, he was facing me at the time."

He stared at her, incredulous. "And you have the gall to stand about waiting for him wake up?"

Huffing in exasperation, she answered, "I try not to give into my cowardly instincts more than once a week. Besides," she jerked her chin in Keilor's direction, "What's he going to do? Kill me?"

Mathin's gaze was long and level. He glanced back at Keilor. "This is one time when I would take advantage of your supposed tender gender and depart, Lady Jasmine." He stood and dusted his hands. "I can distract him for a time until his temper cools."

She crossed her arms and stared at the ground. Tempting as it was… "I would rather see this through," she said quietly, speaking her thoughts. "Seeing him at his worst is preferable to imagining him at his worst, and I can assure you, I have a vivid imagination. Besides, if we…" she trailed off, embarrassed, and chose other words than what she'd intended. "It's better to learn to fight it out in a civilized fashion early on, you know? Saves time later." She looked at Keilor. "Presuming there is a later."

CHAPTER 19

Keilor's eyes opened with a snap, and he was on his feet before Jasmine had time to blink. With a snarl, he yanked her down across his bent knee and spanked her three times. When he was sure he had her attention, he pulled her to her feet and shook her.

"*What in the name of all that's holy did you think you were doing?*" He shook her again, ignoring Mathin and the others. In all his years *no one*, especially not someone under his training, had ever dared to have such cheek. Had she been a man he would have pulverized her, but since she was a woman the best that he could do was blast her with words.

"You deserved it!" she shouted, and kicked him in the shin.

He released her, afraid of what he might do if he did not.

Tears of fury glittered in her eyes. "You were being a jerk on purpose!" she accused him.

He narrowed his eyes. Very coldly, he reminded her, "You asked for my help."

Shoulders heaving, she answered with contempt, "I asked someone I thought was my friend for help." Her eyes raked him with disdain. "I won't make that mistake again."

She started to brush past him and he caught her arm. He wasn't finished.

Unfortunately, she was.

"*Release me*," she ordered him, in the tone no Haunt could resist. Of their own volition, his fingers opened, and she stalked away.

Furious at his inability to follow, he looked around, seeking a target.

The other Haunt melted away with prudent haste.

Mathin just shook his head in sympathy. "Women and war don't mix, my sorry friend. Come and have a drink."

"She asked me for help." Keilor thumped his glass on the redwood table and poured a third shot of rye liquor. "I fail to see what she had to complain of." The windowless taproom in the bowels of the citadel was busy serving lunch, but was not nearly as boisterous as it could become with the after dinner crowd. They could converse easily, and there was enough space between tables to ensure a sense of privacy.

"Perhaps you don't wish to see it," Mathin observed as he leaned back on his chair. He caught the eye of the least ugly waitress and smiled with promise. She hurried over, and he inspected her with lazy satisfaction.

A little breathless, she asked, "Can I get you anything, sir?"

He gifted her with a dazzling smile. "Something solid, I think, to soothe my hunger. I've got a powerful appetite this afternoon."

Blushing, the woman took his order and hurried off to deliver it to the kitchen. The men watched as the other two waitresses conveniently converged on the bar at the same time and talked in whispers and giggles. The boldest even glanced back at the two warriors and smiled.

"When women are petted, they purr, and their friends purr, too," Mathin said, a pleasant smile on his face. "Dampen their spirits, however—" he made a clawing motion with his hand.

Amused in spite of himself, Keilor still had to
inquire, "And if they ask to be taken out in the rain?"

Mathin sighed and shook his head at him. "She's a
woman, imbecile. You can't expect her to react like a
soldier. Galling as it might be for a warrior, she's one
student who'll never come close to what we regard as
perfection." He paused and stretched his long legs. "So
give her what she wants. Surely there's something she
might master." His eyes danced with thinly veiled
amusement. "She appears to be fairly promising with a
gun."

"Go away!" Jasmine shouted at the door. Her bottom
smarted and her pride still stung, and she wasn't about to
let Keilor come inside and inflict more damage. She
wasn't a child, and if he wasn't bright enough to figure
that out then he could just go to—

"Jasmine," Keilor said again through the door. He
was beginning to sound exasperated.

Urseya smirked over her teacup. "Perhaps you should
just let him in." She took a sip, savoring it. "Besides, if
he's come to grovel, I, for one, wish to see it."

Hmm. She does have a point, Jasmine thought.
Urseya had witnessed the entire fiasco earlier, and when
Jas had stalked off, she'd joined her on the way back to her
room, complimenting Jasmine on her spectacular aim.
Then she'd casually remarked that if Jasmine truly wished
to unman a man, she'd be more than happy to teach her
every trick she knew.

Jasmine had stopped, stunned, and scanned her face
for an ulterior motive, but she'd quickly been convinced of
Urseya's sincerity. It seemed when it came to proving men
were inferior beings, Urseya rose to the occasion.

In light of that… "Come in if you dare," Jasmine
called.

Keilor wasted no time with subtleties. "Urseya." He nodded to his cousin and took Jasmine by the hand. Before she could react, he pulled her up and toward the door, intent on some privacy.

"Hey!" It was impossible to get any kind of traction on the polished floor, so the best Jasmine could do was yip at him like a toy poodle tied to the back of a Mack truck. "Don't you have any manners, you troll? I have a guest!"

Instantly, Keilor stopped, spun on the balls of his feet and swept Urseya with a courtly bow. Jasmine teetered, and he wrapped a long arm around her and plastered her to his side. "Do forgive us, dear cousin, perhaps we can chat after my love and I have completed our business. Make yourself at home, and don't wait up for us."

Too astonished by his actions to protest, Jasmine allowed herself to be towed along as far as the second door in the hallway before she found her tongue. "Are all Haunt barbarians or am I just terribly unlucky?"

His low laugh made her shiver. "Some day soon you'll find that having a barbarian for a mate can be a very good thing."

Heat pooled in her belly and she stumbled at the sudden ache. Keilor's head rose like a wolf scenting prey, and his nostrils flared. His eyes told her he knew, and his knowledge of her weakness made her tremble. Without a word, he picked her up and carried her the short distance to his room.

The interior was dim, the furniture brown and heavy. His room was half the size of hers, yet contained a microscopic and very cluttered kitchen. The ugly quilt on his narrow bed was ragged, torn, and sliding off the naked mattress, which rested on the floor. Weapons of every description littered the coffee table, furniture, and nested in corners, along with various articles of discarded clothing.

It looked like Martha Stewart's version of hell.

"Take one step toward that bed, and I swear you won't live to regret it," Jasmine vowed, repulsed.

Keilor halted and looked down at her in surprise. "What's wrong?"

Jasmine wriggled, and he set her down on her feet. Wrinkling her nose, she called for lights and made a wary survey of the place. Experimentally, she ran her hand across the back of one of his leather chairs. It came away dusty. With a grimace, she wiped her fingers on her pants, leaving a dirty gray streak. "What is it with men and dirt?"

She moved a crusty plate off of one of his leather chairs. A discarded towel made a good rag, and she dusted the chair before sitting. Stuffing poked out from the frayed upholstery. "I can't believe I didn't notice this the last time I was in here. How can you live in such squalor?"

"I believe you were preoccupied," Keilor reminded her, irritated. Since she had chosen to sit in a chair, he moved to the battered leather couch and sat down, resting on arm across the back. His eyes swept her with restless hunger.

"Forget it," she informed him in a no-nonsense tone. "I am not making it with you in this pig sty." She ignored his narrowed eyes. "You were so eager to talk. So, talk."

He pinned her with a stern look. "What happened this afternoon will not happen again." He paused, but she only watched him warily. "If you have a grievance with me we will talk about it, not attack each other."

"I wouldn't worry about that. Urseya's going to take up where you left off." Her eyes lowered to half-mast to disguise their glimmer. His words brought back her hurt feelings. Keeping her eyes lowered, she forced out through a tight throat, "I doubt I'll feel the need to shoot *her*."

The silence dragged out, and finally she admitted, "I may have been a little rash this morning, but you have to admit, I did catch you off guard." He didn't flex a muscle, so she went ahead and dug her grave deeper. "You were so convinced I would never measure up, I couldn't resist proving you wrong."

He relaxed at last. "You don't need to measure up." When her face darkened, he added, "Not to the standard I am trained to use." His face and voice now reflected his years of experience, the easy command that made him such a daunting warrior.

"I realized this afternoon that what you had asked of me and what I had thought you'd asked of me were not the same at all. I apologize for treating you like a soldier."

Well, this was better. In the light of his apology she could be magnanimous. "It might have been a little childish to shoot you," she admitted. "I'll try not to lose my temper next time." She smiled slyly. "Or at least, not in front of witnesses."

He snorted and returned in kind, "Then I'll try to restrain myself from spanking you...and wait until we're alone to administer an appropriate punishment." It was obvious what sort of torment he had in mind as his eyes heated. His nostrils flared as he caught her scent, and for one heated moment, she almost reconsidered letting him take her then and there.

Whew! They needed a subject change, quick. "When was the last time you cleaned this place, Keilor?" she asked, standing up to circle the room. No point in being too obvious about bolting to the door. Better just to detour and slip out as her circuit brought her close to the exit.

In two graceful strides he was at her side, offering her his arm. Amused, he told her, "You'll reach the door more quickly if you travel in a straight line."

Her reprieve was short lived.

Not five steps from his door, they stopped, and Keilor backed her up against the wall. Loosening her hair from its tie, he smoothed it back and twisted a strand around his finger. He brought it to his lips, and shock waves traveled up the strands to dance around her scalp. "Tell me what you want in a husband," he whispered.

Jasmine drew a ragged breath. She'd never considered making a list. "I don't know." How was she supposed to consider such things when he was making her toes curl?

She felt him smile against her cheek. "I will not beat you, Dragonfly." He took one of her hands from his chest and slid it dangerously low on his hip, letting her feel the ripple of his taunt, warm muscles. "I am a good provider." He moved closer, cradling himself against her hips and burning with every hard inch.

She couldn't help it, her mouth fell open and she moaned.

"It's n-not the...money," she gasped. She'd never expected anyone to provide for her, the last few weeks not withstanding. Truth be told, she'd begun to feel less like a pampered prisoner and more like a parasite every day. She wanted to do something with her life, earn her own way. Besides, with a room like that, how rich could he be?

Undaunted, he took her right hand and slid it under his vest, over his heart. "Then perhaps you'll accept this?" he asked softly. He brushed his mouth against her lips. "It's been yours for some time now."

A lump formed in Jasmine's throat, and her eyes prickled. No one had ever told her what he was telling her, save Rihlia. No man had ever felt as much. She closed her eyes. "I don't deserve it."

For a moment, he simply held her. Then, with words she would remember for the rest of her life, he breathed in her ear, "I don't know what's happened in your life to make you believe that, but I will spend the rest of mine proving you wrong."

She kissed him. There was no doubt of her answer now.

"My feet are always cold," she warned him. "I'll be forever wanting to put them on you."

He chuckled and nuzzled her neck, drawing on the tender skin. "I like the idea of cold feet in bed. I'm always overly warm, myself." His voice dropped an octave. "Besides, I think I can find a few ways to warm you up."

"Um." Jasmine broke away from his kiss with a gasp. "I hate a mess. I'll be forever nagging at you to pick up after yourself."

"I'll survive," he assured her and kissed her with dizzying hunger. She arched into his body, craving more, and he obligingly slid his hand down to cup her breast.

A soft cry escaped her, and her hands slid into his hair. She removed his clip to tangle her fingers in the silky strands. All thoughts of where they were and the likelihood of being caught evaporated from her brain. All she could think about was fusing her body to his and putting out the fierce ache.

Lucky for her, he had a fraction more sense.

Keilor tore his mouth from hers, took her hand and nearly ran to her room.

Urseya was gone, and they wasted no time getting naked. Keilor made it as far as his pants before passion overcame him and he tumbled her back on the quilt, feasting on her mouth as if he'd never get enough. "Give me the words before I go up in flames," he demanded, breaking the kiss to free her mouth for speech.

"I'm yours, for as long as you want me," she scrambled to say. The time for waiting was well past. All she wanted now was completion.

He rewarded her with a melting kiss. "I take your promise and give you mine. I'm yours, heart and soul, until the end of my life or yours. May it be a long time in coming."

Jasmine cried out as his mouth closed over her nipple, sending seismic tremors throughout her hungry body. From her single, failed experiment at loving at nineteen, she'd concluded she simply wasn't one of those women who felt much sensitivity in her breasts. Keilor's feverish tongue and gentle teeth proved her dead wrong.

She squirmed and tugged at his shoulders, desperate to have him inside. "I'm ready! Oh!" she cried out. His hips moved against her in acknowledgment, but his words didn't bring any promise of relief.

"Not yet." His answer was guttural and swift, but plain enough. His mouth switched to the breast he'd just massaged with his callused palm, and she arched underneath him and cried out.

He reared up to watch her, something like surprise and fierce satisfaction in his face. "More," he commanded, and slipped a finger inside her.

This time she screamed.

Thoroughly aroused, eyes bright, he demanded, "Again," This time his thumb circled her sensitive peak as he slid two fingers inside her, fast.

Her response deafened them both.

"Please!" she cried, scrabbling at his back, begging with her words and her body. "Please! I-I can't—"

"Yes," he promised. "I will please you." He tossed his hair over his shoulder and kissed his way down her belly, teasing the sensitive hollows as he went.

"Keilor!" she wailed. What was the man doing? She wanted him, needed him more with each passing second, and all he wanted to do was stoke the fire! What would it take to make him put it out?

By the time he reached her ankles and began to lick his way back up she was ready to kill him. She begged for more with her hands, tugged urgently at his hair, yet he wouldn't—

He reached her inner thigh, and she knew she was about to die. No woman could possibly survive this kind of pleasure. There was no time to consider whether or not she was ready when his burning lips left her thigh and covered her intimately. His tongue darted deep within and she went mad. She twisted and begged him to stop, to not stop, to make *it* stop while her hands tangled in his hair and forced him to remain exactly where he was.

And he loved it.

One look at his riotous eyes was all her overloaded senses could take. A beast knelt between her legs, feasting on her body, deliberately driving her to the edge of sanity. She began to sob. Any more and the barriers she'd constructed around her emotions would vanish, leaving her completely exposed. "I can't take it!"

"You will," he growled against her. He gave her a long, deliberate kiss.

And the walls came a' tumbling down.

Only then, when she was completely spent, trembling, and feeling more shy and untried than at any other time in her life, did he come to her. He stripped off his pants as she slipped under the covers, hiding. It did no good. He simply flung the covers back and pinned her hips to the bed with his own, slipping his legs between her thighs to spread them wide. "I'm going to love you so deeply you'll never get me outside of you," he warned her. "You'll walk from this bed, but you'll take a piece of me with you wherever you go."

She panted as the broad head of his erection parted her slick folds. She wanted him there, but it burned. She knew she'd taken all she could when the burning turned to fierce pain. "Are you done yet?" she demanded, freezing up around him.

He huffed in disbelief. "I've barely begun." He pressed harder, gaining what seemed to be more than enough ground.

"H-how 'bout now?"

Teeth gritted, he forced himself to a trembling halt. "Have you done this before?" His breathing was harsh and getting harsher.

"Once. Four years ago," she admitted with embarrassment, adding defensively, "But it didn't hurt then!"

He growled. "What was he, deformed? You're as tight as any virgin. Never mind," he told her as she tried to hide her face. "All the better that I be the one to break you in."

The actual words were harsh, but she understood what he meant. Reassured, for she'd had no way of knowing what he'd think of her sexual history, she found the strength to endure as he slowly and gently worked his way in.

"That will have to be enough," he said at last. "You can't take any more of me tonight."

Her eyes widened with indignation. What she'd already 'taken' had caused her discomfort enough. The idea of having to absorb more of him at another time displeased her greatly.

Her expression must have said as much, for he laughed, causing vibrations deep within. Giving her a quick kiss, he told her, "Don't worry, sweet, you'll soon have cause to be thankful for a big lover." His eyes darkened, and he became serious. "Tell me if it hurts."

He withdrew a fraction, and she stiffened in pain. The careful return thrust was no better. Switching tactics, he began to rock her gently, neither pushing nor withdrawing, using the least possible friction. The micro movements were bearable as the longer thrusts hadn't been. She began to feel a touch of pleasure in spite of the discomfort, just enough to keep her from asking him to stop. Still, it was a guilty relief when he threw his head back in a silent roar as he shuddered with his own climax.

He held his weight over her for long moments while she stroked his damp back. When he finally gathered his strength and rolled off, drawing her with him, she lay quietly with her head on his chest, thinking.

"So, when do I get to climax?"

Keilor drew back, startled, and peered at her. "Sweetheart, you found your pleasure so many times I lost count."

She propped herself up on her elbow and frowned at him. "I didn't feel like I was exploding, or flying, or anything like that." When his expression grew even more mystified, she explained lamely, "That's what all the romance novels I've read described it as."

He laughed and shook his head at her. He opened his mouth, but words must have been beyond him because nothing came out. Instead, he leaned over and kissed her, grinning against her lips. Then his hand drifted down her body as he worked his potent magic.

This time when the pleasure came, she knew it for what it was.

"Oh," she panted, when the power of speech returned.

"Oh," he agreed smugly, propped on his elbow as he watched her. He smoothed the hair from her face with fingers that smelled of sex. "How is it that such a beautiful woman comes to me almost untouched?" His eyes warmed. "I am grateful, but astonished. Wasn't there anyone?"

Jasmine ducked her head. "No one ever thought of me as beautiful."

"Impossible," he assured her, and gave her another tender kiss. "What of slug tongue?"

She choked with laughter.

He sighed and drew her close, lying back on the pillows. "Their foolishness is my good fortune, and I am a happy man tonight." He kissed her temple. "Go to sleep, wife, in the arms of the man who loves you." He felt her swallow against his chest.

"I love you, too, Keilor."

He kissed her again and settled back with a contented sigh. "I know."

CHAPTER 20

What a view.

Jasmine wasn't one for mornings, but if she got to wake up to *this* every day, she just might revise her opinion.

Keilor leaned against the back of a chair as he watched the sunrise. Pink and gold light delineated every inch of his superbly naked body. It was a sight to make a make a maiden faint, or even a newly made wife.

She must have made some sound, for suddenly she was looking at her first, full frontal view of a naked man. Fire leapt to her cheeks, and she looked down. They might have done *it*, but she'd never actually checked one out before, and she just couldn't stare at it—him—and still look him in the face.

He had no such hang ups.

"Good morning," he murmured and joined her on the bed. He slid down to suckle on one unsuspecting breast. She grabbed his head and arched with pleasure, only to cry out as sore muscles protested.

Instantly he stopped, concerned. "Are you alright?"

She gave him a rueful smile. "Just a little sore, is all. It surprised me."

"Ah." He looked down at the painful area, hidden under the blankets, until she squirmed. He sighed. "I shall have to be very careful with you, I see." Casanova poked his nose at him, asking for attention, and he petted the little villi. As he did he shifted, exposing himself to her.

Jasmine looked away.

He smiled and gave her another sweet kiss. "You have nothing to fear, my love. I like it when you look at me." He took her hand and guided it to him, showed her what he liked. "I like it even better when you touch me."

Given formal permission, Jasmine explored him. She watched as her hand moved from wet tip and silky-hardness to the vulnerable testi at the base. All the while, he neither flinched nor displayed the least bit of self-consciousness. When she began to stroke him with a rhythmic pattern, he wrapped his hand around hers and showed her the proper pressure and timing, then let go and let her have her way. Head back, he reveled in the pleasure. It was beautiful.

He was beautiful.

Afterward they shared a bath. As they cleansed away the exertions of the night, new fires began. She was still too tender to fully appreciate his loving, but still she wanted him too badly to stop. She knew it would get better every time until nothing was left but pure, sweet pleasure.

They ate breakfast and reclined on the bed afterward. Keilor held her against his chest while they talked.

"We'll need to choose a suite," Keilor murmured, drawing her hair away to kiss her neck. "Our rooms aren't suitable for a mated couple." She felt him smile against her skin. "I think we'll have to take this bed and the mirror with us, though."

Some of her drowsiness fled and she turned over to swat him in playful warning. "Don't you dare!" He grinned and nipped at her, then pretended to wrestle, ending their play with a long, drugging kiss.

Reluctantly he drew away, murmuring, "Many more nights." He settled her comfortably into his arms. With his chin on her head, he said, "Jayems' and Rihlia's wedding ceremony is tonight. Maybe you should get some rest. It's bound to be a long evening."

A sudden thought struck her, and she leaned up on one elbow, her head on her hand. "Do we have to have a ceremony?"

He brushed her hair off her shoulder. "Do you want one?" he asked, feeling indulgent. If that was what she wanted, he wouldn't argue. Personally, he'd never favored public ceremonies, and wouldn't feel any more married for it. As far as he and Haunt law were concerned, she was now his wife.

She frowned and looked at the bed. "To tell the truth, I'd rather just skip it. It seems like a lot of bother just to announce to the world that we're, ah, married."

The careful way she said it raised his short hairs. He pinned her with a hard stare. "You gave me your promise, charmer."

It was the wrong word to use.

She wouldn't look at him. "I said I was yours for as long as you want me." She took a deep breath. "In twenty or thirty years—"

He forced her to look at him, to see his anger. "My promise was for a lifetime, wife. And I meant it." She pulled away, and he cursed the fact that she was too new to loving to speak with his body. She needed his possession right now.

Unsure what else to do, he got up and pulled on his clothes, intent on working off his frustration. "I don't understand you, woman," he said grimly. He tugged on the carefully polished boots, so at odds with his careless housekeeping. "One moment you trust me enough to take me to your bed, and the next you are taking me for an honorless animal."

She opened her mouth to protest, but he cut her off, his eyes sparking gold. "You've got something to learn about your new world, *wife*. Haunt men take but one mate, and we don't touch another woman for as long as she lives, unless we wish to go insane. Unlike humans, once mated, for us there is no going back. As soon as the fluids mix, a connection is made that won't bear severance.

"Unlike you, I can never play you false. Do you not think I considered that carefully before I spoke to Jayems?"

"I'm not planning to run off with the butler and the family jewels the first chance I get!" Most of what he said went right over her head. He already thought of her betraying him? Is that what he expected? "I was just trying to give you breathing room, a chance to bow out gracefully when—"

He turned on his heel and stalked to the door. "I'm not listening to any more of this. If I'd known what madness it was to take a human for a wife—" The door slammed, cutting off whatever else he had to say.

Jasmine stared at the door, wondering what just happened. She'd tried to be considerate. He'd never be able to have kids with her, and she couldn't believe he wouldn't be revolted once old age set in. It wouldn't be fair not to let him go.

Her chest constricted, and she flinched at the thought of Keilor taking another lover, or a wife. She'd be better off to think of this as an extended affair.

Her eyes prickled, and she flopped back on the bed, her arm over her eyes. So much for the honeymoon.

The moment Rihlia saw her somber face, she dropped everything. She dragged Jasmine into her old room and firmly shut the door. The lock snicked shut.

The women who'd hovered around her, fussing over her wedding dress, protested loudly. They were ignored.

"Out with it," she demanded, and sat down on the bed. She pulled Jasmine down to the white and yellow quilt. "I know Keilor spent the night with you."

"Ri!" Jasmine rolled her eyes and avoided her friend's curious gaze. She felt guilty for taking her away from her wedding preparations, but she'd needed to talk to someone, and somehow she'd doubted Keilor would appreciate her talking to the door guards.

"So now you're married," she continued, all curiosity, not realizing in her happiness that Jasmine wasn't nearly as thrilled.

"Sort of," Jasmine hedged.

A frown gathered on Rihlia's brow. "Sort of? How can you be 'sort of' married, Jas? Didn't you sleep with him? Didn't he make you a promise?" A golden square of sunlight from the mullioned windows sparkled on the gems in her hair. Their gaiety was a sharp contrast to her expression of concern. No bride should look so serious.

Jasmine picked at the quilt. "Yes, but it doesn't mean anything. I told him I didn't want a ceremony, and he was okay with that. He told me he loves me and that's good enough for me, for as long as it lasts."

Rihlia peered at her in pained disbelief. "As long as it lasts, Jas? You make love sound like the stomach flu."

Jasmine took a deep breath and explained as logically as she knew how. "It's like I told him, Ri, I'm going to get old a lot sooner than he will. I'll waste away, shrivel up. Hey, for all I know, I'll get Alzheimer's and go senile on him. How would that be fair?" She shook her head. "Like I said, I'll take what I can get for as long as it lasts."

She glanced at her best friend and was shocked to see a single tear track down her cheek. "Ri?" she asked, uncertain what was wrong. She reached out to comfort her.

She shrank away from Jasmine's touch and stood up. "Do you know what it is for a Haunt to take a mate? Of course you don't," she said, answering her own question. Her voice was laden with heavy emotion. "You can be with only one person, if you are a Haunt. That's why I could only go so far with men before. My instincts stopped me."

She closed her eyes and fought back tears. "Jas—you have no idea. Once I was with Jayems, once we had been together, made love... Jas," her voice cracked. "He was a virgin, too."

Jasmine stared at her in shock. Jayems, a *virgin?*

Rihlia found her composure. "We can mess around all we want, touching and kissing whomever we please, but the moment we cross that line, we can never go back. That's why it's a marriage. It has to be."

Still at sea, Jasmine said, "I don't understand."

Frustrated, Rihlia searched for something Jasmine could comprehend. Inspiration struck. "Do you remember what you said about your first time?" she asked as she sat on the bed. "You told me it was mildly pleasant, but you felt detached and empty. Remember?" When Jasmine nodded, she asked, "Was it that way with Keilor?"

Jasmine sucked in a breath. "There was no comparison. I had feelings for him, and he clearly.... She lowered her eyes in embarrassment. "He was clearly a better lover." Unbidden, the image of him as he'd been this morning, completely focused and relaxed as he'd let her touch him, came to mind. There had been no barriers of any kind for him. Because he assumed there would never be anyone else?

She felt misgiving as she remembered how her own walls had come down when he'd been killing her with pleasure. In that moment, everything she was belonged to him and only him. Was Rihlia trying to say they were like that with their mates *all the time?*

A frantic bubble of fear rose to her throat and lodged. How could they survive without armor and walls to hold others at bay? She wouldn't, couldn't! Surely he wouldn't expect that of her? She wasn't capable of that kind of sustained vulnerability.

Something in her face must have given her away, for Rihlia said, very gently, "You became a part of him, connected with something deep inside him that no one has ever touched. Something so much deeper than a loss of virginity I can barely describe it. If you ever tried to take that away…" Words failed her.

A little frightened and a lot shaken, Jasmine got to her feet. This was a lot more complicated than she'd thought. "He was a virgin?" she asked, repeating the most difficult of the concepts to accept.

Rihlia nodded.

"A virgin," Jasmine repeated. How could such a confident, competent man possibly be a virgin? She'd heard men use the word as an insult. She just couldn't reconcile her image of innocence and fumbling inexperience with anything about Keilor, or the Haunt for that matter. Her eyes boggled as another thought hit her. "Fallon is a virgin?"

Rihlia grinned. "Every unmated male is a virgin, silly. Every woman, too."

"Urseya?" She still remembered Urseya standing in nothing but a thin slick of mud, boldly flirting with Keilor.

"I never said they weren't experienced, you goober," Rihlia said, giving her a friendly little push. "Sticking it in doesn't take brains or skill. Even amoebas manage to reproduce." She smirked. "I take it Keilor was one hot number."

This time, Jasmine felt her entire body blush. She hid her face in her hands. What an understatement!

Now she understood what Keilor had been talking about with his rantings about exchanging fluids. Armed with the knowledge Keilor had been a *virgin*, Jasmine had several things she urgently needed to discuss with him.

She returned to her room to avoid the flurry surrounding Rihlia, but Keilor didn't show up soon enough to suit her, and pacing only fed her frustration. She decided to seek him out. She checked in his room, but he wasn't there. The mess hadn't improved since the last time she'd visited. She hesitated, looked around. Did he ever let the maids in here?

Since he wasn't around to tell her no, she decided to muck out some of the refuse, starting with the nasty blanket on his gray mattress. Using as few fingers as she could, she drug the icky thing over to the door and started a trash pile.

That mattress had to go, she decided as she viewed the lumpy thing with hands on hips. It looked like it had been slept on by a team of huskies, peed on, and left to dry out in somebody's driveway.

This called for manly muscles. Fortunately, she knew just where to find some.

She threw open the door and surveyed Raziel and Isfael, who were on duty today. Raziel glanced at her from where he was slouched against the opposite wall, arms crossed and one leg slack, obviously bored. His limp red sash and scarlet insignia were the only hints of color about him today. A silver earring dangled from one ear.

Poor Isfael just looked stoic.

For the life of her, she couldn't figure out why Keilor was wasting officers to guard her when even Rihlia only had regular soldiers. They weren't exactly models of discipline, either. More than once she'd walked out and found them at a game of dice. She shrugged it off. They were a likable pair, and they'd gone a long way towards helping her to relax around the Haunt.

She raised her brows at them. "So, when are you two going to get a real job?" Raziel snorted but didn't move. Isfael gave her a toothy and decidedly unnerving grin. Girding her loins, she said, "Hey, I know you guys aren't servants, but I've got something heavy here I need to get rid of. Could one of you give me a hand?"

The pair followed her into the room and she propped her hands on her hips again with a grimace. "Can you believe this mess?" she asked with disgust. "The man runs an entire army and probably tortures his recruits with inspections and stuff, but he can't even be bothered to pick up his socks."

"Rank has its privileges."

Startled, Jasmine whirled around and stared. Isfael and Raziel had shifted into human form. Isfael was uglier than sin, and she thought with a flash of chagrin that the poor guy looked much better covered in hair. Raziel was unremarkable in appearance, except for his piercing blue eyes. Both of them nodded at her with respect.

"Congratulations on your new match," Raziel said, and she realized he was the one who had spoken. "Keilor is a good friend of ours, and we wish his new wife every happiness."

"Happiness and a long life," Isfael seconded.

Jasmine frowned lightly. "Well, I don't know about the long life, but I'm definitely going for happiness. Thank you."

Isfael unclipped a pouch from his belt, flipped up the cover and extracted a folded belt and a black laser gun. He presented both to her with a toothy smile. "We thought Keilor's wife ought to have her own gun. This way, if he gets out of line, you can bring him to heel."

Jasmine laughed and took the holstered weapon. "Thank you," she told them, and tried it on for size. It fit very well. When she looked up again, they had shifted back. She blinked and shivered. "You guys have got to stop doing that."

Shaking her head, she pointed four fingers of her right hand at the mattress, thumb folded in, and then jerked her thumb over her shoulder, indicating that it had to go. The guys each grabbed an end and took it with them out the door to dump it in the hallway.

It was hard to know which of the scattered papers lying around might be important, so she just gathered them into one neat stack and put them on the freshly scrubbed table. Eyeing the crusty dishes, she decided reinforcements were called for, and summoned a maid to attend to them while she gathered up the scattered laundry. There was too much to do all at once, so she loaded it into the washing machine in increments.

Time passed quickly. She had the tub half scrubbed when Keilor found her.

CHAPTER 21

"What are you doing?" he asked with a frown. "The ceremony is in half an hour." He was already dressed in black leather armor and had his dark hair pulled back with a silver clip. A sleeveless, midnight blue robe of velvet trimmed in silver added an air of magnificence. It was open in front and held together with a thick silver chain. There were sparkling blue stones at every other link.

He looked ready to dazzle, and very impatient.

"Oh, no!" Jasmine popped out of the tub in alarm. She dismissed the maid and tossed her rag in the dirty laundry pile. She sprinted for the door, snagging her wedding gift on the way. Keilor was forced into an undignified lope to keep up with her. Since she was well in hand, her bodyguards followed at a more sedate pace.

"Bath!" Jasmine ordered the moment she stepped in the door, wishing her room came equipped with a shower. Why was it cleaning always made the cleanee dirty? She stripped a little self-consciously and took her frustration out on her husband. "You could have found me sooner."

He leaned against the armoire, unabashedly enjoying the view. "How was I to know you would be so enticed by your wifely duties you would forget your own wedding ceremony?"

Crouched in tub, she froze with soap in hand. "It's Rihlia and Jayems' ceremony...isn't it?"

He raised a brow. "There's been a change of plans. We will also take our public vows today." His expression brooked no defiance.

Jasmine remembered the soap and slowly began to use it. "I don't know anything about Haunt ceremonies. Shouldn't we take a little more time to…?" She trailed off at his quelling look. The man could be spooky when he chose.

He disappeared into her wardrobe. Recalled to the need for haste, she quickly finished up, wrung out the end of her hair and toweled off. Keilor emerged from the closet just as she wrapped the towel around herself, a dress she'd never seen draped over his arm. He held it up for her inspection.

The dress itself was a simple black velvet sheath, long enough to reach her ankles but slit to just above the knee for ease of movement. Two silver clips held the three-quarter inch straps to the bodice. The outer robe was a smaller replica of his midnight velvet. Instead of the rearing stags she could now see embroidered into the edges of his clothes, hers had silver leaves and vines with small flowers. In place of snarling volti heads, the chain that clasped her robe had dragonflies. The material felt heavenly against her fingers.

Touched, she looked at him. "You had this made for me." And some time ago, by the craftsmanship. She wanted to ask when he'd commissioned it, but her throat closed up.

He said nothing, but his eyes shone.

She rose up on her toes and clasped her hands around his neck to demonstrate her thanks. His arms slid around her, and their kiss deepened. His hand fisted on the back of her towel and he pulled it from her, leaving her nude. Warm hands drifted down her back and settled possessively on her derriere, kneading and lifting. With a groan, he broke away, and she could tell it cost him much

to step back. "We have to go." Cupping her face, he gave
her a careful kiss and handed her the gown. While she
dressed he moved to stare out the window, giving them
both a chance to cool off.

Jasmine finished, then looked around. "You forgot
the underwear."

Her husband grinned. "It wasn't an oversight."

She rolled her eyes and moved to the wardrobe door,
but he was there before her, blocking her way.

"Keilor! Move." He didn't budge an inch, and her
face flamed. "I am *not* wandering around in public with no
panties."

For a moment he didn't move, gauging the strength
of her conviction. With a disappointed sigh, he stepped
aside. "We really must do something about this shyness of
yours," he complained as she went after her
unmentionables.

Her only reply was a muffled snort.

Deciding to leave her hair down in the interest of
speed, Jasmine brushed it quickly and stashed the brush
back in the armoire.

Keilor stepped behind her as she closed the mirrored
doors. He placed a diadem of linked prismatic silver
dragonflies and blue topaz, amethyst and sea colored gems
on her brow. Her eyes widened in alarm. It was by far the
most beautiful, extravagant gift anyone had ever given her.
"Keilor, no! I—"

He placed one finger on her lips and admonished, "I
am your husband. I can well afford to lavish gifts on my
beloved wife. Would you deny me this pleasure?"

Tears pricked her eyes. "But—"

He flashed her a wicked smile and pulled her against
him. "Of course, I had to sell my favorite stag and
indenture myself to the jeweler to afford these lovely
gems, but—"

She poked him in the ribs, trying to hide her smile under a pout. "It was very sweet. Please don't do it again."

He took her hand in his, and she felt something slide onto her left hand, over her ring finger. "As you wish," he agreed, and then took her hand before she could look and dragged her out the door.

"Keilor!"

The ceremony was blessed by a stocky priest in shiny brown robes. Performed outdoors on a raised marble dais shaded by a tile roof, it was attended by a crowd of hundreds.

Somehow she survived standing in front of a crowd of strangers to exchange vows with Keilor. By the time they were done with the simple ceremony she was glad to leave the dais and descend to the lawn to mingle with the guests.

It was the first time she'd been exposed to a large gathering since her arrival in the Dark Lands, and it was a bit dizzying. Brightly dressed women and black clad men she didn't know wished Keilor well and looked her over with curiosity. Some of the women were overly friendly in a manner that smacked of social climbing, and Jasmine instinctively retreated behind polite reserve with them. Others looked on her coldly, though none seemed to have the gall to cut her with Keilor at her side, and he never left her, not for a moment. Everything went fine.

Until Yesande.

They stood behind an enormous ice sculpture of a battling stag and a volti, enjoying a lull in between well-wishers. Most of the guests had gathered around the heavily laden buffet tables.

"This must have been Jayems' idea. I know Rihlia didn't pick it out," Jasmine said, stroking the stag's icy flank and admiring the frozen flow of muscle. Somebody had talent.

"Actually, it was a contribution from my clan for the wedding," a woman's voice said. A tall blond with eyes of nearly white blue stepped behind the sculpture. "I created it."

An oath sounded to Jasmine's left and she turned to see Keilor bare his teeth in a snarl.

The woman smiled with amusement. "Hello, Keilor. I almost didn't recognize you with your clothes on."

Gold fire leapt into his eyes and for a moment Jasmine feared that her new husband was going to kill the woman on the spot.

The stranger had no such fears. "Lady Yesande," she introduced herself, inclining her head. Soulless eyes perused Jasmine from head to foot. "You need no introduction, Lady Jasmine...and Keilor and I are already well acquainted."

"Past tense," Keilor said in a voice that could have crushed rocks.

Yesande smiled, or her lips did. "And now you are mated to a charmer. Interesting choice. I wonder how you dare it." She glanced at the crowd they were drawing and said with lazy nonchalance, "Given that her mother was a prostitute."

Keilor took a step toward her, but Jasmine grabbed his arm. Deep currents were flowing here, and she sensed Yesande would relish an attack. Something was wrong besides the obvious, and she was afraid Keilor might be too enraged to see it.

Yesande glanced at Jasmine's hand and asked, "Do you have any idea just how much the Haunt despise whores, Lady Jasmine? Almost as much as we used to hate charmers."

The crowd stirred, and Jasmine took a deep breath. "They're not exactly favored by your average human, either, myself included." With her peripheral vision she saw Raziel and Isfael casually position themselves near enough to be helpful in a hurry if need be. Mathin caught her eye from the crowd and held it, a silent warning in his eyes. *Tread with caution.*

Faking a calm she didn't feel, Jasmine looped her arm around Keilor's waist and said, "Keilor isn't worried about that, though. He told me last night he'd kill me if he ever caught me with someone else, and I believe him."

Keilor looked at her in shock as the crowd murmured. The very idea of a man killing his mate...

Feeling reckless, Jasmine added smugly, "Besides, once you've had the best, why bother with the rest? I'm holding on to this wildcat. And speaking of which..." She sent her scandalized husband a provocative look, "...don't we have a wedding night to celebrate?"

"I'm holding on to this wildcat?" Keilor asked incredulously once they reached her room.

"It worked," she said tartly. She was still miffed at the whole scene with his old girlfriend, and she was more than happy to take it out on him. "What I want to know is how she found out about my mother." She took off the diadem and set it on an end table. "It's not exactly common knowledge here."

"I didn't tell her, if that's what you're thinking." Keilor took off his robe and tossed the expensive garment over a chair. His new wife gave him a dirty look and took it to the closet. When she emerged she was wearing a robe with a glimpse of silver showing at the bottom of the vee. Several pieces of black armor littered the couch.

Jasmine put her hands on her hips and glared at him. "Unless you're itching for a fight, buddy, I suggest you take that junk and put it in the closet. You're not turning my room into a pig pen."

He wasn't thrilled with her bossiness, but he did collect his gear and stash it in the closet. He came out wearing loose white trousers that tied at the top and nothing else. It was a terribly distracting tactic to use when she was trying to fight with him.

Striving to remember she was still annoyed, she crossed her arms and sat down on the couch, leaving him plenty of room at the other end.

Keilor took in her mulishness and knew it for what it was. He chose to attack her jealousy with direct action. Ignoring her mood, he stretched out on the couch and placed his head in her lap. "I don't dwell on the men you knew before me, love," he told her gravely. "I expect the same courtesy from you,"

"None of them are likely to rake you over the coals in public." Her eyes narrowed. "Or mention how I looked without my clothes."

Several heartbeats passed in silence. "I did not go to her willingly, Jasmine." His voice roughened as he sat up. "She drugged me." Seeing her horror, he explained, "Libran. Sweet Surrender." A muscle twitched in his jaw. "I believe you've heard of it."

Someone had given him the aphrodisiac that had almost killed her? She placed one hand on his thigh and watched him soberly.

"She took an interest in me when I was still young, but I despised her." His nose wrinkled in remembered distaste. "Besides being unattractive, she had...has, twisted tastes."

Self-disgust hardened his voice. "I was young and inexperienced at the time, and her clan caught me by surprise. When I woke up, I was chained and already drugged. Easy prey."

Jasmine laid her head against his shoulder. When he hurt, she hurt.

He wrapped his arm around her. "I'd likely still be there if Mathin hadn't poured an antidote down my throat and given me a blade."

She rubbed her head against him, her breathing harsh. "Love…" He felt her swallow. "When was this?"

"Thirty years ago," he answered without thinking.

She sat up, startled. "Thirty—how old *are* you?"

Instead of answering, he kissed her. When she was properly befuddled, he told her, "So now you know you have no reason to be jealous."

"No," she agreed, breathless, but still angry with Yesande. "But the next time I see her, I hope I have a gun in my hand."

He kissed her, and a little of the chill left. "You would fight on my behalf?"

"Well…" She forgot whatever it was she'd meant to say as he eased her back to the couch, a hot promise in his eyes. "Wait!" she protested, and placed a hand on his chest. "I almost forgot—" His lips touched hers, and for a breathless moment she nearly forgot what was so urgent. Before he could completely blank her mind, she forced him to let her up.

His expression stated her reprieve was temporary.

She fumbled with the black cord that held her dragonfly pendant and finally got the knot loose. Straddling his lap, she placed it around his neck like a choker, knotting the cord just below the bead that prevented it from slipping off. The black beaded tail trailed down his spine. She smiled, pleased. "Now we've both given each other something unique of our own."

He fingered the pendant. "What did I give you?" he asked, thinking she would speak of the jewelry or clothes, and feeling rather self-conscious and silly with a symbol he was used to associating with her femininity on his neck.

With a shy but satisfied smile, she answered, "Well, you were a virgin the first time we—"

He sat up so fast he nearly dumped her from his lap. "A virgin!" Highly insulted, he asked incredulously, "How in the name of all that's holy did you come to that conclusion?"

She squirmed. "Well, Rihlia—" she stopped, confused. "You said yourself you'd never done it."

"I'd never mated," he said firmly. "But I can assure you I've had more than my share of lovers. I am definitely not a virgin."

"But—" Before she could say anything else to further insult him, he kissed her, stole her words and her silly thoughts. If anyone had been close to a virgin last night, it had been her, and he was more than willing to demonstrate the gaps in their knowledge.

He broke their kiss just long enough to promise with a wicked smile, "When tonight is over, you'll never have cause to question my experience again, wife." Then he settled more comfortably between her thighs and proceeded to blow her mind.

It was several seconds before the pounding at the door registered.

Keilor sat up, cursing the fact that he'd told Isfael and Raziel to take the night off and enjoy the feast. Both Haunt were likely curled up with a woman by now, and he hadn't bothered posting any other guards. After all, Jasmine had him now.

"It had better be a fire or a flood!" he snarled. "Who comes?"

"Knightin," came the instant reply.

Keilor got up and headed for the door. Knightin would not bother him now unless the matter was urgent. He flung the door wide. "What is—"

The Haunt at the door gutted him.

CHAPTER 22

She was so cold.

Jasmine opened her eyes as dawn broke over the mountain camp. She started to shake. She remembered everything. Curled up in her bedroll, she endured the burning tears and grief as she mourned for her love.

Rocks crunched by her head and cloth rustled as someone knelt before her. Yesande stared at her dispassionately. "You'll get over it," she said. "Where we're going, I can supply you with many men to please you. You need never settle for one again."

Jasmine snarled at her, and she smiled. "Such a brave little charmer. No wonder Keilor found you amusing. Don't worry, pet." She traced the curve of Jasmine's ear and Jasmine recoiled. "No one is going to harm you. You're far too valuable." She stood up and called to the Haunt with them, "Break camp. We need to be out of here before Jayems' trackers find us."

Jasmine scrambled up and tried not to think about who had dressed her. At least they'd chosen pants and a tunic.

She'd been drugged, and much of last night was a blur. She pulled on her boots, which were close at hand. She wouldn't find a way to escape lying on her back, and danged if she wanted to give the creepy Yesande or anyone else, ideas. After all, what other use could they have for a charmer?

No one touched her, though, during the seventeen hellish days it took to reach Yesande's citadel.

Stags had never been Jasmine's favorite animals, and she liked them even less after riding double all day, every day, with Yesande for over two weeks. The hide wore off the inside of her thighs and her backside, and she could hardly walk for the first three days. After a week she started to saunter like John Wayne, and she was certain she'd never be able to stroll with her legs together again.

She only had one question for Yesande in the entire time. "How old are you?" she'd asked as they rode along a ridge on the third day.

Yesande had looked at her over her shoulder in inquiry. "Sixty-seven."

Jasmine had said nothing else.

"We'll find her," Mathin promised Keilor.

Keilor closed his eyes and fought against the drugs. "If Yesande has hurt her…." he said, his voice dark with fury and pain. He should be the one going. Instead he was taking up space in a hospital bed while his enemies ran off with his wife.

"Don't worry, we'll bag her and Knightin, too," Raziel promised him. "He made a grave mistake when he splattered your guts all over the floor and neglected to take your head. You'll be on your feet and ready to rip his heart out by the time we get back."

"Jasmine, it's Mathin."

Her eyes moved under her half-shut lids, but she didn't move.

It had taken weeks to track Yesande to this remote citadel, and nearly a day to convince his sister to let him have a go at the charmer. Yesande's medics had yet to isolate the pheromone responsible for her charmer abilities, and they'd begun feeding her drugs to increase her libido in the hopes of increasing production.

Unfortunately, the side affects were hostility and aggression, fed by her refusal to have anything to do with the men Yesande sent her to slake her thirst. Since the men were all unmated, none of them could force the issue, either. All Jasmine had to do was to tell them not to touch her, or to go away, and they went.

Yesande was encouraged by that, since she liked to watch the encounters, and enjoyed seeing the power she planned to make her own.

Still, the charmer's stubbornness annoyed her, and she'd finally agreed to let Mathin try his luck.

Blessing the fact that he was Yesande's brother for the first time in his life, since it allowed him to proceed without an audience, he lifted the charmer's eyelid and peered into one dilated pupil. "Jasmine!"

With a snarl Jasmine clawed at his face. Just as fast, she retreated to huddle in the corner of her cot. He clamped a hand over her mouth before she could order him away. Knowing Yesande was probably monitoring their conversation, he put his lips to her ear.

"Wouldn't you like to leave this padded cell and go with me, Dragonfly?" She froze, and he lowered his hand.

Wary eyes watched him through sweat dampened bangs. "Keilor calls me that."

"Yes." He held her gaze. "He *calls* you that." He hoped her drugged mind would comprehend what he said.

It didn't.

When he rose to his knees on the bed to block what he was doing from possible watching eyes, she shoved at him, her eyes rolling. "No! I want Keilor, only Keilor!"

There was no point trying to reason with her. She was too drugged to understand.

Mentally swearing a filthy oath, he clamped his hand on her jaw and forced her mouth open. He squirted in one of the antidotes the medics had sent with him, just in case. To hide her sputtering and to prevent her from spitting it out, he kissed her ruthlessly, clashing their teeth and bruising both their mouths.

The kiss revolted him, not because he didn't find the woman attractive but because he'd never forced his attentions on anyone. He didn't relish starting with the wife of a friend, even if it was the only way he could think to hide his actions and force her to swallow.

When he was certain enough medicine had gotten down to clear her brain, he let her go. She shrank away with a cry and hid her face in the corner, sobbing.

Pretending to reconsider his strategy, he used his thumb to wiped the blood from his lip were she'd bitten him. He waited for her mind to clear and his body to stop shaking with rebellion.

Her mind cleared first.

In moments her eyes had opened and she looked at him with the cold stare of a wounded cobra. Before she could tell him to go fry in hell, he grabbed her hair, yanked her to him and hissed in her ear, "Your husband sent me, you idiot. He's alive, and if you ever hope to see him again, you'd better play along." He allowed her to pull back. She watched him, openly distrustful, but said nothing.

He figured silence was the best cooperation he was likely to get under the circumstances. He pulled her to her feet, went to the door, and called for the guards to open it.

Yesande was on the other side, flanked by ten of her Haunt, and she was not happy. "You raped her," she said, taking one look at his blood on Jasmine's lips. Her eyes narrowed, and she informed him with cold intent, "She is no good to me mated, fool."

He pulled Jasmine in front of him and grabbed her throat before his sister could order her Haunt to attack.

"She comes with me or you lose her, Yesande." He was not failing Keilor, not after making it this far.

Smirking, Yesande chided him, "Come now, brother. Cease these games. You may have forced the charmer to spread her legs and mate with you—not that I blame you; I agree something had to be done—but you'll not kill her."

Mathin broke Jasmine's arm.

Even Yesande recoiled a step at her shriek.

"Still think I won't kill her?" he asked savagely, trying not retch at her gasping sobs. She deserved better than this.

Yesande took a step back, pallor leaching her already pale skin. "Father's madness," she whispered with horror. "It did carry to you."

He allowed his eyes to gleam golden. This time the Haunt stepped back as well. "Go," she told him hoarsely, too afraid to stand in his way now.

He drew his sword and dragged the moaning Jasmine out of there. No one got in his way.

"What happened to her?" Raziel demanded when they reached the stags.

Mathin touched the sides of Jasmine's neck over her carotid arteries and cut off the blood flow to her brain. It put her out of her misery for the grueling ride ahead. "I broke her arm," he said grimly, and handed her up to Raziel.

Eyes wide, Raziel said, "If we live through this, Keilor is going to kill you."

"He'll have to stand in line," Mathin answered, as angry Haunt swarmed out of the citadel. He spurred his stag for the hills.

It took them nearly two days of reckless dashes and miserable damp as they hid from Yesande's soldiers, but they gained a lead on the other Haunt. By then Jasmine's arm had been set, and she was taking painkillers, but the drugs coming out of her system combined with their grueling pace took their toll.

Humans were never meant to keep pace with a Haunt.

"If we don't do something soon, she's not going to make it back to Keilor," Raziel said quietly as they ate. Jasmine lay on a pallet on one of the higher pieces of swampland. Thin insect netting shrouded her from head to toe, but they could still see her pallor through the veil. Her breath sounded harsh over the calls of insects and swamp birds.

Mathin looked off through the raised tree roots to where Isfael stood guard in the deepening gloom. He was in Haunt, and somewhat protected from the insects by his thick fur.

An insect bit Mathin and he slapped at it, coming away with a hand covered in glowing bug goo. "I know. That's why we're going to start looking for a symbiont."

Raziel dug a shred of giant swamp snail out of his teeth with a sliver of wood. "What's that?"

"A creature that lives in these swamps. They don't have much use for Haunt, but I think a symbiont may be just what our patient needs."

She was dying.

As Jasmine lay next to the giant tree, she found she didn't care. Mathin had gone off to hunt, leaving Isfael and Raziel to guard her. She didn't want him to come back. When he did, they would leave again. Riding hurt.

She was so very tired, and she just needed to rest.

She missed Keilor. Maybe, she thought fuzzily, if she went to sleep she might dream of him again. Her eyes began to close, and she almost thought she saw him, somewhere in her mind, beckoning…

"Here you go," A rude, raspy voice intruded, and Keilor vanished like so much smoke. She opened her eyes and scowled weakly at Mathin, who knelt beside her with a pouch. The pouch moved.

Thinking of the various forms of swamp life he'd forced down her throat, she informed him with as much strength as she could muster, "If that's dinner, you can have my share."

"It's not dinner." He reached into the pouch and extracted a ball of liquid silver. Isfael and Raziel watched with interest. "This, my cranky little charge, is your new best friend."

The blob was about the size of a baseball and moved like a worm, stretching out and up as if scenting the air. Suddenly the creature stiffened, and its "head" slowly rotated in her direction. It reared back, as if in surprise.

Then it zapped onto her.

Jasmine screamed as the creature landed on her chest with a big warm splat and spread out into a sheet of blood warm silver. With her undamaged arm and hand she frantically tried to grab it and pull it off, but the silver flowed through her fingers and eagerly slid down inside her sling. A tingling buzz spread from the site of the break, and then up her arm and over her body. By the time it reached her head and buzzed through her brain she was on her feet, something she hadn't been able to do unassisted for twenty-four hours.

"Mathin!" she screeched, as she felt the wave move down her body to the soles of her feet and back up to settle around her forearms. "Get it off!"

"Why?" He smiled, watching as she franticly tore off her sling and tried to pull the happy symbiont off her forearms. The symbiont now resembled a pair of silver filigree bracelets covering her forearms from wrists to elbow.

"It'll suck the life out of me!"

"No, it will suck the life *into* you," he corrected as he saw her face flush with healthy color. Now he just might be able to get her back to his friend in one piece.

It couldn't happen fast enough for him.

Keilor wiped the sweat from his brow with the back of his hand and sheathed his sword. Perspiration slicked his entire body, and he grabbed a towel to swipe at his chest and flawless abdomen.

He cursed the lingering weakness. The towel dragged on Jasmine's dragonfly choker, and he flung the cloth away with an oath, assailed by painful longing.

It had been over a month since he'd sent others after his wife.

"You're going to damage yourself again if you keep this up," Jayems observed from where he lounged in the doorway to Jasmine's room. Keilor spared him a glance full of self-disgust but said nothing.

Jayems wandered into the room, pausing to pet Casanova. The independent little villi was the only one not concerned about his mistress. "We know they got her out."

"With a broken arm and a bloody mouth!" Keilor snarled.

Jayems winced, remembering his cousin's reaction to that bit of news. Mathin would be lucky if Keilor didn't break every bone in his body when next he saw him. "She was alive. Raziel and Isfael are with them."

"Small comfort," Keilor answered morosely. He looked at but did not see Jasmine's lemon tree.

Jayems froze. "You don't think she would betray you?" he asked in amazement. "She's not the kind of woman to take her promises lightly, and despite the ugly rumors, I don't believe she'd dishonor you." Thanks to spies, they'd had some intelligence on Yesande's doings at the Citadel, none of it encouraging. They knew Jasmine had been drugged with aphrodisiacs, knew about Yesande's experiments.

"It's not that," Keilor said, but his words were half-hearted.

Jayems inclined his head with a touch of temper. "If you think her association with Mathin is likely to foster affection, think again. He can be charming on the surface, but you of all people ought to know that prolonged contact with Mathin is more likely to drive Jasmine into fits of rage, not passion. I've no doubt she's counting the days until she's free of him."

Keilor sighed, a little cheered. The grim warrior in him still wished to brace for the worst, but perhaps it was time to exercise some faith in his woman, as a husband should. It would help if he knew where they were, so he could meet them half way.

This unending waiting was getting to him.

CHAPTER 23

Jasmine pulled at her new "bracelets" and sent Mathin another dirty look. It had been two days now, and they still couldn't get the symbiont off her, not that anyone cared. After all, they weren't the ones feeling a pulsing, breathing, snake-like *thing* occasionally move on their arms.

Mathin ignored her. He'd merely shrugged away her complaints and pointed out that the creature had healed her. It also continued to supply her blood with extra oxygen in exchange for her carbon dioxide and bodily wastes, making her capable of sustaining the pace of the others. Her personal distress was of no interest to him.

She fingered the pistol Raziel and Isfael had given her for a wedding gift. They'd brought it with them at Keilor's request. Even gravely injured, he'd thought of her.

It was a comfort to know he was alive. His friends assured her that Haunt healed quickly. They were able to sustain incredible amounts of damage, even wounds that would kill a human.

She gazed wistfully in the direction of home, wishing she were out of the foggy, muggy swamp. She couldn't see a whole lot in the deepening gloom, and finally gave it up. She needed to apply some more bug repellent, anyway.

Strands of greasy hair brushed her face as she squatted down. She grimaced and pulled out the tie to tighten her ponytail. "If we don't get a bath soon,

Yesande's Haunt are going to smell us coming a mile away."

"You're welcome to take your chances in the swamp," Raziel teased.

Jasmine shuddered. No one was that desperate. Tugging the end of her hair over her shoulder, she began to finger comb the knotted ends, scowling as the split ends slid through her fingers. Apparently her symbiont didn't do hair. "I need a haircut," she grumbled.

"I have a knife," Raziel offered, reaching for it as if she would really use it.

"No thanks," she answered, warding him off with one hand. The last thing she needed was the mess a blade would make of her hair. "What I really need is a sharp pair of scissors, but since we don't—" she broke off, staring as the symbiont on her right forearm slithered down into her hand. It coalesced into pair of scissors joined to her wrist by a thin loop of liquid metal. "Hey," she whispered in astonishment. "Maybe this little guy is good for something after all."

Mathin rolled his eyes. "Just like a woman. Save her life, and she snubs you. Provide her with grooming aides, and you're her friend for life."

The symbiont turned out to be handier than a Swiss army knife. All Jasmine had to do was think of what she wanted, and the symbiont became that thing. Any manner of utensil or hand tool was suddenly available to Jasmine at a thought, including cups and needles. It even formed into a string for cat's cradle.

"There might be some defensive capabilities to this creature," Raziel observed. Isfael, who remained almost constantly in Haunt, signed something back, and Raziel raised a brow. "I agree. A knife or a garrote might prove invaluable against an unsuspecting foe, provided you knew what you were doing. What do you think? Would you like to test your new friend's capabilities?"

Jasmine, who'd caught some of what Isfael had been saying, grimaced. The idea of using the symbiont for disemboweling or stabbing was not appealing, but considering what they might yet face, maybe she'd better get over her aversion. Her life might just depend on it.

So Jasmine learned to kill. Whenever they had time to stop during the nights, her warrior escort taught her new ways to maim and butcher, silence and scavenge, or made her practice what she did know.

She soon discovered Keilor had been right; compared to him, her new instructors were merciless, inflexible, and exacting. They never deliberately hurt her, and physically they were more careful with her hide than they were with each other, but she did accumulate her share of bruises, mostly from learning to fall and roll over uneven ground.

None of them cared if she got angry, swore at them, or cried. As far as they were concerned, she was now a warrior in training, and she could just get over it.

Wonder of wonders, she did.

The symbiont was a big help. Not only did it thrive by absorbing the damage to her person, it lent her a never before known speed and agility. It did nothing for her strength, but her stamina almost matched that of the Haunt, and that was not a small thing.

No amount of grueling exercise could take her mind off of her husband for long, though. With every day that went by her longing grew, until she dared not think of him while riding lest her seat on the saddle—usually behind Mathin or Raziel—become an aching torture.

Oddly enough, none of her companions seemed to be affected by the increased levels of pheromone she knew she emitted at those times. Wondering if her marriage had something to do with it, she finally asked Mathin about it.

He snorted with ill humor. "Isfael merely remains in Haunt, where one never feels the desire to mate, and he can still scent danger. As for Raziel and I..." He scowled.

"We've been taking a sinus blocker since we reached you. We can't smell or taste a blasted thing while using it."

Jasmine's eyes widened. "Is that why you've been such a jackass?"

Raziel roared with laughter. "I don't know what that is, but just the way you said it... It's got to be good."

"A male beast of burden, known for its stubborn refusal to cooperate and its nasty temper," Jasmine supplied.

Raziel grinned wickedly at the glowering Mathin. "A jackass," he repeated, smirking. "I'll have to remember that. However, I'm afraid our Mathin can't blame the sinus blockers for his disposition. You ought to know by now he's just naturally a foul tempered beast."

Mathin curled his lip at him.

Almost two months to the day Jasmine had been taken, they finally came within a days' ride of Jayems' citadel. Instead of growing relaxed as they entered the forest of fern and towering redwoods, however, her escort increased their vigilance. All traces of levity ceased, as did superfluous chatter. Everyone was on the alert for a last minute betrayal.

They needn't have worried.

Within minutes of entering the forest, volti joined them, running just inside the forest beside the bridle path. Jasmine felt a strong sense of deja vu, but instead of fear, this time she felt exhilaration and a sense of homecoming. Only one thing worried her. "Do you think Keilor will be happy to see me?" she whispered.

Three heads, two in Haunt, whipped around to stare at her. "I can't believe you just asked that," Mathin finally got out. Giving her one last suspicious look, as if wondering if she'd left her wits somewhere in the swamps, he went back to scanning the trees for assassins. Shaking their heads, Raziel and Isfael did the same.

Well. That would teach her to ask a man to boost her confidence.

Her tension increased the closer they got to home, and she kept forcing herself to relax her legs from around the barrel of the stag, lest it run. Still damp from her recent bath, her hair flowed loose down her shoulders and began to wave from the wind of their passage.

"Do you think we could go a little faster?" she asked. The men ignored her, and she slouched, sulking. "I could almost get off and run there faster," she muttered, but nobody listened.

Two hours from the citadel, Isfael and Raziel signaled they heard riders, coming fast. Excited, Jasmine leaned to the side, watching the road. Would Keilor be with them?

He was.

"Keilor!" she shouted happily as he thundered into view on a sweating stag. She levered up on Raziel's shoulders and knelt on his halted stag's back to get a better look in a way that must have been very annoying for Raziel. Grinning like a fool, she waved to her husband, almost losing her seat in the process but for Raziel reaching back to steady her.

Keilor snatched her from Raziel's stag at a trot and seated her so she straddled him. He proceeded to kiss her as if about to ravish her there and then. With eager lips and hungry hands, she told him she wouldn't mind.

"I missed you," she gasped, snatching some air before the dizziness he caused overwhelmed her.

He groaned, pulled her head back and told her with his volcanic kiss that he'd missed her, too.

Wrapping her arms around him in a fierce hug, she sobbed against his neck, "I'd thought you were dead."

"Never," he assured her fervently, holding her close as he stroked her hair. "I'm right here, Dragonfly."

At his use of her nickname, the tears came in earnest, and it was some minutes before she even noticed they were heading for the citadel at fast clip. By then Keilor had switched her position so that she sat curled in his lap, supported by his arms. "I missed you," she said again, giving him a hug.

His arms tightened around her. "Good," he answered with fierce satisfaction. "I was beginning to wonder if you were ever coming home when the news came you had entered the forest." His jaw tightened, and he shot a glare of pending retribution at Mathin over her head.

Mathin inclined his head coolly but said nothing.

"How is your arm? We had heard it was broken," he asked with concern. There was no telling what she had suffered on her journey, and the first thing he intended to do was to have her examined by a medic. If Mathin had let anything happen to her…

"Oh!" Jasmine squirmed upright and unwittingly bumped against his groin, forcing a grunt from him. "Sorry," she said, but she couldn't help looking down with a smile. Keilor was as eager to be with her as she was to be with him. The first chance she got…

Forcing her attention away from him, she held up her wrists so that he could see the silver twined around her forearms. "Mathin got me a symbiont that fixed it. See?"

His reaction was not what she'd expected.

Eyes widening, Keilor bared his teeth in rage and snarled at Mathin, "As if we did not have enough problems! By what right did you do this to her? How dare you use my wife to cause trouble?"

Mathin's rough voice was glacial. "She was dying, maggot brain. Had I not 'caused trouble' you would not be holding her now."

Worried, Jasmine's gaze swung between the two men. "What's wrong? It didn't hurt me, Keilor."

"You've done nothing, love. Be still," Keilor told her, and said to Mathin with barely restrained violence, "She would not have been in that condition if you hadn't botched your job in the first place. What kind of savage—"

Mathin's eyes ignited gold and he leaned towards Keilor with a curl to his lip. "I am not invincible, any more than you are," he said in warning. "Could you have fought off Yesande's garrison and guaranteed you could have brought a sick woman through unscathed? I think not. I traded a small hurt for her life, and a complication for the same. You could not be there to see to her, so do not judge me."

Before Keilor could say more, Jasmine clamped a hand over his mouth. "It was *my* arm, Keilor, and I forgive him. Maybe there was another way, but I wouldn't have gotten out of there on my own. I'm just glad—" She choked up, fighting to beat back the remembered terror. "The drugs were making me…" She closed her eyes, feeling again the nightmare images. "I wanted only you, and I kept saying that, and making them go away, but I was losing my mind, and beginning to see you, and if he hadn't—" A tremor wracked her body, and he pulled her close, stroking her back soothingly. "Please don't fight. Just take me home. I just want to go home."

Out of respect for Jasmine's feelings, Keilor and Mathin ignored each other for the rest of the journey. They would resolve matters between themselves at another time, where Jasmine couldn't see it. In the meantime, Keilor wanted to know everything that had happened to Jasmine while she was away.

Tucking a stray bit of her hair behind her ear, he asked, "So what did you think of the swamps?" He surveyed her ragged tunic and badly patched pants. "They don't seem to have agreed with you."

Rolling her eyes, she nevertheless sat up, glad to share her adventures with him. "What's not to like? Eating mystery creatures—I swear, if anyone says the word escargot to me, ever again…" She grimaced. "These guys might be handy with a sword, Keilor, but the next time, could you send someone who can cook?"

He grinned. There would never be a next time, but he wouldn't interrupt his wife while she was being entertaining.

Looking stoic, she said without enthusiasm, "I now know about twenty-five different edible plants that grow in the swamp and how to find and prepare them, but not one of them tastes worth a darn. It doesn't matter anyway, though, because after Mathin gets a hold of them, they all come out tasting like salt."

Disgusted, she went on, "Finding clean water is a chore in itself, and you can almost forget about taking a bath—not that I could, with three guys constantly under foot, and none of them willing to leave me alone for even five minutes."

"We turned our backs," Raziel, who'd shifted back to normal, protested vehemently what was obviously a sore subject. "Your woman has a bizarre fixation with modesty, Keilor. Even in the middle of nowhere, without a stranger in sight, she insists that all present turn their backs just so she can wash! I've never seen anything so peculiar."

"Yes," Mathin chimed in, forgetting for a moment his truce of silence. "And the one time she saw poor Raziel washing in the morning she screamed and threw a tantrum that nearly brought Yesande's hunters down on our heads." He glowered. "We had to ride hard that day to avoid them."

"Oh, yeah?" Jasmine countered, deciding to air her own grievances. "At least I wasn't the one who nearly got us eaten by that water snake." Eyes huge, she told Keilor, "It was as big around as a barrel, and he insisted after it swam by it wouldn't come back for some time and it was safe to cross." Disgusted, she said, "Well, he was right, *it* didn't, but he hadn't counted on the one that was following it, just two minutes behind. I've never been so scared in my life!"

By the time they reached the citadel, Jasmine had managed to paint her companions as heroes and friends using unflattering words and grumbled complaints.

Keilor began to feel a little jealous. Maybe taking his wife to the medics would be the second thing he'd do.

As they approached the busy stables with a jingle of bits and the huffing of hard working stags, Jasmine finally remembered to ask, "How is Rihlia?"

"Pregnant," he answered succinctly, leaping off and lifting her down. Suddenly boneless, she stared at him, and he grinned. "Don't look so surprised. Jayems has been working hard on that particular project since the moment they mated."

Jasmine blushed and allowed him to take her hand and tow her toward the citadel. Rihlia was pregnant? She was going to be an aunt! She was so preoccupied, she barely noticed where they were going in such a rush. Keilor opened the door to her room just as she asked, "When? How—"

Slamming the door closed with one booted foot and locking it, Keilor shut off the flow of words with his hungry kiss. His loving was fast and needy, but then so was hers. He, however, was quicker at stripping her. Her hands kept getting distracted by the sight and intoxicating feel of his bare arms and naked chest.

They didn't make it to the bed.

CHAPTER 24

Jasmine was slick and ready, but she cried out and stiffened as her husband slid in fast. Instantly he stopped. "What's wrong?"

She ducked her head. "Um, it's been a while."

Keilor cocked his head and moved a fraction in experiment. His eyes flared. "You're a little tight." A shimmer obscured his vision, and he eased off his wife, untangling his pants from his ankles to hide his reaction.

A dark part of him had writhed with fear that while she'd been away from him, she'd learn to scorn him for his failure to protect her and turn to another as more worthy. This physical evidence of her loyalty both humbled and shamed him. She deserved so much more—a man who wouldn't shame her.

Since he could never tell her his thoughts, he showed her instead. With infinite tenderness he kissed her and carried her to the bed, showing her with his body how much he cherished her and the gift of her fidelity. Hearts and souls communed through hands and lips, speaking of a connection that was more than skin deep. It was a beautiful moment, and when he finally took her body, they truly became one.

A long while and much loving later, Jasmine snuggled with sleepy satisfaction against her husband, reveling in the feeling of being held. Her languidly stroking hand encountered her dragonfly pendant, and she smiled, fingering it. Sighing with pleasure, she told him, "You sure know how to spoil a girl, honey."

Keilor chuckled and hugged her in response. "I've thought the same about you." Remembering the agony of the last few months, he felt the need to reassure her, "It will not happen again."

Jasmine rose up and looked at him, frowning. "My abduction? I wouldn't worry about that, hon. It's not likely to happen twice in a lifetime."

He sat up, spilling her off his chest and leaving her bewildered. "It should not have happened once."

"How could we have known what was going to happen?" she protested, watching him pull on his pants, arming himself. "It's not your fault."

Pulling on his vest and answering her with a carefully neutral tone, he asked, "Then whose was it?" Before she could defend him further, he went on, "I am not only your husband, but Master of the Hunt. Your theft was my responsibility." He went to her wardrobe and collected a clean pair of pants and a shirt for her. "Come, I want the medic to examine you." He glanced at her forearms. "We will see if he can remove the symbiont while we are there."

Troubled by his attitude, Jasmine pulled the covers closer and asked with deceptive quietness, "What if I don't want it removed?"

A muscle ticked in his jaw. "That is not an option, and you are seeing the medic regardless. I want to be certain of your health. Come." Again he held out her clothes, and this time she reluctantly took them, responding to the note of genuine concern in his voice. They could fight about the symbiont latter.

"She's in perfect health," the medic pronounced, looking at his clipboard. "In fact, she's better than ever. Her blood contains more oxygen, her lungs no longer function below average, her circulation has improved, and...." He looked at Keilor significantly. "Pivotal changes have occurred in her reproductive organs."

A muscle ticked in Keilor's jaw. "How pivotal?"

"Crucial," The medic answered just as cryptically.

Keilor's face darkened. "Can you remove the symbiont?"

There was a pause. "Well, if—" the medic began, but Jasmine cut him off.

"What are you saying?" Jasmine demanded. Had the symbiont somehow made her fertile? Hope surged within her. Maybe... "Can we have children now?"

"No," Keilor answered, and turned to exit the medic's office.

Alarmed, Jasmine hopped off the examining table and bolted through the door after him. What was the matter? "Keilor! Wait." He slowed a bit, but he didn't look at her. "Don't you want to have kids?" she asked anxiously. If so, why would he be angry about it, unless...

"There will be no children," he told her flatly.

She jerked to a halt, her face paling as she absorbed the shock of his rejection. Feeling wooden, she followed him, holding in the hurt, and a tiny piece of her spirit walled itself away.

"There are political repercussions to your producing a child I am not willing risk at this time," he explained, his eyes facing front.

Jasmine halted and grabbed his vest, forcing him to face her, uncaring that their escort could hear every word. "I don't care about politics," she told him, her throat tight. She searched his eyes for something of his feelings. There was nothing.

"I do," he told her with cold-blooded calm, not a trace of hesitation in his manner. Jasmine's heart shriveled within her, and when he made no move to walk on, she left him.

"I'm two months pregnant," Rihlia informed Jasmine with a radiant smile. She'd nearly squeezed her to death when she'd first seen her and scolded her about taking so long to come home, as if it had been in her power to hurry up. "If it's a girl her middle name will be Jasmine."

Jasmine smiled and hid the sadness in her eyes by reaching for a cookie she didn't want. "I bet your mother is ecstatic."

Rihlia grinned. "And then some. I catch her looking at my stomach and tearing up all the time. I swear she's walking on air. And Jayems…" She sighed dreamily. "He's like a little kid counting the days until Christmas.

"But enough about me! Keilor almost drove us crazy, running around as grim as an undertaker the entire time that you were gone. I'm surprised he's let you out of his sight already."

Jasmine's smile froze. "We've already said our hellos, and he had some important business to take care of, so I came to see you." Then, before Rihlia could ask any more, she launched into a recounting of her adventures, exaggerating and playing down the danger where appropriate. By the time that she was through, her trek through the swamp had taken on the glamour of an adventure, and Rihlia was completely enthralled.

"Wow," she breathed. "I had no idea when Jayems told me about the People-Who-Came-Before, the Ronin, I'd ever get to see one of their critters up close."

Uncertain what her friend was referring to, Jasmine frowned.

Seeing her confusion, Rihlia exclaimed, "The Ronin are the humans who found this place, and the symbionts, before the Haunt arrived. There was a big war over who would keep the land, about sixty years ago. Finally it became clear there wasn't going to be a winner in the situation, and both sides decided it was a stupid waste of time. They moved into the swamps after signing a treaty with us."

Looking like she was about to hand Jasmine a gift, she leaned forward and told Jasmine, "Because of the symbionts, they live as long as we do."

Jasmine stared at her, ramifications and possibilities jogging through her mind. "Are they still there?"

"Sure." Rihlia leaned back and smiled with satisfaction. "I'm surprised you didn't see any."

Jasmine stared out her window, watching the sunset gloss the sky over the sea with bright fuchsia and gold. Her room had been thoroughly cleaned and Keilor's stuff transferred back to his old quarters. The door was locked, and she was in the mood to reinforce her solitude with charmer commands, if necessary.

She would not be the one rejected this time.

What a shame she hadn't figured out Keilor's game before she submitted to a "marriage" with him. Nice and tight, legal and binding, at least here, or so he'd led her to believe. Thanks to a little investigation, she'd discovered that wasn't true. The bond they'd created could be severed with about a year's worth of abstinence.

Tonight would be day one.

No doubt Keilor would put up a fuss. Her lip curled. Honor or some sense of ownership would compel him, not affection. This morning had proven that.

Keilor halted in shock when he saw the red rune of divorce on Jasmine's door, between two unhappy guards, there for the world to see. It had taken most of the day to collect himself after the crippling blow the medic had dealt. To know that his wife could have his children, but to be unable to give them to her because of a law passed years ago...

The devastation had nearly killed him, and he hadn't been as kind to her as he should have been. There had been no way he could have explained to her at the time, though. He'd hadn't had the strength.

Closing his eyes to still the fear and hurt the sight of the rune caused, he stiffened his spine, prepared to erase the battle lines between them. As soon as that was done, he'd erase the cursed rune and get on with their lives as if it had never appeared.

His loose hair brushed against his back as he called through the door to the wife he knew still loved him. Knowing how much she loved it, he'd worn it loose for her. "Dragonfly?"

"You have been served with a divorce, Lord Keilor, given by authority of the Lord Jayems on the basis of your refusal to provide your wife with heirs," his wife's cool voice answered. "It will not serve you to use that name now."

A cold rush flowed through him, but he forced the worst of it back. Jayems hadn't had a choice. No doubt Jayems had already tried to dissuade her with the facts, but Keilor told her anyway, "There is a law against me doing so, as well, *wife*. The penalty for breaking it is fatal." When she didn't answer right away, he added, putting as much conviction in his voice as he could manage, "I would anyway, if a way could be found—"

"There's no law on my world," Jasmine answered.

Betrayal slapped him. How could she ask him to go to a place where his kind was hunted and feared? To give up the Haunt? What kind of life could he or their children have there? "I have no place on your world," he answered, his voice taunt. "Is our desire to conceive children worth starting a war?"

"Do you really want my answer to that?" came her flippant reply.

"So speaks a woman who has never seen blood!" he snarled, pressing his palms to the door. "Have you ever been in battle? I remember the Symbiont Wars. I will not be the cause of another."

Why could she not understand? The very creature that gave him the ability to give her his child also made her his political enemy. Peace depended on strict segregation of two such volatile races, and as the Master of the Hunt, he couldn't ignore that.

"All the more reason to go our separate ways," came the slightly shaky response.

Hearing her uncertainty, he pressed, "I do want children, Jasmine. There is still no reason why we can't adopt—" Something heavy slammed against the door, shaking it, and he snatched his hands away.

"That's not the issue!" she yelled back.

"*Then what is?*" he roared, frustration getting the better of him. Thundering rains, what was her problem? No answer came, and he reached for the door. Enough of this. She was his wife!

One of her guards, looking extremely unhappy, got in his way, and the other tensed in readiness. White-hot fury slashed through him as he realized he was legally bound to remain outside his own wife's door until given permission to enter.

Only a lifetime's discipline kept him from thrashing the soldiers—his soldiers!—and doing it anyway.

Instead, he banked his rage and called to his woman with the age-old challenge of the wronged husband. "You are my wife. I am your husband. Promises given, promises taken, Jasmine. You will acknowledge me again, once and for all time. That is *my* promise." The guards grinned fiercely and saluted him. Keilor nodded back and spun on his heel.

He had a battle to plan.

Jasmine soon found she had no supporters. Her best friend wouldn't speak to her, her adopted family was coldly polite, and all of Keilor's friends, with the exception of Mathin, whose brooding face discouraged discourse, shunned her. Urseya was the only one willing to spend time in her presence, for the express and pointed purpose of fulfilling her promise to train Jasmine.

Keilor did not ignore her. Everywhere she went, she felt his eyes on her, until she began to feel stalked. A week went by, but he never said a word to her, just joined her as she strolled in the gardens, watched her as she practiced with Urseya, or mounted his ugly brute of a stag when she chose to practice riding. He was as unshakable as the plague and as impervious to chill as a mountain.

There was nothing cold about his eyes, however.

Constantly she felt his eyes strip her, and they spoke eloquently of the touches that followed in his mind, torturing her with reminders of a desire that never died, only grew until it coalesced in a seething ball of fire that threatened to escape her command at any moment. Constantly she saw his eyes ignite and his nostrils flare as he drank deep of the scent of her desire. The sight caused her to tremble, and the tiniest of cracks appeared in her wall.

All her life she'd wanted something of her own, something good she'd created that no one else could ever take away. Her logical mind began to nag at her that Keilor and her marriage was that something good, a creation worth saving, but her emotional self refused that logic, bringing the image to her again and again of Keilor's face when he'd asked if the symbiont could be removed. He doesn't want you, that other self whispered.

Rejection. Humiliation. Old foes with heavy chains bound her. Days went by as she let them torture her, wallowing in emotional filth until she couldn't remember what it was like to feel clean and bright and full of hope.

Nausea began to plague her, and she didn't want to eat. The exercise she forced on herself in her attempts to forget Keilor wore on her, and she took to sleeping until nearly noon.

It wasn't until two weeks into her emotional paralysis that she finally noticed how tender her breasts had become and recalled that her period should have occurred some time ago.

Relief swamped her. The decision had been taken out of her hands. She was pregnant.

There could be no divorce.

Isfael slapped Keilor on the back, nearly sending him sprawling over the scarred tavern table he shared with Mathin. "I never doubted you for a second!" he told Keilor, grinning fiercely as he claimed a seat.

A waitress set down a pitcher full of strong barley beer, avoiding Raziel who thumped Keilor with bruising enthusiasm. "I have only one question," he said, spinning a chair around and straddling it. "What are you doing here when you could be bedding her?"

"Who?" Keilor asked with a frown, totally in the dark and a little annoyed at the pounding. What were these fools going on about?

"Your wife, you fool!" Raziel retorted, taking a swig of amber beer and wiping his mouth with the back of his hand. "The symbol's off her door."

Keilor froze. It had still been there when he'd walked by, just an hour ago. "What?"

Raziel smirked. "The stubborn woman has finally come around. Go get her!"

Wary, yet hopeful, Keilor rose from the table with the merry jests and naughty suggestions of his friends ringing in his ears. Could it really be this easy?

CHAPTER 25

Keilor entered his wife's room as though it were his own and caught her unaware.

Jasmine spun around to face him from her position at the fountain. "Keilor," she said somewhat uncertainly. She flinched when he shut the door—hard.

"You do realize," he told her sternly, "that you only get one chance at divorce."

She swallowed hard and nodded. Arms wrapped around herself, she shifted, causing the white satin of her dress to mold around her slack hip and thigh. "I...should not have..." She bit her lip and said in a rush, "I shouldn't have done it, and it wasn't fair—" she broke off and stared at him nervously.

His eyes narrowed with suspicion. He'd never seen Jasmine so rattled. Was she afraid? He allowed his eyes to drop for a moment, something he would never do with an enemy, in reassurance. "I told you once that I would never beat you."

She drew in a breath. "There are some things worse than beating." Since she was looking at the floor, rubbing her arms, she missed his sharp look. "That first day, outside the clinic, I thought that since you were rejecting...other things," her face spasmed, betraying pain, "It seemed clear to me that you had no real use for me, either. Other than the obvious," she finished stiffly.

Torn between compassion and anger, he fought to contain his temper. "I explained myself."

"You did," she jumped to agree. "But...what my ears hear and my brain understands doesn't always make it to my...heart." She spoke the word 'heart' with great difficulty, almost as if she'd rather skim over the entire explanation.

"You doubt my love," Keilor said, and her hesitation and heightened breathing set his teeth on edge. His left hand wrapped around his sword hilt, the index finger tapping out his displeasure. Did all married men suffer these grievances, or was he simply unlucky?

Still she refused to look at his face. "You warned me, so I won't blame you if you don't want…." Taking a shaky breath, she rushed out, "I'm pregnant already." Finally she turned her white face to him.

He stared at her belly, his thoughts stalled on that one word.

She must have taken his dumbfounded expression completely wrong, for she blurted out, tears in her voice, "I can go back to my world and have the baby there, and you won't have to worry about us messing up your life. Really. We—"

She broke off as he drifted to her, unable to take in her words at first. Realization of what she was saying hit just as his palm flattened over her stomach.

His head snapped up. "You will do no such thing. I will not have my wife and child wandering around a hostile alien world without me. You are staying here, my child is staying here, and no more words will ever cross your lips denying me my rights, do you understand?"

Heartbreaking, bewildered eyes blinked at him. "You want us?" she whispered, as if a louder tone might break his trance and cause him to change his mind. "After what I did, you still…?"

He crushed her to him, touching her for the first time in far too long. "Woman…." Words failed him. He stroked her hair, kissed the top of her head. "Dragonfly, I told you

I wanted children, didn't I? Why would you think I would reject my own child?" She started to cry, and then he understood. Her mother.

"Thundering rains." He picked her up like a child and sat down on the couch with her in his lap. What damage had she suffered before coming to him? Stroking her hair in a soothing rhythm, he cradled her, saying, "I am Keilor, and no one who came before. You know me, Dragonfly. Would I do these things you accuse me of?"

A shuddering breath escaped her, and she shook her head against him, sniffing. "No."

He made her sit up and look at him. "Would I—no, look at me and don't think of another," he chided her when her gaze turned inward. "Would this man you know send his baby away? His son or his daughter? His wife?" he finished softly, letting a trace of the hurt he felt color his voice.

"No," she answered, just as softly, and rested her head against his. "I'm sorry."

He sighed. "We'll put it down to pregnancy. Breeding woman are known to do all manor of odd things." She scowled at him, and he smiled, glad to see a return of her spirit.

He stood up and carried her to the bed, laying her on top of the quilt and arranging the light blanket folded at the bottom over her. "Rest for a little while. I'll be back to join you very soon, but first I have to speak to Jayems." He kissed her. "I won't be long."

"I won't allow harm to come to them."

Jayems cocked his head. "Since when do you think I became capable of sentencing an innocent woman and an infant to death?" He smiled faintly. "Not to mention the trouble I would have just getting to her. I assume you have Raziel and Isfael guarding her again?"

Keilor nodded, smiling as he remembered the shock and relief, and then the congratulations his friends had offered. Isfael had teased him, thanking him for not getting her pregnant before their adventures in the swamp. "If she's this grumpy with her husband, I'd hate to think what we would have suffered if she'd been breeding in the swamps."

Serious again, he pointed out, "The others are not likely to support us, Jayems. The law is an old one."

"And foolish." Jayems removed his feet from his desk and reached for a document. "Take a look at this," he said, handing the sheaf of papers to Keilor.

Keilor scanned it quickly. Brows raised, he asked, "Are they serious?"

Jayems nodded. "The Symbiont people wish to open negotiations with the Haunt. If I send an affirmative reply, their representatives will be here within two weeks. Your wife would make the ideal ambassador," he suggested.

There was silence as Keilor considered the implications. The Haunt could hardly afford to alienate Jasmine under those circumstances. Unfortunately, if he were to allow her involvement, she would be exposed to too much danger. Knightin had not been found. Yesande was on the loose, and his own people might very well attempt to kill her for the crime of carrying a half-breed child.

He did not like his choices.

Eyes closed, he pinched the bridge of his nose. He couldn't just keep her hidden away for the rest of her life. She deserved so much more, and for all he knew she'd love to be involved with the Ronin. "The choice shall be hers," he finally said.

Jasmine's eyes got wide with delight. "You mean it?" she breathed. "The Ronin are coming here? I could really be an ambassador?" Keilor nodded in affirmation, and she hugged him with glee. "That's great! Now I can finally be of some use around here. I've got to talk to Jayems." She started to scramble from the bed.

Keilor blocked her with his body and used it to lower her back down to the mattress. One of his knees rested between her thighs, and he allowed just enough of his weight to settle on her to make her eyes flare. "I've been married to you for three months now, yet have only shared your bed twice. Has that been enough for you?" he asked, his eyes smoking.

An involuntary tremor raced through her, and her breathing quickened. She shook her head. "Never enough," she whispered, and it was true. Still, her body stiffened with uncertainty. With all that had come between them, could it still be good? Had Keilor really forgiven her?

Sensing her hesitation, Keilor rolled over on his back, bringing her over him. He kissed her lightly, but with enough hunger to wring a moan from her. He settled back with his hands laced behind his head. With a wicked grin, he told her, "I'm all yours, Dragonfly. Do your worst."

Eyes dark with feminine power drifted down his body, and her eyebrow quirked. "My worst, huh? Are you certain you can take it?"

His grin widened. "Oh, I can take it, love, but can you?" His hips heaved once, bringing his arousal against her, and she cried out at the sudden rush of flame. He subsided with a naughty smile.

Challenged, Jasmine sat up and slowly unfastened the gold clasps holding her sleeveless gown at the shoulders, letting the white silk fall to reveal the flaming red overnji, minus a bandeau, underneath. Keilor's eyes widened, and he started to reach for her. She grabbed his wrists and forced them back behind his head, leaning just out of reach.

"I have been weeks without you," he growled in warning, staring at her breasts. This could not be part of their game. He had not envisioned such a wicked cheat when he'd proposed the match. How was he to keep his hands off her?

"You started it," she taunted, holding his wrists and slithering down his body to reach one sensitive ear. Her hot tongue darted out to trace the edges and then darted into the center, wringing a groan from him. He tried to turn his head to capture her mouth, but instead she forced his face aside with her head and took his lobe in her mouth, deliberately making sexy little moans.

Fiery kisses trailed down his throat, and she sucked on the sensitive skin and released his wrists to slowly unbuckle his vest. He could have done it in a quarter of the time, but nothing he could have done would have matched the fever she created as she lightly dragged her nails down his chest. They flowed across his ribs and down his ridged abdomen to separate and score his thighs.

It was outside of enough. Quicker than thought, Keilor rolled her under him and began to devour her. Lips, breasts and belly fell willing victims to his voracious hunger, and when he finally rid them of unnecessary clothing, his wife was as hungry as he, and just as demanding. All differences were forgotten in the hot rush of pleasure, and Jasmine's reserve couldn't stand before the tidal wave of pleasure her husband called forth. What barrier was fear to the power of lightning?

In many ways, their marriage really began that night. They talked about the past, their future…

"I've never asked. What kind of schooling do kids get here?" Jasmine inquired, snuggling against her bare husband.

"Mathematics, science, history, horticulture," Keilor answered, his hand tracing distracting patterns on her arm. "Some art, animal science, domestic skills…" His lips dusted kisses under her collarbone, above the blanket. "...two years of military service for the males and then trade school."

Jasmine scowled and pushed him back. "Are you saying women aren't taught trades?" she asked, indignant.

Sighing, he propped his head on his arm and answered, "Women may learn whatever they choose and are encouraged to do so. It is only that many marry and begin families of their own, and it's difficult to care for children and work at a trade, too."

"Hmm." She pursed her lips in thought, and Keilor leaned over to take advantage of her momentary quiet, but she beat him to the punch. "If the baby's a boy, I suppose you'll want to stick a sword in his hand and throw him up on a stag as soon as he can walk, huh?"

Slightly exasperated, he tugged her to him, levering himself over her body. "Not for the first five years," he answered, tossing his dark hair over his shoulder and out of the way. Then he slid home, cutting off all further questions for the next half hour.

It wasn't until the next morning that they returned to questions of children and domestic life, and this time it was Keilor who brought it up.

"Today would be a good day to choose new rooms," he said over breakfast. He waited to see her reaction.

Jasmine paused in the act of drenching her hot cereal with nut cream. Slowly she resumed, spooning a good quantity of brown date sugar over the cream. "Won't that be kind of expensive?"

His brows shot up. "I am entitled to any rooms I choose to make my own, lady wife, as are you." His lips twitched. "Free of rent." A soft sound of derision escaped her, but she looked uneasy. "Jasmine," he said, reaching for her hand. "What is it? I can assure you we don't live on charity." He searched her eyes. "Would it ease your mind if I told you that I own the patent to the energy blades, passed down to me from my grandfather, or that half the stags in the citadel's stables are mine?"

Her lips parted in surprise. Enjoying her naiveté because it marked her disinterest in his financial affairs until they directly concerned her, unlike so many others, he continued, "I intend to provide you with a regular quarterly allowance, as well as any additional money you may require."

He named an amount that made her goggle. "That's...I couldn't spend that much in a year, Keilor," she rasped.

"Not if you don't get out and start shopping," he teased, choosing to ignore her reaction. He had confidence that, being a woman, she'd not only learn to spend her allowance, but quickly wheedle him into giving her more. Not that he would begrudge it. "As soon as we're done eating, I'll take you for a walk through the marketplace. Would you like that?"

Her eyes lit up, but in spite of her excitement, she didn't eat much of her breakfast.

Frowning at the half full bowl, he asked, "Shouldn't you be eating more than that?"

"I'm a little queasy."

Concerned, he looked away for a moment, not wanting her to recognize his sudden fear. "We'll stop by the clinic first. I want to make certain that you're...that everything will be all right."

She smiled in reassurance. "I wouldn't worry about it. After all, what could go wrong?"

"I don't want her worried," Keilor informed the medic outside the examining room door. "If the baby makes it here in good health, fine. But I can't see how tormenting her with dire predictions would do anything but harm."

The medic didn't even blink. "As you wish. At the moment there is no sign of rejection. The symbiont is taking care of that. There are no guarantees the child won't have problems after its birth, however. Once contact between its mother and her symbiont is severed, anything can happen."

Keilor nodded sharply. He understood too well.

There had been a few rare children conceived between Haunt and human in the days when they still shared a world, but none had ever survived the forth month. The genetic differences were just too great, the mother's body too alien to support the mysterious changes the infant underwent at that time. It was a fear he hadn't shared with Jasmine, believing that the other—very valid—reasons he'd given her would suffice. Her life was too precious to him to needlessly put in jeopardy.

Now matters had been taken out of his hands. But he could spare his wife from grief that might only hasten the inevitable.

With a forced smile, Keilor entered the examining room with the medic and put an arm around his wife while the medic told her that all was well. It was true.

For now.

"Great!" Jasmine hopped off the table. "Then let's go shopping!"

CHAPTER 26

Jasmine couldn't believe she'd spent so much time at the citadel and was only now getting to see the marketplace. Some of the shops were indoors, but many were set up in booths outside. The wide streets were busy, but not crowded, and the shoppers courteous.

Delicious smells teased her nose, and splashes of red braided chilies caught her eye. Making her way across the flagstones to the first booth, she admired the long, beautiful braids of orange, yellow, green, black and scarlet dried peppers, garlic and onions, and savored the scent of wreaths and bundles of sage, lavender and bay leaf, as well as herbs she didn't recognize.

Smiling with delight, she picked up a bottle of vinegar packed with artfully arranged slices of clove pierced lemons, and another of herbs, garlic and chilies, admiring the pretty tones of the liquid. Then a two foot high bottle of kumquat vinegar caught her eye, and she knew she had to have it. "It would make the most beautiful living room decoration," she told her husband with excitement. "Can we get it?"

Keilor eyed the jar askance and shook his head, smiling at the hopeful merchant. "Whatever she wants," he said.

They left with half the booth on its way to their room.

A wide smile on her face, Jasmine explored the vegetable and fruit stands, exclaiming over the many different kinds of produce for sale, and purchasing quite a few. The jewelers received a quick glance, but it was the display of sparkling crystals at the next stall that captured her attention. She chose a snowflake prism from that collection.

By the time they'd watched a weaver working on a tapestry, seen a glassblower create a rose and green swirled goblet, and witnessed a potter at her wheel, Keilor was looking rather peaked, though he never said a word. Taking pity on him, Jasmine suggested, "Why don't we take a break? I'm starving."

Visibly relieved, Keilor took her hand and led her through the crowd. He chose a restaurant with wide windows and a pleasant odor of sweetness and steaming seafood. Mouth watering, she surveyed the buffet. Mounds of snowy shellfish, swimming with vegetables, orange crustaceans arranged on leaves of kale, and seafood salads in bright red and white radicchio bowls tempted her as breakfast hadn't. Avoiding the tentacled dish and what looked suspiciously like jellyfish, Jasmine loaded a plate with moist baked fish smothered in lemon sauce, enough stir fry and crustacean to sink a fishing boat and retired to a table to await Keilor.

"Hungry, are you?" Keilor asked with amusement when Jasmine began wolfing down her second large plate of food.

She stopped in mid-bite to glare at him. "Watch it, buster. I'm just making up for breakfast."

In the interests of continued domestic bliss, he changed the subject. "Would you like to choose new rooms after this? We'll need somewhere to put all these acquisitions."

Eyes wide with worry, she stopped eating. "Am I getting too much? I know we didn't really need that rug, but—"

"I like the rug," he assured her, "And I wouldn't mind if you bought a hundred of them, but…" He smiled ruefully, "I'm afraid I lack your stamina for shopping." The smile turned mischievous. "I'm sure Isfael and Raziel will love it, though."

Jasmine snorted. "Somehow, I doubt it, but never mind. I can always come back with Rihlia." She frowned. "I presume we're on speaking terms again."

"I wouldn't worry over it. After all, pregnant women do odd things," Keilor answered, looking at her over his mug of steaming sage tea.

Chagrined, Jasmine finished her meal in silence.

They were almost to Jayems' and Rihlia's suite when Keilor abruptly froze, dragging Jasmine to a halt with him. He motioned for silence and hit a red button on the small black box all the guards carried. He moved in front of her, drew his gun and fired an arc of blue light all in one seamless motion. The Haunt at Jayems' door crumpled before they knew what hit them.

"Draw your gun, Jasmine," he ordered her, and she did as he said, her heart thumping. "Stay behind me in the doorway if there's firing, wait until the others get here, and don't get in my way." He spared one grim glance at the fallen soldiers, and then he shifted.

An icy finger of fear slid down her spine at Keilor's seamless transition from husband to warrior beast. Even witnessing Isfael, Raziel and Mathin transform had not prepared her for this final proof of what he was and of the kind of child she carried.

There was no time to dwell on it. Keilor positioned her a little to the side and burst through the heavy doors as if they were balsa wood, firing rapidly.

Taken completely by surprise, the Haunt assassin dropped Rihlia before delivering the death strike he'd been poised to deliver, the remnants of his head splattering

Rihlia's face with gore. His partner went down with a hole the size of a man's fist where his heart used to be.

Rihlia was badly hurt. She lay where she had fallen, curled into a fetal ball as a bright red stain spread on her skirt.

"No!" Jasmine moaned, running to her, trailing Haunt guardsmen in her wake. While Keilor and the others searched for more assassins, Jasmine dropped to her knees beside her friend, wiping gore from her eyes with a shaky hand. Her symbiont stirred, touched Rihlia's face, but didn't leave Jasmine.

Wild hope sprung up in Jasmine even as the blood spread on Rihlia's skirt. "Heal her," she told the symbiont. "Fix her like you did me." Sluggish movement and a vague sense of apathy were the only responses. The symbiont was sated, and more than content right were it was. It had no interest in a Haunt, anyway.

"Heal her!" Jasmine hissed, frightened by Rihlia's growing pallor and lack of response. The symbiont stirred again, responding to her desperation. Almost with repugnance, it extended, gingerly touched Rihlia and retreated with a symbiont shudder. "It's not going to kill you. Just do it!" Jasmine snarled at it. Something like a put upon sigh brushed through her emotions, a primal communication of squeamishness. The symbiont extended, leaving a loop of liquid metal securely wrapped around its host's wrist as it touched the dreaded Haunt.

Through the sudden echo of nausea in her gut, Jasmine felt the symbiont slowly and with great difficulty stop the hemorrhaging in Rihlia's womb, saving the tiny child clinging to life within. The entire process took only seconds.

Satisfied it had complied with the spirit of its host's directive, it withdrew, retracting slowly back around Jasmine's wrist. There it slumped, turning a sickly shade of green.

Jasmine hadn't reckoned on the slow dump of noxious, almost indigestible Haunt material that oozed into her bloodstream from the nearly helpless symbiont. Vertigo assailed her, and her eyes glazed over as she slumped over Rihlia's legs, shivering as her temperature dropped. Cold sweat broke out on her clammy skin, and the blood slowly drained out of her head.

That was how Keilor and the medics found them. Jasmine breathing shallowly, and Rihlia an unmoving ball of quiet misery.

At first Keilor didn't understand what had happened to his wife. He thought she'd fainted, or was suffering from some kind of shock. It was Mathin who figured it out.

Mathin had come running along with the rest of the Haunt on duty when the alarm had sounded, and he hissed at his first glimpse of Jasmine, limp in her husband's arms. "Look at the symbiont," he said, pointing to the sagging strands of greenish metal. "She tried to heal Rihlia. She poisoned them both."

"How do you know?" Keilor demanded, even though he believed Mathin. Thundering rains, all he had to do was look at the symbiont for proof, now that he knew.

Mathin avoided his eyes. "I've spent a great deal of time in the swamps, picked up some useful information." He focused on Jasmine's chalky face, looking worried. "What she needs is another symbiont to help bleed off the poison."

"Do I look as if I have one?" Keilor snarled, taking his rage and distress out on the nearest target. He cradled his wife to his chest and strode out of the room, heading for the infirmary. "The People Who Came Before won't be here for nearly two weeks, and unless you can fly—" He shut up. Mathin didn't deserve this.

Unfortunately, he couldn't take his temper out on his shivering wife. Not only was it worse than useless to yell at a semi-conscious woman, she hadn't known the consequences of her reckless gamble. Not that it would have mattered, he acknowledged with a stab of dread. She'd do anything for a friend.

Today, she might die for one.

Keilor sat in the chair next to his wife's bed with his hands steepled against his chin, his eyes closed. They burned from staring at the slow rise and fall of Jasmine's chest.

There wasn't anything the Haunt medics could do. The symbiont flowed like water through the fingers and instruments that tried to remove it from Jasmine's arms, and Jasmine thrashed in delirious panic whenever it had been attempted. Finally Keilor had ordered them to stop trying.

Rihlia was not much better. Although Jasmine had managed to save her baby, possibly at the risk of her own, she had been badly beaten, and even the natural resilience and speedy healing of her Haunt body could only do so much against loosened teeth, cracked bones and bleeding organs. Jayems stood grim vigil over her this night, no doubt wracked with guilt and self-loathing Keilor knew too well.

Tonight he wasn't feeling guilty, though; only sad, and a little proud of his Dragonfly's selflessness. He did not have to ask her to know she wouldn't have counted the cost too high had she known what her attempt at healing would demand.

Swallowing hard, he dropped his head onto his clasped hands and shut his eyes, trying not to think of what tomorrow might bring.

The Symbiont delegation arrived in style.

The morning after the assassination attempt, just after dawn, a silver ship with fifteen passengers glided into

Haunt waters and docked. As soon as its passengers had disembarked, the ship broke apart, coalescing into fifteen silver hover cycles. Before the astonished eyes of the Haunt escort, the cycles sent silver tendrils around their rider's legs to the knee, anchoring them in place.

Jayems, who had been alerted only a bare hour before of the change in plans, grabbed Keilor. He informed him what was up as they hurried to the field between the arms of the citadel. They were waiting there as the Symbiont riders arrived.

There was only one woman in the group, and the men were without exception of warrior stock. All the males wore their hair cropped short, and even the woman's blond hair was only long enough to touch her shoulders. They wore black pants of heavy cloth, boots and jackets of suede suitable for traveling at high velocities. Each rider wore a sheathed knife and a black gun and watched the Haunt with a wary expectancy. The leader, a man of only slightly above average height but tremendous presence, inclined his head to Jayems and Keilor.

"My name is Jackson." He slid a glance at Mathin, who remained mounted on his snorting stag. "We were informed that you have a medical emergency we might be able to assist with?"

Jayems glanced aside at Keilor, leaving the decision up to him. The center of attention, Keilor eyed the new arrivals, their leader in particular, his nostrils flared to take in their scent. He snorted silently in self-disgust. As if that would help him any. He could read nothing in Jackson but fearlessness.

"She rests in the clinic," he told Jackson reluctantly. "My wife tried to heal our cousin with the symbiont, but it poisoned her."

Jackson dismounted in one easy motion. "We can help her, but we'll have to use one of the big symbionts. It might be easier if she were brought outside, if that's possible."

"We will move to a courtyard closer to the citadel while Keilor goes to get her," Jayems offered while his cousin strode away.

Keilor did not like this, but what was he to do? Let Jasmine or the baby die because he couldn't bring himself to trust a stranger? So far it had been their allies who had betrayed them.

"Jasmine," he said, touching her cool forehead and smoothing back her hair. "I've found someone who can help you."

Her eyelids fluttered. "Keilor...help her."

He grit his teeth and tamped down on his concern. She was still delusional. "Rihlia is...fine, Dragonfly," he said, skirting the fact that she was still in intensive care. She was alive, after all. "But we need to get you some help." Careful not to jar her, he picked her up, blanket and all.

This had better work.

"The symbiont will not touch her as long as you do," Jackson warned Keilor. He held out one hand. "Your choice."

Keilor stared at Jackson's shoulder as he fought the instincts that clamored at him not to let this stranger, this one-time enemy, touch his helpless woman.

Jasmine moaned and shivered as she burrowed against him in a vain search for warmth. Her symbiont hung loose on her wrists.

The symbiont riders winced, and the woman murmured something sympathetic.

Keilor's face softened at the sight of Jasmine's pain, and he placed her in Jackson's arms.

She cried out, muttering something nearly incomprehensible about drugs and 'only Keilor', but

Jackson ignored her, holding her firmly as he stepped up to his silver cycle. For a moment nothing happened. Then the giant symbiont flowed and completely enveloped Jasmine.

Keilor hissed and instinctively grabbed for his sword, stopping just shy of drawing it. Thin streaks of pale green and brown flowed out of Jasmine's body and were absorbed into the large creature. It worked on her for several seconds and then withdrew, coalescing back into a blurred image of the silver cycle. It settled on the ground with a soft whump.

Jasmine opened her eyes, ascertained that the man holding her was a stranger, and twisted out of his arms. She shoved him away with surprising strength, considering her wobbly stance. "Who are you?" she demanded. A breeze teased her legs and she glanced down at herself with horror. Snatching up the blanket that had fallen away from the silver nightgown she wore, she whipped it around her shoulders. "What's going on? Where's—Keilor!" she squealed, as her husband caught her up in a crushing hug. "Let me breathe!"

His arms loosened, even though he did not let go. "I thank you," he said hoarsely, looking over her head to Jackson, who inclined his head in acknowledgment.

"For what?" Jasmine turned to see whom he was talking to. Her frown turned to an expression of surprise when she caught sight of the cycles. "Hey! A motorcycle!" She took a step toward it. Keilor's arms tightened a moment and then released her. "Cool," she said in awe. She reached out to touch it and then withdrew her hand to glance at Jackson for permission.

Jackson did not hesitate, but his answering nod was noticeably curt. In light of that, Jasmine kept her hands to herself, but her circling inspection was no less thorough.

"Nice," she pronounced with approval and then, "How fast does it go?" with a gleam in her eye.

"Don't even think it," Keilor growled, taking her by the shoulders and steering her away from temptation. "This is Jackson," he said, planting her firmly in front of the man she had pushed and ignored in favor of his symbiont. "His symbiont saved your life."

Rattled at her lack of memory, Jasmine frowned and unthinkingly asked, "Why?" Keilor's fingers tightened on her shoulders in disbelief.

Jackson's left eyebrow twitched. "Good manners?" he suggested.

Jasmine put her fingers to her temple and rubbed, as if that might bring back the memory. "I don't remember," she muttered. "Just guns and...Rihlia!" She turned as if to run to her friend. "She's hurt!"

Keilor stopped her with an arm around her waist. "You already helped her, and she's sleeping right now." It didn't calm her down, and he grunted as her elbow connected with his sternum. "Be still!" he ordered, squeezing off her air with his arm until she quieted, panting. He glanced sharply at Jackson, who spread his hands in ignorance.

"I've seen it before," one of the other Ronin offered, stepping forward. Jackson introduced the stocky fellow as Ma-at. "It's just the last of the poison working out of her system. A little sleep should clear her head."

"Very well," Keilor scooped up his uncooperative wife. "We'll talk later," he told Jackson, nodding his farewell. He headed for their room.

"I can walk," Jasmine grouched, struggling and completely oblivious to their audience.

"Later," Keilor answered. "Right now you're going to take a nap. Then we'll have a nice, long chat about manners…"

CHAPTER 27

"So, what say we ditch these guys and see if we can't go scare up a pizza?"

Leo, the female Ronin, and the only other female in the council chamber, stared at Jasmine, startled. There was a lull at the table around them as the men broke off their tense verbal sparring to stare.

Jasmine didn't care. Ever since she'd woken up from her nap and joined the group in the council chambers, her temper had been slowly climbing.

The Symbionts wanted to open up negotiations for military cooperation with the Haunt. It seemed the cities they'd constructed beyond the swamplands were under attack by monsters from the East. Not only did they wish to drive the beasts off, they wanted to strengthen their position with the Haunt to ensure peace.

The Haunt princes who'd assembled at Jayems' command weren't adverse to peace, but they stubbornly refused to budge from the principal that isolation made good neighbors. Jayems himself remained silent as his Haunt peers dredged up ancient history about the bloody Symbiont Wars, as they called it, slapping down reason after ancient reason why the Symbiont nation was not to be trusted. Even Jackson's impassive face began to darken.

Figuring that it was either exit the place gracefully or run screaming from the room, stark raving mad, Jasmine decided to rescue the equally miserable and silent Leo while she was at it and leave the men to fight it out.

Dropping a quick kiss on Keilor's lips, she stood up.
"Gentlemen, it's been fun, but I'm afraid my feeble female
mind has become dizzy with your dazzling intellect.
Besides, I drank too much water," she admitted. "So if
you'll excuse us…" Taking Leo's arm before she could
object, Jasmine half-dragged the young woman with her as
she strode from the room.

"Have you ever seen such a bunch of idiots?" she
muttered as soon as the doors had closed behind them,
drowning out the sound of obstinate male voices.

"Jackson is my brother," Leo replied.

"I was referring to the Haunt."

"Ah. Well, in that case…" A suspicion of a smile
crossed her face. "Perhaps I could be persuaded to agree."
She cast a sidelong glance at Jasmine. "How is it you came
to be matched with one of them, if I may ask?"

"Sounds like you have little use for them."

Leo turned her eyes to the hallway. "Our people have
never known peace."

"A non-answer if I ever heard one," Jasmine
observed, a little of her frustration seeping back. She hated
this verbal sparring. Couldn't they just skip it?

Leo must have perceived her annoyance, for she said,
"I do not know these Haunt anymore than they know me.
For now I will try not to let my prejudice blind me."

Cheered by that, Jasmine led Leo to the mud spa after
collecting Casanova and a couple of bottles of juice from
the cooler in her room. She directed Leo to sit by the
waterfall so that neither the two Symbionts who'd
discreetly followed them nor her own Haunt guard could
hear what they spoke about.

Jasmine popped the cap on her own juice and took a
swig, staring at the moving water. "So tell me, besides the
fact that you're Jackson's sister, how is it that you're the
lone woman here? Isn't it a bit unusual?"

There was a moment of tense silence. "I convinced the council that I would be a good choice," Leo finally said. Jasmine just looked at her, daring her to evade the question. Leo sighed with disgust. "If you must know, it's because I was the one who followed you through the swamps, and am thus the one most familiar with you."

At Jasmine's raised brows, she added, "Your party was trespassing, and I was...curious. We rarely see strangers in our swamps, and the combination of a human woman among three male Haunts was most unusual. Unprecedented, in fact." She took a long swallow of juice. "It's due to my information that my brother decided the time was right to approach the Haunt. It was thought your presence might indicate softening prejudice."

"Hm." Jasmine scratched around Casanova's nubby horns and his ears went limp with pleasure. It was something to do to avoid a reply. Politics, especially those involving her, were never Jasmine's favorite subject. Casanova folded himself down with a sigh and laid his head in her lap, eyes closed in bliss.

Would she ever be able to trust so easily? "But why did you want to come so badly?"

Leo stared at her boots, clutching her bottle. "I had my reasons," she said.

Jasmine decided to let her keep one secret.

"My clan will not ally themselves with a parasite-laden pack of humans!" Tor Maphin, one of the assembled Haunt lords, shouted, rising from his seat.

Tilus, who was seated next to him, pulled him firmly back down, but his words were no more encouraging. "There has been peace between us for the past fifty years because of our segregation. The Haunt are strong enough to hold our own lands. If you are not, return to Earth."

The Ronin beside Jackson, Armatris, growled. Jackson quelled him with a look.

Keilor, who, like Jayems, had said very little until now, said mildly, "Even Haunt band together against a common enemy, or to trade, Tilus."

"Who should speak but the Haunt who's sired a half-breed abomination in the belly of his charmer?" sneered Tor Maphin. "We shouldn't wonder that you'd take their side. You and Mathin the Mad, with his fool's talk of alliances."

A muscle ticked in Keilor's jaw, but it was Jayems who said with cool challenge, "The charmer is not only my cousin, Tor, but she saved my wife's life and the life of my child. Show some intelligence and cry peace."

Mathin said nothing, but his very posture breathed menace.

Tor Maphin looked away sullenly. "I withdraw my complaint." Still, the tension in the room did not abate, and this time it also centered on Keilor.

"If everyone has formed an opinion then I suggest that we adjourn this meeting for now. Any objections?" Other than some sullen mumbling from Tor Maphin, which he ignored, there was none. "Very well." Jayems rose, and the rest of the table stood as well.

"As my guests," he said, addressing the Symbionts, "you'll be sharing the meal with me. I'm certain your journey has tired you, so I'll have you escorted to your rooms to refresh yourselves first."

Not until the council room was empty did Keilor allow a snarl to twist his lips. "Who made that mewling cub a council member?"

A wry smile twisted Jayems' lips. "We knew this meeting might be worse than fruitless."

Keilor crossed his arms. "There is truth in what Tilus says."

Jayems stroked his fisted index finger with his thumb as he regarded Keilor impassively. "Perhaps. What of our own kind, though? Recent events have proven they can be as treacherous as any foreign enemy. At this time I am not averse to strengthening my clan with human ties. Your wife has proven they can be loyal."

"It's possible my wife is an exception," Keilor murmured. "I am concerned that her delight at meeting others of her kind will weaken her judgment."

"Maybe it will, for a time. It's easy to trust in the familiar, but she is your wife now. She will listen to you."

Keilor slanted him a look. "You think she would accept it if I told her that I will not ally myself with the Ronin?"

Jayems' eyes slipped downward, conceding to Keilor's very valid concern. The Ronin had a valuable ally in Jasmine, and no doubt knew it. "I know you're in a difficult position, Keilor, but I will support you. I will not command the same from you, but…" He did not need to say what was already understood. Together they could stand firm against the rest of the Haunt, divided… division might be disastrous.

"I need to find my wife," Keilor muttered so he wouldn't have to answer Jayems. He knew what his answer would be; the one that might make him a traitor in the eyes of his people. But if that was what it took to secure the future for his family then so be it. He could do nothing less for his wife and child. If he had to choose whom to protect, his family or his race, his race could fend for themselves.

He was a family man.

"This is for you." Keilor handed Jasmine a black box like the one he wore on his belt. "It's coded with your personal frequency."

Jasmine took the summons box and lifted a brow. "My, what lovely presents you bring me."

He smiled a little. "Until I say otherwise, I want you to wear your gun every time you leave this room." She opened her mouth, but he cut her off sternly, "Every time, Jasmine."

She took a deep breath. "*All right.* I can just imagine how stupid I'm going to look at nine months pregnant, toting a gun…" Muttering, she took his hand and tugged him down to sit beside her on the bed. Since he remained tense, she rose on her knees behind him and began to massage the rock-like muscles in his shoulders. "Is this about the Ronin?" His muscles tensed under her hands, and she grimaced. At this rate she'd wear out before he did.

"Among other things." He was silent for a moment. "Be careful. Just because they're human doesn't mean they can be trusted."

"I'm not completely stupid, you know," she grumbled, pausing in her ministrations. "I think I can figure that out."

Turning around, he took her hands in his. "You aren't stupid, only ignorant of some of the dangers we face, dangers you now need to know about." Careful not to edit out even the worst of Tor Maphin's insults, though he wanted to, he repeated what had been said at the council. She needed to know.

She took it better than he'd expected.

"That homely sack of dog puke!" she exclaimed. "He's lucky you didn't carve him up into stew meat."

"I was tempted," he said with a quick smile. "But now you see why I'm concerned. Tor is not our only enemy." His gaze softened, and he stroked her cheek. "Be careful, love, but don't be afraid. I will keep you safe."

Safety was overrated.

"You're certain your husband would not object to this?" Ma-at asked again, a frown marring his stolid face. He glanced at Isfael, who stood nearby with his arms crossed and a scowl on his face, but made no move to stop her. No support there. He tried again, "He didn't seem pleased by the idea when we first arrived."

Jasmine slung a leg over the Symbiont cycle and grabbed Leo's waist. She'd practically begged to ride the cycle, humbling herself with shameless determination, and she was not about to miss this chance. "That was then, this is now. Besides, Keilor's an understanding kind of guy."

Isfael snorted and rolled his eyes. Ma-at and Scoir, who'd accompanied Leo, frowned, but before they could do anything, the silver cycle whipped tendrils around its rider's legs, and Leo gunned the throttle.

Just in time to shoot past an angry Keilor and a startled Jackson.

Jackson watched the pair without expression. "Leo is a good rider, her Symbiont dependable."

The look Keilor shot him was pure murder. Then his eyes narrowed back on the moving blur that was his wife.

What fun!

Jasmine shouted with delight as the cycle took the curve of the practice field with dizzying speed. "This thing *rocks!*" she yelled, relishing the wind tugging at her ponytail. "Rihlia would kill to ride this baby," she gloated.

"Can't," Leo shouted back over her shoulder. "It won't take Haunt." She slowed to a more sedate pace, conserving the symbiont cycle's living strength, allowing it to 'breathe'. Unfortunately, the slower pace brought the glowering male faces of their small audience into focus. Leo dared only two more passes before she slowed the creature down to park directly in front of Keilor.

Knowing the value of first attack, Jasmine leapt onto the packed dirt and flung her arms around her husband, giving him a quick kiss. Then she started chattering, far too fast for him to speak. "Did you see me? Can you believe it? That thing must go a hundred miles an hour! Can I—"

Keilor touched two fingers to her lips, cutting off the flow off words. "I am pleased you enjoyed yourself, but I think it would be best to wait until after the baby is born before you go tempting fate again, yes?"

Encouraged by the slight amusement lurking in his eyes but chastened by his very real concern and the shades of anger clinging to his mouth, she ducked her head and nodded in agreement. "I promise not to go so fast again until after the baby is born, unless it's life or death. Deal?"

Danger flashed in her husband's eyes. "We will talk about it further." Nodding to the riders, he took her arm and walked toward the citadel at a rapid pace. Jasmine smiled and sent a jaunty wave to Leo, not particularly concerned.

Keilor's hand tightened at her nonchalance and then relaxed a hair, careful not to bruise. As soon as they'd passed out of earshot, he said in a tight, contained voice, "I thought I'd made my wishes very clear last night."

With a verbal shrug, Jasmine answered, "I'm a grown woman, Keilor, even if I'm not as old as however old it is you are. I knew the risks, and I certainly don't need a grandfather telling me what to do at this late date."

Golden flames danced in his Haunt eyes. "You took the risk in the name of fun, and to prove your independence. My concerns were never an issue to you."

There was a heartbeat of silence. "Well...they did pass through my mind. But come off it, Keilor, what are you going to do, beat me?" She dared a glance at his face and faltered. He did look kind of mad.

"See that we are not disturbed," he told Isfael and the guard who was filling in for Raziel. Once in their room, he locked the door.

CHAPTER 28

Jasmine unbuckled her gun belt and laid the weapon on the table. When she turned around, he was there, already divested of his own gear. A startled rush of air escaped her as he backed her up against the table, picked her up and deposited her on the top. Closing the distance between them with a decisive movement of his hips, he took hold of her waist. Holding her eyes, he whispered, "My wishes are my commands, Dragonfly. I am not only your husband, but your lord, and you will obey me as such."

She cocked her head, trying to hide her rapid breathing. "Getting a little dramatic, are we—Oh!" In seconds she was naked, with little idea how, and this time there was nothing between her bare bottom and smooth, hard wood. "You animal, you," she breathed, excited but attempting to remain in control with a show of worldliness.

Dumb move.

Keilor grabbed her hips and pulled her to him, bringing her tender parts flush up against the rough material of his pants and his potent arousal. His stinging nip on her tender throat made her jump, but the suction he applied to soothe her skin left her panting.

It was when she started to wind her arms around his neck and rub against him that she understood Keilor wasn't playing a game. He caught her hands and placed them flat against the table, holding them there while he resumed his play at her throat, slowly moving lower.

She moaned with frustration and tried to rub against him, but he moved back, just out of reach, and resumed his teasing. "Keilor," she said in warning, becoming annoyed. "Let me—ah! Stop with the nips all–*ohh*…" His hot, wet mouth closed over one nipple, driving out all her breath, and his restraint of her hands only made her more aware of how much she wanted to touch him.

Using the only part of her that was free, she tried to wrap her legs around his waist, but he broke away and stalked off to her closet, returning with two long sashes and a white fur coat. He tossed the coat on the table and lifted his shocked wife, laying her down on the unbearably silky fur.

"What are you doing?" she demanded, alarmed when he began binding the sashes around the table legs. She tried escaping, but he was much too quick for her, and in less than a minute she found herself on her back, her hands securely fastened above her head.

For a moment Keilor merely looked at her, his eyes drifting down her body and fastening with potent awareness at the slick place between her thighs, making her tremble with both embarrassment and desire. "Stop it," she whispered, closing her eyes.

The door of the cooler in her room opened and shut, and then there was a rustling in the cupboard by the table. Two clinks sounded, just above her head, out of sight and reach. Then the table shook a little, and her eyes opened in time to see Keilor vault onto the top.

He took off his clothes, and he was very, very slow about it.

By the time he'd removed his pants and dragged them over her quivering thighs, she was in a sweat, and fighting not to twist on the fur, knowing its silky caress on her naked skin would be her undoing.

He tossed the pants. Dropping to his knees, he crawled over her, straddling her body, but touching very little of it. Then he parted her thighs with one knee and slowly slid down the length of her.

She clenched her teeth at the sensual assault, but a long, tortured hiss escaped anyway. "Patience is not always a virtue," she rasped, and lunged up, trying to capture his lips. The restraints stopped her a hair's breadth from his mouth.

Cool dark hair caressed her as he teased her lips, nibbling and licking but refusing to deepen the kiss, to let her respond. She twisted in frustration, snarling at him as his mouth slid aside to torment her ear. "Now, man, NOW!" she shouted, wrapping a leg around his hips and surging upwards.

Instead of complying, he rolled aside and propped his head on his hand as he watched her with masculine satisfaction. "Who is your husband?"

"You are, blast you! You scurvy, bloodless—"

"What is my name?" he interrupted, circling one dusky nipple with lazy possession.

She moaned, and her head rolled to the side. "Keilor."

"Mmm," he said, and rewarded her with a brief, too shallow kiss. "And who is your lord?"

"God!" she snapped, just to irritate him.

"Among men," he allowed, amused. His finger trailed down her belly and slowly circled her navel.

Shivers began and would not stop, but danged if she'd give him the satisfaction. "You really get off on these domination games, don't you, babe? So sorry to disappoint you, but—" She broke off as he reached above her, bringing a bottle of dark cinnamon oil, packed full of the curled bark, and a decanter of rich caramel sauce into view. "What are you doing with that?"

272

He winked at her and uncorked the oil, pouring a generous pool into the palm of his hand.

Nearly mesmerized and a touch horrified at what that stuff was going to do to her control, she whispered, "That can't be good for fur."

He chuckled, and a moment later his slick hands came down on her body.

It was far worse than she'd imagined. She pleaded and begged, hollered and swore, but he was relentless. Every square inch of her body was treated to a heated, merciless torture.

All but the one place she needed him the most.

It was the kisses that were her final undoing.

"Will you obey me?" he whispered against her lips, teasing her with butterfly kisses when what she needed was hard contact. "Am I your lord?"

"Mercenary!" she snapped, too close to losing the skirmish.

"Marauder," he agreed, amused. He rubbed his hard length against her, stealing another gasp. He licked the inside of her mouth.

A woman could only take so much. "Yes!" she gasped. "My lord, you can be my lord. Please!"

Triumph flared in his eyes. "I am your lord, and you will obey me."

For a moment the words stuck in her throat, but it only took one teasing touch of him at her swollen entrance and she started babbling, "Yes! Oh, God, *yes,* please, you're my lord, I'll obey, I'll—" A scream tore from her throat as he slid deep, deep inside her, pinning her squirming hips to the table.

He kissed her long and sweet. "Thank you," he murmured, and began to love her with a gentle passion that soon turned to flaming need. He could not get enough, and she strained against her bonds until he set her loose. She lunged up, wrapping around him with arms and legs, sinking her teeth lightly into his shoulder until screams and sobs of pleasure forced her to let go.

The pleasure that came then was the best they'd ever known.

"What did you get that out for?" Jasmine asked later, snuggling against Keilor with sated affection.

He took up the decanter of caramel sauce and gave her a wicked grin. "Let me show you."

Keilor was surprised to find Raziel leaning against the opposite wall when he exited. Then he remembered it was time for his shift to begin.

Raziel smirked, his blue eyes twinkling as he toyed with his earring. "Is it safe to return to Haunt? The noise coming through the door was too much even for poor human ears."

A rare flush bronzed Keilor's cheekbones. "I'm out here, aren't I?"

"So you are." Raziel inclined his head in merry acknowledgment.

Keilor snorted, choosing to ignore his friend's imprudence even as a smile teased his lips.

They *had* been rather noisy.

"We seem to be making a bad habit of this," Jasmine joked, sitting down in the chair beside her friend's bed two days later. "How are you doing, Ri?"

"I'm beginning to understand why you were such a grouchy patient." She shifted against the mattress, grimacing in discomfort. "Between Jayems' hovering and my mother trying to cheer me up, I'm slowly going mad. Tell me I wasn't that bad."

Jasmine grinned. "Worse. Just be glad you don't have to live on liquids for a week," she said when Rihlia groaned in dismay. "The important thing is you're going to be okay, the baby is doing fine, and you'll be on your feet in time to watch your toes disappear under your baby belly."

Rihlia glared, but then her look softened. "Thank you, Jasmine. If it hadn't been for you—"

"You would have done the same for me," Jasmine interrupted before Rihlia could grow maudlin again. The pregnancy was really turning Rihlia into a bawl baby. Jasmine shuddered. She'd count herself lucky if all she suffered from was bad temper.

Rihlia picked at the covers. "I suppose you heard that one of the assassins was Knightin?"

Keilor had told Jasmine they'd uncovered evidence that Knightin had been receiving bribes during the last year, possibly longer. A discreet investigation had begun to search for other possible traitors.

"Jayems is talking about moving me to a safer place until all of this is over."

Jasmine looked up, surprised. "No one has said anything to me."

"He just brought it up today. I was too tired to fight about it much, but I don't want to go, especially now of all times." Tears shimmered in her lowered eyes. "I don't want to leave him right now."

"I'd be happy to talk to Jayems for you, if you like," she offered.

Fresh tears of gratitude sprang to Rihlia's eyes, and Jasmine jumped up, rushed her goodbyes, and beat a fast retreat.

God save them all from pregnant women.

Jasmine commandeered a bench at the side of the training area where Keilor was instructing a group of soldiers in the art of the sword. She'd never watched him at work, and it was a novel experience to see him through the eyes of his students.

They worshiped him. He asked the impossible, and they delivered because it was he who asked. He was curt, but never cruel. He didn't accept excuses, merely worked patiently with a student until that student understood what he wanted of him, demonstrating where necessary. The beauty of it was, his demonstrations were always matter-of-fact and instructional, never an outlet to showcase his own skill.

And he was skilled. Every fluid movement and graceful gesture spoke of strength and stamina, both in battle, and—

"Mind if we join you?" Urseya, dressed in a stunning brocade gown of rust and gold, joined Jasmine on her bench without waiting for an answer. Leo, accompanied by two of the Symbiont riders, took the remaining space on Jasmine's other side.

An unaccustomed stab of jealousy groped at Jasmine's heart, but she pushed it aside. There was no reason to feel that way, and she wasn't about to start playing the clinging, insecure wife at this late date.

"I understand that congratulations are in order." Urseya glanced at Jasmine's stomach, and for a moment a flash of something dark and glacial surfaced in her eyes before swimming away from the light.

Jasmine stilled and searched her face. Her brain had instantly labeled the dark thing malice, and her every instinct told her not to relax, to search below the surface of Urseya's now placid face. "Yes."

"I suppose Keilor is very happy," she said, watching him demonstrate a movement without expression. "If the child survives, I'm certain that its...mixed blood will barely bother him."

"Why wouldn't it survive, Urseya?"

Indifferent eyes moved again to Jasmine's stomach. "We've only the history of the by-blows, of course, but the odds of you carrying the baby through the third month are astronomical. No human woman has ever carried a Haunt child past the fourth month. Didn't you know?"

Leo cleared her throat. "The symbiont might make all the difference, Lady Jasmine," she said quickly, touching Jasmine's shoulder. "You've seen yourself what they can do. I wouldn't concern yourself too much about it."

Urseya's voice dripped false concern. "I'm certain Keilor only wished to protect you by not telling you this."

A low sound of fury escaped Jasmine's lips as she rounded on Urseya. "Do not pretend to be my friend. Now leave!"

"Do not presume to order me around, charmer," Urseya sneered, allowing gold to flicker in her eyes. Isfael took a warning step nearer, and she eyed him with contempt, standing up. "Do not worry for her, charmer's pet. She faces no danger from me." She cast one more mocking look at Jasmine's belly and turned on her heel, leaving in a swirl of rust brocade.

Still simmering, Jasmine saw Keilor approach from the corner of her eye. "Your best defense is silence," she warned him before he could say a word. Standing up, she told him with barely suppressed fury, "Now if you'll excuse me, I have to go check on the fragile sticker apparently glued to my forehead. I think I feel it peeling off."

Keilor, of course, did not leave her to simmer, but fell into step at her side. "It's a well known fact that even strong women behave oddly when they're breeding. Just look at Rihlia."

"I did, I have, and I'll forgive you on those grounds this time only. Do you understand? This is my body, Keilor! You can't just demand courtesy without giving any in return." She took his silence for agreement. "Now, don't you have a class to run?"

"What did Urseya say to you?" he asked, ignoring her hint.

Her lips tightened. "I think you got the gist of it."

A gentle but firm hand on her arm pulled her to a stop in the shadow of a garden archway. "I'm not interested in the 'gist' of it, Jasmine. I need to know details." His serious, concerned expression told her without words why.

"You're afraid that she…" she whispered, unsettled. She wanted to protest, to say that even Urseya wouldn't sink so low as to betray her family, but the words died unspoken. With everything that had happened, dare she dismiss Urseya's actions as simple jealousy? She touched her stomach, remembering the dark thing in Urseya's eyes, and clenched her jaw. "Why don't we go find some privacy?"

Jayems rubbed his lips with his thumb, his face grim as Jasmine finished repeating her brief exchange with Urseya.

"I've already assigned the necessary personnel to look into it," Keilor assured him, crossing his arms as he waited for Jayems to respond.

Jayems glanced at Jasmine, who was seated in a chair in front of his desk. His gaze cut to Keilor. "Are you prepared to use the option we discussed now?"

Keilor closed his eyes and sighed in frustration. "Jasmine."

She looked at him expectantly. She'd never seen him so tense, and she braced for the worse. "Yes?"

"Knightin is not dead. We have him in custody." When the blood drained out of her face, he took her hand and knelt at her side. "Easy. He can't hurt you now."

She nodded. She trusted him.

"But he has given us no useful information, and right now we need detailed, accurate facts. You could help us with that, if you're willing." At her mystified look, he explained, "You could command him to speak, to tell us what we wish to know."

Misery settled over Jasmine's expression. She'd thought she'd left that sort of thing behind when she'd married him. *Do I have to?* her expression said, but out loud she answered, "I guess so."

He was silent for a moment, and then he touched her cheek. "I'm sorry."

CHAPTER 29

Keilor did not like taking her here, to the interrogation room on the prison level. It went against his every instinct to expose her to this white-walled dungeon, even if, with the exception of Knightin, she'd never see the prisoners.

Knightin was already manacled to a chair when they entered the bare room, and before he could register his danger, Jasmine did as she'd been instructed, saying quickly, *"Don't turn to Haunt."*

Knightin blinked at her.

Flanked by Jayems and her husband, Jasmine sat down in the chair across the table from Knightin and studied him for a moment. His long red hair was unkempt, hanging loose around his shoulders, and his face sported the beginnings of a beard and fading bruises, but his blue eyes held a startling lucidity.

She cleared her throat. *"Tell us the names of those who've worked with you against my family."* Obediently he began to rattle off a list of names. Jasmine watched him for nearly a minute. "He's lying."

"How can he be?" Keilor asked, sending her a sharp look. "He's not mated."

"Look at his eyes. No dilation," Jasmine insisted, even as Keilor started swearing. Jayems called for a guard and began questioning him, but Jasmine barely paid attention. "Who's the girl?" she asked, looking into Knightin's mocking face.

He blew her a kiss.

"Enough of this." Keilor took her arm and assisted Jasmine out of her chair. A medic entered the room with a syringe and Keilor subtly maneuvered so the instrument was out of her sight. "Call me when you need me," he told Jayems, leading her out the door.

Jasmine craned her neck to get another look at the needle, but Keilor hurried her on. "What was that?" she asked, a sick feeling in her gut.

"Truth serum," Keilor answered, never slowing in his brisk walk.

"Why didn't you use it before?" Jasmine asked, puzzled. "Why bother with me?"

His nostrils flared. "It's clumsy, as well as fatal. He might not have given us the information we needed before he expired."

Jasmine froze in her tracks. "You're going to kill him?"

"It is what we do with traitors and murderers."

She shivered. When he'd led her out of the prison level and into the sunlight, she broke away and jogged towards a bench set up in a nearby grove of orange trees. She sat down and hid her face in her hands.

The general public did not see condemned men in the society that had raised her. She'd always believed in the code 'an eye for an eye', but seeing that code in execution brought death much closer to home than it had ever been before. Even her near-death in the swamps had been a dreamy, almost peaceful thing. The stark walls and ugly needle she'd just witnessed were no dream.

A vision of Keilor's sword came to mind, and her breath hitched and came much faster than it should have, making her dizzy. He'd been in a war. He'd spoken of killing, but she'd never connected his words with the vision of carnage spilling into her mind at that moment. Blood on sparkling steel, blood everywhere...or would the energy blades cauterize the wounds? Then there would only be piles of mangled bodies...

Keilor put his arms around her. "I'm sorry you had to see that."

She buried her face in his chest. "Would you have killed me, too, if Rihlia hadn't made you promise? I understand now—you hated what I was."

He stilled. It was a while before he spoke. "It's better not to look back, Dragonfly. I don't want to think about it."

She sighed heavily. It was as she'd thought.

He met her eyes and brushed her hair gently behind her ear. "Would you like to visit my parent's memorial? It's past time I introduced you."

She gave him a sad smile. "I'd like that."

He offered her his arm. After they'd walked a little while in silence, he said, "I've never taken a woman to see them."

"Well," she demurred, "You've never had a wife before."

"I was engaged once, a long time ago," he said, surprising her. "She never saw them."

"Oh." The rest of the walk was made in silence.

The memorial was one among many in a lovely plot of mossy ground. It was nothing more than an obelisk of polished granite with a plaque, but Keilor caressed the stone with tenderness and a hint of longing. "My father, Dais, my mother Jacqueline and my brothers, Ellis and Mick. My mother was pregnant with my little sister, but she never had a name."

Jasmine took his hand and kissed it. "I've always liked the name Rain."

His brows shot up. "You wish to name her?" he asked, as if the idea had never occurred to him.

She shrugged. "Why not? It beats calling her baby, doesn't it?"

He inclined his head with a wry smile. "Rain it is." He pulled her to him, resting his hand against her stomach, holding her close.

His life had come full circle.

Keilor had further business to attend to that afternoon, so Jasmine decided to pay Rihlia another visit. Heaven knew she must be bored out of her gourd being cooped up in bed so much.

Rihlia's mother, Lady Rhapsody, was just leaving as Jasmine arrived, and she looked relieved to see her. "Jasmine, dear, you're just the person I needed to see," she said, taking Jasmine's hands. "I am so worried about my daughter. Could you spare a little time to take tea with me? There are some things I'd like to discuss with you."

"Uh, sure," Jasmine agreed, pulling her hands discreetly from Rhapsody's dry grasp. She'd never been comfortable around the stately older lady, something she'd attributed to the aura of royalty that cloaked her. However, if she were worried about Rihlia, Jasmine would be glad to give her all the help she could.

The suite of rooms that belonged to Rhapsody was close by, and within a minute Jasmine entered the main living quarters. It was very...white.

Snow-white walls broken only by crystal framed pictures of family members held a room full of ivory wood and white upholstery. The carpet was white. A regimented row of white statue-topped pedestals marched along the walls.

Jasmine felt as if she'd stepped inside a snowball. It was not a comfortable sensation.

Rhapsody directed her to sit in one of the wing chairs while she prepared the tea, and Jasmine twiddled her thumbs and eyed her colorless environment, trying not to shiver. Oh, what she'd give for a bucket of paint and a few brightly woven Indian blankets. Naughty thoughts of redecoration schemes involving stuffed moose heads, loud slip covers and a few busts of Elvis kept her occupied until Rhapsody returned with the tea tray bearing unadorned white china. Come to think of it, she was wearing white today as well.

I bet I can guess your favorite color, Jasmine thought, biting her tongue so she wouldn't say it. She might have grown up a hooligan, but she still had a healthy respect for her elders. "Thank you," she said instead, accepting the scalding cup of tea and setting it on her saucer to cool. "So what's on your mind?" she inquired as Rhapsody made herself comfortable in the chair opposite the tea table.

Looking a little surprised at Jasmine's disregard for the formalities, Rhapsody folded her hands in her lap and surveyed her guest. "I'm concerned with my daughter's despondency. She has been very emotional since the attack, and I can't seem to make her open up to me."

Jasmine raised her thumbs and shrugged her right shoulder. "Well, there's your problem right there. You don't *make* Ri do anything. Nobody does."

A hint of coolness slipped into Rhapsody's voice. "She responds well enough for Jayems."

Staring at the colorless tea set, Jasmine laced her fingers together over her stomach and twiddled her thumbs. "Granted, but there's elements there you just can't duplicate."

"She loves him, is that it?"

One look at Rhapsody's tight lips was enough to convince Jasmine that she was on shaky ground. "I'm sure she cares for you, too."

It was the wrong thing to say.

"Platitudes will not serve me."

Jasmine suppressed a shiver as her hostess took on the unyielding nature of one of her statues. If she'd ever harbored any doubts that Rihlia's mother disliked her, they were all wiped away in that instant.

Stalling for time, she dipped a finger in her too hot tea, started to raise it to her lips and then froze. She reached for her bone white napkin and carefully wiped her finger clean, and it was not because she'd suddenly remembered her manners.

The tea was poisoned.

She sat back, staring at Rihlia's mother for a long moment. Finally she said, "It's a bit harder to poison a girl when she's wearing one of these." She raised her clenched right fist, the back of her knuckles facing her would-be murderess, and the symbiont flashed with silver anger. It was comfortable, fat and happy, and it did not like threats to its tasty hostess. It had been the one to sense the danger and send a warning tingle of awareness to Jasmine.

The *change* came so quickly that Jasmine almost missed Rhapsody's shift from human to other. There was barely time to register shock at the sight of a white Haunt before she leapt for Jasmine's throat, claws bared.

There was no time to leap away.

The force of the dive took both Jasmine and the chair over backwards, shattering china and splashing poisoned tea on the way.

Keilor's friends had been even better teachers than Jasmine realized. Without thought, Jasmine's body braced for the fall even as her legs came up to shove Rhapsody off with surprising force. The white Haunt went flying, and Jasmine just made it to her feet before Rhapsody rushed her again. Forced to act, Jasmine sidestepped and slashed at her with the long knife her symbiont formed, and the Haunt hissed as raw wounds opened across her arm and abdomen, leaving the white gown in tatters.

Hammering started at the heavy door.

"That's two," Jasmine warned her grimly, blocking out the sound as an irritation that could cost her life. Mathin would have had her head for such hesitation, but

285

she'd never taken a life, and she didn't want to start with her best friend's mother.

"Don't make me kill you," she grated, her voice raw. For her child's sake, she couldn't afford to hesitate again.

Rhapsody's lip curled, and a frightening madness flashed in her eyes as she charged.

The symbiont flashed as Jasmine struck back, aiming for the white Haunt's stomach. A second later her adversary was clutching her abdomen, trying in vain to hold in the spill of intestines. Blood ran down her legs, a spreading crimson stain on the white carpet.

The door burst open, and the Haunt barely checked before coming to Rhapsody's aid. One rough hand closed over Jasmine's right biceps just as her knees buckled.

Unfortunately, her faint lasted less than ten seconds, and she came to just in time to be hit full in the nose by the smell of slaughter. Dazed, she found herself on her knees beside the steaming body, emptying her guts. The blood from the carpet soaked onto her hands, and with a whimper, she crawled two feet away and pressed her head to her forearm, waiting for the surging darkness to stop.

"Here," someone said, grabbing her hair and coaxing her head up. Raziel wiped her mouth with a damp napkin. "What happened?"

"Poisoned tea," she stammered, so softly no one else heard. He let her go and went to collect a sample from the wreckage around the tea table.

The next few minutes were a confusion of raised voices, screams and accusations as Rhapsody's sister arrived on the scene and started demanding explanations and Jasmine's execution.

"*She killed her!* How can you just stand there? Do something!" Lady Portae shrieked, kneeling at the body of her sister, who would forever remain in Haunt. Keilor might have survived a similar wound, but he was young and fit. There was no hope of that here.

Jasmine hid her face in her hands, forgetting the blood until she'd smeared it all over her face.

"What happened?"

Jasmine looked up at the sound of Keilor's stern, concerned voice. His lips tightened at the sight of her pale, blood-smeared face and contracted pupils. He'd already heard Raziel's report and sent him off with a sample of the tea, but he needed more details. "What happened?" he asked again, more gently.

Jasmine looked up, saw Rihlia's stricken face, and her throat closed over the words. How could she tell her best friend that her mother had tried to kill her, twice? Instead, she closed her eyes and bent her head, trying to will her ears shut. The sound of Portae's shrill voice faded as somebody dragged her off. Silence roared in the white room.

"Talk to me, Jasmine," Keilor said again, a hint of fear for her in his commanding tone. "Tell us what happened."

"Nothing," she whispered, and winced. Those weren't the words he needed, were nothing close to what he wanted from her, and she knew it.

He took her by the chin and raised her face, giving her head a little shake when her wild eyes darted to the tense Jayems and pale, bright-eyed Rihlia.

"I am in charge of justice, here, wife, and you will tell me what happened. I want the truth from you, and I want it now. What happened here?"

A low groan escaped her at his compelling command, and she wrenched her bloody face away, trying to escape his will. Maybe she was in shock, but Rihlia seemed to be the priority now. She didn't want to hurt her.

He stood up, looked at her and circled the room, studying the furniture. "You sat here, didn't you?" he asked with implacable purpose, pointing to the overturned chair. "It carries your scent." She nodded, biting her lip.

Wariness churned inside her, but it wasn't a betrayal to answer questions whose answers he already knew, was it?

Cocking his head, he studied the overturned table and tea service, his face thoughtful, dangerous. "The direction this table tipped tells me that Rhapsody leapt over it to get at you, likely knocking the chair over at the same time." He moved closer until he was stood over her, studying her scared face. "What made her do that, wife?"

Jasmine closed her eyes, shutting him out, trying to ignore the way he kept calling her wife, reminding her of his intimate authority over her. "She just did."

He stared at her, the fathomless darkness in his eyes weighting her, making it difficult to breathe. "Before or after you brought up the poisoned tea?"

"It wa—" she snapped her mouth shut, choking off the denial. She couldn't lie to him. But what could she say that wouldn't hurt her friend?

It didn't matter. He drew his own conclusions anyway. His expression savage, Keilor glanced at Jayems. "Are you satisfied with what went on for the moment, Lord Jayems? I can bring you more information after I question…" he trailed off, considered Jasmine, and finished, "The witness."

"But—" Rihlia tried to break in, bewildered.

Jayems cut her off. "Go," he told Keilor, jerking his head towards the door. "I will deal with the rest here."

He said nothing on the way back to their rooms, but the moment Keilor opened the door, he rounded on her, hissing, "Are you trying to get yourself killed, woman? Is that what you want?"

Cold lips trembling, she said nothing, just stared up at him and shook with shock.

Swearing, he called for a bath and then looked away for a moment, clenching his fists. Taking a deep breath for patience and another for his fraying nerves, he told her, "Do you know what would have happened to you at the hands of another Haunt, wife? I can think of many that would use your silence as an excuse to get rid of you forever. Why are you being stubborn about this? You are risking not only yourself, but our child."

A defeated sigh escaped her. "Wiley doesn't deserve this," she whispered, her shoulders slumping.

The bath shut off with a click, and Keilor shut his eyes and shunted his adrenaline to the task of undressing his lover, who was still covered with the gore of her kill. "You accomplish nothing for Rihlia by holding your tongue, Dragonfly. Jayems will make certain that she is told everything."

At the endearment, her breath hitched, and she flung herself at Keilor, half naked and crying.

"Hush, little one," he soothed, stroking her back. "Just tell me what happened. I know it wasn't your fault." He could not relax until he had every detail. Then and only then could he deal with her emotions, and almost as urgently, his own.

She pulled away a little, and he stripped off the rest of her splattered clothing, helping her into the bath and sitting on the edge. Slowly her shaking stopped as he bathed her, and she finally told him the complete tale. Only then did the tension of duty drain from him, leaving behind a flood of feeling and a need for comfort that could only be dealt with in one way.

Jasmine was just as frantic as he was when he urged her from the hot water and into his arms, uncaring that his clothes got soaked, encouraging her as she ripped them off in her frenzy to get to him. He dried her with his hands and the heat of their passion, giving her love, making everything all right again.

Need. Heat. Wanting.

They took each other in the depths of the big bed, and satisfied them all.

Jasmine felt half dead with emotion afterwards, barely rousing herself to whimper a protest when her lover withdrew, leaving her only half of a whole.

"Shh," he told her, kissing her temple and pulling her into the comfort of his arms. "I have to go, but not for a little while. You need to rest."

For a while there was quiet. Then, "Is it always so hard, Keilor?" She could not forget Rhapsody's death; she could still see the blood.

Sighing, he gathered her closer for a moment, understanding immediately what she was asking. "No, and more's the pity."

CHAPTER 30

Jayems' face was savage as he paced in front of his desk. "How many more vipers are we going to find at our ankles, Keilor? Or should I be asking how long before one of them sinks its fangs in again?"

Keilor crossed his arms and waited. He was not the only one tired of murder attempts centering on his wife. A thought struck with sudden force. "Does Rhapsody have anything to do with Yesande, Jayems?" He shook his head, answering his own question. "Of course not. She would not approve a strike against her own daughter, or would she?" he asked, leveling a questioning look at his cousin.

"Who can say now? 'The dead are notoriously tight lipped'," Jayems said, quoting a grisly proverb. "A search of her rooms revealed nothing, not that I thought it would, considering how our luck has been running."

He put his fists on his desk and leaned forward, allowing his loose hair to fall forward, concealing his face. "How are they getting past us? We're neither fools nor innocents. I'd swear on my soul that Knightin was a good man once, and he gave us nothing—*nothing!*— under the truth drug."

Shoving his hair back, he straightened and looked at Keilor with hard eyes. "I have never seen anyone resist Nerasia the way he did today. It was almost as if—" For a moment he became utterly still. Only his eyes moved, as if visually tracing a thought.

When he looked up, his eyes glittered with a solution. "Jasmine said Yesande experimented on her, didn't she? Took samples of her blood?"

Keilor nodded. He did not like to remember that time.

Jayems leaned forward. "The Ronin, our symbiotic friends, are human. We've had so little contact with them; who's to say they don't still breed charmers?"

Keilor closed his eyes, considering the unthinkable impact of that possibility. "That would be a very bad thing." His eyes snapped open. "But it would explain their sudden interest in opening communications with us. Yesande discovering a cache of charmers, craving their power, conducting experiments… If several of our women suddenly went missing, I would be looking for a way to infiltrate the enemy and scout around, too."

"And Jasmine is a charmer…"

"A natural lodestone for them, and a possible ally," Keilor finished. "No wonder they risked bringing a young woman with them. Considering what Jasmine will do for a friend, it was a thundering good strategy."

"And just how did they know about that little trait of hers?" Jayems asked knowingly, and Keilor inclined his head. "This is all starting to come together, cousin, and I think it's about time we had a little chat with our visiting dignitaries. And Mathin, of course."

A dangerous smile curved Keilor's mouth. "Of course."

Fifteen Ronin, four Haunt and Jasmine sat around Jayems' table, prepared to play a game of poker involving people's lives.

Jayems opened the game by dealing Jackson a question. "Have you had any strange disappearances among your people recently? Women, in particular?"

Jackson's head came up. "We were given to understand they were charmers." His impersonal gaze flickered over Jasmine. "Not that we're able to tell one way or another."

"And you, Mathin? What do you know about this?"

"I confirmed that at least one of the missing women was a charmer. I'd met her before. I'm guessing about the others, but given Yesande's interest in Jasmine, the blood tests that she took, and all that we know about her, it seems a good guess that she's after the pheromone."

Jayems glanced at Keilor. "Any chance she's already got it?" He quickly explained about Knightin and the Nerasia and Rihlia's mother.

"But I saw Knightin," Jasmine protested. "His eyes were perfectly lucid. He didn't have that stoned look."

"Stoned?" Keilor inquired.

She colored. "Drugged, half-stupid." When his eyes narrowed, she leaned over and whispered in his ear, "Don't worry. I was far too busy trying not to drool over you myself to notice if you looked dazed."

He lifted a brow, but the scowl left his face just the same.

"That still doesn't explain his resistance to the truth serum," Jayems pointed out. "Did you notice anything strange about Rhapsody?"

A gray storm cloud drifted through Jasmine's heart, freezing her to the spot. "She bled a lot." Someone gasped, and Jasmine opened her eyes to stare at the shaken Rihlia. "I'm sorry. No, there was nothing."

Keilor squeezed her hand under the table, giving her support and comfort.

"Still, it doesn't rule out outside influence. We don't know what knowledge her experiments might have given her. Regardless, if she's behind the disappearances, something needs to be done," Jayems said, steepling his hands and touching them to his upper lip. He raised his head and his tented fingers rested against his chin. "Any ideas?"

"Yesande would not welcome me back, so I can't go openly, but I am still familiar with her lair," Mathin offered. "I could always seduce some information out of one of the women there."

"Rather sure of yourself, aren't you?" Leo suggested with a raised brow.

Mathin just smiled.

Jasmine cleared her throat. "Why bother going to her? She seems to go to great lengths to get her hands on charmers. Why not make it easy for her? Wave a charmer under her nose and she's sure to pounce."

"No," Keilor said in tone that brooked no argument. "You will not play bait." She opened her mouth to protest, but he squeezed her hand under the table in warning.

"She wouldn't have to," Leo offered, standing up to move beside Jasmine. Without a word, she reached out and took Jasmine's free hand.

"Leo, no!" Jackson shouted, standing up, but it was too late. Their symbionts flowed together; forming one interlocked whole, and pulsed. Jasmine jerked in surprise as a warm buzz flowed through her body, concentrated in her left arm, and then flowed out through her symbiont and into Leo's. The symbionts separated and streamed back to their respective hosts.

"Neat trick," Mathin growled, his nostrils flaring as his eyes dilated.

Jackson took one look at Mathin's hungry expression and ordered his sister with a killing look, "*Purge it right now!*"

"That would be foolish," she returned, standing firm, if wary. "The plan is a good one."

Jackson's hard eyes swept the assembled Haunt. "Did you not think of what might happen to our women if word of this gets out?" he demanded of her.

"I wonder if this stuff could be transferred to a man?" Jasmine murmured, eyeing her husband with speculation.

"Don't even think it," her husband growled.

"Enough! Jasmine, stop making trouble; Mathin, behave," Jayems ordered. "You don't have to worry about any of *us* making use of the information, Jackson. Yesande is the only one who would desire an army of lust crazed fools."

Mathin glowered at him and slid his gaze back to Leo.

Unnerved, her eyes flickered away and settled with determination on her brother. "Do you have a better way to end this, brother? Who will it be next time, your wife, our little sister?"

"Uh, Leo," Jasmine interrupted. "Just so you know, you're letting yourself in for a pack of trouble with this charmer thing. I do hope you can turn it off as easily as you turned it on, otherwise it might be best to consider other options."

Jackson tensed, and Leo bit her lip. "I'll be all right for a while. The symbiont won't work the pheromone into my genetic makeup for at least a month."

There was a tense moment of silence. "Three weeks," Jackson finally bit out. "I give you three weeks, and not an hour more, understood?" Still very angry, he dropped back into his seat, and Leo followed suit. "Now what?"

"Is it always like this?"

Jasmine glanced at Leo, noted her unease, and smiled with sympathy. "Actually, it's been a great deal better for me since Keilor and I, uh…" She waved a hand. "Since I got married and started bleeding off a little of...whatever it is that makes them do *that*." She indicated the nearly slavering Haunt males thronging the marketplace. Eyes lingered on Jasmine, but they positively glued to Leo, much to the consternation of her Ronin escort. Jasmine's

Haunt bodyguard handled it with stoic resignation. They'd been through all this before.

All but Mathin, of course, who'd appointed himself one of Leo's protectors, in spite of Jackson's none too subtle hints to take himself off. Leo's persistent suitor wasn't in sight at the moment, but Jasmine caught glimpses of him from time to time, and she knew he was nearby, watching.

Leo knew it, too.

"What does he think he's doing?" she muttered in irritation as she caught a glimpse of Mathin through the crowd. "I hardly need another protector; Jackson is bad enough."

Jasmine looked at her askance. "What? Don't you recognize lust when you see it?" Leo's face grew fiery with rage, but Jasmine said anyway, "Mathin's not such a bad sort. Granted, he's a lousy cook, but he's worth his weight in platinum when you find yourself in a jam."

"You can say that, after he broke your arm?"

"Given the choice between that and remaining Yesande's permanent guest, I'll take Mathin's way, thank you very much. It's crude and it's rude, but you've got to admit it's effective." The scent of oranges reached out and seized Jasmine's nose, so she stopped and bought a couple of them. Handing one to Leo, she peeled it as they watched the basket weaver under the striped awning next door make a laundry basket.

Juice spurted as she dug her nails into the peel, releasing a delightful whiff of citrus. "So, do you have a sweetheart back home who'd object to all this male attention?"

Pretending great concentration on her task, Leo shook her head. "No, but that's not the point. I don't like being stared at, and it's infuriating to know that their interest is merely a chemical reaction."

Jasmine nodded. "Hard on the ego, isn't it? Not to mention danged annoying. But hey, look on the bright side, at least *you* can get rid of it." She popped a juicy orange segment into her mouth and then umphed!, as though something important had occurred to her. Rolling her eyes as she chomped quickly, she finally cleared her mouth to ask, "Speaking of getting rid of things," she held up her forearms, "What about these?"

Gaping as though Jasmine had suggested killing the pope, Leo asked, "Why would you wish to do such a thing?"

"Relax, Leo, I'm just curious. Now that I've gotten used to the little guy, I kind of like him, but let's just say that something came up, and I needed to get him off. Then what?"

"It's not done," Leo answered in consternation. "The symbionts extend our lives, bring health, and provide all manner of help. They define who we are as a people. Why should anyone wish to shed one?"

Jasmine raised an imperious brow, unknowingly picked up from her new Haunt family. "I define who I am, Leo, and no one else. I like being one of a kind, knowing there's no one else just like me."

"But don't you need a connection with someone? With others similar to yourself?" Leo pressed, sucking the juice out of the end of an orange wedge and licking an escaping drop, oblivious to the intensity of her audience with her attention focused on Jasmine. "Don't you have a need to belong?"

Jasmine noticed the male Haunt's fascinated stares, and smiled. A teenage boy who was watching Leo and not his feet ran into his mother when she stopped to admire some cloth, and earned himself a scolding.

Her smile grew. "I do belong." She placed a hand on her belly. "I belong to Keilor, and he belongs to me. If I never had anyone else, he would be enough."

Leo looked away and shook her head. "I don't understand that." Noticing her admirers, she scowled. "How can you know it's you he loves and that he's not caught in the spell of the charmer?"

Shrugging, Jasmine answered, "We're past all of that. He's said he loves me and I believe him. It's there in his eyes, in the way he treats me. It's in his kiss, like nothing I've ever experienced, and it has nothing to do with skill. I believe even if I'd never been a charmer, we still would have come together. The pheromone isn't irresistible. It doesn't command the heart." Jasmine grinned as she caught sight of Mathin, who was headed straight for them, and pitched her voice a tad higher. "It might have brought him to heel quicker, though."

Dark eyes caressed Leo with unnerving intensity. "I'd be pleased to be at your heels anytime, sweet charmer." He leaned in closer, bridging her personal space, and murmured against her ear, "or your knees, or even—"

Leo shouldered him out of her way and stalked on, blond ponytail switching, hips swaying angrily. A low hum of appreciation vibrated from Mathin.

Jasmine caught his arm. "She doesn't like you, Mathin."

"Hm. The way you didn't 'like' Keilor?"

Flushing, she crossed her arms. "That was different."

Mathin smirked, "Did your husband ever tell you that we can smell a woman's arousal?" Her eyes widened, and he flashed her a wicked smile of assurance. "Leo *likes* me very much, I promise you." Pulling away from her slack grip, he followed after Leo.

Jasmine blinked. So that was how it was. Still, she liked Leo, and she didn't want to see her get hurt. Not that her watchful Ronin escort would ever allow Mathin to get Leo alone...but still. Jasmine knew how such dogged pursuit could weaken a girl's heart.

With a fatalistic sigh, she shook off her concerns, promising herself she wouldn't interfere. Love was a messy thing, but those two were both adults, and they'd just have to fight it out like everyone else.

CHAPTER 31

The one walk through the marketplace was Leo's last. Her presence had been scented and witnessed, and now all they had to do was wait.

"Seventeen days there, seventeen days back," Jasmine said, shaking her head. "Unless Yesande has taken up residence in the neighborhood, or unless she's got someone closer to home keeping an eye on things, you're going to have to purge the charmer thing, Leo."

Jasmine picked up one of the long sticks that speared the marinated meats and vegetables on the tray nearest her. She moved from the table to the bonfire Keilor had built in the fire pit. The fire was the only light in the darkened and deceptively unprotected garden. Fireflies danced and whizzed through the rare black night, but did nothing to illuminate the six people around the fire.

Mathin shook his head, taking the stick from her and laying it on the grill. The faint, flower scented breeze ruffled a lock of hair that had escaped his queue. It caught in the faint stubble at his jaw and he brushed it away with impatience. "It won't matter. Now the word's out, and she'll come for her. If she finds Leo is no longer a charmer, she'll be that much more piqued, and even more determined to get her hands on her. A power that comes and goes? It will smack of control, and Yesande could never resist that."

Keilor shot a quick look at Jackson, saw his jaw was clenched, and looked away. "The sooner, the better. We're ready for her. Though *you—"* he pulled Jasmine back into his arms, settling her between his bent knees as he stroked her gently rounded belly, "—will stay well out of it."

"Bossy, aren't you?" she teased, turning her face into him and rubbing her head against his chest. It was covered in a dark green silk shirt and not his uniform vest for once. "I wouldn't worry about it." She affected a lofty tone. "Yesande wouldn't dare tangle with me again. After all, I thrashed her so badly the last time we met, she wouldn't risk the humiliation of a rematch."

Keilor snorted in amusement, and Mathin raised a brow and looked at her askance. "And which time was this?" She stuck her tongue out at him, and he shook his head, chuckling. He rotated the shish kebabs, and the fire snapped and sizzled as their fats and juices dripped into its flames.

"Do you ever miss your world?"

Jasmine looked at Leo, surprised by the sudden question. "Why?"

Leo shrugged. "You gave up a great deal to stay here. I was wondering if you have regrets."

"Hmm...I haven't really thought about it, so I guess not."

Leo frowned and poked a stick at the fire, raising sparks. "There must be something you regret leaving."

Smiling, Jasmine snuggled deeper into Keilor's arms. "Nothing worth giving up this. Believe me, I've got the better end of the bargain."

Leo grunted, unconvinced. "I don't care much for the swamps, but I wouldn't leave my family just to be with a man. Besides, we need every Ronin we can get to take back our homelands from the beasts."

"You still have that choice. After all, you're not in love. I would have thought the same thing if I'd been asked before being yanked into the Dark Lands." Jasmine watched the fire. "Love isn't something that's easy to resist. Sometimes it's a pull stronger than the fear of the unknown."

Mathin slanted a glance at Leo, and she quickly looked away, scowling. "I'd just as soon avoid it."

Jasmine laughed and chanted, "Run, run, as fast as you can. You can't catch me, I'm the gingerbread man." When the others looked to her for an explanation, she dismissed it with an airy wave, "It's nothing. Just an old nursery tale. Are those done yet, Mathin?"

They were, and he distributed the skewers, adding more to the grill as he munched with one hand.

"What I want to know is, now that you've gotten what you really came for— help ending the kidnappings— are you guys still going to keep to your trade agreements?" Jasmine asked after she'd finished her first shish kabob. "It's still worthwhile, isn't it?"

There was a moment of uncomfortable silence, with neither side wishing to speak first. Finally Keilor said with caution, "I would not be adverse to trade, provided the Ronin are still willing."

Jackson studied his denuded skewer. "We might be willing, on a trial basis, and on a much smaller scale than originally agreed upon." He slid a wary gaze to Mathin. "We would require that all transactions occur at this citadel, however. The swamps are difficult at best to penetrate without a symbiont, dangerous at worst. We would not like to be responsible for any casualties."

Jasmine grunted. "No offense, but you can have your swamps. I, for one, will die happy if I never have to see them again."

Her words lightened what had essentially been a warning against trespassing, and Keilor relaxed behind her. "I think we can handle that, provided you leave an agent here to deal with any business that may come up. Preferably someone capable of acting as an ambassador, as well."

For the first time that evening, Ma-at spoke up. "I am willing."

"I need you at home, Ma-at. You're too valuable to me to leave behind," Jackson objected. "It would have to be someone else."

"I'll stay."

Jackson glowered at his sister. "You're too young."

"I'm twenty-four," Leo gritted out. "Hardly a child."

"Hail the elder," Jackson retorted with a sitting half-bow. "Sorry, white-hair, but you'll be going with us. I can't spare the men to watch over you."

"Jasmine is my age, and look what she's done. Perhaps certain offices call for youth and flexibility," she contended, setting her jaw.

"She has a point," Ma-at said, interrupting what looked to be the beginnings of a royal argument with the ease of long practice. "I can stay with her, as well as two or three of the others. Besides, if she were back home, you'd only waste your energies finding things to fight about. Apart, you may actually get something useful done for the rest of us."

"We wouldn't like to see her get hurt," Keilor assured him. "If you chose to let her stay, we'll watch over her as well. You have my word."

There was nothing Jackson could say without giving offense. Instead he said in a tone that brooked no argument, "We'll talk about it later."

It must have been a doozy of a talk, because when Jasmine next saw Leo, she was not happy. In fact, she was quietly simmering. She tried to discuss it with Keilor, but he had concerns of his own.

"Whether she goes or stays matters little at this point," he said, leveling a stare at his wife across the dining table in their new suite of rooms. "What I want to know is when are you going to start visiting Rihlia again?

It's been weeks, and still you two don't speak unless thrown together."

All appetite abruptly fled. Jasmine twiddled her spoon as if fascinated with the play of light. "She hasn't been feeling well."

"All the more reason to visit. You can cheer her up."

She squirmed. "Keilor…"

He set down his cup of cinnamon tea with a sharp *click*. "Do you think allowing Rhapsody to kill you would have made Rihlia happier? I swear I am sick to death of this foolish dance you two are having. Do something! Scream, yell, fight about it if you must, but get it over with. Jayems and I have had enough!"

Jasmine tossed down her spoon. "What do you recommend I say to her? 'Gee, fine weather we're having today. You're looking well in spite of the dark circles under your eyes and that nasty pallor. Oh, and by the way, I'm so sorry I *killed your mother*!'" Her voice rose at the end, and she shoved her chair away from the table, hurrying down the three steps from the dining level to the sunken living area. She plopped onto an overstuffed chair.

Keilor pried her hands away from her forehead and held them as he knelt before her. "We all do what we have to, my love. I'm glad you are still whole, still safely carrying our baby.

"You were willing to cross worlds for Rihlia. Could she not cross this barrier for you?"

In spite of Keilor's assurances, Jasmine did not go easily into the lion's den. He had to all but drag her to Jayems' suite and deposit her inside Rihlia's room.

He and Jayems stared at the closed door. When no one bolted out, they exchanged a wary glance. "How is it on your end today?" Keilor inquired.

A muffled shout came from behind the door, and Jayems answered, somewhat distracted, "She grows more depressed and miserable each day. If I see one more tear I may have to run and hide."

Swearing, foul and loud, issued from the door. "I hope that's your wife," Keilor murmured. "I'd hate to think my own woman could out-swear the entire garrison."

"It's mine," Jayems said with a scowl as a particularly forceful word drifted out, followed by a rapid spate of invectives and denials. "That's one of her favorite words when she's either angry at me or for me." A faint smile tugged at his mouth. "But hanged if I know half the phrases your wife is answering her with."

Keilor just glowered. He would have a talk with his wife later about her foul tongue.

Silence descended. Keilor caught himself straining to catch a hint of conversation and shook his head in disgust. "Come on," he said, clapping Jayems on the shoulder. "We would be better off otherwise occupied. Let's look over the Ronin trade proposal. I understand they have prismatic silver…"

Jasmine crossed her arms and waited with grim forbearance, her back to Rihlia. She needed a moment to rein in her temper, and to steel herself against her friend's anger. From experience she knew Rihlia would be a real witch until she'd exhausted her emotion. Only then would the real issues surface.

As they did now.

"I never did love her."

Jasmine turned around and stared at her remorseful friend. *That* was what was bothering her? Guilt over a lack of affection for her mother?

"I wanted to blame you for taking her away before I could find some feeling for her. It was childish, I know, but what kind of a monster doesn't love her mother? I didn't want it to be my fault."

Jasmine shook her head and approached the bed. "I didn't love my mother," she said quietly. "Sometimes I even hated her. Then I hated myself for caring at all."

"That's different. Your mother—"

"Oh, stop with the guilt trip!" Jasmine snapped, dumping herself into a chair. "You barely knew the woman. Then when you did finally get to know her, she came on too strong, making you want to retreat, not open up. I'd have done the same thing. Besides," she looked away. "Look how she turned out."

A shaky sigh came from the bed. "Jayems thinks there's this drug—"

"Drug, smug. No chemical would put the hate I saw in her eyes," she retorted, chopping her hand through the air, unable to hide the strain she felt. "I gave her every chance I could to stop, Ri, I swear to you! I did *not* want to hurt your mother, and I really didn't want to hurt you."

"I know," Rihlia whispered.

Jasmine closed her eyes. "It's still so vivid; all that red against all that white. Warm, sticky blood on my hands, drying on my face." She shuddered. "God." It was a prayer and a plea for forgiveness all in one. "I didn't want to do it. I *really* didn't want to do it."

"It's ok, Jas." Rihlia touched her hand, gripped it. "It's all right."

Jasmine wasn't sure of that. This was a big thing for even their friendship to overcome. Even if Rihlia hadn't been able to care for her mother the way she'd wanted to, she must have felt something.

"I didn't," she answered, reading Jasmine's mind in the way of long-standing friends. "I'm not sorry you defended yourself, and I'm not sorry it's you who lived and not her." Her voice gained strength and she gripped Jasmine's hand harder. "Don't beat yourself up over this, kid. You deserve to be happy. I *want* you to be happy."

A slight smile tugged at Jasmine's mouth. "Who are you calling kid, old lady? Surely you're not ready for the old folk's home just yet."

Rihlia frowned with mock severity. "I will be if you don't stop scaring the crap out of me."

"Aw, you're just feeling feeble from lying around in bed all the time. Why don't you get up and take a walk with me? It'll do you good."

Rihlia's smile faded to seriousness, and she let go of Jasmine's hand. "I can't. I'm paralyzed from the waist down."

"What!" Jasmine stared at Rihlia's lower half in shock. It was covered with blankets.

"Now don't panic, the doctors said it's only temporary. Just until after I have the baby and my body can start working on repairing me. It'll be a piece of cake."

"But—"

Rihlia threw up her hands in a calming gesture. "Hey, I'm an alien, remember? We can do all kinds of freaky stuff." She smiled in assurance. "Even heal a broken back."

Biting her lip, Jasmine eyed her. "Hey, don't be getting all cocky on me, now. I'm pretty impressive myself these days, thanks to this little guy." She waved one hand, drawing attention to her symbiont.

"You still can't see in the dark," Rihlia said with a smug smile.

"Maybe, but I don't sprout hair when the moon is full, either," Jasmine laughed as her friend scowled. "It's good to have you back, Ri," she said with heartfelt joy. Rihlia raised her hand, and Jasmine clasped it, palm to palm, as tears sparkled in their eyes.

"This is a very good thing," Rihlia whispered, her voice hoarse. "A very good thing."

Keilor and Jayems both shot to their feet as Jasmine closed the door behind her. Her amused smile told them all they needed to know. "What is this? Two big bad wolves anxious over a minor womanly dispute? What will your friends think?"

"Bite them. Are things well between you two again?" Keilor asked, coming towards her.

"Never better," she said with a smile that faded to a warning look. "But why didn't you tell me that she was paralyzed? All this time I've wondered why she stayed holed up in her room, and you never said a word."

"She'll be fine," Keilor assured her, looping one arm around her waist and giving her a little squeeze. "There was, and is, nothing for you to worry about."

"We're talking paralysis here, not a broken leg. How do you know—"

"I've been paralyzed a time or two myself, Dragonfly. It's a little inconvenient, but no big deal. She'll heal."

Jasmine stared hard at him. "When was this?" When he said nothing, merely looked amused, she demanded, "Just when are you going to tell me how old you are, anyway?"

Steering her towards the door, he answered, "Never."

"That's not fair!"

"Life isn't fair."

"I'll make you tell me…"

CHAPTER 32

It started out innocently enough.

Jasmine watched as one of the big symbionts fed off a sick stag. The living metal partially enveloped the snorting animal, calming its prey with a release of endorphins as it sucked the putrefaction out of the stag's foot. The process took only moments. When it was finished, the symbiont released the stag and turned back into a cycle.

That was when she had her great idea. "I wonder if one of these big guys could turn into a hang glider?" she mused out loud, watching the snorting stag prance with restored good health.

It narrowed its eyes at them and stamped a cloven hoof in warning, swinging its spiked tail. She and Leo moved away from the pen.

"A hang glider?" Leo inquired, blond brows raised in inquiry behind her dark glasses.

"Sure. I've always wanted to try it." Jasmine patted the silver cycle as it glided to a stop beside them. "I'll bet that you could, couldn't you, big guy?" she crooned, stroking the cycle's 'tank'. The symbiont rippled in approval of the caress.

Leo stroked her jaw with the backs of her fingers. It was a mark of her adventurous spirit that she didn't even bat an eye at the suggestion. "Hm. We could try it." She glanced around at their escort, but men and Haunt were standing back far enough that their speech was private.

"We'll need a high point to launch from, though. The symbiont will have to take a run at it solo first, to test the waters."

"How about the top of the citadel? I've been up there once. It's pretty high, and we could go up in the lift," Jasmine suggested, tilting her head back to study the rocky cliff that made up the citadel.

Soon they were on top of the citadel, looking out over the forest and the sea. For a moment they were silent as fingers of wind teased their hair. It slid over feminine skin, sighing at the pleasure. It was a smooth steady wind off the ocean, and carried the wild scent of salt tang and green forest.

Leo called her symbiont over and explained via touch what she wanted to do. The symbiont responded, but instead of the hang glider, it took on the form of a giant silver bat. Spreading its enormous wings, it leapt fearlessly from the precipice. Awestruck, its audience watched as it banked into the wind and soared.

Ribbons of light reflected off of its smooth silver surface as it flew in front of the sun, becoming a black shadow limned by fire. It banked again, returned to the citadel, and slowed just enough to catch Leo and Jasmine in ribbons of silver. The ribbons retracted, lacing them to its body as it glided past. Then they were out over the ocean, the terrified cries of their bodyguards quickly lost in the rush of wind.

It was scary, but also exhilarating as they swooped and soared, at one with the sky. The symbiont dived with dizzying speed, spreading its wings to arch upward again ten feet from the ocean waves. "Are you controlling this thing?" Jasmine called over the wind, her stomach somewhere in her throat.

"How could I? I don't know how to fly!"

Jasmine's eyes got big at that pronouncement. "In that case—"

"Done!" Leo answered, and indeed they were swooping back to the roof of the citadel and a pale bunch of men and Haunt.

Keilor was one of them.

For long seconds he said nothing, simply looked her over, seeking injuries. Finding none, he took her arm in a firm grasp, saying nothing as he ushered her to the lift. His trembling hand said it all.

Jasmine cringed and dragged her heels. Opening her mouth seemed like a supremely foolish thing to do at that moment.

She did it anyway. "Would it help if I said I was sorry?"

"It's a start." That was the extent of their conversation until they entered their rooms. He released her and paced in a circle, then sat on the arm of an overstuffed chair.

"Where do I even start with you?" he demanded wearily. He ran his hand through his hair, uncharacteristically rattled.

Jasmine cringed with guilt. She had this coming, and she deserved every word. Instead of words, he stood up and turned his back on her, going over to stare out the window.

He stood there for a long time.

He didn't come to bed that night or the next.

Jayems told her that he was working with the volti, but nothing else. He wouldn't discuss her problems with her, either. "Some things should stay between a Haunt and wife. I can do nothing for you." He refused to leave the room when she went to visit Rihlia, effectively blocking that outlet.

Raziel wouldn't discuss it. "It's not my place. Speak with your husband."

Isfael remained in Haunt, and she didn't know enough sign language to bother him. Fallon was typically absent, Mathin was gone, and Leo was unavailable.

About the only ones who wouldn't run from her were Casanova and Keilor's family.

"I don't understand him," Jasmine confessed miserably to the obelisk from the overturned bucket that she was using for a stool. It said nothing, but it made her feel better to talk, even to the long dead and unknowing. "I mean, I wasn't doing anything *really* dangerous."

The column stared back.

"Ok, so maybe it was, a little, but why would he be so upset about it now? I've done stuff like this before." *Yeah, but nobody cared then, and you weren't pregnant.* She winced at that bit of inner wisdom and rubbed her face. This exploring the self stuff was not fun.

In truth, she didn't want to think about being pregnant. She wasn't ready, and it was scary. A part of her thought if she put it from her mind and went on like always, there would be no change, and she could forget, but it wasn't working. That morning she'd gotten up and found herself unable to button her pants and the illusions had shattered. She was pregnant and getting more so every day.

It was one thing to want a baby in the nebulous future and another to have one tomorrow. In the future she had time to become worthy of the task, to become a better person. Today the poor kid would be stuck with her as she was, and she wasn't ready!

She got up to pace, enumerating her failings. She'd never changed a diaper, and she knew nothing about nursing. Babies got sick a lot, didn't they? Needed shots? Clothes? A college fund? What was she doing out here, moping? There were a thousand details to see to, things to get ready for the kid's arrival, and here she was sitting around, talking to a rock!

With a new sense of purpose, she collected the bucket she'd brought the jasmine flowers in and hurried from the garden.

She had a lot to do.

Luck was with her. The first person she asked, her maid, had grandchildren, and yes, she was willing to let Jasmine visit them with her.

Her maid lived in a nice little cottage carved into the arm of the mountain, and her grandsons, aged seven and nine, adored Raziel and her Haunt escort. It was the four-day-old baby girl, though, that interested Jasmine the most.

"Her mother stepped out to do some shopping," the maid explained when Jasmine arrived. She picked the blanket-wrapped bundle up out of its crib and pulled back a corner of the quilt, exposing the sleeping face of the baby girl.

"She's so small," Jasmine said in consternation as she stared at the little one.

Her maid laughed. "She'll grow. Would you like to hold her?"

Jasmine's eyes widened. "Oh, no! I'd probably break her."

The woman snorted and handed the baby to her anyway. "Nonsense. Simply support her head and her little bottom and you'll get on just fine. Yes, there. Now have a seat in the rocker and make yourself comfortable while I go and make certain the boys aren't pestering your Haunt."

A stab of panic flashed through Jasmine at being left sole caretaker of the child, but in seconds she was alone with the babe. The little one slept on, unconcerned. Taking courage from that, Jasmine nudged back the blanket and examined the infant's hands, marveling at their small size. Her fingers were perfect, the nails exact replicas of an adult's, but so very tiny!

At that moment, it finally hit her. That was what her own baby was like, growing inside of her. Wonder blossomed in her heart, and a fierce protectiveness. Was that what had scared Keilor so, the thought that she was risking his baby so heedlessly? Shaken, Jasmine closed her eyes, feeling lower than low. It wasn't just her body anymore, was it? She was sharing it with a little one like this, whether she was ready or not. Everything she did from here on out was going to affect it.

Near tears, she carefully laid the little one back in her crib and found her hostess, thanked her for letting her hold the child and quickly took her leave.

She had a lot of thinking to do.

Keilor came home that night, smelling of sultry forest and wild air. He showed up just as she was getting ready for a solitary dinner, striding in with his hair loose and a volti at his heels.

Jasmine's eyes got wide and she scrambled up on her chair, kneeling on the cushion as she peered over the chair back. Casanova ran under the table, hiding behind her.

A half smile turned up the corner of her husband's mouth. "She won't eat either of you. Terza is here to protect you."

Not a bit reassured, Jasmine peered at the huge creature that watched her with smirking and far too-intelligent amusement. "Uh, what happened to Raziel and Isfael, and the rest of the bodyguard?" she croaked through a dry throat. "They were doing a pretty good job, I thought."

His eyes cooled. "Terza has offered to take their place. They will no longer be needed."

Terza yawned, exposing a mouthful of fangs, and licked her chops. She closed her jaws shut with a snap and a small snarl. Her far too-human eyes mocked her new charge's fear.

Jasmine swallowed. They understood each other.

Like some enormous house pet, Terza stretched out by the fireplace, roasting herself at its heat. A spicy wild smell wafted from her coat to permeate the room, scenting the air with exotic danger. The same scent clung to Keilor as he moved closer with an innately sensual grace.

Jasmine's eyes dilated, and her body grew languid and weak, hungry for him. "What did you do?" she whispered as passion fogged her brain. Was this what he felt around her?

Lightning zinged from his touch, scorching her. "You're not the only one who can inspire passion, wife."

Far into the night, he proved his claim, and Jasmine reveled in his possession.

Morning came too quickly, and with it, responsibilities.

"I'm sorry, Keilor." Jasmine rolled up on one elbow and regarded her doubtful bedmate. "I have been too reckless lately, and…." She gritted her teeth, made herself say it. "…selfish. You don't need to sic the volti on me. I've already decided to mend my ways."

"She stays," he said, flinging the mussed covers off and getting up. Sun-lit dust motes danced around his lean body with distracting glee. "Are you hungry? I haven't eaten since yesterday afternoon."

Expelling a breath of frustration, Jasmine got up and threw on her clothes. "You're determined not to trust me, aren't you? All right, fine. I'll just have to prove it to you."

"I'll welcome your efforts," he said in the grim tone of a man who was hearing an empty promise. "What would you like for breakfast?"

The rest of the morning didn't go any better. Jasmine asked for his opinions regarding the baby crib and gear, and he politely offered her his thoughts, giving her his full attention before returning to his paperwork. When she mentioned going to see if Leo would like to go shopping, he didn't even look up from the document he was examining.

"She would not," he answered, and his tone was final.

"I beg your pardon?"

He laid aside his pen. "You are restricted from seeing her without Jackson or myself present until after your pregnancy. Then you may do as you wish."

Jasmine put her hands on her hips. "Are you telling me I'm grounded?" she asked, almost more amused than annoyed. "Aren't I a little old for that?"

"I could lock you in your room."

Tilting her head, she mocked, "Ah, well, glad to see you're not completely lost to reason. I would stay away from her big symbiont, you know."

"I know you will," he answered, implacable. He stroked the end of his pen against his fingers, waiting for her to lose her temper.

It was a very close thing, but she mastered it, stuffing it away until she could deal with it in private. "All right. I'll see you later."

He raised a brow, mildly surprised when she closed the door without slamming it, and that she only frowned a little at Terza, who padded after her.

Sitting back in his leather desk chair, Keilor contemplated the door. His brief absence while he mastered his temper seemed to have chastened his recalcitrant wife more than he would have expected. For all he knew, she might even mean her words of repentance.

Unfortunately, he doubted it. Whatever the reasons for her carelessness, he'd had enough nerve-wracking experiences lately that he was taking no more chances. Hence, Terza. Not only would no one dare to cross a volti in her prime, but a volti was also one creature he never had to worry about Jasmine charming into complacency.

He had another reason for accepting her offer of assistance, however. Yesande was on the move, and had even dared to brush the borders of volti-patrolled forest, tempting death with reckless presumption. Raziel and Isfael were needed elsewhere, and since he couldn't be at Jasmine's side constantly, Terza was the next best thing.

Of course, the best thing would be for Jasmine to exercise some caution and common sense, but since that was unlikely to happen...

He was a little encouraged by her visit to see her maid's grandbaby. Raziel had said she'd looked shaken, so perhaps she was finally beginning to realize the seriousness of her responsibilities. Or not.

With an oath, he grabbed another paper and got back to work. Time would tell him soon enough whether or not she'd really changed.

CHAPTER 33

"What is *that*?"

Jasmine glanced sourly at her silent shadow, who'd followed her into the gardens where Rihlia had been taken to get some air. Hellish eyes full of golden fire stared back at her from the shade of a tall hedge. "My newest nanny, Terza the Terrible. Why, don't you like her?"

A low, rumbling growl came from the beast, and Rihlia's eyes widened. "I don't think you ought to bait her, Jas."

She sniffed. "Keilor should have thought of that before he sicced her on me. After all, he's the one so concerned about me taking risks. It would serve him right if he found her snacking on me." Remorse stabbed her the moment she'd said it, and her friend's horrified expression didn't help.

"I didn't mean that," she sighed. "Just ignore me. You know how I get when I'm mad about something, and this infernal bitchiness I've felt ever since I got pregnant— no offense," she said, widening her eyes with arch disrespect at the volti, "is driving me crazy. And now Keilor's all but said that he doesn't trust me to be careful of the baby…"

"Can you blame him?" Rihlia broke in. "I'd have killed you if I'd been him."

Jasmine winced. Close friendships had their drawbacks.

"You don't take those kind of risks with a baby, Jas, ever."

"I wasn't thinking of it like that; not then. It was only yesterday that I finally realized that I wasn't just pregnant, I was carrying a baby."

Rihlia stared at her. "I just know I'm going to be fascinated by this explanation."

Jasmine leaned forward. "The day before last I had a *condition*. Yesterday it finally dawned on me that my condition was a baby."

Rihlia blinked. "Sometimes I try to figure out how your mind works, Jas. Other times I'm a little smarter and decide to give it up." She shook her head as if ridding it of a bad dream. "Have you explained any of this to your poor husband?"

Plucking a leaf from the hedge, Jasmine started to shred it. "I don't think it would matter right now. He's pretty well convinced I'm a reckless fool up to no good. I think the hang glider stunt really shook him up."

A snort of amusement escaped Rihlia, but she didn't take the bait. "Have faith. Even reckless fools can change. Heck, before you came here you thought shaking hands during flu season was taking an awful risk. I have faith you'll revert back to normal in no time."

"A phase, huh?" Jasmine asked doubtfully. She shrugged. "Well, that's as good of an explanation as any. I promise you though, I'm through taking risks, and this time I mean it. From now on, it's the straight and narrow path for me, all the way."

Virtue was very boring.

Jasmine caught her attention wandering again and yanked it back to Sousa, her domestic instructor, who was teaching her how to make a lemon sauce for the seafood they'd just laboriously cooked and shelled. It was fascinating, really. It was just that her difficult husband had just entered his glassed in office with Raziel and Jackson, and she really couldn't pay attention to something as mundane as cooking when something so interesting was going on across the room.

Keilor looked up, saw her, noticed she wasn't paying attention to Sousa, and gestured to Raziel. The shades came down, blocking Raziel's amused face and leaving her nothing to stare at.

"I raise my bet two more prismatic silver." Raziel said, turning from the closed blinds. "She'll never last the week."

Keilor snorted as he drew a folded map forward and opened it. "Two weeks. I'm giving her the benefit of the doubt."

"I have doubts my sister will last as long. Already I've caught her twice sneaking off towards the rooftops with her symbiont, seeking to go scouting for Yesande," Jackson muttered. "Regardless, tomorrow is the day she purges the pheromone from her system, and we can't stay much longer. I don't like the reports from home." He did not share what might be in those reports, and no one asked.

"You won't need to," Keilor assured him, spinning the map so he could see. "We've found her camp, and it's only a day's ride from here. We would have taken it already, except she is not in it."

"A decoy."

"Yes." Keilor pointed to the map, drawing his finger across two routes. "The only roads past the volti are on this river here, and over these mountains here. The mountains are treacherous, especially with the storm season coming, but if Yesande could master them and get out with her prize, no one could come after her until after the storms. Should she dare the river, she'll have to contend with the water beasts, as well as row upstream."

Jackson shook his head. "Unlikely, even with a symbiont boat. You're focusing on the mountains?"

"We are. Isfael and Mathin are out there right now. I only wish Fallon hadn't gone off on business again. We could use him right now."

Raziel snorted. "What business is it that takes him away for weeks at a time, just when he could be of the most use?"

"Family business," Keilor said, staring his friend down. He was well aware of Raziel's opinion of Fallon as useless for anything other than entertaining women, but Raziel was ignorant of several important facts. He couldn't share those facts, even with one of his best friends, but he wasn't about to let his cousin be slandered.

Raziel broke eye contact first, mostly out of politeness. "You would know. About those mountains— we estimate Yesande has twenty men with her, give or take one or two. Whatever she plans, you can depend upon it; she already has help lined up inside this citadel. How are we going to combat that?"

Before Keilor could answer, there came a knock on the door. "Come."

Jasmine opened the door, balancing a tray bearing tiny cookies with one hand. "Thought you might be getting hungry," she said with an innocent smile.

"How thoughtful. Thank you." Keilor came around the desk, a suspicion of humor twitching at his lips, took the tray, and then remained to block the doorway. "Dinner smells delicious, too. I'm looking forward to it."

When he refused to budge, her eyes narrowed. "You're welcome," she said, and then very, very carefully shut the door with a soft click.

Raziel took a cookie and popped it into his mouth with a grin. "One week, ha! I'll have my money tomorrow, my friend, and you'll be that much the poorer."

Keilor only smiled.

Later that evening, as he watched his virtuous wife nearly bite her tongue off during dinner to prevent herself from asking about his meeting, he had to admit he was enjoying this contest of wills. Wild curiosity was such a part of her nature, and suppressing it was clearly killing her. Just for the thrill of it, he'd been prolonging her suspense, but now he took pity on her. "Yesande is near. We were making plans to ensure her capture and the safety of yourself and Leo."

Her head snapped up. "Yeah?" Her eyes sparkled with questions, and he could see her holding her breath.

Laughing, he tossed down his napkin and moved to her side, taking her hand and pulling her into his arms. "You're trying too hard." Offended, she scowled and tried to pull away, but he had a secure hold on her. "Not that I haven't been impressed, mind you, but I don't like to see you suppressing yourself like this."

When she stared at him, unsure, he smiled and stroked her hair. "I want you to be yourself, Dragonfly. Do the things you love to do, just do them safely for our baby's sake. Do you see? Can you do what I'm asking?"

Wounded, she answered, "I said I would, didn't I?"

"Yes." He kissed her lightly. He lingered, teasing at her lips. "You did," he murmured, distracted.

She pulled away, a bit breathless, and demanded, "What about Yesande?"

"We will take care of Yesande when she comes," he reassured her, meaning his warriors and himself, but avoiding an argument by letting her think she would be included. When she still looked troubled, he led her to the couch, sitting down and arranging her on his lap. "I assure you I won't be taken unawares twice. You'll be as safe as the Master of the Hunt and a citadel full of soldiers can make you."

Jasmine smiled. "I'm sorry, I just get worried. Every time that I think about—"

He touched her lips, silencing her. "I feel it, too, Dragonfly. But don't let the past rule you. You are safe, here and now, and I'm here and whole. We will win this time, I promise you." He kissed her hand, offering comfort and support. When she nuzzled into his touch, seeking more, he slid down on the couch, prepared to deliver.

His summons box clicked.

He sat up and grabbed it off of his belt to check the code. Adrenaline poured through him as he saw it was the one he'd been expecting.

Jasmine's hand tightened on his hip. "What is it?"

He gave her a quick kiss before bounding to the closet to collect his battle gear. "Nothing to worry about, but I want you to stay here. No visitors until I get back, all right? That includes family. Rihlia won't be visiting at this time of night, and there is no one else who needs to see you. I don't even want you opening the door unless I give the all safe code, is that clear?"

She only hesitated a heartbeat. "All right. But what if—"

"Terza is here, and Isfael is just on the other side of the door, along with reinforcements. If you need to see what's going on for some reason, you may use the view screen to watch the hall." He buckled on his weapon's belt and took her in his arms for one last kiss. "Keep the bed warm for me, Jas." And then, with the click of a door, he was gone.

It was a moment before her mind cleared enough to assimilate what he'd said. Her eyes narrowed. Great. *Stay home, be a good wife, and don't worry about me maybe getting my head blown off, little lady.*

Rolling her eyes, she cleared the table and settled down with a deck of cards for a game of solitaire.

It promised to be a long night.

Keilor raced through the moonlit night, his long legs pumping with exhilarating efficiency, sending adrenaline charged blood through his pounding heart.

Battle. At last.

Taking a deep breath of the sultry night air, he checked the scents of those who ran beside him—all friends. As he neared the stable, he saw his stag among the many battle-ready mounts, his night vision equal to all but the deepest of shadows.

In her arrogance, Yesande had assumed she would be safe if she clung to the mountains until the very last and then used the river to carry her nearly to the walls of the citadel. She'd strike near dawn, forcing the series of gates guarding the ground level seafood hatcheries that helped assure fresh meat in times of siege or storm.

She hadn't reckoned on the prowess of Jaymes' scouts.

He reached the aqueduct gates just as Yesande and her men docked their boat. Their feet no sooner touched ground than the surprised group was surrounded by silent Haunt who melted from the shadows on every side.

"Good evening, Yesande. Rather late in the year for boating, isn't it?" His voice lowered to a rough growl. "I'm sorry to inform you that Tor Maphin won't be joining you this evening. He's been...delayed." He flashed her a smile of challenge as he took on the Haunt, his sharp white teeth gleaming in the light of the triple moons.

A silent roar of rage was her only answer as she and her men dashed for the woods as one body, firing as they ran.

They were cut down like so many scurrying bugs.

Mathin personally took his sister's head.

A kink in her neck woke Jasmine. She stood up and stretched. If she was going to be bored to sleep then she might as well do it while lying comfortably on the bed.

She was determined not to worry about Keilor. She'd learned enough about Haunt honor and the male mind in recent months to know he'd find her lack of faith distressing.

She knew he still tormented himself over her kidnapping and that he viewed the capture of Yesande as his redemption. His unwillingness to forgive himself for that tore at her. It wasn't his fault, but he was too good a man—and too much in love—to easily believe that.

Determined to show her trust, both in him and the men he'd surrounded her with, she prepared for bed.

It was the least he deserved.

"I'm sorry to see you here, cousin."

Urseya stopped, startled by the voice in the shadows.

Jayems melted out of the darkness of an alcove in the only corridor leading to Jasmine and Keilor's suite.

The corridor she was just turning down, with flash grenades hidden in her suddenly sweating palms. Jayems' nostrils flared, and she knew he'd scented them as his eyes flashed golden fire.

Evasion was useless, so she drew herself up, shifting the glass grenades carefully to her left hand and settling her weight on the balls of her feet. "You don't have to be a part of this, cousin. Your wife needs you, doesn't she? For her sake, if none other, remove yourself."

His teeth gleamed in a humorless smile. "Your fate was set the moment you came here, Urseya, but I'll make this quick, for your mother's sake." With blinding action, his blade cleared its sheath, flaring into a blue arc even as her hand came up. There was a hiss, a shriek, and a blinding explosion of blue as his blade shattered the glass balls, negating most of their destructive energy. Urseya's thumb went flying through the air, but she barely had time to feel it before Jayems reversed the arc of his blade and severed her head.

Sounds of battle erupted just down the hall and were almost immediately extinguished. Raziel rounded the corner, retracting his blade. "Such poor sport," he complained, glancing behind him with contempt. "All clear."

Haunt spilled out of the hallway behind him and checked, disgruntled at being left with nothing to do but clear the bodies. One of them slung Urseya's body over his shoulder and bent to scoop up her head by the hair, carrying what was left of her off.

"Shall we see how Keilor fares?" Jayems suggested, leading the way. The sooner this night was over, the better.

Keilor entered the rooms he shared with Jasmine, careful to do so silently. If she were sleeping he didn't want to wake her. She didn't need to see him as he cleansed away the blood of battle. It would only upset her.

He eased the door quietly shut and paused a moment, listening. Her respiration remained steady and deep, unmistakably that of deep slumber. Satisfaction brought a smile to his face. It pleased him greatly that she would trust him so well.

She'd left a light on for him. It was a sweet gesture, and wholly human, for no Haunt would ever stumble in the shadows. Still, the thoughtfulness warmed him. He had a very good wife.

It was just as he was finishing his bath that Terza lifted her head and growled. Keilor froze in the water, listening. His eyes narrowed. Something was scrabbling down the chimney.

Still naked, he slipped from the bath, water dripping from his body to slick the tiles. A motion of his hand warned Terza to silence. He retrieved his blade, staring at the chimney above the still smoldering fire.

A long reptilian head emerged from the chimney, its slit yellow eyes blinking to clear the smoke.

Keilor didn't give the poisonous lizard time to focus. One swipe of his sword and its head thumped into the fire, followed closely by its body. The coals sizzled as blood dripped and flowed over them, evaporating in a cloud of noxious smoke.

He glanced at his sleeping wife, doubly glad he was here. Even Terza might not have stopped the reptile before its poison overcame her. Keilor looked at the fireplace, his thoughts grim. Even with the Haunt he'd send swarming up to check the roofs, it was doubtful they'd catch the culprit. Yesande and Tor Maphin were dead. Who was still alive who wanted Jasmine dead?

CHAPTER 34

The symbiont delegation left the next day, hurrying to get home before the storms began. They left none behind.

"Maybe you'll get to come back for a visit," Jasmine told Leo, a little sad to see her go.

Leo glanced at Jackson, who was mounting his symbiont cycle, her expression doubtful. "Maybe."

Jasmine stopped her with a touch to her suede swathed arm as she was about to mount. "A calling card, just in case you need a friend," she said, handing Leo a dragonfly pin made of iridescent silver. "Things sound rough back in the swamps. Let me know if I can lend you a hand, or if you need a place to hole up for a while, ok?"

Something suspiciously like tears sparkled in Leo's eyes. "Thank you," she murmured. She cleared her throat and mounted up for the short ride to port.

She was the only one who looked back as they rode away.

The hard rains came the next day, and continued without mercy for weeks, occasionally morphing into deadly hurricanes. No one was more relieved than Jasmine when they finally left. The hormones from her pregnancy had made her more and more irritable as each day passed, until even the indomitable Keilor began to keep a wary eye on her when he entered the room.

Rihlia gave birth to a healthy baby daughter, and shortly thereafter she was back on her feet, just as the doctors had promised.

"Glad to see they're not born furry," Jasmine teased, holding her charming little niece.

And then it was her turn.

After the first ten minutes of her high-pitched screaming, Keilor turned an alarming shade of eggshell and quickly found some ear protection—earning a glare from the medic—but bravely stayed to await the birth.

Nearly ten months to the day of her return, Jasmine gave birth to a pair of twin boys. One was born with dark hair and his father's eyes.

The other, the second born, emerged wearing a tiny symbiont.

The End

About the author:

I'm a stay at home mom with three kids, a dog and an active imagination. I spent the first 34 years of my life in Alaska, land of the midnight sun, but these days I'm located in Washington, and am enjoying a much warmer sun :)

I'm married to my high school sweetheart, John, who is known to bring me flowers "just because".
My leisure time is filled with gardening, sewing, art and reading.

Connect with me online at:
www.autumndawnbooks.com
http://authorautumndawn.blogspot.com

Books by Autumn Dawn:

Spark Series:

No Words Alone Dorchester
When Sparks Fly Dorchester

Solar Flare

Anthology for the *Mammoth Book of Time Travel Romance*:

Hemlock & Iron

Indie books:

Dark Lands Series:

The Charmer
Dark Lands: Homecoming
Scent of Danger
The Golden Bell
Ghost in Her Heart
Beast Wars

The Woman Inside
The Other Woman
Through the Looking Glass

Ride The Stars
Careful, He Bites

Interstellar Lover

CPSIA information can be obtained at www.ICGtesting.com
Printed in the USA
LVOW130235210612

287039LV00008B/2/P